Praise for
The Last Bastion of the
Living

Unique, potent, unnerving, and full of action, The Last Bastion of the Living will leave readers in a daze. **- Xpresso Reads**

It was so creative and packed full of action. The characters are awesome and the love story is to die for!! Read this book! **– The Literary Darling**

Fan-freaking-tastic! An absolute bloody amazing novel with a seriously wacked ending! **– Gizmo's Reviews**

I can totally picture this being made into a badass movie. **– Sweet Tidbits Review**

Frater lights up the plot with conspiracies, treachery, coups and a bucket load of political fucktards to last through a nuclear explosion (since, you know, they are like roaches). **- Smash Attack Reads**

"Rhiannon Frater's Last Bastion of the Living is a welcome shot in the zombie arm. A tense and exciting tale that manages to deliver a very human story. Don't even hesitate to read this book."**- Timothy W. Long, Author of** *Among the Living*

"Night of the Living Dead meets super badass Maria Martinez, Tomb Raider style! Fierce, unrelenting in it's intensity... Frater demands attention with The Last Bastion!"
– The Bookish Brunette

THE LAST BASTION OF THE LIVING

A FUTURISTIC ZOMBIE NOVEL

RHIANNON FRATER

The Last Bastion of the Living
A Futuristic Zombie Novel
By Rhiannon Frater

Original Copyright 2012 by Rhiannon Frater
All Rights Reserved.

ISBN-13: 978-1475206319
ISBN-10: 1475206313

Edited by Felicia A. Sullivan
Cover artwork by Claudia McKinney
Interior Formatting by Kody Boye
Cover Typography by Ashley Dawn

http://rhiannonfrater.com/

Author's Note

The story you are about to read is probably one of the most challenging ones I have ever written. Not only is it a combination of multiple genres, but it's also my first standalone novel in a very long time. Just in case you thought this is another AS THE WORLD DIES novel, let me quickly state for the record that it's not. The universe of The Bastion is a different reality from any other novel I have written. It's completely self-contained and not part of a trilogy or a series.

In many ways it was odd to write about a form of zombies again after spending so many years in the AS THE WORLD DIES universe. Plagued by nightmares of the shambling undead throughout the six years I was working on THE FIRST DAYS, FIGHTING TO SURVIVE, and SIEGE in all their incarnations, I was ready to be zombie free.

I did write another volume in my VAMPIRE BRIDE series and a few short stories about other types of monsters, but the idea for this book constantly haunted me. Based on an incredibly vivid dream, I wanted to write about The Bastion, but couldn't muster up the emotional energy to tackle another universe filled with the undead.

On a whim, I posted a poll online asking my fans which I should write first: a futuristic zombie novel or the sequel to my modern day vampire tale, PRETTY WHEN SHE DIES. I was surprised when the final votes were tallied. The futuristic zombie tale won hands down. I've told many aspiring writers that sometimes it takes an extra push to get a writer through a story. That poll was the push I needed.

Originally, I tried to shove this tale into a short story. That didn't work. I next attempted a novella, but quickly realized that wasn't going to work either. I gathered up all my false starts and started again. This time I found the magic that every writer dreams of and finally wrestled this idea into a novel. I absolutely love the story and I'm so happy to finally present it to you.

I hope you enjoy it.

Rhiannon Frater

Other Novels By Rhiannon Frater

Zombies

As The World Dies Trilogy
The First Days: As The World Dies Book 1 (Tor)
Fighting to Survive: As The World Dies Book 2 (Tor)
Siege: As The World Dies Book 3 (Tor)

Untold Tales Series
As The World Dies Untold Tales Volume 1
As The World Dies Untold Tales Volume 2
As The World Dies Untold Tales Volume 3

Living Dead Boy and the Zombie Hunters

Vampires

Vampire Bride Series
The Tale of the Vampire Bride (Vampire Bride 1)
The Vengeance of the Vampire Bride (Vampire Bride 2)
The Rise of the Vampire Bride (Vampire Bride 3) (release date 2013)

Pretty When She Dies Trilogy
Pretty When She Dies
Pretty When She Kills (release date in 2012)
Pretty When She Destroys (release date in 2013)

Short Story Collections
Blood & Love and Other Vampire Tales
Cthuhlu's Daughter and Other Horror Tales (release date in 2012)

Dedicated with much love and affection to my husband for his love, support, and inspiring me to take a risk with this novel

Special thanks to
Tim Kirk, a personal hero, who helped create the Constabulary.
So glad you're home safe from Afghanistan.

The sound of her labored breathing filled her helmet as Special Sergeant Maria Martinez snapped the rifle harness to her body armor. Her fingers trembled as she hooked the rifle to her vest. She hated the outward manifestation of the fear that gripped her and tried to steady her hands. Taking a deep breath and slowly releasing it, she mentally counted to ten, attempting to distract herself from the impending battle.

The deployment of the military was in the shadow of the great wall that protected The Bastion, the last city of the living. Maria glanced over her shoulder at the vast metropolis looming beyond the staging area. In the early dawn, it was shrouded in gray with only the lights on the ten-story high wall gleaming in the mist. Somewhere in the endless sprawl of aging buildings, her family was praying for her safety. She hoped God was listening.

Today was the last great battle against the creatures that had wiped out nearly all of humanity. Today would either ensure the future of generations to come, or start the countdown to human extinction. Almost every last bit of fuel, ammunition, and resources within the city's stores had been poured into this operation. It *had* to succeed.

Soldiers snatched up ammunition and equipment from the dispensers while massive machines slid on treads toward the large aircraft that would ferry them to the battle zone. The blades of the tiltrotors that served as troop transports whined above the din as they lifted off from the loading platforms.

Double-checking the clasps on her helmet, Maria gave her head a firm shake to guarantee it was secure. Like the rest of The Bastion, the armor was very old and prone to malfunctions. She tapped her right wrist and the helmet display flickered to life before her eyes. She swept her gaze over the readout and was satisfied that all her body armor systems were online.

"Keep moving, Martinez," Vanguard Ren Stillson ordered, his huge body looming over her. With his deeply tanned skin and shaved head, he was an imposing sight.

The mass of gray armored bodies shifted around her as she joined the rest of her squad. She greeted those closest to her with a brief nod of her head. As the soldiers were herded forward to the loading platforms, she checked her weapon again and fought down the fear gnawing at her nerves. She wasn't alone in her anxiety. An unusual silence dwelled among the gathered soldiers.

Through the thick plastic visor of her helmet, she saw the commanding officer, Chief Defender Dwayne Reichardt, watching the squads from his vantage point in the command center. He was an imposing man with keen blue eyes and the lines of his face spoke of his years of hard service. She didn't envy his position. To be responsible for the lives of so many had to weigh heavily upon him.

A nudge in her side drew her attention to Special Constable Lindsey Rooney, one of her squad members. Maria lightly bumped her helmet against her friend's in greeting. They had enlisted at the same time and were firm friends. Standing side by side, the two women waited for their turn to board a tiltrotor.

The speaker in her helmet hissed as the com units came online. The steady scroll of information to the right side of her vision bore the news that they were about to move out. Despite her determination not to be afraid, Maria could hear her breath shortening as her heart sped up. Gripping her weapon firmly in her gloved hands, Maria pinned her gaze to the loading platforms rising above her. This is what she had trained for since enlisting.

A one-on-one battle with the Inferi Scourge.

Special Constable Ryan Sherman bumped her arm as he stepped up beside her. His boyish grin and twinkling eyes behind his visor didn't reveal a shred of anxiety. Blowing her a playful kiss, he winked. He constantly flirted with her in hopes of a hook up. With golden hair and deep brown eyes, he was not bad looking. In fact, he was quite handsome. Maria had been more than tempted to indulge in a little physical activity with him, but she knew Lindsey had her heart set on him. She would never betray her friend.

Pointing to her then himself, Ryan mimed drinking.

Rolling her eyes and shaking her head, she veered away. Out of her periphery, she saw Lindsey snarling playfully at Ryan. The teasing and good humor of the moment was a balm to her nerves. If they survived the day, the three of them would end up at an underground bar swilling bootleg liquor all night.

Vanguard Stillson pushed his way to the head of his squad as they shuffled forward. A couple of tiltrotors lifted into the air as two more drifted downward to take their place. As the squad drew closer to the platform, Maria craned her head to stare up the tall expanse of the great wall. It obscured most of the pale blue sky above. Despite the sounds of the military mobilizing around her, she could hear the cries of the Inferi Scourge just beyond the wall.

"Are you scared?" Lindsey asked, her voice barely heard over the din.

Maria nodded her head once in the affirmative.

Lindsey's grip on her weapon visibly tightened. "Me too."

"Keep moving, Rooney and Martinez," Vanguard Stillson's voice barked in her helmet.

Maria sucked in a breath, held it, counted to five, and slowly exhaled. The silence was eating at her nerves just as much as the cries of the Scourge.

"Move forward!"

Vanguard Stillson's hulking figure raised a hand, signaling his squad. Trudging across the concrete to the steel stairs that led up to the loading platform, Maria lifted her eyes to the command center again. Chief Defender Reichardt was pointing to several screens before him and gesturing emphatically to the older man beside him. Maria recognized the officer as Commandant Young.

She wondered if something was wrong.

Stomping up the stairs to the platform, she managed to stay close to Ryan and Lindsey. The rotors sliced through the air above their heads as they loaded onto the flying beast. Quickly sliding into a harness near her friends, Maria watched as the other members of the squad took their places. She exchanged smiles with a few while others took the time before liftoff to meditate and pray. Though these were the same men and women she trained with every day and patrolled with on the great wall, this was their first actual battle. None of them had ever seen the Scourge up close. The simulations in the training room had been unnerving, but what would it feel like to actually face the resurrected dead?

Beside her, Lindsey and Ryan were engaging in a wildly pantomimed conversation. A smile flitted across Maria's lips as she watched them. A few squad members laughed out loud, but the chuckles faded the second Vanguard Stillson swung up into the transport. Buckling into his place just behind the pilots, he swept his dark eyes over his people.

"Keep focused. Stay on target. Do not fear. You know what to do, people, and I know you're more than capable of coming out of this day victorious," his deep voice intoned through the feed in her helmet.

Maria knew the plan by heart. The daily drills and debriefings had her dreaming about her role in the battle. It was a nightmare she woke from every night. Yet, she craved the coming violence against the undead. They had destroyed the world and trapped her within the city. She longed for a world without the Scourge and was willing to fight for it.

The tiltrotor lifted off the platform and tilted sharply as it swooped low over the city before ascending to join the other tiltrotors already in formation. Maria felt her stomach drop as the tiltrotor climbed and grinned despite her nerves. Ryan winked at her and Lindsey gave her a thumbs up. The simulations they had all experienced were nothing like reality. Maria found the sensation of flying a little disconcerting.

As the tiltrotor rose above the great wall, the valley that would be their battlefield came into view. The Bastion was tucked into a man-made valley carved out of an imposing mountain range that created a natural barrier of protection. The only pass into the valley had been guarded by a twelve foot thick, ten-story tall gate. The walled city itself had been designed to give shelter to two million people. The valley had contained seven farms, cattle ranches, a lake fed from an underground river, a hydroelectric station, and settlements for the farmers, ranchers, and miners. Originally, the valley had provided everything humanity needed to survive: water, livestock, a mining facility, power. It was humanity's greatest achievement in the aftermath of the Inferi Scourge infection.

Peering out the front window of the tiltrotor, Maria could see in the distance the enormous gate that had failed to keep out the Scourge. It was a mocking reminder of plans gone awry. Five years after the last survivors of humanity had taken refuge in the valley, the gate had failed. In one terrible day, the farms, ranches, mining, and hydroelectric facilities were lost, along with thousands of people who lived and worked outside the city. No one knew why the gate had failed. It was a mystery none had solved.

Ever since the city had been cut off from its most valuable resources, it had been dying slowly.

"We're moving into position," Vanguard Stillson announced. "Remember to dispatch quickly."

The tiltrotor stopped its ascent and hovered. Through the cockpit window, Maria could see other aircraft carrying the large machines that would create the new perimeter moving into position.

And below...

The massive ocean of the Scourge filled the land before the great wall, their upturned, screaming faces reducing Maria's insides to jelly. The Inferi Scourge Plague Virus (ISPV) victims, the walking dead, the Inferi Scourge, reached toward the massive machines looming over their heads. The crowd of Scourge reached into the foothills and Maria wondered how they could possibly establish a foothold on the land outside the walls.

Ryan's hand settled on her shoulder and she gave him a slight smile.

"Piece of cake," Ryan said, his voice muffled through their helmets since he wasn't using the feed.

"Walk in the park," Maria answered.

"A park infested by insane dead people," Lindsey added.

Nervous laughter was glared into silence by Vanguard Stillson.

Maria's helmet readout abruptly turned red.

The battle had begun.

The sound of the Maelstrom Platforms on the walls erupting into action startled the soldiers crammed into the tiltrotor. Twisting against their straps, they watched through the ports as the large superposed load platforms (or SLPs) reduced the crowd of Scourge outside the immediate walls into so much bloody pulp. The large, long rectangular guns perched on the city walls were boxy in appearance due to the many barrels packed on top of each other. They were capable of firing four thousand rounds in two seconds flat, and they shredded anything in their path.

The aircraft with heavy machinery payloads drifted out over the destroyed bodies as the Maelstrom Platforms continued to pulverize the Scourge near the walls. In a perfectly timed synchronization of actions, a Maelstrom Platform would fall silent just as an aircraft dispatched its heavy payload onto the blood-drenched ground below. Immediately, the dispatched machine rolled into position on its massive treads and extended long unfolding steel mesh wings. The first to land immediately attached to the city wall and the ones that followed lined up to create a perimeter. Each squat machine was a cog in a mobile wall that the military engineers hoped to use to extend outward into the valley to push back the Scourge.

"Unbelievable," Ryan said in awe, watching the action below.

More machines landed and extended their walls. Turrets slid out of the tops of the squat forms and opened fire on the Scourge swarming toward the newly erected perimeter glinting in the sunlight. The new walls latched onto the machines landing as the tiltrotors above performed a graceful ballet, while the Maelstrom Platforms alternately fired. A few hundred meters had been carved out of the Scourge masses by the time the final machine extended its walls.

Maria swallowed hard as the tiltrotor dropped in altitude and flew toward the wide expanse of bloody land that had been cleared. Already, the Scourge struggled to reach the new perimeter. The Maelstrom Platforms fell silent as the tiltrotors ferrying the troops headed into the fray. The energy expenditure for the Maelstrom Platforms was high. Each individual bullet was ignited by an energy spark and with so many platforms firing, the already strained grid was forced to go dark in some areas of the city.

The turrets on the mobile wall continued to fire below. The tiltrotor began to descend into the new staging area, and Maria lost sight of the Scourge.

Glancing toward her friends, Maria could see the tension in their faces. Ryan gave her the thumbs up while Lindsey blew her a kiss. The jolt of the landing reverberated through her legs, then Maria was free of her harness and hurtling out the hatch.

The Scourge had long ago trodden the grass and foliage as they had milled around the wall. The ground beneath Maria's feet was a muddy mix of pulverized flesh, bone and dirt. As she rushed to her position amidst the rest of her squad, her boots sloshed through the gruesome mess. Shallow craters pockmarked the ground were the salvos of the big guns had impacted. The remains of the thousands of bullet rounds flashed in the sunlight before being trampled into the mud.

The military engineers were busy at work ensuring the new perimeter was erected properly while reinforcing the locking mechanisms. The steel mesh comprising the walls was supposed to be the strongest ever created.

The troops spread out along the perimeter as the howls of the Scourge filled the air now that the Maelstrom Platforms were silent. Other weapons and equipment continued to be offloaded as The Bastion soldiers quickly erected their new base outside of the city.

A tiltrotor dropped a heavy payload in the designated spot near Maria's squad. Maria and Ryan grabbed a crate by both ends and lugged it toward the new, high wall. Popping the latches on the container, Maria felt sweat starting to pool between her breasts and slide down the back of her neck. Her armor's cooling unit was obviously not working properly. Ryan and Maria punched in a few codes into the panels on both ends of the container and darted back as it rose up into a catwalk that attached automatically to the mesh perimeter.

Scaling the ladder, Maria felt her chest tighten as she neared the top. Reaching her post, she hooked her safety line onto the catwalk, then finally dared to look upon the enemy.

The Scourge panned into view, screaming and thrashing about as they rushed over the shattered remains of their comrades. From above, the new wall looked terrifyingly thin and vulnerable to the crush of bodies swiftly approaching.

"Keep them back from the wall!" a voice barked in her helmet.

It was Chief Defender Reichardt. He stood in the center of the claimed territory directing the deployment of weapons and equipment.

Maria raised her rifle and took aim at the creatures surging toward the new perimeter. The turrets continued to fire as the soldiers who had never faced true battle stared into the faces of the victims of the ISPV plague. This wasn't a holographic projection in the training rooms, but the true, deadly Scourge. Their cloudy eyes, tattered clothing, tangled hair, and seeping wounds were the only indicators that they weren't human. Maria could now vividly understand why the ISPV victims had originally been perceived as wounded living beings. How easily their cries must have been interpreted as appeals for help.

"They look so human," Maria muttered. Her trigger finger hesitated as the face of a young woman filled the scope. Her muddy blond hair and dirty face obscured a pretty face. The Scourge woman looked horrifyingly alive as she screamed.

"Keep then back from the wall!" the order came again.

Maria realized she wasn't the only one hesitating in firing. Beside her Ryan kept readjusting his aim.

The crowd was now a few hundred meters from the walls.

The news vids flashed through Maria's mind, images of the Scourge attacking the living...

The sharp bark of Ryan's weapon released her paralysis. Squeezing off a shot, she saw the young woman's face disappear in a gout of blood. Immediately, she aimed at the next Scourge and fired. It was woefully easy to keep pressing the trigger once the first few rounds had been fired.

The air hummed around her as another aircraft set down more of the mobile wall units. Behind her on the sodden ground, she knew the military engineers were swiftly hooking the units together and preparing to expand the wall again. The tensile strength of the expandable walls would prevent collapse, but Maria was leery of the mesh-like structure into which Commandant Young was placing so much faith.

Beside her a turret died and a soldier rushed to reload it. The one just beyond Ryan also went silent. Maria felt her stomach clench as the Scourge gained ground now that the two turrets had ceased firing.

"Hurry with those turrets!" Chief Defender Reichardt's voice barked through the feed.

Maria switched her weapon to full auto and strafed the Scourge charging the wall. Ryan and the other members of her squad followed suit just as Vanguard Stillson gave the order.

"Expanding the wall," a voice announced over the feed.

Maria focused her attention to demolishing the Scourge below. Blood, bone and viscera poured onto the dry soil. The Scourge slipped and fell over their brethren, but kept coming.

The turret beside Maria sprang to life again, but the Scourge had advanced further than anticipated in the mission briefings. It was a matter of seconds before they hit the wall.

"Beginning wall expansion."

"This is a bad idea," Maria muttered, gripping the handhold next to her.

The catwalk shuddered as the military engineers activated the mobile wall units. The connected catwalks also came to life, the treads pushing forward as the wall expanded. A cluster of the machines were connected to the apex of the wall and rolled forward as the wall unfurled like a blossoming flower. Maria crouched, glancing over at Ryan. He tried to get off a few shots before giving up. It was too difficult to aim with the wall moving. The wall shuddered as it met in an unyielding mass of flesh, and Maria clutched the handhold with both hands.

"We need the Maelstrom Platforms loaded and firing!" Chief Defender Reichardt's voice commanded.

The overwhelming wave of the Inferi Scourge pressed against the perimeter and the engines whined furiously as they tried to gain traction on the slippery ground. A few tiltrotors roared overhead as the flight crews strafed the crowd, but most of the air support had already retreated to the safety of the city. The fuel reserves were too low to keep the tiltrotor fleet up in the air for extended periods of time.

Commands barked over the feed as the tiltrotors firing at the Scourge were ordered back to the city. The mobile wall trembled again as it continued to unfurl. The treads of the units rolled over the sodden ground, struggling over the pockmarked terrain. The turrets continued to fire bursts as the soldiers feverishly reloaded them.

The massive Maelstrom Platforms finally opened fire, pulverizing the Scourge a hundred yards from the expanding perimeter.

"The simulation wasn't this bad!" Ryan shouted, trying to fire over the edge again.

The muddy, bloody, sloshing ground was gumming up the treads. Maria could feel their catwalk shuddering as it struggled through the muck. Scanning the staging area set up behind the mobile wall, Maria saw panic beginning to spread as some of the mobile units strained to move forward. The units were synchronized to move out in formation, but a few were already lagging behind. Some of the depressions that had been carved out of the ground by the Maelstrom Platforms were deep and several of the machines whined as the viscid mud clogged the treads.

Maria gripped the handhold and managed to get to her knees. Firing at the Scourge, she fought the fear threatening to engulf her. The display in her helmet was filled with a flow of information that was scrolling too quickly to even read. Another burst from the Maelstrom Platform sent clouds of blood into the air, the wind sweeping the bloody mist over the fighting soldiers.

"Fuck me!" Lindsey shouted, trying to clean off her helmet visor.

"Keep firing!" Vanguard Stillson shouted. He was moving along the inner catwalk, laboring to stay on his feet.

As Maria reloaded her weapon, Vanguard Stillson fired on the Inferi Scourge as the roar of the Maelstrom Platforms sounded. Maria felt Stillson's hand briefly on her shoulder as she opened fire again, then he moved on.

A massive shockwave rippled through the perimeter wall, tossing soldiers off their feet and onto the catwalk, or over the wall into the Scourge horde below as one of the mobile units twisted around in one of the deeper craters and wrenched another unit completely about. The torsion between the two units sent another shudder through the perimeter wall and Maria clung to the catwalk as Ryan fell on top of her. Together, they rode the catwalk to the ground, tumbling into the mud. Maria immediately scrambled to her feet and gasped.

The steel mesh had torn free of one of the units and the Scourge were shoving their bodies through the frayed opening. The squads closest to the breach opened fire. The mesh wall shimmered as it wavered under the onslaught of the undead. The mobile units continued on their designated course to their next position, ripping another hole in the mesh wall.

"Fall back!" someone ordered as the Inferi Scourge shoved through the widening openings.

Ryan grabbed Maria's shoulder and dragged her toward a section where the fallen catwalks formed a barrier along with some of the unpacked supply units. Lindsey scrambled to follow. The squads formed a line, shooting at the Scourge coming through the gap. For several agonizing minutes, they were successful at holding the howling creatures back.

"Tiltrotors are en route!" a voice intoned in her helmet.

Sweat poured down Maria's face as she reloaded. Ryan lobbed several grenades toward the breach as Lindsey fired over Maria's head.

"About that date..." Ryan said, grinning despite the fear in his eyes.

Maria slid around him into a better position and aimed at a Scourge trying to scale the fallen edge of the wall. "You're supposed to give me a reason to live, dumb ass," she groused.

Another soldier landed in the mud beside her and helped her obliterate the Scourge trying to scramble through another widening tear in the wall.

"This was a stupid plan!" she shouted.

"It seemed like a good one when we planned it," the soldier answered.

It took her a full second to realize it was Chief Defender Dwayne Reichardt.

"Sorry, sir," she said quickly.

He shook his head, still firing. "Let's just live through this!"

The Scourge pushed further into the perimeter. Maria knew now it was only a matter of minutes before they were all dead. She tried not to hear the screams of the soldiers overcome by the Inferi Scourge. The Scourge tore at them, ripping at their body armor, trying to reach flesh so they could bite and infect. One soldier was pulled free of a group of Scourge, his armor still intact as his comrades gunned down the creatures that had attacked him.

Vanguard Stillson lobbed a grenade at a catwalk's treads and the explosion toppled it over onto the Inferi Scourge.

They were losing ground swiftly and chaos ruled. No one was listening to orders barked over the feed anymore, but were just trying to survive. The perimeter wall attached to the city wall still stood intact with the catwalks still secured to it. Many soldiers clambered onto it, trying to escape the ground. Maria, Ryan, Lindsey and the Chief Defender started to fall back, providing cover to those trying to reach higher ground.

Rappelling ropes started to fall from the high wall. Frantic soldiers gripped the lines and climbed upward, their muddy boots slipping against the steel surface.

Maria tripped, falling on her ass, and the Chief Defender hauled her up swiftly. The Scourge were everywhere now, smashing through the clusters of soldiers, howling. Maria fired point blank into the face of one as it charged her. The Chief Defender knocked another one back with the butt of his rifle. Together they charged through the mud toward the city wall.

Ryan and Lindsey were just ahead of them and nearing the remaining catwalks when Maria saw a flash of light. A massive force slammed into her and sent her sprawling through the air. Blackness surged up to claim her, and she fought not to drown in it. Pulling herself onto her elbows, her body felt numb and her helmet was gone. Beside her, the Chief Defender struggled to get up. His armor was punctured with shrapnel and blood poured through the tears.

Lifting her weapon, Maria aimed toward the creatures trying to climb over the corpses of Scourge and soldiers the grenade blast had killed. Pulling the trigger, she felt the rifle pulsing as it hurtled bullets into the bodies of the rampaging dead.

"Tiltrotor!" Ryan's voice screamed near her.

She kept firing, but flicked her gaze to one side to see Ryan carrying a badly-wounded Lindsey over one broad shoulder. The churning wind pulled her gaze up to the aircraft slowly descending over the fray.

Beside her, the Chief Defender fell over onto his side, unable to get up. Maria grabbed his arm and shifted her body under it. Rising to her knees, she pulled him upright. He screamed. Together, they managed to get to their feet as Maria fired at the Scourge drawing closer.

Vanguard Stillson's huge body moved through the crowd of Inferi Scourge like a rampaging elephant, tossing them left and right, shooting a few as he went. His helmet was gone and his armor was smoldering. Maria could see the shrapnel from the grenade had sliced away parts of his face. Yet Stillson kept fighting. The Scourge were so intent on him, Ryan and the others were able to skirt past the mob and head toward the aircraft.

Casting one last look at Stillson, Maria gasped as a Scourge grabbed the man's thick neck and bit into his cheek, infecting him. Usually the Scourge abandoned a victim successfully infected with the virus and moved on to another, but this one kept tearing at Stillson, chewing and appearing to devour his flesh.

Reichardt stumbled, forcing Maria's attention away from Stillson's demise. Pulling her superior up to his feet again, she continued to fire at any Scourge rushing them. Around her, other soldiers continued to fall, fighting the undead to their last breath.

"Keep moving, Chief Defender," she urged him. "I don't want to die today."

"Neither do I, and my name is Dwayne," he said crisply, his voice filled with pain and determination.

"I'm Maria."

"Nice to meet you, Maria. Now, let's not die," Dwayne said

"Is that an order?" Maria kicked over a Scourge and shot it in the face.

"Without a doubt," Dwayne answered with a grin.

Ryan led the way through the grim terrain, firing at the Scourge charging from every direction. Lindsey hung lifelessly over his shoulder. Maria shot anything that moved toward them that was not uniformed. Dwayne managed to draw his sidearm to help fight.

Another aircraft zoomed low nearby, its engines sputtering as its fuel ran dry. Maria watched as the pilots hurled themselves out of the hatch just before the aircraft hit the ground and slid through a mass of Scourge, crushing them beneath it.

The remaining tiltrotor was already packed with soldiers, but the crew kept hauling more up into the interior. The pilots of the other tiltrotor managed to reach it and clamber on board just as Ryan reached the tiltrotor and tossed Lindsey inside. Maria saw her friend's eyes flicker open for just a moment to gaze at Ryan.

"Ryan!" Lindsey cried out weakly.

"Get out of here, Linds," he answered, then Ryan grabbed the Chief Defender and pushed him into the arms of another soldier.

"There's no more room!" Maria exclaimed.

People were piled on top of each other nearly to the roof and she felt panic fill her.

Ryan grabbed her rifle harness on her vest and wrapped it around the handhold outside the hatch a few times before clamping the end to her armor. The tiltrotor began to rise.

"Get ready to fly, Maria," he said with a grin and kissed her passionately.

A mob of Scourge was almost upon the tiltrotor.

They were torn apart as the tiltrotor ascended.

"Ryan!" Maria gasped, reaching for him as the tiltrotor lifted her away.

"I'll catch the next airlift!" he shouted, firing at the Scourge leaping for the tiltrotor.

Just before the airship managed to gain more altitude and swing away, Maria saw Ryan look up at her, wink, then disappear under the onslaught of the Inferi Scourge.

Dangling from her harness, Maria stared at the decimated remains of the perimeter wall. An arm wrapped around her waist, pulling her dangling body closer to the doorway.

Looking over her shoulder, she saw the devastated expressions of the other soldiers.

The blue eyes of the Chief Defender met her gaze steadily. It was his arm wrapped around her waist, holding her.

Lindsey, weak and wounded, lay on top of some other soldiers. Her friend's eyes were full of unshed tears and Maria stretched out her hand to her. Lindsey clasped her hand, closed her eyes, and sobbed.

"We failed," Maria finally said.

"Never give up hope," Dwayne answered above the roar of the wind.

The tiltrotor's engines began to sputter as it flew over the enormous wall surrounding The Bastion.

Chapter 1

The fan sputtered, then died as the rolling blackout hit her section of the city. With a groan, Maria peeled the covers from her damp body and sat at the edge of the bed. Her silky black hair fell over one shoulder, covering her bare breast. The heat was already rising in her small flat. The metal walls and high windows made the narrow room claustrophobic and, once the power cut out, stifling.

"Another glorious day in hell," Dwayne muttered beside her. He peered at her from under the arm thrown over his face to shield his blue eyes from the sunlight beginning to pour through the window above the rumpled bed.

Maria yawned. "You mean a glorious day in the last great bastion of humanity?"

"That speech last night really did suck," Dwayne decided, laughing.

"Our fearless leader is full of shit." Maria stood up, stretching out her lean, muscular body. "President Cabot isn't the best liar. That whole line about 'our time of crisis being at an end' was ridiculous."

She sensed Dwayne making a grab for her ass and easily stepped out of reach. He groaned with frustration, then dragged his body out of bed. Scars crisscrossed his muscled arms and chest, a terrible reminder of the day he had almost died while fighting the Inferi Scourge. She had her own scars, her darker skin rising into hard keloids. They were fading slowly, but would never completely leave her.

A panicked soldier had tossed a grenade at the wrong time during the last great battle against the Scourge. Only their battle suits had kept Maria and Dwayne from being ripped to pieces, but some of the shrapnel had managed to pierce through the aging armor. It had been a terrifying twenty-four hours before they were cleared of the ISPV infection. Oddly, it was the time in the hospital that had laid the foundation for Dwayne and Maria's relationship.

"Our fearless leader may be full of shit, but it's in everyone's best interest to keep the civilians calm. We don't need riots in the streets again," Dwayne said, yawning.

"I'm just tired of being lied to. And to make it worse I have to defend those lies because it's my duty." Maria twisted her hair back from her face and flipped it over one shoulder. She wasn't vain by nature, but her hair was the one aspect of her looks she actually cared about. It was very long, glossy black, and thick with just a slight wave to it.

"We all do what we have to," Dwayne answered with a sigh.

She plugged the coffeemaker into her small generator to brew what little coffee remained in her precious stores. Dwayne slid his arms around her waist and pressed hard kisses against the back of her neck. She leaned into him, feeling his erection against her back, and toyed with the idea of dragging him back to bed. With a sigh, she pushed that thought away. Duty called in just two short hours.

"If you keep doing that, we'll both be in trouble," she teased, turning her head to catch a kiss.

"Tomorrow is our day," Dwayne promised.

"I can't wait," Maria answered, then returned her attention to rigging her ancient coffee maker.

"I have meetings all day today. Something is up with the high command," he said in her ear.

"I have to go stare out at a whole fuckload of Scrags howling at me all day," she answered, using the military slang for the Inferi Scourge. "I kinda think I'm the lucky one."

"You have no idea," Dwayne muttered, then let her go. "I think I'd rather deal with the Scrags all day." He stepped into the small shower in the corner of the room and slid the plastic door shut.

Maria winced when he yelped as the cold water hit him. They had overslept, and with the power down there was no way to heat the water in the reserve tank. Glancing out the narrow window over her tiny kitchen counter, she could see the long stretch of rectangular gray buildings reaching out toward the high steel walls that enclosed The Bastion.

It was an ugly, rank home. Lines of drying wash were the only bits of color in the city. On the edge of the far west of the city were bands of green where the fruits and vegetables were grown along the wall.

The Bastion was the only world she had ever known and she hated it.

Her silky black hair fell down around her face as she fumbled with the packaging for her daily protein ration. There were only so many ways to disguise tofu. Today it had a chickenish shape. The frozen lump would be a boring dinner unless she could pick up some herbs and vegetables in the market. Rations were enough to keep someone alive, but it was the produce and herbs from private gardens maintained on rooftops and in small courtyards that added flavor and spice to meals. Breakfast was either going to be bland oatmeal mixed with protein powder or a protein bar. She frowned at either option, shuffling her meager stores around in the cabinet.

Dwayne emerged from the shower, dripping and shaking his head. "Ugh. Cold shower. Hot room."

"These rolling blackouts are not doing anything for morale, especially mine. It's freaking summer. It's too hot to be without air conditioning." She finally settled on the oatmeal and emptied the packet into a bowl of water.

Dwayne sighed, shoving his hand through his hair, slicking it back. The silver hair at his temples and sideburns had increased recently. The silver strands had started to appear soon after his promotion to Castellan. He was a war hero and his promotion had been a political one. As Castellan he was in charge of protecting The Bastion, but Commandant Pierce of the Constabulary made his job difficult. He was often kept out of the loop on some of the more urgent matters. He had a good twenty-five years on Maria, yet he was ruggedly handsome, and his smile made her knees weak.

"Yeah, well, there is a lot more going on than they're letting us know." He began to shrug on his dark blue uniform, looking grim. "The Bastion is falling apart. Everyone knows it, the government just won't admit it. Well, actually, they can't admit it."

"The Scrags may never get into the walls and slaughter us all, but we're all slowly dying in here. In the end they *will* win," Maria decided grimly.

"I hope it never comes to that, and if I have any say about it, it won't," Dwayne vowed.

"I sometimes I wish I could crawl inside your head and know what the world was like before the Scrags destroyed the outside world. What it looked like...smelled like." She sighed, sitting at the edge of the bed. Her panties stuck to her tan skin and her hair tickled her bare breasts.

"I wish you could, too." He leaned down to kiss her cheek, smelling of soap. "I wish I could show you the world I knew when I was a kid. But it was far from perfect. The Scrags were already destroying parts of the world when I was born."

"But you knew a life where you didn't have to live in this damn broken down city," Maria reminded him.

Dwayne chuckled lightly, a twinge of bitterness to its tone. "Yes, but that only meant I witnessed the great fall of humanity and our exodus here. Not pleasant."

"True," Maria exhaled. "I hate feeling this way! But that speech last night..."

The night before, Dwayne had arrived just in time for them to curl up in her bed and watch the live broadcast. It was the anniversary of the great battle that had ended in defeat and the death of hundreds of soldiers. Maria and Dwayne had almost lost their own lives, and Maria still missed Ryan. It had been rumored that the speech would announce new victories against the Inferi Scourge and advancements in food production to boost morale in the city. Instead, it had been another charismatic but empty speech, full of false promises of a bright future that was not reflected in the everyday lives of the inhabitants of The Bastion.

"You and I know differently because we see it. But to all the people who never see what lies outside of the walls of this city, it gave them hope," Dwayne reminded her.

"But it's not real," Maria protested.

"No, but it's what they need." Dwayne lightly touched her cheek. "You give me hope. You're what I need."

Smiling slightly, she whispered, "You're my everything."

His lips caught hers and they shared a long, lingering kiss. Despite her tough exterior and reputation as a bad ass, she felt terribly vulnerable when she was with Dwayne. He owned her heart and soul completely.

"When will you be here tonight?" she asked as he resumed dressing.

"I have to swing by the divorce lawyer later today to sign more paperwork. Barbara has made a few more demands," he said, averting his gaze.

"She still doesn't know about me, does she?"

"And she won't. Not for a while. But I know all about Bob, don't I?"

She knew he loved her, but the bitterness in his voice made her wince.

"Not that I care. I haven't really cared for years. It's more of an ego thing, I guess. While I was risking my life in an attempt to defeat the Scrags, she was off..." He shrugged. "I guess a teacher is a better mate than a soldier."

"Unless you're a soldier."

Buttoning his jacket, he nodded solemnly. Catching a glimpse of her expression, he took her face between his hands. "Never doubt for a moment that I love you. I don't think I ever really loved anyone before you."

Kissing his palm, she sighed. "And I love you. I know you love me. It's the heat, the smell, you and me being a secret: everything getting to me. I just want to be somewhere with you, safe, sound, away from all of this. And I know it's not going to happen."

He kissed her again. It was the sort of kiss that made her want to drag him back into bed. "I love you."

"I love you," she whispered back.

"Your brown eyes are what keeps me going each day. That look inside them when you see me makes it all bearable."

"Don't make me cry! I'm a hard ass!"

He laughed, straightening. "I'd better go." Pulling a protein bar from his jacket, he headed toward the door. "Take care out on the wall."

"Unless the Scrags learn to fly, I'll be fine."

Dwayne smiled, then was gone.

The flat seemed painfully empty and small without him. It was one long narrow room with a long counter along one wall that served as her kitchen. Simple storage units were tucked under it, full of her food stores, clothing, and her few personal effects. Her bed was tucked into the opposite corner. The small shower and toilet closet were two feet away from the end of the bed. Despite its small size, she felt very lucky to have a flat all to herself. Most enlisted single people lived in the military facilities, but because of her status as a war hero, she had been allowed to live on her own in one of the residential sections of the city.

The vid screen on the wall over the counter next to the windows chimed twice then flicked on. It was the daily morning update that all the citizens of The Bastion were required to watch. Maria ignored the beautiful woman's face filling the screen as she shoved the oatmeal into the small oven on the counter.

"*Good morning, citizens of The Bastion. Though the Inferi Scourge continues to gather outside the walls of our fine city, the citizens of The Bastion continue to live their lives freely without threat. Several pivotal victories against the Inferi Scourge have...*"

Maria turned on the shower to drown out the lies and half-truths delivered by the mouthpiece of the government she no longer trusted. The anchorwoman, Raquel, was even more popular than President Cabot and people trusted her implicitly. Maria didn't understand the blind devotion.

Stepping into the shower, she braced herself as the freezing drops pelted her skin. The cold water washed away the last vestiges of sleep, awakening both her body and mind.

When she moved out of the shower into the muggy warmth of her flat, the fresh smell of coffee filled her nostrils. Naked, she poured the rich brew into a small cup, spooned in generous heaps of the raw sugar Dwayne had managed to procure, and gulped down the strong mixture. It was almost hot enough to burn her tongue, but the rush of caffeine and sugar really hit the spot. The vid screen had shut off after the morning dose of propaganda. Enjoying the quiet, she leaned her hip against the counter while she stared out the narrow window to the busy streets below.

Pouring herself a second cup, she couldn't help but feel a twinge of remorse as she saw children rushing through the morning crowds to school. Though she had never really thought about being a mother, the loss of her reproductive system due to her battle injuries had sealed that door forever. Dwayne had twins, a boy and a girl, about to celebrate their eighteenth birthday, and an older daughter that he had a difficult relationship with. Aware of her infertility, Dwayne was silent on the issue of them having children. She suspected he was waiting for her to bring up the subject. They could always adopt or apply to have themselves cloned, but Maria was uncertain about bringing children into this dismal world.

Of course, the government was always pushing for more children despite the shortages. The ratio between men and women continued to be worrisome. Only a third of the population of The Bastion was male. A large number of the deaths when the gate failed had been men.

Maria hated to admit it, but ever since the battle she had given up hoping for something more than her dreary life. Only Dwayne made life bearable and if not for him, she was certain she would have drowned in despair by now.

Sliding her finger over the face of her wristlet, she activated the screen. Every resident of The Bastion wore the device from birth. It expanded as the person grew, keeping a snug fit to the wrist, and couldn't be removed. Paper-thin, two inches wide, with a silver sheen to the metal, it was not only a communication device and personal computer; it was the government's direct link to the citizens. The life signs of every citizen were constantly monitored by the Science Warfare Division, and the instant someone died a squad was dispatched to destroy the body immediately. The ISPV was not airborne, but the government didn't want to risk a possible mutation. The implementation of the wristlets had been controversial in the days before the Inferi Scourge had finally destroyed civilization, but now the civilians of The Bastion were comforted by its presence on their wrist. It provided a connection to relatives and friends living on the far edges of the city, as well as kept them informed of the latest updates on food distribution, weather, and government news.

Like many, Maria simply regarded it as an extension of herself.

The screen lit up and she quickly tapped in her password. Her orders for the day appeared, unchanged from the night before, but she furrowed her brow at a new message from only an hour earlier. Sliding her finger over the message, it unfurled, filling the screen. Reading it over twice, she slowly lifted an eyebrow.

It was two short sentences ordering her to report to the Section Officer's office to meet with a representative from the Science Warfare Division after her patrol. The message was marked as top priority and top secret. Staring at the words, she couldn't fathom why she would be summoned by the SWD. Before her release from the hospital, she had been cleared of all contamination by the ISPV.

Still frowning, she quickly dispatched a coded message to Dwayne letting him know she'd be home late. Pulling her heated oatmeal from the small oven, she shoveled the nearly tasteless food into her mouth, suddenly feeling quite nervous about the day.

* * *

Hurrying up the long, winding metal staircase to the elevated monorail station, Dwayne finished eating the last of his protein bar. The flavorless meal left a chalky residue in his mouth and he couldn't wait to snag a decent cup of coffee at his office. Arriving at the station, Dwayne glanced over his shoulder at the sprawl of the city. Below, the inhabitants of The Bastion rushed about in a frenzy of activity. The morning sky was heavy with the promise of rain. The threat of storms always had the populace scurrying in preparation for the possibility of buildings leaking, power outages and flooding. A government drone wound its way through the streets broadcasting the latest news on the war against the Inferi Scourge on its screens while urging the citizens to remain diligent. Dwayne noticed that a few people stopped to watch the update, but most continued their morning routines without a second glance at the drone.

The station was off limits to civilians and only a few low ranking officers were milling around, sipping lukewarm coffee from a vending machine. The old benches, upholstered in black vinyl, were torn and cracked, revealing the padding. It was just another reminder of the slow decay of the once gleaming city.

A slight tingle alerted him to an incoming message and he quickly checked his wristlet. Entering his password, he watched a series of communiqués download. Stepping away from the other commuters, he read through the messages. Most were from the brass canceling all the meetings previously scheduled for the day. One was from his soon to be ex-wife reminding him to speak to his lawyer once he was off duty. The last was from Maria informing him she would be delayed in the evening.

"What the hell is going on with today?" he muttered.

Dwayne glanced toward the military complex that took up nearly all the southern quarter of the city. The tall steel buildings were as gray and ominous as the approaching storm, but there didn't appear to be any unusual activity. Yet, the cancellation of all his meetings with the upper brass and even Maria's mysterious delay didn't sit well with him. The grind of the daily routine was one of the things Dwayne could depend on, and any changes, usually due to some unexpected occurrence, was a concern.

In this terrible world they lived in, disruptions to the carefully attended balance of the city could cause major problems. The last time all his meetings had been canceled it was due to the food riots.

His gut told him something was not right, and it took all his willpower not to rush down the steps and into the streets to find Maria.

Closing down the screen of his wristlet, Dwayne looked up to see some of the other officers staring at their own orders with perplexed expressions on their faces.

Sweat began to bead his forehead, not because of the muggy air, but because he suddenly feared that the Inferi Scourge had finally breached the walls.

Chapter 2

The narrow hallway was stiflingly hot and the smell of boiling laundry was strong and acrid. Through the open door of one of the flats, Maria caught sight of two older women stirring a large stainless steel tub on a makeshift stove. Rose Bergman waved to her while Rose Garcia scowled into the mix of soap and water. Maria always thought of the sweet couple as 'the Roses,' but she found it easier to call them by their last names.

"Be careful on the wall!" Ms. Bergman called out.

"Don't tell her what to do, Rose," Ms. Garcia snapped. "You're always so bossy."

"I'm showing concern for her wellbeing, Rose," Ms. Bergman pouted.

Feeling obligated to make an appearance, Maria stepped back into the doorway and waved. "I'll be fine, Ms. Bergman. Thank you."

The older woman with the unruly silver curls smiled at her sweetly while Ms. Garcia scowled. The couple loved to squabble and Maria found it endearing. Both appeared to be in their sixties and wore their hair long under colorful headscarves. They worked long hours cleaning laundry for most of the people living in the building. Maria paid them in credits while others paid in food and other wares.

"We'll have your laundry ready tonight," Ms. Garcia informed her. "We're running a little behind. The blackouts set us back."

"We had to get out the propane stove," Ms. Bergman explained.

"It's all good. I don't need my things until tomorrow anyway." The pungent fumes from the soap were making her eyes water and she suppressed a small cough.

"We'll drop it off at your flat tonight," Ms. Bergman promised.

Pulling out her wallet, Maria fished out a few credits. "Here let me pay you now."

"Oh, we couldn't," Ms. Bergman protested.

Ms. Garcia plucked the money from Maria's hand and thrust it into one of the pockets of her heavy apron.

"Rose, we can't!" Ms. Bergman chided her. "Not until we're done with the job."

"You need your pills," Ms. Garcia said, her heavily sweating face set with determination. She continued to stir the laundry, ignoring her partner.

"It's fine. Really." Maria slipped out of the doorway. "You get your pills and I'll see you tonight."

"Oh, Maria," Ms. Bergman called out, rushing out after her. "I just wanted to thank you so much for all you're doing."

"It's no problem paying early."

"No, no, I meant about the speech last night. It was so wonderful to hear that we're close to defeating the Scrags. It's the first time in so long I feel any hope!" Ms. Bergman clutched Maria's hands in her strong, callused ones. "I keep telling Rose that things will be so much better once the Scrags are gone and we can return to the outside world. I do miss it so."

Swallowing hard, Maria mulled over her words before responding. "We're just doing our best out there. I do my part. That's all I can say."

Ms. Bergman's big blue eyes stared into hers searchingly. "We're close to winning, aren't we?" Her voice wavered slightly.

Not wanting to see hope die in her sweet friend's eyes, Maria squeezed her hand. "Of course. Closer and closer every day."

An enormous smile burst onto Ms. Bergman's round face and she giggled like a girl. "I keep telling Rose that, but she is always so cantankerous."

"I can hear you!" Ms. Garcia called out.

"Don't worry. We're doing our best," Maria declared, letting go of the woman's hand.

Clapping her hands, Ms. Bergman rushed back into her apartment. "I told you, Rose! We're winning!"

Turning, Maria hurried down the hall, half-smiling as the two wives continued their argument. The door to the outside was propped open with a broken cement block in a futile attempt to circulate air through the hallway. She stepped out onto the metal staircase that led down to the street and held tightly to the handrail as she descended the creaking stairs.

All the buildings in The Bastion had their primary entrances on the second floor. There were no windows or doors on the ground level of any of the buildings as a security precaution. The stairwells were collapsible, which was becoming a hazard as they grew rickety with age and the mechanisms sometimes gave way.

Striding into the street, she immediately noted the lack of open stalls along her pathway. Usually people were hawking their wares and services as soon as the sun rose, but with the impending storm rolling over the high mountain summits the businesses would remain closed until it passed. No one could afford a loss of inventory.

Most of the citizens of The Bastion were unemployed. Every citizen was provided with a home, rations, and basic living necessities from the city's wares. Those who were able to find employment fared a little better, able to purchase services and wares with Bastion credits. But there were no opulent homes to save up for, no cars to buy, no luxury goods. Therefore, most of the citizens created their own work like the Roses had done with their laundry services. For the citizens who ran the stalls barter was a way of life. Maria was one of the few able to pay with credits.

A drone rolled past her on its narrow treads, its screens flashing scenes of the military firing on the Inferi Scourge. Old footage, Maria noted. Soldiers patrolling the walls were not allowed to fire any of the precious ammunition stores unless absolutely necessary, and patrols outside of the walls didn't exist. She sidestepped the drone and plunged down a busier side street. It was packed with government officials rushing to the monorail system to catch the train. Usually the final train scheduled to run in the morning was the least packed, but people always ran late during bad weather.

The first drops of rain fell as she reached the stairs to the station.

Clutching the slick handrail, she pounded up the metal steps. Her long braid felt heavy against her back as she pulled the hood of her gray uniform over her head. As she stepped onto the platform, a hand gripped her arm. She almost jerked away, then realized it was Dwayne.

"I thought you left on the earlier train," she said.

Under the brim of his hat, his blue eyes were vivid and full of concern. "All my meetings were canceled for the day."

"Why?" Maria arched an eyebrow.

"I'm not certain," he said in a low voice, pulling her away from the rest of the commuters. "I think something is up."

Maria was startled to feel hope swell within her. "Do you think it's true then? That we're close to defeating them?"

Dwayne exhaled slowly, then leaned toward her. "I think it may be that we're *not* close to defeating them."

Sighing as the spark of hope died within her, Maria nodded her head. "And the president made so many promises last night..."

"The brass may be scrambling to make his promises a reality. I'm not sure. I don't rank high enough to be in the know." Rain beaded on the visor of his cap, then trickled off. "Why are you going to be late tonight?"

"I have a meeting after patrol." She wanted to tell him it was with the SWD, but she didn't dare with so many people milling about.

Frowning, Dwayne glanced toward the wall. "Just be careful today. Something doesn't feel right and it's not just the storm."

The monorail train rushed into the station, gliding to a quiet stop. The doors on the sleek white train slid open and the waiting commuters surged forward.

"Whatever is going on, we'll deal with it," Maria said.

Dwayne smiled slightly. "We will."

Together, they moved toward the train, their shoulders brushing as they walked. Maria wanted to touch his hand or have him wrap his arm around her, but discretion was best. Inside the train, most of the seats were occupied, so she found a corner and grabbed hold of the strap above her head. Dwayne joined her, holding onto the pole beside him. The doors closed with a hiss and the train lurched into motion.

The storm raged over the city, sheets of rain falling in great bands. Maria peeked out of the window and saw that most of the streets were empty. Lightning sliced across the sky as thunder rumbled.

"It's right over us now," Dwayne noted.

The buildings of the military complex rose higher than the rest of the city. They were ugly, dreary buildings, with black windows on only a few floors. The complex hugged the high wall and occupied a good portion of the southern part of the city. The government buildings nestled closer to the center were more impressive with sleek glass faces and more ornate styling. The capital building strongly resembled an elongated pyramid. The only ornamental garden in the city surrounded the capital. All the other parks or gardens that had been part of the original design of The Bastion had long been turned into housing complexes after the gate failed and the survivors from the valley had taken refuge inside the walls. As the train swept past the only part of the city Maria found even remotely attractive, she turned her gaze away. The building only reminded her of the president's speech full of empty promises.

"We're both in a mood this morning," Dwayne mused.

"It's the storm," Maria answered, even though they both knew it was much more than the weather causing them concern. The Constabulary was going to be hard pressed to bring the President's speech into reality. No president of The Bastion had ever made such bold promises before.

Dwayne gave her a slight smile that made her want to press kisses to his lips, but she fought the urge by looking at her wristlet. Just a few more minutes and she would be on the wall.

There was a sharp inhalation of breath from nearby, and then several people let out gasps of surprise.

"Look!" a man exclaimed, pointing out the window.

The commuters flooded to the sides of the car, faces and hands pressing to the glass. Being taller than most of the people on the train, Maria simply had to stand on tiptoes to peer over their heads.

"Dwayne!" she gasped.

"I see it."

A tiltrotor was swooping low over the city heading toward the capital building. The last tiltrotor Maria had witnessed in the air was the one that had rescued her a year before. Soon after, all the aircraft had been grounded due to lack of fuel. Her heart sped up at the sight of the black shape moving across the sky, its rotors repositioning to land.

Several people clapped just before the train swept into the main terminal of the city. Excited conversation filled the air. Quite a few of the commuters were already tapping away on their wristlets with great excitement.

"What does it mean?" Maria wondered aloud.

"I'm not sure," Dwayne answered, the lines in his face deepening.

The monorail train slid to a stop and Maria reluctantly started toward the doors. Dwayne dared to lightly press his hand against the small of her back as they shuffled along at the rear of the crowd. The mood in the train had been muted until the appearance of the aircraft and now the ecstatic expressions and joyful chatter seemed oddly out of place on such a dreary morning.

As she was about slip through the doorway, Dwayne whispered in her ear that he loved her. She smiled at the familiar words of endearment, then joined the throng of people moving through the long glass tunnel to the main terminal. Glancing back, she saw Dwayne heading in the opposite direction.

The main terminal was not nearly as busy as it had once been when all the trains had been running and had been open to the general public, but it was still fairly crowded. She quickly wove her way through the rush of people, avoiding the drably dressed professionals hurrying to the government facilities. Joining a group of other soldiers, she spotted a familiar face.

"Another day, another credit," Lindsey joked, falling in step beside Maria. Heavily favoring one leg, she leaned on her cane as she walked. The blond soldier had been terribly wounded in the last assault on the Scourge and now manned communications. Before the fall of humanity, her injury would have been easily repaired, but with resources low, she was disabled for life.

"It never ends, huh?" Maria answered.

"Nope. Day after day, same old, same old. Though, according to the president, things sound like they're looking up," Lindsey answered with a wink.

"The biggest load of bullshit I've heard in a long time," Maria groused.

"I almost believed him," Lindsey admitted, shrugging. "Then I remembered what I hear every day when I'm on duty and I stopped being a dumb ass."

"Something's gotta give soon. They have to figure something out," Maria said, her dark eyes scanning the crowd thoughtfully.

"They've been saying that ever since the first Scrag outbreak," Lindsey reminded her with a shrug of her shoulders.

"True. And the last time they got a great idea on how to push the Scrags out of the valley Ryan died."

Lindsey pressed her lips together, her eyes lowering. It was difficult for her to talk about Ryan. "They're talking about shutting down another train. I also heard a rumor about mandatory blackouts at sunset."

Maria shook her head. "Then why did President Cabot make all those promises?"

"Maybe he knows something we don't?" Lindsey shrugged again. "We can hope."

"Hope is all we got," Maria decided. "But I did see something weird on the train on the way here."

"What was that?" Lindsey asked.

"An aircraft."

Lindsey's eyes widened. "They were grounded."

"I know, but everyone on the last train saw it," Maria answered.

"That's what I get for taking the ground tram. Damn. I would have loved to have seen it. The sky has been empty for over a year." Lindsey lightly chewed on her bottom lip.

"Everyone got so excited when they saw it, but I'm not sure how I feel," Maria admitted.

Lindsey leaned heavily on her cane as she slightly frowned. "Maybe it's a good sign. If they're running the aircraft maybe we're close to something big."

They reached the end of the terminal where the transports were loading up soldiers and whisking them to their assigned duties.

"We need to get a drink soon," Lindsey decided, "catch up."

"Yeah. Definitely. Send me a message and we'll hook up," Maria answered before swinging herself up onto the transport that would carry her to the wall.

Leaning on her cane, Lindsey gave her a small smile. "And if I find out anything on that aircraft, I'll let you know."

"Rumors are going to be flying," Maria reminded her.

"I have a way of finding out what isn't bullshit," Lindsey assured her, then walked on.

* * *

As Dwayne passed through security and into the main building that housed the leadership of The Bastion Constabulary and their staffs, he noted the absence of the usual hectic bustle. This didn't bode well. The last time he had witnessed this sort of inactivity in the HQ was right before the last disastrous push against the Inferi Scourge. Between the aircraft, the president's speech, and the abrupt cancellation of all his meetings, his growing sense of unease definitely didn't seem without merit.

Tucking his hat under his arm, he strode down the long corridors that would lead him to his office. Like the rest of The Bastion, the hallways and offices were austere with black tile floors, pale gray walls, and very little ornamentation. Only the flag for The Bastion and the crest of the Constabulary decorated the main corridor. He noted that there was definitely tension in the air as the lower officials of the Constabulary spoke in hushed voices. A few glanced in his direction, but quickly averted their gaze. He was most likely the highest ranking officer in the building today and people didn't want to be seen gossiping.

Reaching his office, he glanced at the doorway across the hall that led to Commandant Pierce's office. The doors were shut.

"She didn't even come in today," Petra, his assistant informed him as she stepped into the corridor to greet him.

"Something's up," he decided.

He slipped past her into the small block of offices where his staff worked. Petra followed, her pad in her hand.

"Absolutely," Petra agreed.

She was efficient, smart, and tenacious. Very tall, a little too thin, and fine-boned, she reminded him of an avian predator. Her slightly hooked nose and narrow face only added to that impression. Her thick curls were pulled back from her face into a braided bun and her uniform was immaculate.

As he hooked his hat on a metal coatrack and slid out of his wet jacket, he inclined his head toward her pad. "I know you have your ear to the ground. Talk to me."

"I admit I have been in communication with a few sources," she said, the corner of her mouth quirking upward.

He entered his personal office and flipped on the coffee maker in the corner. He desperately needed caffeine. "And what did you discover?"

"Commandant Pierce didn't come into the office this morning, but her assistant sent a communiqué informing me that all her meetings were canceled, including the one with you. Then word began to filter in that all the echelon of the government was canceling meetings." She tucked her long body into a chair, her pad resting on her lap.

Dwayne slid into his somewhat comfortable chair behind his big ugly desk. "All divisions?"

"Every single one. I did some sleuthing and found out that an aircraft picked up the president's counsel and delivered them to the capital. Which is where they have been since early this morning," Petra informed him.

"I just saw an aircraft heading toward the capital."

"Ah, now, the interesting part is that the aircraft you saw was seen landing and departing from the SWD." Her fingers lightly caressed her pad. "I received that information right before you arrived."

"The Science Warfare Division? Interesting. They've been incompetent since the beginning of all this. I wonder what's changed." Dwayne set his hands on his desk and tapped the surface. The keyboard display popped up and he entered his password. Scanning through the communiqués being sent out by the senior officers, it was obvious they were all in the dark. "Do you know anyone in the Science Warfare Division?"

Slightly inclining her head, Petra affirmed what he suspected. "I have been in contact with a few people I know. They're scrambling for information as well. There are rumors of a covert operation being implemented by the SWD, but there are no specifics about what that operation may be."

"I hate being in the dark," Dwayne complained.

"I will attempt to remedy that," Petra vowed.

"You really are a tenacious creature," Dwayne mused.

"I would have made a fantastic investigative reporter before humanity fell," she conceded. "Of course, there will only be so far I can go before the information I secure for you will be considered top secret."

"That has never stopped you before," Dwayne said wryly. "You know how the Constabulary works."

"Unfortunately, yes."

"If I'm going to be efficient in my role as the Castellan, then I need to know what my dear Commandant is up to and she's not going to tell me herself." Dwayne folded his arms over his chest, feeling grim and uncertain.

"Understood. I'll report back as soon as I have something." Petra slid out of her chair and moved toward the doorway. "Will you need anything else?"

Dwayne shook his head, staring at the empty slots in the calendar glowing on his screen.

Petra shut the door behind her as Dwayne twisted his chair about and stared out the narrow window toward the capital building.

Chapter 3

As she hurried up the narrow cement staircase toward the heavy steel door at the top, Maria dragged in deep breaths of stale, humid air, preparing herself mentally. It was always hard to face what lay beyond the high walls of The Bastion. No matter how many times she patrolled the walls, her heart always sped up during the first few seconds on duty.

Her body armor was heavy and slightly claustrophobic. She hooked the strap of her weapon onto her armor, and it settled against her chest, a comforting, familiar weight. Her breath reverberated in her helmet as she swung around a landing and headed up the next flight of stairs. Above her, the door to the outside slid open and dark shapes blotted out her brief glimpse of the low-hanging, gray sky. The shapes morphed into soldiers descending the stairs after a long shift on the walls. They wore somber expressions inside their helmets as the hurried past her. Maria fiddled with the strap on her weapon one last time, then took the last few stairs in a rush.

Walking out onto the platform, her breath caught in her throat. The sky spread out in a panorama of dark clouds. Lightning flashed deep within the storm, and thunder echoed through the valley seconds later. Before her, the endless sea of the Scourge filled the wide expanse of the valley all the way to the foothills of the mountains towering above The Bastion. The creatures of her nightmare howled into the storm winds, their voices rising up to greet her. The sound of the Scourge crying out sent chills flowing down her back, her muscles seizing, and she forced a deep breath into her lungs. It was difficult to see them and not remember the terrible day that she had lost Ryan and almost her own life.

The virus that had brought back the dead also did a superb job of preserving them. Though many of the Scourge wore the grievous injuries that had killed them, they still retained a startlingly-fresh appearance. Wounds still wept blood and their flesh was remarkably free of decay. They looked disgusting, smelled rank, but were not rotting. They were dead, feral corpses that could survive the extreme heat of the summer and the terrible cold of the winter. The ISPV was potent and horrible in its power over the dead.

Swallowing hard, Maria hurried past the silent Maelstrom Platforms toward her post.

"Fucking goddamn Scrags," Special Constable Kurt Jameson grumbled next to her as they took up their positions.

"Same old, same old. Never changes," Maria answered, understanding his frustration all too well. It felt fruitless to stand on the walls day after day and stare down at the monsters humanity had become.

Jameson made a big show of hocking up a wad of phlegm, leaning over the rail, and spitting at the upturned faces far below. The action disgusted Maria and she averted her gaze. Beneath her, the Scourge howled and raged.

"Man, I wish we could just unload on them. Just fire away, watch their fuckin' heads explode. Instead, we gotta just stand here so the civvies feel we're doing something to protect them. It's all show,

Vanguard. I signed up to kill me some goddamn zombies," Jameson said, resorting to outdated slang to describe the Scourge. He was bitter that right after he had joined the armed forces the brass had clamped down on ammunition expenditures. The stores were running low with no way of replenishment.

"Hey, you know we're not supposed to use that word," Maria chastised him. "And we do what we gotta for the people we serve. It makes them feel comfortable and safe to see us up here."

Jameson shook his head with agitation. His face was young and handsome under his visor with strong cheekbones, a square jawline, and large brown eyes framed by thick, dark lashes. Fastening his intense gaze on her, he said, "You got to see action. You're one of the lucky ones. You actually got to kill some of them."

"The final campaign was a failure," she said tersely.

"Yeah, but it was an all-out assault on the Scrags right outside the wall. The engineers almost got the perimeter up before you got swarmed."

"And causalities were high," Maria reminded him, trying not to lose her temper. "I was lucky to get airlifted. I still have nightmares." Her voice sounded harsh, but she couldn't help it. So many had died in the fruitless push against the Scrags.

"We should just open fire on them. Kill them all." Jameson waved at the masses of Scourge reaching toward them. Sometimes they would push up against the walls, crushing the bodies of their undead comrades into pulp. "I don't know why they keep holding us back."

"The tiltrotors don't fly anymore. We wouldn't have air support. And you know how every bullet has to be accounted for. Ammunition is scarce. You know we can't fire without due cause or we get reprimanded."

"There has to be a way," Jameson persisted. Though he was always too exuberant in his desire to kill, she had never seen him so agitated. The president's speech had them all on edge.

"Orders are orders, Special Constable. We do our jobs," she answered after a brief hesitation. Expressing her frustrations wouldn't be conducive to their time on the wall. It was mindless work, but it had a purpose. The well-trained soldier inside her struggled with just being an object of display in order to give a sense of security to the populace of the city. Looking down at her weapon, it felt ineffectual in her hands. The clip was loaded, but she wouldn't be firing it. She would unload her weapon at the end of her patrol and turn in the full clips.

"C'mon, Vanguard, the orders are shit." Jameson shook his head, his helmet bobbing up and down on his dark hair.

"Keep your opinions to yourself. Don't let the Section Officer hear you, or it will be your ass."

Jameson grudgingly obeyed, but his sour look reflected her own mood.

With a sigh, Maria looked back over the throngs of the Inferi

Scourge filling the valley. Standing on the massive steel wall, she felt insignificant and overwhelmed.

* * *

"You asked to see me, sir?"

Maria ducked through the narrow doorway and into the small sweltering office where the Section Officer could usually be found. Today she was nowhere to be seen. A stranger sat in her place.

The thin man behind the desk glanced up. "Vanguard Martinez?"

"Yes, sir."

"Take a seat." He gestured to a chair.

The military headquarters was a massive stone building built flush against the wall. It was heavily fortified with reinforced steel. The interior was claustrophobic with low ceilings, thick walls, and warm air. Sitting on the uncomfortable metal chair, she tried to concentrate on anything but the sweat trickling down between her shoulder blades. Her dark hair fell over her shoulder in a long braid and her uniform clung to her moist skin. The armor had coolers, but the building was stifling. A fan whirled in the corner, lightly ruffling the short blond hair of the man before her. He was dressed in a white civilian suit, but had the aura of a man with power. Intently studying the scrolling information on his notepad, he lightly tapped his stylus against the desk.

"I'm the assistant to Admiral Kirkpatrick. Do you know who that is?"

"Head of the Science Warfare Division," she answered. She didn't want to add that that arm of the military hadn't done jack shit for the Constabulary in decades.

"Correct. My name is Mr. Petersen. I am here because you were selected by your superiors. I have been told you have an excellent record, are in perfect health, and can be counted on to perform to the utmost of your abilities."

"Thank you, sir," was all she could think to say.

"You're of Dominican descent, I see," he continued, his index finger lightly brushing over one of his pale eyebrows as he read the pad.

Maria was uncertain what her ethnicity had to do with her performance as a soldier and tried not to bristle. Instead, she nodded. "And Puerto Rican. But my family was located in San Antonio in the Republic of Texas when the plague started."

"Most Latino families are very tight knit," Mr. Petersen continued in his bland voice. It was completely devoid of any inflection she could use to determine his intent.

Slightly shrugging, she answered, "I guess. I can only speak for my own family."

"I see your father, Vanguard Mariano Martinez died fighting the Inferi Scourge when they invaded the sewer system a few years ago."

Swallowing hard, Maria slightly inclined her head in the affirmative. It was still difficult to discuss the death of her father.

Mr. Petersen turned his gaze toward her when she didn't verbally respond.

"Yes," she answered, her emotions threatening to choke her. "Yes, he died fighting the Scrags."

The man behind the desk regarded her for several long moments before returning his attention to his pad. "I see you have several siblings and your mother is still living."

"Yes, sir."

"Are you close to them?"

"As close as I can be."

"Clarify that statement."

Maria shifted in her chair uncomfortably. "They live on the far west of the city. It's hard to get over there more than a few times a year. Since the trains shut down, it's difficult to find transportation. It's a full day's walk to reach that side of the city."

"Yes." He tapped the stylus on the screen a few times. "You're single. Never married. Correct?"

She thought of Dwayne, but she nodded in the affirmative. "Yes, sir."

"Are you presently involved with anyone?"

"I don't see-"

"Are you presently involved with anyone, Vanguard?" Mr. Petersen's gaze was unnerving.

Maria shook her head. "No."

"I see you can't have children due to a grievous wound you received in battle. They removed your uterus and ovaries."

Swallowing hard, she answered, "Yes, sir." She was uneasy with the personal aspect of the questions.

Mr. Petersen moved the stylus over the pad, making notations and sorting through several files she could see glowing on the screen. "Are you happy?"

"Sir?"

"Are you happy? Do you find your life satisfying in the city?"

Maria rubbed her lips together.

"It's not a difficult question."

Reluctantly, she answered, "No. I'm not."

"Do you find your patrols on the wall to be a waste of your time?"

"It's not for me to judge my orders," she answered briskly.

"But do you find your patrols on the wall to be a waste of your time?" Mr. Petersen's gaze was piercing.

"I am aware that a show of strength is important for the morale of the citizens."

"But you feel ineffectual?"

Nodding tersely, Maria glared at the man across from her. He was picking at her wounds, making her angry and vulnerable. "I do not

30

understand the line of questioning."

Mr. Petersen leaned over the pad and made a few more notations.

"I am a good soldier," Maria continued. "I am well decorated for my bravery in the field. I have done my duty without question."

"You're questioning now," Mr. Petersen pointed out.

Maria pressed her lips together, considered her words, then said, "You want truthful answers. So do I."

Slightly arching one brow, Mr. Petersen slowly set his stylus down. Clasping his hands together, he leaned toward her. "What I am looking for, Vanguard Martinez, are soldiers that will be willing to spend an extended period of time on a special mission. If they're single with not many attachments, they will fare much better than someone with closer familial ties."

Maria narrowed her eyes slightly, but didn't respond.

"You fit those criteria." Mr. Petersen's intense gaze didn't falter. "Don't you?"

Reluctantly, Maria answered, "Yes, sir."

Mr. Petersen picked up his stylus and made another notation. He waited a few moments and then Maria caught sight of a communiqué flashing across his screen. Opening it, Mr. Petersen read it, and then set his stylus aside. Raising his eyes, he said, "Would you be interested in volunteering for a mission that will save the city and all its inhabitants and let us reclaim the valley from the Inferi Scourge?"

Maria hesitated as visions of Ryan being overwhelmed by the undead churned in her mind.

"I see you're a little hesitant." Mr. Petersen gave her a tight lipped smile. "You were involved in the last great battle against the Inferi Scourge, Vanguard Martinez. You were almost killed. You were rendered infertile. Don't you wish to seek revenge upon them?"

"I would like to see them destroyed. I would like for humanity to be free again."

"That isn't an answer to my question." Mr. Petersen leaned toward her, narrowing his eyes. "Or is it not the Inferi Scourge you blame for your losses? Perhaps you blame your superiors for an ill-conceived battle plan?"

Maria flicked her gaze away from the man with the uncomfortable stare and carefully formed an answer. "I did what I was ordered."

"But you feel the battle plan was faulty, no?"

Maria's mind lingered on the mobile walls getting stuck the in the mushy ground and the steel mesh ripping free. She remained silent.

"You can speak freely with me. In fact, I insist on it. It's vital that I understand you, Vanguard Martinez."

Lifting her eyes, Maria answered carefully, "I believe that certain factors were not taken into consideration when the battle plan was formalized."

Mr. Petersen gave her an unexpected smile, bobbing his head. "I concur! The SWD never supported the battle plan and was absolutely opposed. Commandant Young and the President's council were adamant that a seventy-two percent probability of success was more than acceptable. We disagreed. In fact, we asked for more time to perfect our own plan to eliminate the Inferi Scourge from the valley and restore order."

"If the plan was faulty, why did they do it?"

Mr. Petersen tilted his head and gave her an amused look. "You're a very smart young woman. Why do you think they did it?"

"We're running out of resources and time."

"Exactly. It's not so hard to surmise. Just walk through the streets of the city and see how much has been lost just in the last twenty years. Soon the city will go dark and humanity will be lost."

"How is your plan any different?" Maria asked pointedly. "What makes the SWD believe they can be successful?"

"Simple." Mr. Petersen flashed a wide, unexpected smile. "We found a way to allow our soldiers to walk among the Inferi Scourge without fear of attack or infection. We have found a way to deceive them into believing you're one of them."

Maria gasped and slumped back in her chair in shock.

"Our newly developed serum requires the healthiest of bodies. Our plan demands the strongest of minds. Once the serum is administered, you will leave the city and systematically clear the valley and close the gate."

Maria let out a breath she hadn't realized she was holding. "Oh, my God."

"Amazing, isn't it? Just when it seems we're on the verge of extinction, *science* has delivered us from evil." Mr. Petersen picked up his stylus. "Now, would you be interested in volunteering for a mission that will save the city and all its inhabitants and let us reclaim the valley from the Inferi Scourge?"

Maria nodded her head adamantly. "Yes, absolutely."

Mr. Petersen smiled.

Chapter 4

Maria was dozing lightly when Dwayne crawled into bed with her. The fans around the bed hummed softly, and her body was cool beneath the thin sheets. As Dwayne's naked body stretched out next to hers, she rolled over and kissed him.

"You're awake," he said, surprised, and wrapped his arms around her.

"You're late," Maria replied. She ran her fingers down over his face, feeling the light poke of his stubble against her skin.

"You got my message, didn't you?" Dwayne asked worriedly.

"Uh huh. Dinner with the kids."

"The twins wanted to see me." Dwayne's hands gently pushed her hair back from her face, his fingers gentle as always. "Even Caitlyn joined us."

Maria knew that Dwayne's eldest daughter was usually unavailable. She was an assistant to one of the president's council members. "How was she?"

"Argumentative as always. I felt like I was on trial. She should have been a lawyer. It was exhausting. I just wanted to get back here and see you."

"Just see me?" Climbing on top of him, she whispered softly to him in Spanish, knowing he loved it.

"I don't know what the hell you're saying, but it sounds great," he said with a little moan as she rubbed her bare breasts over his chest and kissed his neck.

Soon he was hard and inside her and they gasped as their bodies rode together. Dwayne wrapped his fingers in her hair and kissed her deeply as they came together, perfectly matched as always.

"I like that greeting," he finally whispered in a husky voice.

Resting her forehead against his, she smiled slightly. "Me too."

"I should get delayed more often," he teased as his hands slid over her hips.

Maria's hands traced over his muscled chest lightly, the light smattering of hair tickling her palms. She could sense Dwayne tensing as his expression grew concerned.

"Maria, why are you awake?"

"I have something to tell you."

"Okay," he said cautiously.

Sliding off of him and tucking herself into his side, she drew a breath, then said, "I volunteered today for a new program with the Science Warfare Division."

"What? With the SWD? Why?" Sitting up, Dwayne frowned. "Explain it to me."

"Technically, I'm not supposed to," Maria replied, pushing herself up to face him.

Dwayne narrowed his eyes, his gaze growing steely. It was a look she remembered from when he had once been her commanding officer. It used to terrify me, but now it just made her want to comfort him.

"Cut the bullshit, Maria. We both know the SWD hasn't done anything effective in years. If they want you for some sort of special ops, I want to know what it is. Petra was busting her ass all day trying to find out what is up with the SWD and the secret meetings today, and she came up empty. If you know something, I want to know. Not just because it concerns you, but because upper echelon has a tendency to leave me out of the loop when it matters most to our people. We already break enough rules being together, so spill it."

Maria shoved her hair back from her face and sat cross legged in front of him. Pulling the sheet over her legs, she took a deep breath. "Fine. Fine. It's a big operation and it has the full support of the president. It's huge, Dwayne. I think this is why the president is so optimistic about finally beating back the Scrags."

"Tell me more." His voice was like steel and his gaze was intense.

Maria hesitated, knowing that what she was about to relate would only antagonize him more. "They asked me to volunteer because I'm physically fit, unattached as far as they know, and I'm not 'breeding stock' and therefore, not important to maintaining our population."

"That's a shitty way to put it."

"I didn't care much for his wording either. But the really big news is this, Dwayne," she said, reaching out to take his hand, "they think they found a way to fool the Scrags into not attacking the living. It's like an antidote. They said even if the Scrags did bite me, I wouldn't get infected."

"If they swarm you, that won't matter. You'll die." Dwayne's voice was clipped, his expression concerned.

"But if they think I'm one of them..." She flicked her dark eyes up to meet his vivid blue ones. "...they won't swarm me."

"They never attack each other," Dwayne admitted, realizing where the conversation was leading.

"I could walk among them, kill them, and walk away without being attacked." Hearing the words coming from her own lips made her shiver, but the excitement of being able to fight the Inferi Scourge without fear was like electricity in her blood. "I'm going to help clear the valley and close the gate."

"So they forcibly conscripted you into doing this." Dwayne shook his head.

"No. It's volunteer only. They didn't tell me the mission until I volunteered."

"I should have known." He leaned back on the pillows, covering his face with one hand. "The canceled meetings, the aircraft, the SWD being involved, and you being late back from your patrol."

Maria tenderly rested her hand his chest. "I have to do this. They'll give me a plot of land once the valley is cleared and the gate is repaired and shut. I can pick anywhere I want. I'll get a standard settlement deal - one prefab house and furniture." She leaned her chin on his shoulder and stared at him. "I want out of this city, Dwayne. I want those fuckers gone. I want a life with you. Maybe we can't have kids, but we could have a good life if those things aren't out there."

Lifting his hand, he settled it against her cheek. "How long?"

"The serum will give us four to six months to clear the valley. They think I'm unattached, so..."

Dwayne held her tenderly against him. "Other people will do it. You don't have to go."

She was silent, unsure of how to answer.

Dwayne chuckled, shaking his head. "What am I saying? Of course, you do. You've been going batshit crazy with the rolling blackouts and shortages just like the rest of us." He kissed her brow, smoothing her hair back from her face. "The one thing you can't stand is not being able to *do* anything."

"Exactly. So now that I *can* do something..."

"Once you're back, the divorce will be settled, the twins will have graduated from high school, and we can concentrate on us. We *will* get married."

"And move out to a nice prefab house near the lake," Maria added.

"Absolutely." He swept her hair back from her face. "I'll miss you."

"I'm doing this for us."

"I know, but I'll still miss you and worry about you every second you're gone." He sighed, then asked, "When are you going to leave?"

"In forty-eight hours," she answered, her voice catching. Rubbing her palm against his chest, she struggled not to cry. "I love you, Dwayne Reichardt."

"I love you, Maria Martinez." He slightly frowned. "Forty-eight hours, huh?"

"Uh huh."

"You won't be doing much sleeping," he decided and dragged her over on top of him.

* * *

The small flat was refreshingly cool in the early hours of Maria's last morning in her home. The air conditioner whispered above her head as she scrubbed the counters and sink. The last of her coffee stores percolated in the old coffee maker and the remains of her monthly rations were packed in a box near the door. She planned to give it to the Roses before she left her flat for the last time.

It felt odd packing up and preparing to leave, but when her duty was complete she wouldn't be living in the city. Instead a house near the lake would be waiting for her. She had already reviewed the designs on her personal pad. Dwayne had sat at her side as she had studied the various floor plans before making her final choice. He'd left the decision entirely up to her. Again, she was reminded of why she loved him.

"You're fighting for it. It's your house. Just give me a recliner, a vidscreen, a beer, and I'll be fine," he promised her.

A long tendril of hair fell into her face as she finished rinsing out the sink and she pushed it back with a damp hand. Looking over her

35

shoulder, she surveyed the flat one more time.

All of her uniforms were neatly packed in one small bag and her personal items were in another. She'd never decorated her tiny space and her personal possessions were meager. She was allowed only a few small mementos out in the field, but she was fine with keeping her possessions in storage until her return. As long as she had a life to return to that was all that truly mattered.

Straightening, she tossed the sponge she was using into the recycle bin and set her hands on her hips. She considered changing her clothes before calling her mother, but decided against it. Her final change of clothes before she left the flat would be into her uniform, and her mother had never approved of her enlisting.

Angling the vid-screen to face the bed, she slid her personal pad into the port in its side and dialed her mother. Sitting at the edge of the bed, she tucked her hair back from her face and took a deep breath. This was not a conversation she was looking forward to. The "Call Connecting" screen remained much longer than she expected. When it flickered alive, her brother appeared.

"Hey, Mariano," Maria exclaimed in surprise, not expecting to see him.

"What you up to, sis?" Her brother's dark kinky hair, big dark eyes, and charming smile were a welcome sight. He was the oldest in her family and strongly resembled her father. Like Maria, he was also named after their father.

"I need to speak to Mama. It's important. Is she around?"

"Yeah. Give me a second."

Her brother vanished from the screen. The camera transmitted a good view of her mother's living room. The furniture was old, overly stuffed, and covered with brightly colored throws. A huge block of ice sat in a basin slowly melting as a fan whirred behind it. The wall was decorated with pictures of the family arranged around an enormous picture of the Virgin Mary. It was familiar and comforting. Maria felt a little tension leave her shoulders. Her mother entered the scene, sat down in her recliner and fussed with the fan so it would blow icy air over her.

"Hey, Mama!"

"It's not Sunday. Why are you calling early? Are you okay?" Her mother frowned at her, her shapely lips turning downward. Lourdes Martinez's hair was just as dark, thick, and beautiful as Maria's, but with fine strands of silver. It was braided and coiled into a fancy bun on the top of her head. The resemblance between Maria and her mother was quite strong, down to the stubborn set of their chin.

"No, Mama. Nothing is wrong. I just wanted to call to let you know that I am going on a special assignment for around six months. I am not going to be able to contact you and I just wanted-"

"Where are you going?" Lourdes demanded, her eyes flashing.

"Hey, sis, what's up?" Mariano leaned into view.

"All I am allowed to say is that I am on a special assignment authorized by President Cabot," Maria answered truthfully.

"I don't like it," Lourdes decided. "Tell him no."

"I can't, Mama, I already said yes. I'm getting ready to leave now," Maria answered, her hand sliding nervously up and down her arm.

"No, no. You tell him no. I already lost your father to the Scrags. Don't you go and get yourself killed, too!" Lourdes wailed, slamming her fist onto the armrest of her recliner. "You almost died in that last battle!"

"Mama, I can't. I made a vow," Maria answered quietly, her voice rough with emotion.

"Calm down, Mama, and listen to her," Mariano urged.

"I am listening and I don't like it!" Lourdes shouted. "You never come to see me! I hardly see you, and then you call to tell me that you're going to do something stupid and get killed!"

"Mama," Maria exclaimed, standing up sharply. "I just wanted to tell you how much I—"

"If you go, I don't want to hear from you ever again! I already lost your father! Isn't that enough?" Lourdes sprang out of her chair and stormed out of view.

Mariano swiftly moved into frame. "She doesn't mean it, Maria. She's just upset. She never wanted you to go into the service," he said, trying to console her. "And when you got wounded..."

Despite her best efforts to control her emotions, tears streamed down Maria's cheeks. "I know, I know. But I need to do this. Not just for me, but for you, for her, for everyone."

Mariano nodded, his dark eyes studying her. "Just keep safe. Come home safely. She'll forgive you then."

"Don't be angry with me."

"I'm not. I'm proud of you. And scared for you," Mariano admitted. "Be careful, okay?"

"Tell her I love her, please," Maria asked. "And I *will* come back."

Mariano flashed his beautiful smile. "I know you will. You're a bad ass. *Te amo*, sis."

"*Te amo*," Maria answered just before the screen flashed to black.

"That could have gone better," Dwayne's voice said, startling her. He stood just inside the narrow doorway in his dark blue uniform, his expression one of concern.

"I don't know why I ever expect it to go well when I talk to her." Maria yanked her pad out of the vid-screen and angrily tucked it into her bag of personal possessions.

"Mothers have a way of making their kids crazy. I see it with Barbara all the time. Hell, my mother did it to me, too." Dwayne reached out and touched her cheek lightly. "But she loves you. She wouldn't be so upset otherwise."

"I know that, but it doesn't make me feel any less shitty." Maria wiped at her face with irritation. "I just wanted this one conversation to go well and not end with her yelling at me."

Wrapping her up in his arms, Dwayne held Maria close, kissing her forehead.

"And I hate crying! And she always makes me cry and feel like a stupid little kid. I'm not a stupid little kid, Dwayne. I'm a bad ass. I'm a decorated war hero. I shook the hand of the president! But is that good enough for her?"

Dwayne listened in silence as she raged.

Maria clenched her hands at her sides, stepping away from him. "She is always going to hold it against me for enlisting. Hell, she even blames me for getting wounded. The last time we argued she claimed I had killed her future grandchildren because I chose to become a soldier. At least she didn't throw that in my face this time."

Dwayne sighed as he sat on the edge of the bed. His blue eyes gazed up at her with such tenderness, Maria felt her rage start to ebb away. It wasn't his fault she had failed in all of her mother's expectations of her. She had betrayed her mother by following in her father's footsteps, and for that her mother would never forgive her. Rubbing her hand over her stomach, she could feel the ugly scars beneath her shirt.

"I don't know what to say other than I believe in you and what you have chosen to do. I'm scared, too. That's most likely why she's lashing out at you. I'm not saying she's right to do so, but I do understand how scared she must be that she's going to lose you." Dwayne touched her hand lightly. "*I'm* scared I'll lose you."

"You won't. I promise. This will work. We'll kill the Scrags and be free of them. Then you and I will go live in that house by the lake." Maria plopped onto the bed next to him, covering her face with her hands. "I just wanted to have a good moment with her before I head out there. I wanted to tell her I love her."

Rubbing her back lightly, Dwayne said, "At least she knows you were thinking of her before deployment."

"True. I almost didn't call her. I thought about just sending her a message. But she would have killed me for that." Maria ran her hands over her hair and turned her gaze toward him. "Did you get your errand taken care of?"

"Yes, I did," Dwayne answered, smiling slightly. He pulled a small black box out of his pocket. "I'm not going to lie. I don't like the idea of not having any communication with you while you're out there. I hate that they're disabling that aspect of your wristlet."

Sighing, Maria nodded. "I don't like it either. It's going to be the hardest part of the mission."

"Well, I went to see someone that gave me a solution." Dwayne held out the box. "It's for your wristlet. I am leaving this up to you, though. All you have to do is connect it to this device and it will download a program that will create a back door for us to communicate through."

Maria took the small box, flipped it open, and stared down at the small device. "If I got caught..."

"Exactly. That's why I said it's your choice. I'll download the same program, of course."

"We'll be jail breaking our wristlets," Maria said in a solemn voice.

"Which is against the law," Dwayne added, his keen blue eyes gazing into her dark ones.

Maria ran her finger lightly over the slim silver stick thoughtfully. Running her hand over her wristlet, she activated the screen and slowly tapped in her passcode. She could feel Dwayne watching her, waiting. Pulling the device out of the box, she tilted her head to gaze at the man she loved.

"I'm willing to risk it if you are," she finally said.

The corner of Dwayne's mouth quirked upward as he nodded. "I'm absolutely ready to risk it."

It took only a few minutes to install the program and Maria was relieved when it disappeared into the depths of the wristlet's operating system. Together, they experimented with pulling up the hidden program and giving it a test run. They were both pleased when there were no problems.

"She's the best," Dwayne decided with a grin.

"And how do you know this hacker?" Maria wondered.

Grinning, Dwayne destroyed the device, grinding it under his boot. "I've been around a long time. You meet people along the way and find out their special talents."

"She's one of us?" Maria said.

"Maybe. Does it matter?"

"No, no." Maria smiled as she ran her fingers over the slim wristlet. "Whoever she is she just made this job not seem quite so bad."

"The new house on the lake wasn't enough to make it bearable?"

With a shrug of her shoulders, Maria lay back on the bed. "It was enough to keep me motivated, but this actually makes me happy."

Dwayne settled down beside her, his arms around her waist and his face tucked into the crook of her neck. "I'm going to miss you."

"I'm going to miss you." Maria noted the time and her stomach coiled with nerves. Rolling over onto her side, she rested her palm gently against Dwayne's cheek. "I have to go in two hours and the hardest part of all of this is leaving you."

Dwayne stroked her hair as he kissed her lips softly. "Two hours, huh? Let's make it count."

Laughing, Maria dismissed her fears, her doubts, and her heartbreak as she lost herself in making love to the only man she had ever loved.

Chapter 5

The painful scene before him reminded Dwayne of the night he had packed his bags and walked out of his old home. It held a finality that bothered him.

Maria slowly moved through her flat, checking each cabinet, the closet, under the bed, every location she might have left one of her small possessions. The tension that had settled between her eyebrows had her forehead knotted. Clad in her charcoal-colored dress uniform, her hair braided down her back, she looked lovely, yet stern.

Standing near the door, Dwayne waited for her to finish her last round through the flat. It was spotless, sterile, and empty. It made him ache to see it so barren.

For the last year, this place had been his safe haven from a bitter, soon to be ex-wife, surly teenage twins, an angry adult daughter, the pressures of his career, and the unyielding stress of knowing the Inferi Scourge were just outside the wall. Now it was over and he couldn't help but feel afraid when he watched Maria heave her bags over her shoulder.

Her strength of will always amazed him. All too vividly he remembered her rousing him after the grenade had exploded and hurtled them both through the air. He couldn't even see or hear at first. Blood had filled his eyes and he had been deafened by the explosion. Though badly wounded and bleeding profusely, she had kept firing at the Scourge streaming toward them. Unable to get to his feet, his mind numbed and his body yet to feel the full brunt of his wounds, he had been dependent on her to rescue them. He would never forget her expression when she had seen the tiltrotor swoop down to airlift them. She had been unbelievably beautiful in her joy. He was fairly certain that was the moment he fell in love with her.

Now watching her stand in silence as she regarded her flat for one last time, he grappled with the fear that he would never see her again once she walked out the door.

"I think I'll miss this old rat cage," she said at last.

"You're what made it special," he reminded her.

Drawing in a deep breath, she closed her eyes. As she slowly exhaled, he watched her features soften and the tension disappear from her brow. She was amazing at keeping herself calm and collected when all the rest of the world fell apart around her. Right now he felt close to shattering. Despite his resolve, his eyes felt damp and he folded his arms over his chest and swallowed hard.

Maria opened her dark eyes and her gaze settled on him. She strode the few steps over to him. A smile slightly pulled on her lips even though her eyes were rimmed with unshed tears.

"I have to do this," she said at last.

"I know," he answered in a low voice, his emotions kept in check. He wouldn't make this harder on her.

"If I can help destroy the Scrags in the valley and reclaim it for us, I have to. I can't stand not being able to do anything but wait for the city to completely run down, or for them to get in."

He knew her speech was more for her than for him and he let her talk without interruption.

"I will not fail," she finally added after a long beat. "I will make this work for you and me and everyone else in this city."

"I know you will. I have no doubt in your abilities. Hell, you dragged my ass onto that tiltrotor. I wouldn't be here if not for you." He lightly touched her chin. "Your stubbornness sets into your jaw and once that happens, I know nothing will stop you."

That made her grin and she wrapped her arm around his waist.

Dwayne kissed her mouth, her cheeks, and her forehead before drawing her against him and inhaling the fragrance of her hair. They were almost the exact same height and she fit so perfectly against him. Despite their age difference, life experience, and backgrounds, they were perfect for each other. They completely understood each other. And because of that, he wouldn't shed a tear in front of her or let her know how terrified he truly was.

"I need to catch the train," she said at last, pressing her lips to his cheek.

"Keep in contact when you can," he urged her.

"I will. I promise." She kicked the box of provisions with her foot. "Please make sure the Roses get this."

"Are you sure you don't want to do it yourself?"

"They'll ask too many questions and I don't think I can deal with that right now," she answered truthfully. "Give them my love. And if they ask you where I went, tell them I'm doing my job."

"I will."

"And can you check up on them once in a while? I don't think Ms. Bergman always has the credits to get her medicine from the herbalist."

"Did they run out of her meds?" Dwayne knew the shortages were growing more rampant, but he didn't realize it had hit the medical sector.

"She's on a very long waiting list. But luckily the herbalist has some sort of concoction that helps her. Even if it is a placebo, she swears it works."

"I'll check on her. I promise." Once again he was reminded of how Maria tended to watch over those around her while often ignoring her own needs. It was a stark contrast to his ex-wife who always demanded so much from those around her.

Falling into silence, Maria shifted her bags and stepped closer to the door. Her shoulders set and he saw her jaw tighten. Turning toward him, he saw her strength and resolve take firm hold of her countenance.

"I'll see you, Dwayne Reichardt."

"And I'll see you, Maria Martinez," he answered in a rough voice.

Her fingers lightly caught his for a second, then she shoved the door open and slid into the hall.

Fighting the urge to follow her, he folded his arms over his chest and took in a deep, ragged breath. Lowering his chin, he waited as the echo of her footsteps faded away. He took a breath, released it, lifted the box of rations, and stepped out of the doorway. Looking over the empty flat one last time, he clenched his jaw to reign in his emotions, and shut the door.

* * *

"Spring rolls! Fresh spring rolls!"

Maria glanced over at the street vendors as she walked through the throngs of people filling the market. All around her people were hawking wares, homemade crafts, or food made from their own small rooftop gardens. Refurbished battery powered fans and reconstructed lightweight clothing were the big sellers. Children scrambled around the silent, dry fountain on the street corner while a man strummed a guitar as a woman beside him sang in a sweet, high voice.

A government drone circled the square flashing the latest updated news. The screens showed scenes of the Inferi Scourge being gunned down by the valiant defenders of The Bastion. Maria paused, clutching the strap of her bag. The screaming, torn faces of the Scourge made her skin crawl and she looked away.

The city streets were hot, stifling, smelly and overwhelming.

Looking up, she stared at the bright blue sky visible between the tall grey buildings surrounding her. The top of the wall was barely discernible above the roofs. It was a far departure from the historical vids of people living in high rise apartments, driving sleek cars, dressed in fancy clothes, decked out in the latest tech, and living lives free from the Inferi Scourge.

Jostled by the crowd hurrying past her, Maria was drawn out of her ruminations. She swept her gaze over the people busily going about their business. She almost felt like laughing as she felt the futility of her mission wash over her. How could she save all these people? How could she even be certain that her mission would succeed?

Taking a deep breath, filled with dust, humidity and the stink of the city, she forced her doubts away. She was a soldier of The Bastion Constabulary. She wouldn't doubt. She wouldn't fear.

"No going back now," she murmured, and rounded the corner heading to her destination.

The side streets were narrower, congested with people, and stifling. Someone poured their dishwater out of a high window and drenched some of the passersby. Shouts of anger rose as Maria hurried around the corner, grateful the dirty water had missed her.

Ducking down the stairs into the now defunct subway station, she shifted the bags on her shoulder. She had a few minutes before the only running subway train would pick her up. It was used exclusively by the military and would be stopping just for her. All the stations were now restricted areas. Squatters had been removed and the trains shut down as a security precaution after the Scourge had infiltrated the sewers.

Swiping her wristlet over the locks on the heavily barred doors, she heard an ominous click as they unlocked and opened. She entered the gloom beyond the gaping doors, leaving behind the heat and sunlight. Lights flickered on as she walked across the cement floor to the platform. The doors clanked shut behind her.

It was cooler down here. She sneezed in the stale air and rubbed her nose. Her wristlet caught her eye and she ran her fingers lightly over the smooth silver surface. The screen activated, flashing that it was locked, ready for her commands. She tapped her finger lightly over the edges, her password unlocking the device. She had no additional orders. Nothing had changed. Maria felt both relief and trepidation.

Noises in the pitch black tunnel startled her. Instantly on alert, her body tensed as her heart began to pound. The sound of approaching footsteps reverberated through the station. *Running?* Her hand automatically slid to her side, but she had no sidearm.

Mentally chastising herself for panicking, she nonetheless let her bags slide to the floor. The last breach of the wall had been years before when her father had died fighting the Inferi Scourge in the sewer system. The footsteps were moving swiftly in her direction. It had to be a maintenance crew, but why would they be running?

Maria knew that her panic was born of her experience outside the walls. Ever since the defeat of the Constabulary military forces, she had been suffering from post-traumatic stress disorder just like all of the rest of the survivors. A few months of therapy and drug treatment had greatly reduced her anxiety attacks, but her body was absolutely singing with adrenaline as she listened to the sounds emanating from the darkness.

Backing away from the bags, she sought out a hiding place. The old station was devoid of any decoration and all the benches and vending machines were long gone. There was no place to conceal herself. She considered calling out, but decided against it. If there was a breach, the last thing she wanted to do was draw attention.

An alarm sounded, announcing the arrival of the train within a minute's time. She shot a quick look over her shoulder toward the locked doors. Should she flee up into the market and risk the Scourge breaching the door, or hope the train arrived in time?

"Oh, shit," she muttered.

It couldn't be the Scourge. They couldn't be in the system.

Backing toward the doors, she drew a deep breath.

"Out of the hole, soldiers!"

It was a woman's voice.

A search and destroy squad, dressed all in black, bounded out of the tunnel. Their heavy masks made them look like insects as they moved in perfectly synchronized motions. With striking ease, they leaped onto the platform and fell into formation. Two members of the squad dragged what looked like a body bag up off the tracks and dropped it at their feet. The leader was the last up onto the platform. She acknowledged Maria's existence with the curt nod of her helmeted head.

Maria stared at the group uneasily. They were heavily armed and carried extra clips of precious ammunition on their belts.

The sound of the train roaring toward the station lured Maria back to her bags. She yanked the straps over her shoulders as the leader of the squad scrutinized her. They were of equal rank, but the other woman was from the SWD, not the Constabulary. There was little love lost between the two divisions.

Hot air blasted out of the tunnel as the sleek train skimmed to a stop. The train consisted of only two cars plus the electric locomotive. The doors of the second car slid open and a short male with dark curly hair stepped out.

"Vanguard Martinez," he called out.

Still under the watchful eye of the squad leader, Maria stepped forward. Lifting her wrist, she swept it over the pad the conductor extended. Reading the results displayed on its surface, the man gave her a short nod of his head.

Once onboard, Maria took a seat, still watching the squad as it stood silently waiting for the train to depart.

The conductor glanced at the search and destroy squad, but said nothing as he took his seat. He was from the SWD, but his black uniform didn't have any signifiers of rank or even a name tag. The train sounded an alarm then pitched forward, the station platform swiftly disappearing from Maria's view.

The dim lights of the car did nothing to enhance the dull gunmetal color of the floor and walls. The seats were thinly padded and had long ago stopped being comfortable. The monitors that had probably been used at one time to entertain the passengers were silent and dark on the wall. Maria adjusted her bags, straightened her uniform and peered out the window. It was completely black outside the glass. Not even emergency lights illuminated the tunnel. Only the bright blue lights on the train's exterior glowed weakly into the darkness.

"How often does the train run?" Maria asked.

"When it's needed, which isn't often," the nameless man with the curly hair and ambiguous uniform answered in an equally featureless voice.

"Who are you?" she asked impulsively, swiveling in her seat toward him.

"Your escort," he answered.

She became aware of the pistol strapped to his thigh and arched her brow. He ignored her. She fought the feeling of discomfort slithering into her soul. Folding her arms over her breasts, she glowered at her shiny boots. She had nothing to fear. All would be well once she was outside the wall, immune to the Inferi Scourge, and slaughtering them.

Ten minutes later the train's alarm sounded. Glancing out into the darkness, Maria started when the glow of the train lights flowed over the form of a person standing next to the tracks. The impression of a tattered uniform and ragged face made her jerk away from the window.

"What is it?" the blank man asked.

"I saw someone standing near the tracks."

"Maintenance," the man answered dismissively.

She replayed the image in her mind's eye and suspected that her mind had filled in the other details. She was still tightly wound from her earlier scare. He was probably right. She had seen a maintenance worker and her mind had altered him into an Scourge.

Maria grasped her bags while the train slid past heavy blast doors that clanged shut the instant the last car was clear. The SWD station was filled with light as the train slid to a stop. Another heavily-armed search and destroy squad stood on the platform.

Suddenly, Maria wasn't too sure she was imagining things. She gave the man beside her an accusatory glare. "They're in the subway system, aren't they?"

The doors opened and her escort gestured for her to depart without responding to her allegation.

"What did I see in the tunnel?" she persisted.

"Someone in maintenance," he answered imperturbably.

"Then why all of this?" She indicated the waiting squad.

"Routine patrols." Again, he motioned for her to disembark.

Unnerved, Maria exited the train. A quick examination of her surroundings revealed two machine gun nests positioned on a second level facing the heavily fortified blast doors that sealed off the tunnel.

The search and destroy squad brushed past her as they filed into the train.

"Routine, my ass," she muttered.

Her wristlet beeped and she tapped it.

"Welcome to the Science Warfare Division Facility. Please proceed to the terminal." A simple and to-the-point message.

Following the directions, Maria departed the station and bounded up a narrow stairway that led to another set of heavy doors. A guard scanned her wristlet, keyed open the door, and waved her through.

Stepping into the main terminal, Maria swallowed hard. It was filled with seek and destroy patrols.

Chapter 6

Mr. Petersen emerged from the gathering of SWD patrols, his starched white suit a vivid contrast to the all-black armor of the soldiers. He slightly inclined his head as he approached Maria.

"Seems you have a lot going on around here," Maria said, her voice sounding a bit clipped even to her own ears.

"There is some excitement," Mr. Petersen admitted, slightly shrugging. He was as unperturbed and collected as he had been during their previous interview.

"I saw something in the subway tunnel," Maria said boldly.

"Did you?" Mr. Petersen started to walk.

Maria fell into step beside him, shifting her bags to her other shoulder. They thumped against her back as she wove her way through the squads waiting to be dispatched. "They're in the tunnels, aren't they?"

"We can never be too vigilant when fighting against the Inferi Scourge," Mr. Petersen answered vaguely.

"How did they get in?"

Guiding her out of the main terminal, Mr. Petersen tucked his hands behind his back and studied her expression. "Whatever makes you believe they're in the tunnels?"

"I saw something."

"What did you see?"

Maria started to answer, but faltered. The truth was, she wasn't really sure if she had seen one of the Scourge, or if it had just been a maintenance worker. "I saw a search and destroy squad at the station where I was picked up. They had what looked like a body bag, and something was in it."

"There are regular patrols in the tunnels. The teams take equipment to run a variety of tests. I am certain that is what you saw them carrying."

"And all of the squads back there? Where are they going?"

"Routine patrols for all the tunnel systems under the city. Sewer, maintenance, subway..." Mr. Petersen shrugged. "You just happened to arrive on a very busy day." Stopping before a lift, he swiped his wristlet over the console and the doors slid open. "After you."

The cold sterility of the SWD headquarters and all she had seen had her on edge. Staring into the lift, she felt her gut twist. Maria's instincts were fine-tuned, and she believed in them implicitly. The action of boarding the elevator unexpectedly had a finality that unnerved her to the core of her being. She inhaled through her lips and steeled her resolve.

Maria entered the elevator after Mr. Petersen. Turning on her heel, she faced the closing doors.

"The mission you volunteered for is going to go down in history," Mr. Petersen said in a warmer tone. It was as if he sensed her discomfort. "It's a brave and wondrous task, and will have far-reaching ramifications for all of humanity."

Unable to find the right words to speak, Maria opted to nod her head instead. There was no indicator as to whether the elevator was rising or descending. Only the steady hum of the elevator motor and slight vibration gave any hint of its movement through the shaft.

When at last the elevator doors opened, Maria was struck by the glaring whiteness of the walls. She was so used to the dingy grayness of the city, the bright lights reflecting off the sterile white walls was almost blinding. Her boot heels echoed as Mr. Petersen led her down a corridor devoid of any activity, which was disconcerting after the constant crush of bodies and cramped living space in the rest of the city.

"I will show you to your room, and then you will be summoned for the examinations to prepare you for the inoculation," Mr. Petersen informed her.

"I don't understand. What do you mean 'prepared'?"

"Though your recent medical examinations reveal you to be in perfect health, we will be taking one last look at your vitals before administering the antidote," Mr. Petersen explained. "Nothing too invasive. Just a simple physical exam."

Her hands felt clammy and she realized she was far more afraid than she had believed she would be. "And you're sure this will work?"

"Of course," Mr. Petersen responded confidently. "We wouldn't want to imperil one of our best, would we?"

After several turns, he finally opened a door that led into a much shorter corridor. Doors lined both sides in regular intervals; security cameras rotated slowly overhead.

"This one is yours. I advise you to quickly unpack and change into your fatigues," Mr. Petersen said as he swiped his wristlet and the door opened.

The room was long and narrow with the shower, sink, and toilet stall at the far end. A simple bed was tucked into a recess in the wall, and a small desk with a matching chair fit into a corner next to a narrow wardrobe. It wasn't much smaller than her flat.

Maria stepped into the room and slung her bags onto the bed. The door hissed shut behind her and she was grateful to find herself alone. Mr. Petersen unnerved her far more than she cared to admit.

Before slipping out of her uniform, she quickly stowed her personal effects utilizing the bins tucked under the bed. Taking great care, she hung the charcoal-colored trousers and matching jacket in the wardrobe. She tried to smooth out the slight wrinkling with her hands and was careful to make sure the jacket was hanging correctly so it would retain its shape. The Roses had always done such a great job caring for her uniforms. As she thought of her sweet neighbors, she felt a twinge of regret that she had not visited them one last time.

A small black box that held her medals and her miniature Bible, a gift from her father, was placed on the top shelf of the wardrobe. Inside the Bible was a folded photo he had given her on her sixteenth birthday. It was a snapshot of a ten year old Maria dressed up in her father's uniform. A wide smile graced her tiny face that was dwarfed by his helmet and the sleeves and trouser legs were rolled up with a belt cinching the jacket. Being an old-fashioned sort, her father had not only printed the photo, but had scribbled a message on the back. As a teenager she had not understood why he hadn't just transmitted the image to her wristlet, but ten years later, the tattered, wrinkled photo was a treasured possession.

Once her personal effects were tucked away, she washed her face and freshened up. The lighting over the sink was quite bright, and as she peered into the mirror, she studied the faint scars decorating her neck and cheek that were clearly visible in the harsh light. Thankfully, the marks were not nearly as noticeable as the thick keloids decorating her stomach, side, and back.

The wristlet hummed on her arm, alerting her of an incoming message. For a moment she hoped it was Dwayne, but it was from Mr. Petersen informing her that he would be escorting her to the lab, and was on his way.

When he arrived exactly ten minutes later, she was dressed in her casual trousers, t-shirt, blouse, and heavy combat boots. The journey to the lab was short and silent after his initial greeting. Again, she noticed the disturbing lack of people and noise in the long corridors.

At last, they entered an examination room filled with various types of medical equipment. A large vid-screen took up one whole wall, and a very tall blond woman stood before a work station studying the data scrolling across the surface of the monitors before her.

"This is Dr. Beverly Curran. Beverly, this is Vanguard Maria Martinez," Mr. Petersen said by way of introduction.

Beverly Curran glanced at Maria briefly before returning to her work. "Good evening, Vanguard Martinez. Please take off your blouse and get on the treadmill," the doctor said, gesturing toward the exercise equipment nestled amidst the monitoring machines. Her eyes didn't stray from the screen before her.

Obeying, Maria couldn't help but wonder what was holding the doctor's rapt attention. After hanging her blouse from a hook set into the wall, she stepped onto the treadmill.

Finally pulling her gaze away from her readouts, the doctor strode over to the treadmill, quickly activated it, and set the controls.

"You've done this before, you know how it works," Dr. Curran said simply.

"Yes, I do."

Dr. Curran nodded, then returned to her station. Mr. Petersen didn't leave the room as Maria had expected, but lingered at the doctor's side.

The large screen flickered to life, readouts beginning to scroll as a thermal image of Maria's body appeared. Maria glanced at it briefly, then concentrated on her breathing, finding her running rhythm. Having endured countless tests before she had been allowed to return to duty, she was a little bored by the whole process, but not particularly worried. Except for her scarring, a missing kidney, and damaged reproductive system, she knew she was in good health. As the treadmill's speed increased, she easily matched its pace.

"She's in perfect health despite her past injuries," Dr. Curran murmured.

"Her readings are superb," Mr. Petersen agreed.

"Excellent readings on her cardiovascular system," Dr. Curran noted.

As Maria listened to the two people discuss the status of her health as if she wasn't even in the room, her thoughts began to drift. She could see the image changing and at one point was fascinated to see her internal organs animated on the screen.

Sweat trickled down her spine and between her breasts as the pace continued to accelerate. The heavy thud of her boot heels against the belt was a steady beat.

The doctor lowered her voice as she spoke to Mr. Petersen and their hushed conversation lured Maria's attention to them. They both appeared excited and pleased with the data scrolling across the large screen.

After the treadmill, Maria submitted to a variety of tests and watched as samples she provided were examined and evaluated. As the hours wore on, Dr. Curran appeared increasingly pleased with all the results. The blond woman's stern expression even broke into a smile a few times.

"Excellent, excellent," she muttered to Maria.

"So I'm a good candidate for the serum?" Maria finally asked after being instructed to don her blouse.

"Absolutely," Dr. Curran responded, giving her a slight smile.

Up close the doctor appeared older than Maria had first thought, with fine lines around her eyes and strands of white mixed in with the blond. The woman's face was narrow with high cheekbones and a long nose. Her gray eyes were striking, but her thin mouth tended to frown, already forming lines in the corners.

"Good. I'm ready to do this," Maria assured her.

"Let's have a talk, shall we?" Dr. Curran suggested, gathering her pad and striding toward the door.

Mr. Petersen walked behind Maria as she followed the doctor. Dr. Curran moved with a quick gait, her long hair flowing behind her. She led Maria through several thick doors, moving her deeper into the SWD facility through lab areas, offices, and corridors filled with doctors and nurses. The noise and bustle was welcome after the disquieting silence upon her arrival.

Dr. Curran entered a small room with a table set in the center and several chairs circling it. The metallic walls were highly reflective and Maria noticed her form was a fractured image on the surface.

Taking a chair, Maria rested her hands on her lap. The sterile environment and grueling tests had worn on her nerves. She was uncertain what she had expected once she had reported for the mission, but her level of discomfort surprised her. She felt as though she were being kept in the dark about something. That some important bit of information was not being divulged.

The doctor and Mr. Petersen sat across from her. Mr. Petersen folded his arms over his chest, his bland face expressionless while Dr. Curran entered some final notes into her pad.

"May I ask a question?" Maria asked as she finally grasped what was bothering her.

"Of course," Dr. Curran answered, not looking up.

"This is a safe procedure, this serum...what you're giving me. It's safe for me to take?"

"It is," Dr. Curran assured her.

"And it will make me immune to the Scrags, correct?"

"Yes."

"Then why aren't you giving it to everyone in the city?"

Dr. Curran lifted her eyes to scrutinize Maria, then folded her hands on the table. "The serum we're giving you and the other volunteers requires a healthy body. It's a vaccination that uses a modified version of the Inferi Scourge Plague Virus. You will become very ill for a short period of time before your body builds up a sufficient immunity. You're in superb physical shape whereas many in the city are not. There would be a good chance that a lot of our citizens would succumb to the serum and become Inferi Scourge."

"And there is no danger of that happening to me?" Maria asked, rubbing her suddenly damp palms over her knees.

Dr. Curran stared at Maria for a long moment, then said, "Do you really think we'd risk our best soldiers if we were not certain of the serum?"

Before answering, Maria considered the intensive medical examination to which she had just been subjected. "No. I don't."

"Precisely," Dr. Curran agreed. "It's much safer for everyone in The Bastion if only a few take the Inferi Scourge Plague serum, clear the valley, and close the gate instead of risking our elderly, infirmed, and our children."

The doctor's words made perfect sense. "I understand. When will I be given the vaccine?"

"Tomorrow, but I would like to take this time to discuss the Inferi Scourge with you."

Shifting in her seat, her sore muscles aching, Maria lifted her eyebrows. "Oh?" She'd rather return to her quarters and take a shower than discuss the Inferi Scourge, but her curiosity was sparked. "What about the Scrags?"

"What do you know about them?" Mr. Petersen asked.

Maria's mouth quirked into a sardonic smile. "Other than that they want to destroy us?"

"Exactly," Dr. Curran answered.

"Well, I know what I was taught in school..."

"Which is?" The doctor settled back in her chair and crossed her long legs.

"That they're the product of the Inferi Scourge Plague Virus that was created by terrorists over a hundred years ago." Maria took a cue from the doctor's more relaxed posture and slumped slightly in her chair, trying to relax her sore body.

"Continue," the doctor urged, "tell me the history."

Mr. Petersen didn't appear to blink as he watched Maria.

Maria switched her gaze back and forth between them. Perhaps this was some sort of test of her cognizance or psychology. She cleared her throat.

"The first incident was in India. The Inferi Scourge appeared and ravaged the country. Within days the Scrags had the upper hand. Pakistan fired their nuclear arsenal on India claiming that they had to protect themselves. What remained of India's government fired back, and the area was decimated. The world thought that the Scrags had been destroyed, and then they appeared in Israel a few months later. Israel's government initiated a kill order. Anyone infected was immediately destroyed. The Arab nations attempted to invade while Israel was dealing with the Scrags; Israel used their nuclear arsenal on their enemies." Maria furrowed her brow, trying to recall the details. "I believe that is when the world started an embargo against the Middle East."

Dr. Curran nodded. "Go on."

"I don't see why-"

"Please continue," Mr. Petersen urged.

Maria folded her arms over her chest, trying to recall her lessons. "I believe they traced the virus back to the Russian mob, or maybe it was the Chinese. The ISPV became the most popular terrorist weapon in the world. Every time there was an outbreak, it was stopped until around sixty years ago when it took hold in South America and Europe. It got to the point where no one could control it, and that is when the world started building walls. Eventually, there were more of them than us. The walled cities began to fall. Forty years ago a coalition of nations created The Bastion and airlifted the last surviving people here."

"Basically, you're correct. The ISPV was a terrorist weapon. It had a chilling effect on the nation it was being used against. It was difficult to fight. Do you know why?" Dr. Curran tilted her head, studying Maria.

"Because the Scrags are dead humans that the virus revives," Maria answered. "I remember reading something about it being very hard for people to kill the Scrags when they first appeared because they thought they were just ill, not the reanimated dead."

"Exactly," Mr. Petersen agreed. "They look basically human except for their wounds."

"And their eyes," Maria said quickly. The eyes of the Inferi Scourge haunted her. They were blank and cloudy like the dead.

"You've fought them up close," Dr. Curran said.

51

"Yes."

"Did you find it hard to kill them?" the doctor asked.

Maria pondered the question. The Scourge didn't decompose, and therefore they looked like wounded people in need of help. But their screams, their whitish eyes, and clutching hands were a nightmare. "It was hard at first, but I saw what they can do when there are enough of them." She could still hear the screams of Vanguard Stillson as he died. "They eat us."

"Actually," Dr. Curran said with a slight smile, "they don't."

"I saw it," Maria snapped.

"The virus that reanimated them prompts them to spread the virus. It's transmitted through saliva, so they bite. And they bite hard enough to rend flesh," Dr. Curran explained. "If there are enough of them trying to infect a victim, then yes, it would appear that way. But they do *not* actually eat us."

"The ISPV created creatures that resemble some monsters from old horror vids from a very long time ago," Mr. Petersen said with a slightly pompous expression. "People jumbled the facts with the myths of those old movies and altered the truth about the Inferi Scourge. The media was especially guilty of this."

Shifting in her chair, Maria considered correcting them, but realized it would be fruitless. She *had* seen the Inferi Scourge not only attack, but start to eat Vanguard Stillson.

"The question remains: did you find it hard to kill them?" Dr. Curran persisted.

Maria shook her head. "Not after the first shot. Then it was easy."

"Do you think it was easy because you didn't know any of them? In the original days of the infection, many people struggled to kill loved ones that were turned," Mr. Petersen said.

"Maybe. I don't know," Maria answered truthfully. Could she kill Dwayne or her family members if they were infected? Her mind told her that she could, but her heart whispered a solid *no*. "Why are you asking me this? The Scrags out there have existed since before I was born."

"Yes, with the exception of the fallen soldiers from the last attempt to push back the Inferi Scourge. We never did recover their bodies," Dr. Curran pointed out. "They're still out there."

She felt her jaw drop as the words punched into her gut like a sledgehammer. Ryan's smile slashed through her mind. Forcing her mouth closed, she lowered her gaze to her hands. Could she hold her weapon and pull the trigger on Ryan?

Dr. Curran tapped the table, pulling Maria's attention back to her. "So, from what you have told us about the past, you do understand what the Inferi Scourge are - the dead reanimated by a virus that does not let them truly die. And you understand that actions taken by the nations that existed before The Bastion failed for a variety of reasons. Israel and the Republic of Texas were two of the last countries to fall due to their strict kill orders. If the rest of the world had followed their leads, perhaps there wouldn't have been a need for The Bastion." Dr. Curran let her words sink in as she leaned forward and placed her elbows on the table. "Therefore, should you see some of your former friends and fellow soldiers out there among the hordes of the Inferi Scourge, the question is simple: Can you kill them?"

Maria drew in a sharp breath, then slowly exhaled. She could remember the names and faces of each fallen soldier like they were her own family. She thought of Ryan, grinning at her, and winking in the face of death. Then she thought of the Roses, Dwayne, and all the people crammed into the dying city. "Yes. Yes, I can."

* * *

Maria woke with a start when her wristlet purred against her skin. Sitting up, she quickly tapped in her passcode. Accessing the hidden program buried within the operating system, she held her breath. She was relieved to see Dwayne's face appear.

"Dwayne," she breathed.

"Are you okay?" he asked immediately. His face was tiny on the screen, but she could see the concern in his expression.

"I was sleeping," she answered, "but I'm so glad to hear from you."

"Rough day?"

"Really rough," she conceded. Snuggling down on her bed, she held the wristlet so she could clearly see him and he could see her. "They ran a lot of tests."

"We can't talk long." Dwayne gave her a gentle smile. "I had to see you before going to sleep. It feels wrong to be going to bed alone."

"I know how you feel. I wish you were here."

"Are you having second thoughts?"

Maria pondered his question, then shook her head. "No. No. I need to do this. I want more for us than living in a squalid flat in the middle of this dying city, but I'm realizing this may take a lot more out of me emotionally than I thought."

"What do you mean?"

"Did you ever think about the people we left behind after the final assault? The ones that didn't make the airlift?"

"The ones that died," Dwayne said somberly.

"And came back. Because they did come back, you know. I didn't really think about it until today when they asked me if I could kill them when I see them." Maria swept her hair back from her face as she watched Dwayne process what she had just said.

"Can you?" he asked, raising his eyebrows.

"For us, for the city," Maria replied sorrowfully, "I can do it. But it's going to hurt like hell."

"I'm sorry, darling. I never thought about that aspect of this mission."

"Neither did I."

"You can do this though, Maria. You can make it through. I believe in you. And if you want out, I will find a way to get you out."

"No, no. I'm in this for the long haul. I can do it, Dwayne. I just need to get my focus and not be afraid. When I said yes to this mission I was just so desperate to do something I really didn't think through all the possible ramifications of that decision."

"Our time is up," Dwayne said regretfully. "I'll call you tomorrow."

"I love you," Maria whispered, her fingers from her other hand touching his image lightly.

He touched his screen, too. "I love you."

The screen flashed black then returned her to the main menu.

This was going to be the hardest part of being on the mission: being away from the man she loved.

Rolling onto her back, Maria covered her face and fought back tears. She could almost feel his presence nearby, comforting and loving. Her body yearned to feel him pressed against her side. Closing her eyes, she pretended he was laying next her, his breath matching her own as they fell asleep together.

Chapter 7

The next morning she awoke to a call from Dr. Curran informing her that she would be sent for in two hours' time. Crawling out of bed, she pushed her body through her morning exercise routine before taking a hot shower. Breakfast was delivered to her room on a tray by a young male nurse. He stared openly at her scars as she took the tray.

"Thank you," she said, dismissing him before he asked any stupid questions.

He backed out of the room and the door slid shut.

Uncovering the tray, she was surprised to see eggs and bacon, toast, orange juice, and a thermos of coffee. She was certain the meat and eggs weren't the real thing, but the food smelled amazing. Picking up a slice of bacon, she nibbled on the end curiously. It didn't taste at all like flavored tofu. Suddenly ravaged by hunger, she dug into the meal, eating each bite with great relish. Nothing she had ever eaten had tasted quite so amazing. When she finally finished, she poured herself a cup of coffee and sipped it slowly. It was the best she had ever tasted.

After she finished, she retrieved a second set of fatigues from her locker and took a shower. The water was hot and helped ease her aching legs and arms. As she soaped her skin, she studied the scars that had so fascinated the nurse. She supposed she had grown used to their appearance. The knots of hard flesh were a part of her now and she could barely remember what it was like not to wear them as a badge of honor. Her fingers traced over the especially savage wound over her lower belly. This was the injury that had robbed her of any chance of motherhood. It didn't do any good to mull over the possible future children she could have had with Dwayne if she hadn't been hit by the flying shrapnel, so she pushed those thoughts away.

Once out of the shower, she dressed and braided her hair. Despite her fabulous breakfast, her stomach was fluttering. For the thousandth time she reminded herself that she had no reason to be afraid.

Dr. Curran came for her personally. Today her long blond hair was wound in a bun on top of her head and she was clad in a white jumpsuit. There was a much more official air about her and her voice was clipped when she spoke.

"Are you ready?"

"Yes, ma'am," Maria answered, trying to not sound like she was lying.

"Very good," Dr. Curran said briskly and led her down the hall to the wing with the labs. Her heels clicked against the floor as she strode swiftly ahead of Maria. "Did you sleep well? Did you eat all your breakfast?"

"Yes, yes. It was all good," Maria answered.

"I arranged your breakfast. Real eggs and bacon. A rarity in the city, but obtainable for special purposes."

"Like last meals, huh?" Maria joked.

Dr. Curran gave her a sharp look that gave Maria pause. "Something like that."

Outside the lab, there were four SWD special officers on duty. The previous day there had been one. Dr. Curran and Maria were quickly waved through security, but the nurses preparing to enter behind them were immediately stopped. Glancing over her shoulder, Maria saw the guards scanning the wristlets on the nurses, their expressions grim.

"More security today," Maria pointed out.

"Today is an important day," Dr. Curran answered.

When they entered the lab area, Maria noted that even more doctors, nurses, technicians and the like were bustling about than the day before. A few threw curious looks her way before hurrying on. Dr. Curran took hold of Maria's arm and pulled her down a new corridor, moving her swiftly past the onlookers.

"Why are they staring?" Maria asked in a low voice.

"They know who you are. This is a big day for the SWD. This is the first step in our push against the Inferi Scourge. The success of your mission will ensure the continuation of humanity. You're very important, don't you realize that?" Dr. Curran shot her a curious look, obviously surprised that Maria hadn't recognized this on her own.

"I'm just a soldier doing her job," Maria answered.

"You're more than that now," Dr. Curran assured her. "Much more." She swiped her wristlet over a control panel set in the wall, and a set of doors hummed open. Entering, she motioned for Maria to follow.

Inside was another disturbingly white room. An examination table surrounded by monitors and equipment was the center of attention for several technicians. A few stole peeks in her direction, but most were fiercely concentrated on their tasks. Several robotic arms extended from the ceiling, swiveling about as they obeyed the commands of the technicians below. Satisfied, a technician pointed upward and the arms retracted into their bay in the ceiling.

"What's all this for?" Maria asked, intimidated by the sight.

"You're going to be extremely ill for about ten hours. We're going to have to monitor you closely. Because of the raging fever that you will experience, we're going to sedate you."

"And this is safe? You've done it before?"

Dr. Curran turned and gazed into Maria's eyes. "Yes, we have done this before. You will be safe in here."

Maria's misgivings didn't fade with the doctor's assurances. Though she discerned sincerity in Dr. Curran's expression, she felt as though the entire truth of the situation was not being revealed.

Striding over to the technicians, Dr. Curran motioned for Maria to take a seat on the examination table. "Please remove your blouse and boots."

Complying, Maria took deep, discreet breaths, steadying her nerves. The tension between her shoulder blades was starting to be a burning pain. With a quick roll of her shoulders, she focused her concentration on exorcising any anxiety while keeping her goal firmly in mind. A technician took the discarded blouse and boots when Maria sat at the edge of the examination table.

"Everything is looking very good, Vanguard Martinez," Dr. Curran assured her. "Please lie down and get comfortable."

As Maria swung her legs up onto the table, her gaze swept over the faces of those gathered around her. Their white jumpsuits and austere hairstyles made them appear cold, remote, and just as robotic as the mechanical arms retracted into the ceiling overhead. She pulled her braid over one shoulder as she lay down. A technician touched the table and a small panel lit up. Guiding Maria's wristlet over the panel, the technician gave Maria's hand a gentle squeeze.

"You'll be alright," she said. Her green eyes flicked toward Maria's face before she returned her attention to creating a link between Maria's wristlet and the monitoring equipment.

"We've established a connection," the technician informed Dr. Curran after a minute or two.

"Excellent," Dr. Curran replied.

Another technician said, "Data is in the stream."

Dr. Curran rested her hand on Maria's shoulder. Her fingers were icy cold. Maria realized the Doctor was far more nervous than she had let on.

"It's almost time," Dr. Curran stated, her gaze locked to one of the screens. "Everything is going just as we'd hoped."

The door hissed open and Mr. Petersen appeared in Maria's peripheral vision.

"We're almost ready," Dr. Curran said in a voice that was surprisingly curt.

Mr. Petersen inclined his head. "Very well. Everyone has arrived and is waiting for you to proceed."

Frowning, Maria searched the corners for cameras, then her gaze settled on a wall to her left. It was bare of any equipment and the technicians were careful not to linger on that side of the examination table. She wondered if it was a hidden window.

"Someone is watching?" Maria asked. "Why?"

"Don't worry about it," Mr. Petersen replied.

"It's just a few of the higher ranking officers of the 3WD. You don't need to worry about them," Dr. Curran assured her, but the glare she cast in Mr. Petersen's direction was tinged with anger. "Mr. Petersen will be joining them now."

Without a word, Mr. Petersen turned and left the room.

"We're ready," a male technician informed Dr. Curran.

"Very well. Clear the room," Dr. Curran ordered. She leaned over Maria, her expression suddenly far from cold and remote. There was concern and warmth in her eyes. "Don't be afraid." After giving her hand a light squeeze, the doctor followed her team out of the room.

Alone, lying on the table, staring up at the robotic arms, Maria felt dread wash over her. She clenched her teeth together, fighting her fear.

One of the monitors began to beep faster and she realized it was her heart rate. Ashamed of feeling so afraid, she closed her eyes and took several deep breaths while she waited for the doctor to return to administer the vaccine.

Instead, the robotic arms above her came to life, uncurling from the ceiling. The hum of their rotors compelled her to open her eyes and she gasped as one of the mechanical hands lightly pressed on her chest. Abruptly, clamps slid up out of the table, encircled her ankles, wrists, elbows and knees, and locked. Unable to move, Maria started to hyperventilate. Despite all her attempts to push away her misgivings and fears, she was utterly terrified and convinced she had made the wrong choice.

"Dr. Curran!" she called out as she watched one of the robotic hands tap a code into a stainless steel refrigeration unit marked 'Biohazard.' "Dr. Curran!"

"Please remain calm," the inhuman voice of the machine commanded her.

"Dr. Curran! Why are you restraining me? What is going on?" Maria demanded.

"Please remain still and do not struggle," the machine answered.

The refrigeration unit hissed open.

"Dr. Curran, please, talk to me. I don't understand why you're restraining me. What are you doing to me?" Maria twisted her hands, struggling to get free, but the clamps only tightened. She could hear the heart monitor's beeps accelerating.

The robotic arms continued their task, the whirring of their movements adding to her terror. This didn't feel right. Something was terribly wrong and in that moment she was absolutely certain she had been lied to.

One of the robotic arms withdrew a syringe with a very long needle from the refrigeration unit and swiveled toward her.

"Modified ISPV is ready to be administered," the robotic voice droned.

"You may proceed," said a male voice Maria didn't recognize.

Straining to break free, Maria watched the syringe in horror as it was poised over her torso. One of the other arms moved, and a metallic hand pushed down her head, then turned it to one side. Out of the corner of her eye, Maria saw another arm with a different needle descending toward her. Her eyes sought out the one identified as the modified Inferi Scourge Plague Virus. It hovered just out of sight, waiting.

"Please don't," she gasped.

The second needle plunged into her chest, just below her right breast, sliding between two of her ribs. She screamed as it burrowed deep within her. Liquid fire spread through her body. Gagging, she arched her back as the burning pain filled her. It was unbearable. Maria felt as if her body was being consumed.

The heart monitor's beeps were racing.

The arm holding the modified Inferi Scourge Plague Virus moved into position over her.

"Please don't," Maria whimpered.

The heart monitor suddenly went silent as the world turned black and cold.

* * *

The world was full of icy darkness. Maria struggled to move and gather her bed covers over her, but she found she couldn't move. She was restrained, and her mind wondered if Dwayne had her pinned with his arm and leg like he sometimes did as he slept.

Trying to say his name, she found she couldn't speak, couldn't find her voice. Her mouth was dry and her tongue felt heavy and coated.

Struggling to open her eyes, Maria again tried to move. This time she could feel something warm and heavy pressing down on her wrists.

"Dwayne," she whispered, "get off me."

"Did she say something?" a familiar male voice asked.

"Vanguard Martinez, wake up." It was Dr. Curran.

Eyelids fluttering, Maria tried to pull herself up out of the darkness. It was so cold it hurt and she struggled to draw a breath.

"Open your eyes, Vanguard Martinez. You can do it."

Shapes swam above her. Dark forms hovered beneath an ocean of white. Pain pulsated behind her eyes, then faded as her vision slowly cleared.

Dr. Curran leaned over her with Mr. Petersen at her side. "Vanguard," Mr. Petersen said in a short tone, "identify yourself."

Maria tried to swallow, but her throat felt painfully dry. "Vanguard Maria Martinez," she answered groggily.

"Well, she can speak," Mr. Petersen said.

"They could all speak," Dr. Curran answered in a terse voice. "Maria, please look at me."

It was hard to focus. Her brain felt muddled and her thoughts were like fleeing ghosts. It was hard to concentrate.

"Maria, look at me," Dr. Curran ordered again.

Maria finally rested her gaze directly on Dr. Curran, but it was Dwayne that filled her mind's eye. She missed him with all her soul and couldn't understand why he wasn't here with her.

"Where am I?" she rasped, confusion still snatching coherent thoughts away from her. Images of the last few days flashed through her mind, but avoided being strung into a cohesive narrative.

"You're in the SWD facility. You volunteered for a special mission to fight the Inferi Scourge. Do you remember?" Dr. Curran asked.

Like puzzle pieces snapping together, her memories began to interlock, completing the picture. "Did it work? Am I immune now?"

A whisper of a smile touched the doctor's face and she slightly nodded. "We believe so. We just need to complete a few more tests."

Pulling on the restraints, Maria struggled to stretch her body.

Though she was certain she was now completely awake, her body felt strangely remote. She could feel her limbs straining against the restraints, but felt disconnected from the action.

"Please, let me up," Maria gasped.

"We can't do that yet," Mr. Petersen answered.

"I feel...odd," Maria complained, blinking her eyes against the harsh light, her voice scratchy. The robotic arms began to move over her and she gasped. "Please! No more shots."

"We just need to do a few tests," Dr. Curran assured her.

With the delicate touch of a well-trained nurse, the robotic hands took skin samples, hair, blood, and a swab from the inside of her cheek. Maria shivered at their touch, trying to shirk away from them, the memory of the painful needle too fresh in her mind.

"It burned," Maria whimpered.

"What did?" Mr. Petersen asked.

"The first shot. It burned. It hurt so bad I thought I was dying." It was hard to speak above a whisper.

Mr. Petersen smirked.

"You don't believe me?"

"Oh, I believe you."

"How do you feel?" Dr. Curran asked, turning her gaze away from a screen to study Maria's expression.

"Numb. Like my nerve endings are shorting out or something. I don't feel like I'm really connected to my body yet. When does it wear off?"

"It doesn't," Mr. Petersen said with a slight shrug. "Get used to it."

"Would you mind not speaking to my patient right now? I don't need you upsetting her," Dr. Curran said sharply. "In fact, I suggest you leave the room."

"You know I am under orders to observe, Dr. Curran."

"You can watch the proceedings with the others."

"I am fine here."

"I insist," Dr. Curran asserted. "In fact, let me escort you. I need a word with you. *Now.*"

Maria could hear the two people march from the room and the door slide shut behind them. Pulling on her restraints again, her anger began to get the best of her.

"Could someone please let me go?" Turning her head, she tried to look around the room. No other technicians or doctors appeared to be in the room with her. "Dammit."

Relaxing her arms, she closed her hands into tight fists. The action felt remote and odd. Curious, she slowly dug her fingernails into her palms. She could feel the pressure, but not the sharp slice of a fingernail against skin. She pushed the tips of her fingers into her flesh even harder, but still felt nothing but the steady pressure.

The room was strangely silent and it wore on her nerves.

"Hello? Dr. Curran?"

She flexed her toes and wiggled her fingers. Something wasn't right. The silence tormented her.

It had been so loud in the room before that horrible needle had sliced into her chest. At least she wasn't in pain from that part of the procedure.

The terrible taste in her mouth was not going away and she kept struggling to swallow.

The room was so quiet. The robotic arms were withdrawn into the ceiling and the monitors weren't even beeping.

Maria's eyes widened as the implications of the silence became clear to her. Turning her head, she strained to see the monitoring screens on the equipment. A few were still showing data, but one was ominously silent, a straight line cutting across its width.

An involuntary cry broke from her lips as her hands beat against the surface of the examination table. The stillness in the room only matched the stillness in her chest.

The heart monitor was silent. Her heart was not beating.

"No!" she rasped.

She wanted to cry, she wanted to scream, but all she could do was let out a terrible gasping sob. Forcing air into her lungs, she felt them expand then contract. She held her breath and waited for the terrible burning agony of her body raging for oxygen, but it never came.

Maria returned her gaze to the monitors, straining to read and understand what she witnessed. Trying to control her growing terror, she focused on the monitor nearest her. It was for her respiratory system and it was silent. The next was cardiovascular; it too showed no data. The one with the constant feed of data was for her neurological system.

"Please, please, please," she whispered, hoping this was all a nightmare. Maybe she was delirious with the fever the doctor had told her about. Perhaps she was in the throes of her illness and this was a terrible nightmare. That had to be the truth. The truth couldn't be laid out on the screens. It couldn't be.

Staring at the silent screens, she wished she could cry, but tears wouldn't come.

The world felt so cold.

Chapter 8

The snap of fingers before her face pulled her out of the darkness. Maria's eyes focused on the form of Dr. Beverly Curran. The doctor was across a table from Maria, her face looking pale and tired.

Seated, but still restrained, Maria sat with heavy cuffs holding her wrists and ankles flush against the armrest and legs of the chair. A restraint was also across both her chest and her waist. Confusion filled her as she tried to recall the moment when she had passed out. All she could remember was screaming.

"Maria," Dr. Curran began gently, "I'm sorry I left you alone to discover what you are."

"You made me into a fuckin' Scrag," Maria rasped. Anger filled her and her hands twitched.

"A different sort of Inferi Scourge," Dr. Curran corrected. "A *thinking* Inferi Scourge, a *speaking* Inferi Scourge. You're Inferi Boon. You're exactly what we need to defeat the Inferi Scourge."

"Why am I restrained if I'm what you wanted?" Maria spat out furiously. Her voice sounded raw. A part of her newly-restored brain was trying to adapt to her condition and she realized she was taking short intakes of breath so she could speak.

Dr. Curran ran her fingers lightly around the edges of her pad. "When you see me, what is your first desire?"

"To punch you in the face," Maria answered truthfully.

"The one desire all Inferi Scourge have is to spread the virus," Dr. Curran said. "We need to make sure that we were successful in removing that from the strain we gave to you. You're being monitored right now as we speak." Dr. Curran lifted the pad. Information was scrolling across the screen.

Maria blinked rapidly, wishing she could cry, but her dry eyes just ached. "So, what are the results telling you? Huh? That I'm pissed off?"

"I understand your-"

"No! No you *don't*! I don't have a heartbeat! My body doesn't feel right! *I* don't feel right! I feel like my body is wrapped up in cotton and I can't quite feel it! Do you know how that feels? No, you don't, because you're alive and I'm not!"

"You're alive in a new way," Dr. Curran assured her. "Who you were before death still remains."

Maria howled in anguish. "You killed me!" The sound was terrifyingly like that of the mindless Scourge Scourge.

Dr. Curran visibly shrank back in her chair. The fingers that were clutching her stylus trembled. "Yes, we did. But it's the Modified Inferi Scourge Plague Virus we gave you that brought you back to life. You're not like the others."

Emotions boiling, Maria fought the urge to scream again and keep on screaming. The rational part of her brain sliced through the maelstrom of fear and anger. She could still reason, could still talk. Despite the numbness of her body, she could still move. Her still heart yearned for Dwayne and his reassuring touch. Despite what had been done to her, she was still Maria Martinez. Desperately, she clutched to any shred of hope she could find.

"Can you change me back?" Maria whispered.

Dr. Curran's attention never diverted from the screen of the pad as she answered, "We have an antidote."

Maria let out a cry of relief.

"You're doing quite well, Vanguard. That you're this coherent and capable of processing what is happening to you is a very good sign that this endeavor against the Inferi Scourge will be successful. The modified virus has taken control of all your vital functions and you're operating at a much higher level than the original Inferi Scourge."

The doctor's words were not quite as comforting as Maria supposed the scientist thought they would be. Though the restraints on her body were pulled taunt, she didn't feel any aches or pain. The small twinges from her previous injuries were gone. But then again, so was her heartbeat.

"Once we're done, we'll get the antidote and come back to life, right?"

"Our agreement with you stands, Maria. Once you're done with your duty, you will receive all that was promised to you," Dr. Curran assured her. She surprised Maria by reaching out and touching her hand lightly. "I realize this is terrifying, but I am doing the very best I can to ensure that this process goes well not just for you, but the other soldiers who will be undergoing the procedure."

"Am I the first?"

"Yes, you are."

"Why didn't you tell me you were going to do this?"

Dr. Curran made a few more notations in her pad, then slowly raised her gaze. "There was some discussion about that, but it was decided that we wouldn't end up with a volunteer force if we informed you that you would die and come back as a modified Inferi Scourge. Forcibly conscripting soldiers to do this task would have significantly decreased the chances of success. We need all of you to want to make this mission be a success or it's destined to fail."

"You should have told me," Maria insisted.

"Would you have volunteered if you knew?"

Maria considered the question, then answered honestly, "No."

"There you have it." Dr. Curran slid her stylus over the screen. Maria saw it alter to now show what looked like the scan of a brain.

"How do you know this will work? You modified the virus, but how do you know the Scrags will see me as one of their own?" Maria asked.

The blond woman hesitated in her imputation. Averting her eyes, she slid the pad into the pocket of her uniform as she stood. "We're about to find out."

"What do you mean?" Maria demanded, fear beginning to swell within her.

On what appeared to be an impulse, Dr. Curran leaned toward Maria and said in a low voice, "It's the only way to know for sure. Security is watching. Don't be afraid."

Understanding flooded Maria as she watched Dr. Curran turn and walk from the room. "No, don't! Don't!"

The restraints snapped off her body with a sharp click. Maria gripped the edge of the table and pulled herself to her feet. She was certain there was a slight delay between her thought processes and her body's response. It was throwing off her equilibrium. Staggering from the table, she found her center of balance and managed to stand.

"Don't do this! Let me out!"

She could barely feel the coldness of the floor under her feet. On impulse, she pinched herself. All she felt was a dull twinge.

There was a loud snapping sound then a whine as the floor before her yawned open. Slowly, a platform rose out of the shaft below. An Inferi Scourge stood in the center of it, shackled, chains securing it the platform. It rolled its head about, its white eyes shifting back and forth in their sockets. It was a male. Its clothes were mere tatters over a body that had once been fit and athletic. Covered in years of filth, it barely looked human with its scarecrow hair. It snapped its teeth together over and over again, shifting its weight from foot to foot. It let out an ungodly howl as the platform leveled with the floor.

Maria stared at it in horror. Whereas in the past she had found herself breathless with a racing heart in the face of the Scourge, her lungs and heart were now silent. She considered calling out, but the Scourge had yet to look in her direction. Instead, she stood in silence, not daring to move, hoping that this test would soon be over and the Scourge would be lowered back into the bowels of the SWD facility.

Instead, the restraints on the creature snapped off and receded into the platform with a loud clanking noise.

The Scourge howled.

* * *

Maria instinctively backed away from the Scourge as it wailed. Her back impacted with the wall and she used her hands to brace herself. Feet apart, she watched the creature of her nightmares howl again. With terrifying swiftness, it launched itself at the door. The force of the impact busted the creature's chin open, spilling blood from the wound. Slamming its hands against the door, the Scourge's cries grew in intensity. It was if it knew that its prey was just on the other side.

Her gaze skimming over her surroundings, Maria noted that the chairs and table were bolted to the floor. The walls were smooth and seamless except for the one door. If she could actually breathe, she'd be hyperventilating. Instead, she remained utterly still, watching the Inferi Scourge hurl itself against the door.

Either it was blind and couldn't see her or it truly didn't identify her as human. Even if it was blind, if she moved it might hear her, so she remained against the wall.

The Scourge howled and rampaged against the door for a few minutes before staggering back away from it. Twisting its head one way then the other, its dead eyes moved over her without recognition. With a grunt, it struck out with one hand, slapping its palm against the wall. Slowly, it began to walk along the wall, its hand slapping against the cold surface. Maria had the impression it was seeking a weakness in the barrier between it and the humans in the rooms beyond.

Impacting with a corner, it pushed its face into the narrow crook, then continued its journey along the next wall. Maria studied the ceiling, searching for the cameras, or a possible exit. It was as smooth as the walls except for the panels that illuminated the room. Even if she stood on the table and jumped, she wouldn't be able to reach the lights.

The Scourge let out another spine-chilling howl as it reached another corner. It turned, now walking along the wall that Maria was pressed against. Daring to make a sound, she tottered on her tiptoes to the center of the room.

The Scourge didn't acknowledge her presence. It continued its trek around the edge of the room, slapping its hand against the wall as it grunted. It left a trail of blood drops and bits of its clothing and hair, swaying from foot to foot as it walked. Every few feet it would let out another guttural howl.

Backing against the table, Maria pressed a hand to her still chest. Her fear was gradually diminishing as the Scourge started its second rotation around the room. Daring to drop her gaze, she studied her hand. Her skin had a faint undertone of gray and her nails were tinged with blue. Her scars gave her limb a faintly-ghoulish appearance. Slowly, she lifted the hem of her tank top and stared at the mass of scars over her chest and belly. Running her hand over the hard welts, she looked up at the Scourge, rage beginning to pour into her as her fear vanished.

"I'm not one of you!"

The Scourge tilted its head in her direction, its white eyes rolling around in its sockets as it sought out the source of the voice.

"I'm not one of you!" she screamed again, her emotions surging through her like a tidal wave.

With a grunt, the Scourge swiveled about, surveying the room.

"Do you hear me, fucker!" Enraged, she rushed forward and shoved the Scourge into the wall.

It fell back, lost its balance and crashed to the floor. With a screech, it bared its teeth as its eyes darted around the room.

There was no fear now. Only rage. Maria grabbed it by its matted, filthy hair and heaved it to its feet. Its eyes kept swiveling, seeking, searching, for the source of the human voice. With a scream of despair, Maria hurled it across the room. It flailed, then fell again. Running after it, Maria grabbed it by the arm and wrenched it upwards. The creature howled in confusion. Pivoting on her heel, she shoved the Scourge headfirst into the table. Its forehead cracked against the corner, blood oozing from the wound and filling its eyes.

Standing over it, Maria could see its confusion as it clawed on the floor, its eyes searching frantically for a human. It never acknowledged her even when looking directly at her.

Maria pulled in a deep breath of air and screamed.

It joined its howl with her cry.

The Scourge always answered the call of their own.

Infuriated, she grabbed the Scourge again by the hair and hoisted it upright. It bayed again, calling out. Her wrath reducing her to a wordless state, she smashed its head against the table over and over again, decimating its face, then crushing its skull.

Anguish filled her as she finished killing the Scourge. It slipped from her grasp, the bloody remains of its head flopping with a wet sound onto the floor. Blood, brains, and bits of bone littered the table and chairs.

Looking down, she saw that thick, blackish blood covered her hands and arms. Numb and overwhelmed, she fell into a chair, resting her hands on her thighs. There was neither heart to calm, nor breath to still. She was empty inside.

"I'm not one of you," she muttered to the dead creature at her feet.

In silence, she waited for Dr. Curran to return.

Chapter 9

Awareness sliced into her mind like a rapier. Reality assaulted her senses, consuming Maria. Her brain struggled to process her surroundings as fear filled her. Blinking her eyes, she twisted about in the chair she was seated upon and discovered her feet were secured to the floor and her wrists were fastened to the armrests.

Before her rose a bank of screens. She was no longer in the room with the dead Scourge.

"What are you doing to me?" she demanded, her voice sounding raw and fragile.

"A few tests, Maria," Dr. Beverly Curran answered as she stepped into view. The room was dimly lit and the walls were plain and gray. The blond woman looked tired and a bit strained, but her smile held a hint of genuine warmth. "I know you're still adjusting to all of this-"

"You have no idea what I am going through," Maria snarled. "No idea! You locked me in a room with a Scrag, for god's sake!"

Sitting on a stool near Maria, Beverly nodded her head. "Yes, I did. And I know it is no reassurance for me to say that I knew it wouldn't attack you, but it proved to you and to us that the procedure was a success. You're a walking, talking, thinking Inferi Boon that Inferi Scourge will see as one of their own. You have now become the most important weapon against the Inferi Scourge humanity has ever had. Do you understand that?"

Averting her eyes from the doctor, Maria stared down at her lap. Her chest was still and her lungs empty, yet she was alive. Alive enough to want to cry and to miss Dwayne.

"You lied to me."

"We twisted the truth."

Maria fastened her gaze on the doctor and glowered. "You took away my life."

"To give life to others."

Maria rubbed her dry lips together and wished she could clear her throat. Her mouth and esophagus felt horribly dry. "Tell me again that there's an antidote. Swear to me that you can bring me back." Leaning as far forward as she could, Maria stared into the eyes of the other woman, seeking out the truth.

"We can bring you back," Beverly stated in a firm, calm voice. She met Maria's gaze without wavering.

Sagging in her restraints, Maria closed her eyes. "I just wish you had given me a choice."

"I understand that. I didn't want to deceive you, but I'm not the only one making decisions around here. Protocols were decided upon and adhered to."

Beverly did appear remorseful, which helped calm Maria's nerves just a tad. Glancing toward the monitors, she asked, "What are those for?"

"More tests. We need to check on your responses to various stimuli."

"Trying to see how human I am?" Maria asked wryly.

"Honestly, yes. The virus reanimates a human brain and body at a base level. We altered the virus in order for our test subjects to retain their cognitive skills and personality."

"Test subject," Maria echoed tersely.

Beverly pursed her lips slightly then said in a rather tired tone, "A wrong choice of words."

"But that's what I am. A test subject. You said I am the first one that has received this virus. So all these tests are to see if it's safe to give to other soldiers. Am I right?"

"Yes, you are."

Beverly's admittance of the truth was not any sort of comfort to Maria, yet she was satisfied to some degree to be conversing with the scientist openly.

"Will the others have a choice?" Maria asked.

"A choice as to whether or not to take the serum?"

Maria laughed darkly. "No, no. Let me rephrase my question so that I am very clear and you can't twist my words around. Are you going to tell the other people who volunteered for this mission that you're going to kill them and revive them as a thinking, talking Scrag?"

Beverly sank back in her chair and regarded Maria thoughtfully.

"I take it by your silence that you weren't considering that as an option."

"You're a soldier. You take orders."

"That's true. I did vow to give my life to The Bastion, but that life has been given. You *took* it from me. I think it's only fair that if you're going to be taking our lives, you let us know what you're giving us in return. I want to help defend The Bastion and its people, but your actions have fucking pissed me off!" Maria wished she could pound her fist on the table, but instead strained at the end of her restraints and glared. "If you want me to cooperate with you with all your tests, I want to know that the others will know what you're doing to them before you kill them, too!"

The scientist remained impassive. She set her stylus down and stared directly into Maria's eyes. "Is that what it will take for you to cooperate?"

"Yes. And I want to hear it from Mr. Petersen. Not you. I know he's the higher ups' lackey and I want to hear it from him."

A slight smile quirked onto Beverly's lips. "Very well." Collecting her things, she strode out of the room.

Maria found the resulting silence in the room unnerving. She studied the room, wondering where the observation window was located, and settled on an area apart from some blinking equipment. She glared at the empty spot on the wall, hoping the weight of her gaze would have some impact on the men and women who controlled her fate. Maybe she had overplayed her hand. Maybe she had assumed too much when it came to her worth in the program. But she had to believe if she was their first test subject she had to possess some physical or mental attribute that had made her a perfect candidate. Flexing her fingers, she stared at the blank wall, hoping that the powers that be would heed her words and do the right thing.

In silence, she waited.

* * *

Consciousness snapped her back into reality with a disorienting overload of sensory information. Maria shook her head, trying to focus her thoughts. She didn't remember falling asleep. Her last memory was of staring at the wall, hoping that the leaders of the SWD project would see reason in her words.

"I see you're back with us," Mr. Petersen's voice said pleasantly.

Maria lifted her eyes and saw Mr. Petersen sitting across the table from her. Beverly stood behind him clutching her pad. Her expression was stoic and Maria couldn't discern if her situation had worsened or not.

"Why does that keep happening?"

"Care to explain, Dr. Curran?"

Beverly sighed and set her pad down on the table. Using her stylus, she pulled up several blocks of information, including a vid of Maria staring at the wall. "Watch."

Maria leaned forward and recognized that one bit of information was showing her brain activity while another was measuring the stimuli in the room around her. Light, sound, and movement were all being recorded. Maria watched as her image on the screen slumped in her chair just as her brain activity dropped to a startling low. The vid sped forward, then showed Dr. Curran and Mr. Petersen entering the room. Mr. Petersen took out a small electroshock device and pressed it against Maria's chest. Maria's brain activity spiked and she came back into consciousness.

"What does it mean?" Maria asked. The vid was disconcerting to say the least. She had looked like a corpse sitting in her chair.

"The Inferi Scourge have one basic need: to spread the Inferi Scourge Plague Virus," Dr. Curran said. "It's their sole purpose for existence. We removed that need when we modified the virus. Therefore, you're not spurred on by the desire to spread the virus like they are. You don't have their aggression, their need. In the historical vids there is footage of millions of Inferi Scourge standing perfectly in place once the entire city was infected by the virus. They only began to move once they sensed that there was an uninfected human nearby. In other words, the Inferi Scourge become dormant when there are no humans nearby to infect. At first our predecessors thought this would enable us to wipe them out. They left infected cities alone, quarantining them, hoping the Inferi Scourge would remain in their dormant stage. They even attempted to bomb the inert creatures a few times only to rouse the Inferi Scourge and send them on a march in the direction the bombers took on their return flights. That tendency to fall dormant is one of the drawbacks we have discovered in giving you the modified virus."

"What good am I going to be if I keep blacking out?" Maria stared at them curiously. "How did you not see this happening?"

Mr. Petersen smiled, but it held no warmth. "Actually it will be easily remedied with a new program in your wristlet. Once your testing is done, we will install a program that will stimulate your nervous system and rouse you whenever you fall dormant for too long."

"*If* I do the testing," Maria said tersely.

Mr. Petersen regarded her like she was an insolent child, then let out a sigh that indicated how insufferable he thought she was. "Yes, that is why I am here. It has been decided by my superiors that your request makes sense in light of your...reaction to your condition."

"How did you think we would react?" Maria stared at him incredulously. "How did you think we would feel when we woke up to find out that we're not even alive anymore, but Scrags?"

"Inferi Boon," Beverly corrected automatically.

Maria almost cursed at the scientist, but thought better of it and held her tongue. Pressing her lips together, she carefully considered each word before she said it. "I might be a thinking Scrag, but that doesn't make what you did to me any easier to process emotionally. And let me be very clear on this matter. I am fully committed to fulfilling my duties and ridding the valley of the Scrags, but what you did to me was wrong."

Mr. Petersen and Beverly regarded her in silence for a few seconds before exchanging looks. At last, Mr. Petersen returned his attention to Maria and said, "Our superiors will have you record a message for the volunteers to our program once you have finished your testing. It has been decided that will make the transition for the rest of the team a much smoother process."

"You're the first, Maria. What you say and do will greatly help the others when they transition. You will be their guide." Beverly gave her a wan smile. "Is that agreeable?"

Maria nodded. "Yes. It is."

"Now, let's begin our tests, okay?" Beverly motioned to Mr. Petersen, who promptly vacated his chair. Beverly sat down and motioned to the bank of monitors. "Are you ready to begin?"

Nodding, Maria settled into her chair.

* * *

A steady rain was falling over the city again. Dwayne dreaded the trek home to his small flat in the city. He had even pondered staying in his office for the night. He was in a restless and sour mood and wasn't sure if he wanted to deal with the soggy streets. Hunkered down behind his desk, he rubbed his bottom lip lightly with one finger, not even aware of the action. He was deep within his own thoughts, worried and frustrated at the long silence from Maria. It was now three days since he had last communicated with her and the silence was worrisome.

The door to his office slid opened. Petra lingered just outside the room waiting for his acknowledgement.

"Come in," he said at last.

Petra strode in swiftly and stood at the end of his desk. Though her expression was carefully neutral there was a slight puckering between her eyebrows that concerned him.

"What did you discover?" he asked not sure if he wanted to hear her answer.

"Absolutely nothing," Petra admitted, and he could see the defeat in her posture now that the words had been spoken. "The SWD is in lockdown. I couldn't gather not one shred of information from my contacts. I can't even make a casual phone call to a friend inside the facility. All communications coming in or going out of the SWD facility are only allowed with top security clearance. I'm not sure the Commandant could get through."

"You tried her codes, I take it?" Dwayne lifted an eyebrow at his assistant.

Petra hesitated, then nodded.

Dwayne exhaled slowly and tried to calm his fraying nerves. His stomach felt like it had given birth to a black hole that was slowly consuming him. "Thank you for your efforts."

"I could keep trying," Petra offered, clearly not wanting to accept defeat.

"No, that's not necessary. I will see if there is another channel I can utilize." Dwayne's voice sounded colder than he liked.

Petra gave him a slight nod before shifting on her feet slightly. He could see she was grappling with her own questions, doubts, and fears. He had only asked her to find out what she could about recent SWD activity, but it was clear that the security lockdown had her unnerved. "I did uncover one piece of information. You may already know what I'm about to tell you. I'm not even sure if it's related to your request."

"What are you talking about?"

"The commandant signed off on the transfer of twenty soldiers of the Constabulary to the SWD for an unspecified reason. The official reason for their reassignment is 'training' at the East Garrison. Since the East Garrison is basically a housing facility for the soldiers patrolling that side of the wall that didn't make much sense. So I did a little more digging and found that all of twenty of the soldiers were transferred to the SWD. Not officially, of course. I reviewed the list of names. Some of them are war heroes from the last big push against the Scrags. Vanguard Martinez, the one who saved your life, is one of the mysteriously reassigned soldiers."

Dwayne felt a slight chill slide down his spine. He trusted Petra, but she was sometimes a little too perceptive when it came to his motives. He and Maria had always been discreet, but now he wondered if Petra had discerned the truth somehow.

"Interesting," he said at last.

"Isn't it? But, like I said, I didn't find the answer to your question. The SWD is obviously implementing a new program of some kind utilizing Constabulary soldiers instead of their own, but other than that..." Petra shrugged.

"Any ideas as to why they would use the Constabulary soldiers and not their own?" Dwayne had wondered about that aspect of the assignment when Maria had told him about the serum.

"I'll let you know in twenty-four hours," Petra answered, smiling slightly. "I may not be able to get you a direct answer to your question, but I think I can find a back door."

Dwayne chuckled. "I should have known you weren't empty-handed."

Petra lifted her shoulders. "I'm never empty-handed. I just don't always choose to show what I'm holding."

"You're trying to figure out what I know, or don't know," Dwayne said after a beat.

"Do you know anything?"

"I know the SWD is veiling itself in secrecy and that I don't trust them."

"And that is all you will tell me," Petra said.

"And that is all I *can* tell you," Dwayne answered.

There was a flicker of annoyance in Petra's expression, but she didn't let it seep into her voice as she said, "I will report in as soon as I have more information."

Dismissing her with the nod of his head, Dwayne settled back in his chair and let out a low groan as the door slid shut behind Petra. He was beginning to regret not trying to get Maria to reconsider her decision. Her silence was frightening him. Of course, there could be all sorts of reasons why she was not accessing the secret program on her wristlet, but the growing unease within him was not something he could ignore. He trusted his gut.

Activating his wristlet, he checked again to see if Maria had left him a message or logged on. She hadn't. Grimly, Dwayne activated yet another secret program in his wristlet. He sent out a call query and waited.

Seconds later, the other party answered.

"This is unexpected," Lindsey said, rubbing sleep out of her eyes.

"I need your...skills."

Lindsey yawned, then nodded. "You got it. What am I doing?"

"Hacking into the SWD." Dwayne had the utmost confidence that Lindsey could handle it. She was a genius beyond compare.

Scrunching up her face, Lindsey seemed to contemplate the challenge. After a few seconds, she nodded. "I'll get right on it. What do you want to know?"

"Anything and everything you can find out. Some of our people were transferred over there, including Vanguard Martinez."

Lindsey's eyes widened. "Maria?"

"Yes. Can you see what you can uncover?"

"You got it." Lindsey killed the connection.

Dwayne rubbed his eyes and glanced over his shoulder at the gray city shrouded in rain and mist. He yearned for a world without the Inferi Scourge, but he wasn't willing to sacrifice Maria to get it.

Chapter 10

Awareness came swiftly and shockingly every time she was roused out of her torpor. Maria hated the lack of control she had over her mind and body. She wasn't even attuned to the moment when she ceased to function. Each time she woke, she felt as though she was being reborn out of darkness. It was disconcerting. She desperately wanted to return to her room and call Dwayne, but because she had no need to eat or sleep the SWD team kept her busy.

Some of the tests were odd. She was made to watch short films on everything from war to parenthood. Some of the images were upsetting, while others were amusing. Her laughter during one film startled her, but appeared to please the male scientist watching over her. He was young with too pale skin and a shock of black hair. She could see his blue eyes watching her every move. More than once she was tempted to pretend to lash out at him and see if he would jump. Though the scientists working with her appeared pleased, she could see they were unnerved by her presence. She couldn't blame them. She was now Inferi Boon after all.

The hours slid away like water. She lost all track of time as the tests continued. It seemed as though whenever she faded out, she was revived by a new set of scientists ready to send her through a string of tests. Dr. Curran sometimes was in the room overseeing the testing, but other times she was absent.

As the tests progressed, Maria's restraints were systematically removed until only the shackles around her ankles remained. It was a relief to finally be able to move her arms and upper body. Not because she had been in any sort of pain, but because she had felt like a prisoner. The discomfort she would have felt when alive after being seated for so long was absent.

When she was finally allowed to write and manipulate a pad, she began to feel more like an actual person than a test subject. When a rifle was placed before her and she was told to field-strip it, clean it and reassemble it, she couldn't keep from smiling. Though her sense of touch was diminished, she was still able to perform the task efficiently and quickly.

When she finished, Dr. Curran entered the room and the colorless man with the blue eyes slipped out.

"Well, done, Maria. Very impressive." Dr. Curran sat down across from her and set the pad on the table. For once, Dr. Curran was smiling broadly and genuinely. "You have surpassed our every expectation. Every test result is superb. Words cannot express how excited we all are." Surprising her, Dr. Curran laid her hand over Maria's. "You're the most remarkable woman I have ever met. You're the hope of the city now."

Maria fidgeted nervously, trying not to pull her hand away from the startling warmth of the scientist's hand. "I'm doing my job. I believe what I'm doing is right."

"I know you do and it gives me such hope that the others will follow in your footsteps." Dr. Curran withdrew her hand and tapped her stylus on the pad.

The last of Maria's restraints retracted.

Startled, Maria sat in silence staring at her unencumbered limbs. Slowly, she raised her eyes and said, "You're not afraid of me? Even though I'm Inferi Scourge."

"You're not Inferi Scourge, but Inferi Boon. You're the answer to the hopes of The Bastion." Dr. Curran was positively glowing. It was rather troubling. "You're going to be escorted to your room now. Please shower and change into your dress uniform. It's time to show the upper echelon our future."

Maria slowly slid her chair back and stood. Her balance was a little off, but she adjusted her stance and found her center. For the first time she noticed her boots had been set near the door. Dr. Curran rose and watched as Maria quickly donned her footwear.

"I know this has been difficult for you, Maria. Though I sympathize with your predicament, I cannot imagine what you're going through. Your strength of will is inspiring."

"The perfect test subject?" Maria arched an eyebrow at the scientist. She had been unable to hold back that stinging comment.

Dr. Curran nodded. "I won't apologize again for calling you that. The reality is you're our test subject. You're the first of your kind. You're our salvation. You and the other volunteers will give humanity a chance to live and thrive again. I am sorry that we were not forthcoming with the truth of the procedure, but I am proud of the success of this endeavor. I *am* proud of you."

Maria set her feet apart and tucked her hands behind her back. "I won't lie, Dr. Curran. You and Mr. Petersen are not my favorite people in this world. But I *will* do my job to the best of my abilities for the citizens of The Bastion."

"Of that, I have no doubt," Dr. Curran answered, smiling.

* * *

After all the time spent in the testing rooms, Maria was relieved to finally take a shower and have a little bit of time for herself. To keep her from fading into torpor, the wristlet emitted a pulse every few minutes to keep her senses stimulated. It was a little annoying at first, but she soon became used to it. After scrubbing her body and washing her hair, she stepped out into the small room and stared into the mirror.

There was a slightly bluish shadow around her eyes and mouth, and her irises had a strange cloudy appearance. Otherwise, she looked like herself. If only she felt completely alive again. The faint numbness in her limbs was unnerving.

Glancing at her makeup bag, she pondered using concealer to hide the strange discoloration around her eyes, but opted not to. Let them see what she had become to save the last of humanity.

She braided her hair then knotted it on top of her head before starting to dress. Checking the time on her wristlet, she was surprised to see that it was only just past dinner time. It would be a few more hours before she could contact Dwayne safely and discreetly. Despite the many breaks during the testing, she was aware that it had been a very long day.

Mr. Petersen retrieved her from her room. She regarded him coolly as she stepped into the hallway.

"You're very presentable," Mr. Petersen said, and flashed a smile that didn't reach his cold eyes.

"Thank you," Maria answered, her tone slightly wary.

"Considering everything you have endured for the last two weeks, I have to say you look remarkably well. Strong, lucid...almost human."

"Two weeks?" Maria lifted her eyebrows at him as they walked down the hall.

"Yes. Two weeks. They did tell you, didn't they? That you have been being tested for the last two weeks?" There was a cruel light in his eyes and his smile was downright serpentine.

It took all her willpower not to fully reveal her shock. She kept her features as neutral as possible and slightly shrugged. "I don't have to eat or sleep," she answered blandly.

His smile faded around the edges as he studied her face. "That is true. Since you're dead."

As they stepped into the elevator, Maria graced him with a broad smile and said, "Oh, not dead. Inferi Scourge."

She enjoyed his discomfort as the elevator door slid shut.

* * *

The sun descended behind the mountain range that ringed the valley The Bastion was nestled within. Dwayne hurried down the crowded street, ducking around the vendors packing up their wares and the few pedicabs carrying government officials home. It always saddened him to see the makeshift rickshaws attached to old bikes making their way through the streets while the monorail stations remained silent.

Dressed in civilian clothing, he blended in with the rest of the people trudging home. His coat, sweater, and pants were all reconstructed and his boots had been resoled many times. The old battered hat on his head was a gift from Maria. She thought he had looked rather rakish when he had tried it on during one of their shopping trips in the bazaar. This evening he kept the brim tilted downward as he rushed toward his appointment, his chin tucked low to avoid being recognized. He was uneasy about meeting Lindsey at her small flat, but she had been insistent. The last thing he wanted to do was draw unwanted attention to her.

A government drone drifted along the street, its screen depicting the latest updates on the battle against the Inferi Scourge. Dwayne knew it was all rubbish. Usually the inhabitants of The Bastion ignored the drones carrying propaganda to the masses, but tonight several people turned to watch as it passed by. Dwayne sighed, realizing how effectively the president's promises were lifting the hopes of the people. He wasn't sure what to think anymore. The mission Maria had volunteered for sounded like a plausible way to resolve the issue of the Scourge in the valley, but her long silence was worrying. Now he feared she had been lied to and something altogether insidious had happened to her. Lindsey's urgent message had only heightened his growing fears.

Ducking around a corner, he headed into a narrow alley filled with overflowing recycling cans. Halfway into the darkened area was a stairwell that led up to the second floor. It creaked as he climbed and he had to avoid toys left on the steps. A long passageway bisected the pre-fab apartment complex. The walls were grimy and the floor was heavily-patched. Reaching his destination, he rapped on a battered door and waited.

Lindsey manually slid the door open and stepped aside as he entered her small flat. She pulled the door shut and secured it with multiple locks. "Rolling blackouts are a bitch."

The flat was lit with homemade candles and Dwayne's eyes took a few seconds to fully adjust to the gloom. The flat was extremely small. To his right was a small sanitary station. It was an old standard issue. The shower stall had a toilet that receded into the wall when not in use. To the left was a counter space that served as a kitchen. Lindsey's computer station was tucked under the platform that housed her bed and clothes trunk. Pictures clipped from old magazines and books decorated the walls in colorful collages, the glossy paper reflecting the candlelight.

Lindsey's narrow face looked almost ghoulish in the light from the candles. Her blond hair was loosely braided down her back and she was dressed in a sweater over leggings and mismatched thick socks that were mended with several different colors of thread. It took him a second to realize her hand was shaking as she pulled on an electro-cig. The nicotine-flavored mist drifted over her features.

"What is it?" he asked, even more afraid than before.

Rubbing her brow, Lindsey leaned toward him. "You cannot ever tell anyone I uncovered this information for you. I hacked deeper into The Bastion network than I ever have."

"Were you traced?"

"Of course not." She scoffed at him. "My father designed that system. I know it inside and out. They haven't changed any of his old codes, but I made sure there's no sign of me being in the system before I exited." She snagged a folding chair from against the wall and set it down for him next to her worn swiveling computer chair. Taking her seat, she turned on a generator tucked under the desk.

"I can't thank you enough for doing this," Dwayne said as he settled next to her.

"She's my friend, too," Lindsey answered a bit gruffly. "I wanted to know what the hell was going on with her. One day we're planning to go out for the drinks and then she's gone. Off the radar."

"The information that Petra secured for me says that twenty of our people were signed over to the SWD by the commandant along with Maria."

"That record was erased soon after she accessed it," Lindsey answered. "Did she see what I saw?"

"All unattached single people?"

Lindsey nodded grimly as she watched the screens before her come to life. "And mostly veterans of the last push. If I didn't have a gimped leg, they may have come for me, too."

"So what did you find?"

Lindsey tapped away on her desk for a few seconds, then a vid popped onto the screen. "This."

The vid revealed not only the top officials of the SWD seated around a long conference table, but also President Cabot and Commandant Pierce. The vid started just as Maria took a seat near the middle of the table flanked by a female scientist with blond hair and a man in a plain white suit that looked remarkably bland, yet dangerous at the same time. The camera zeroed in on Maria's face and Dwayne inhaled sharply.

Lindsey's eyes glittered with tears in the light emanating from the screens. "They're fucking assholes."

Dwayne had trouble breathing. His hands coiled into fists as he struggled to compose himself. "She looks like an Scrag."

"Because she is. Just listen," Lindsey said softly.

Dwayne's horror only grew as the female scientist, identified as Dr. Beverly Curran, explained in great detail how she had modified the ISPV and injected it into Maria after her life had been extinguished. As the scientist spoke, vids were played for those gathered of Maria's death and resurrection. Dwayne leaned forward, his elbows on his knees as he stared aghast at the screen. The vids also revealed a variety of tests. In one Maria destroyed a Scourge sent into a room to see if it identified her as one of its own. In an even more chilling vid, Maria was in a blacked out condition the scientist called the "Inferi Scourge torpor" when at least a dozen Scourge were released into the same room with her. They ignored her until they were dispatched by SWD security. The camera kept flashing to Maria's face as the briefing continued. Though she remained calm and her expression impassive, Dwayne could see that a few times she was surprised by the information that was being revealed by the slight raising of her eyebrows.

"In closing, we are able to now create a soldier that can dispatch the Inferi Scourge with impunity. They can walk among the Inferi Scourge without fear. They do not sleep. They do not eat. Yet their personality and intellect remains. They're our salvation. The answer to all our hopes. They're the Inferi Boon. Vanguard Martinez is the first of the squad that will help eradicate the Inferi Scourge. With your approval, we will begin transitioning the rest of our volunteers into Inferi Boon," Dr. Curran finished.

"Jesus Christ," Dwayne muttered, and wasn't sure if it was a prayer or a curse.

"Vanguard Martinez," an all too familiar voice said. It was the president. "You have remained silent throughout this debriefing. I would like to hear your thoughts on this matter."

Maria looked as surprised as Dwayne was by the question. She hesitated then said, "I am ready to destroy the Inferi Scourge and do what I must to secure the future of The Bastion."

"And you're willing to sacrifice your life?" the president asked.

For the first time Maria appeared a little unnerved. "It's my understanding that I will be brought back to life and given the antidote for the Inferi Boon Virus."

"That is exactly correct," the man in the white suit said with a smile.

The president appeared surprised, but then smiled as he said, "Well, then I feel a lot better about giving my final approval on this mission."

Lindsey snorted. "He would've approved it even if she had to stay that way."

Dwayne sank back in his chair as he listened to the last few minutes of the meeting. The vid ended with Maria leaving the room and the president congratulating the SWD officials. "I never dreamed that they would kill her," he muttered.

"What?" Lindsey gave him a sharp look. "You knew about this?"

With a short nod of his head, Dwayne reluctantly admitted the truth. "I knew she had volunteered for a top secret mission."

"The program I created was for her, wasn't it? Not your mistress to hide from your wife, but for her?" Lindsey gaped at him.

"She used it only once then went silent. That is why I asked Petra to find out what was going on. I started to fear that they had lied to her. It appears that some of what they promised her was true."

"What did they tell her?"

"She was told that there was a serum that would allow her to walk among the Scrags. That it would make her immune to them and they would identify her as one of their own. Maria volunteered because she is as desperate as the rest of us to be free of the Scrags."

Lindsey stared at him, her eyes examining his expression and his posture. "You're in love with her. She's your mistress, isn't she?"

"I'm getting a divorce. I wouldn't call her my mistress. But, yes, we're involved."

"But the SWD doesn't know that and have no idea that her sudden silence would concern anyone. This is why all those soldiers they transferred are single. They want this as quiet as can be."

"I can't believe they killed her," Dwayne whispered.

Lindsey turned away from him to type for a few minutes. Dwayne suspected she was angry, hurt and afraid. He watched her delete all the information she had so carefully extracted. When she finished, she swiveled her chair toward him. Her expression was so intense, he wasn't sure how to read it.

"The vid is only two hours old. This is updated information. Right now, Maria is the only Inferi Boon they've created. You can stop this."

"You just deleted the information."

"I have a copy I can give you. I just wanted it off my system. You can take that vid and show The Bastion what the SWD is doing. You can show everyone how they're killing our own people to make them into Scrags. You can get Maria out of there!"

"Lindsey," Dwayne said in a gentle tone, "she volunteered."

"They killed her!"

"I know that. And don't think I am not as torn up as you're about this. Frankly, I am horrified, but you saw what she said. I know her as well as you do, Lindsey. Tell me if you think she was lying when she said she would do anything to destroy the Inferi Scourge and make a better future for us all." Dwayne stared directly into Lindsey's eyes. "Tell me that she's not doing exactly what she wants to do right now."

With a frustrated groan, Lindsey covered her face. "She didn't know they were going to kill her. I could see it on her face! She had no clue!"

"I agree with you on that point, but she has accepted what has happened. She wants to do this. Even if we're horrified by what is going on, the truth is that it might work, Lindsey. Maria and the others might destroy the Scrags and save us all."

He could see the turmoil in the eyes of the young woman as she considered his words. Finally, she shrugged and picked up a small data drive off her desk. "Here. Do with it what you will. This just feels wrong somehow. Maria being a Scrag is wrong. She fought so hard against them."

"She's not Inferi Scourge," Dwayne said firmly. "We both saw that."

"She's not alive. Not like she was. She fought so hard to live after we were all wounded and the SWD killed her." Lindsey shook her head grimly. "Maybe she's okay with what is going on, but I'm not sure I am. Are you?"

Dwayne thought of Maria's slightly gray pallor and milky eyes. "No. I'm not. But I know she believes in what she is doing and I will support her."

"When you finally talk to her what will you say?"

"That I love her. I believe in her. And that I know she will do her best to save us all."

A bitter laugh escaped Lindsey's lips. "What sucks is I feel the same way. She's our best damn hope for a future and I hate that."

Tucking the drive into his pocket, Dwayne stood. "I should go. If there is any chance at all I might be able to reach her tonight, I should head home."

Lindsey stared at her screens thoughtfully. "I'm going to try to keep digging."

"You don't have to."

"I want to. I want to know what's happening to her."

Pressing his lips together, Dwayne nodded once in understanding.

Lindsey followed him to the door, hands on her hips. "It's wrong somehow. They're lying. About the serum, about something. I can feel it."

"So can I."

"Do you think she realizes it?"

"If she does, she will ignore it so she can get her job done." Dwayne watched Lindsey unlock the door's many locks. "She's tough. She can handle anything."

Resting her hand against the door, Lindsey said in a much lower voice, "I hope so. I don't want to lose her like I lost Ryan."

"I couldn't agree more."

Once outside in the growing darkness of the night, Dwayne pulled the brim of his hat down over his tearing eyes and rushed home.

* * *

Maria was seated on her bed reading a manual on the bolt weapon created specifically for the Inferi Boon mission when her wristlet indicated there was an incoming message from the hidden program. She quickly accessed it and smiled as Dwayne's face came into view. He smiled the moment he saw her and she was glad she had taken the time to put a little makeup on to hide her condition. She couldn't hide her eyes, but she hoped the dim light in her room would disguise them.

"Dwayne, I'm so sorry I couldn't contact you earlier. It's been a crazy few weeks," she said in a rush of words.

"Honey, don't speak. I know what is going on. I know *what* you are now," he said in his strong, yet soothing voice.

Confusion washed over her as she raised her hand to her face wondering if he could see that she was no longer truly alive. "Dwayne, I—"

"I just want you to know that I love you, and I'm proud of you. I know you'll do everything you can to fulfill your duty. I can't say I'm happy about what they did to you, but I respect your choice." His voice cracked slightly. She realized his eyes were brimming with tears.

"It'll be okay. They can restore me when I'm done. I *am* coming home to you Dwayne." The vow felt sacred as it passed her lips and she meant it with all her heart. "I love you. I'm doing this for us."

"I love you," Dwayne whispered. "And I will be waiting for you to come home."

She wished she could cry. She wished she could feel her heart harshly beating within her chest. Instead she was wrapped up in a stillness that was rapidly becoming her new norm. Though she didn't crave food or sleep anymore, she craved Dwayne. If she could have one moment in his arms, she would feel alive again.

"I won't fail," she said at last.

"I know," Dwayne answered, winking. "You're one hell of a warrior."

Laughing, she smiled at the tiny image of him on her wristlet. "I'm a mean bitch."

"Give 'em hell."

"The Scrags will never know what hit them." It was the literal truth. Maria and the others would be virtually invisible.

"I love you."

"I love you."

"I'll call you again tomorrow."

"I'll be here," she answered.

Then he was gone.

Lying down on her bed, she closed her eyes and thought of Dwayne. Though her body remained not aroused and apart from her emotions, her lips smiled.

Chapter 11

Maria shifted her weight, the chair's leather seat creaking under her movements. Installed in an observation room off of a debriefing room, she watched as the men and women conscripted for the Inferi Scourge Special Ops filed in and settled onto the benches staggered against one wall. She spotted a few familiar faces. She was surprised to see Special Constable Kurt Jameson and the young scientist with the black hair joining veterans of the final pushback against the Scourge. Crossing her legs, she glanced at Dr. Curran, who was making quick notations on her pad. On the screen were the profiles of all the potential Inferi Boon soldiers.

"I thought they were all going to be veterans," Maria said.

Dr. Curran glanced up, her eyes studying Maria's expression thoughtfully. After a slight pause, she answered. "The news vids are filled with the president declaring that the Inferi Scourge will soon be abolished from the valley. Volunteers are overwhelming the recruitment centers. SWD Security Officers petitioned to be included in the mission. We screened a few more potentials and expanded our force to two full squadrons. Forty soldiers in all. Twenty Constabulary, twenty SWD Security Officers."

"That scientist in there..." Maria pointed "...how is he going to handle himself?"

"Gideon's going along to monitor the Inferi Boon soldiers. He will be trained with the rest of you. And yes, he volunteered."

Lifting her eyebrows, Maria sat back and studied the faces of the people in the room beyond the glass. The veteran soldiers of the Constabulary wore placid expressions while the scientist and a few of the newer recruits from the SWD came across as nervous. Jameson looked ready to crawl out of his own skin and his eyes were shining with excitement.

Mr. Petersen entered the debriefing room and took his place on the podium. The vid screen behind him sprang to life, the emblem of The Bastion rotating against a blue backdrop.

"It's good to see you again," Mr. Petersen began, his well-manicured hands resting on the podium. Unlike other speakers, he didn't fidget or shift his weight. He remained almost perfectly still. As always, Maria had the impression that his every word, movement, and expression was carefully calculated to elicit a desired response. "It has been a few weeks since we last spoke. I hope your time in the SWD facility has been comfortable. It's been a bit of a vacation, hasn't it?" A flash of his pearly white teeth and the merriment in his eyes pulled smiles onto the faces of his listeners and a few chuckles. "Alas, it's time to go to work." His grin broadened as the men and women before him looked visibly relieved, excited and apprehensive all at once. "But I know that each and every one of you is glad to hear that at last you will be getting down to the very dirty business of finally removing the Inferi Scourge from outside the walls."

The volunteers cheered as the excitement in the room swelled.

"He's good," Maria remarked, slightly impressed

"Yes." Dr. Curran's voice was clipped. "He is."

"There's no need to reiterate the enormous importance of what you have volunteered to do for humanity. It's no secret that humankind has stood on the brink of extinction since the Inferi Scourge decimated our nations and brought us to our knees." As Mr. Petersen spoke, behind him flashed historical vids of the glories of the old world before transitioning to uncensored coverage of the Scourge rampaging through the cities.

"I've never seen these before," Maria said, unable to look away from the bloody footage of the Inferi Scourge swarming their victims. Once the hapless victim was revived as Scourge, the rabid creatures moved on.

Dr. Curran sighed slightly, glancing up at the proceedings in the other room. "The government felt it was best not to show the more disturbing vids. When the survivors were being airlifted to the city, it was determined that for their psychological wellbeing the more graphic historical vids should be removed from the public archives. This was supposed to be the new Eden. They didn't want to remind the new Adams and Eves of the snakes outside the gate."

The vids running behind Mr. Petersen clearly showed that The Bastion had been heavily promoted as the new Garden of Eden: a utopia in the midst of a dying world. Maria tore her gaze from the vids of the construction of The Bastion to the faces of the men and women that would soon be Inferi Boon soldiers. They were staring in rapt attention at the images being played. Maria had to admit they were inspiring. Mr. Petersen narrated as the vids revealed the extensive work that had gone into creating the new Eden. Mountain passes were destroyed so that only one gated entrance remained into the valley. Scenes of the massive airlift of prefabricated buildings into the valley were impressive, as was the footage of the construction of the city walls.

"This was our new home. Our new Eden. In fact the nickname for The Bastion in those exhilarating first days was actually New Eden. Once it was ready, human survivors from all over the globe were transported to this location from the last remaining human enclaves. I'm sure your own families tell of the harrowing escapes from nearly overrun rescue centers. My own grandfather only escaped because he managed to lash himself to the skids of the last helicopter leaving South Africa when there was no more room inside the aircraft to carry out anymore survivors."

Mr. Petersen was not relating any new information to the people in the room, but he was making it a personal journey. Maria could see the emotion building in the eyes of the people listening to the man in the white suit. Maybe it was because she was Inferi Boon now, or maybe because she wasn't in the room surrounded by her comrades, but she could see how expertly he was manipulating them all.

"This has to be fair," Maria said at last to Dr. Curran. "The choice they make to either become what I am or not should be their own. They shouldn't be manipulated into it."

Dr. Curran angled her head toward Maria. "Is anything he is saying a lie?"

"No, but-"

"You said you wanted them to make the decision you didn't get to make, right?"

"Yes, but-"

"We killed you and brought you back as Inferi Boon. Yet instead of harboring a grudge, you have agreed to go out there and destroy the Inferi Scourge."

Maria nodded, already knowing what Dr. Curran was going to say.

"You're doing it because this city is humanity's last chance. If this city falls, humanity ceases to exist." Dr. Curran's gaze didn't waver from Maria's eyes. "Am I wrong?"

"No, you're not."

"So let Mr. Petersen tell his stirring and patriotic story. Let those men and women in there remember what the stakes are. Let them see how our world almost died and how the last remaining nations of the world did their best to save us all. We stand on the brink of our own extinction. A little patriotism isn't going to hurt anything."

Maria gave the scientist a brisk nod. She didn't like feeling manipulated by the powers that be, but Dr. Curran was right. Even though she was angry at the deception that surrounded her transformation, her feelings seemed petty in comparison to the distress that filled the city. Her death and resurrection could possibly save millions. With or without the rousing presentation Mr. Petersen was giving, she would have volunteered. There was no doubt in her mind.

"For five years The Bastion not only survived, but thrived. The city and the valley were filled with hardworking people who created a new way of life." Mr. Petersen's narration was now accompanied by scenes of cattle grazing in lush pastures, fruit laden orchards, and sprouting fields of grain. "The Bastion was humanity's ultimate success in the aftermath of its worst tragedy." Mr. Petersen took a deep breath, dropping his gaze for a few moments. Lifting them just as the screen began to show the Scourge rampaging through the idyllic farmland around the city, Mr. Petersen said, "Then the gate failed."

Falling silent, Mr. Petersen allowed uncensored footage of the slaughter of the men, women, and children who had once lived and worked in the shadow of the city to play out in all its visceral terror.

Maria averted her eyes, unable to watch the massacre, but her gaze was gradually drawn to the appalling images. It was difficult to comprehend the sheer terror that had engulfed The Bastion on that day. She gasped as a news drone recorded the city gate closing. Countless people tried to scramble inside before the heavy steel doors shut, some being crushed as they closed. The remaining people screamed and beat against the doors as the Scourge tore into them. Shots from above killed both the non-infected and the Scourge.

"In one tragic morning, we lost nearly half our population and all our natural resources." Mr. Petersen rested on hand on the podium, as if to steady himself. "Ladies and gentlemen, my fellow citizens of The Bastion, we must close the gate and destroy the Inferi Scourge outside the city walls. We have no other choice."

"That's your cue," Dr. Curran said, tapping Maria's hand.

Standing, Maria straightened her uniform and ran a gentle hand over her hair, checking that it was smooth and her bun secure. Dr. Curran led the way to a door that she palmed open. Maria followed in her wake, then stepped into the debriefing room.

Immediately she was under scrutiny. Her appearance brought one or two sharp intakes of breath. Jameson's eyes widened as one or two of the veterans who knew her audibly gasped. A few of the soldiers didn't immediately recognize her Inferi Boon condition, but when they did she could see the fear in their eyes. A few of the soldiers looked in confusion between her and Mr. Petersen.

"We promised that you would be able to walk among the Inferi Scourge. That they wouldn't identify you as prey," Mr. Petersen said in a low, but clear voice. "We were not lying to you."

"She's a Scrag!" Jameson exclaimed, the words bursting from his mouth, spittle flecking his lips.

"Yes, I am." Maria moved to stand at Mr. Petersen's side. "But I am a thinking Scrag. My mind and personality are intact. I am still Vanguard Maria Martinez of the Constabulary of The Bastion. I am still strong, agile, and able to defend this city and its citizens to the best of my ability. I can walk among the Scrags and kill them with no remorse. I do not hunger. I do not sleep."

Gideon was watching her intently, his trembling hands tucked under his chin as he listened. Jameson's mouth remained open in disbelief.

A female soldier with dark skin and black eyes that Maria didn't know asked, "How do you know they won't attack you?"

Maria knew that the vid she had helped Dr. Curran edit together was now showing behind her. It would reveal the highlights of her testing, including her standing in a room crowded with Inferi Scourge, untouched by them. "I have undergone a series of tests over the last two weeks. I am the ultimate weapon against the Scrags. Dr. Curran assured me that when we're done purging the valley of all the Scrags, we will be restored to life."

Dr. Curran stepped forward as Mr. Petersen abandoned the podium. "I am Doctor Beverly Curran. I am in charge of the Inferi Boon Project. What Vanguard Martinez has told you is the truth. We can restore you and give you an antidote to destroy the modified virus. You will be able to build a new life for yourselves once the valley is free. Vanguard Martinez is our first Inferi Boon Special Ops. She can answer all your questions and alleviate any of the fears you may have about the procedure." Beverly took a breath as the men and women before her shifted uncomfortably in their chairs and stared at her warily. "This mission still remains voluntary. If you decide to withdraw from the program, you will continue to stay in the SWD facility for the next six months until the operation is over. Consider it an extended vacation, but this mission must remain top secret. Though the city knows that the government has plans to remove the Inferi Scourge from the valley, it has been determined that there will be an outcry if they discover the truth about the Inferi Boon Special Ops. The fear of the Inferi Scourge is deep-seated in our psyche. We don't want there to be any discrimination or fear associated with your returns to society. Therefore, our cover story is that special armor was used to enable you to move among the Inferi Scourge. No one will ever know about what you had to become to save The Bastion. Before entering this mission debriefing, you were all sworn to secrecy. That oath will remain intact whether or not you're on the mission. Once the mission is successfully completed, those participating in the mission will be publically acknowledged by the president. Those who decide to opt out will be listed as support personnel. Am I clear?"

"You're going to make us into Scrags?" Jameson said with disbelief.

"Thinking Scrags," the young woman with the short cropped hair amended.

"You have twenty-four hours to decide," Dr. Curran continued.

"I don't need twenty-four hours," a man said in a clipped accent. He stood up, his broad shoulders and height impressive. His closely-cropped hair was lightly beaded with sweat and despite his imposing looks, it was obvious he was uncomfortable with all he had been told.

"Chief Defender Omondi, I would like to hear your thoughts," Mr. Petersen said in his bland voice.

Maria glanced at the black man and saw his eyes narrow dangerously.

"I am ready now for the procedure," Omondi responded.

"So am I," a woman with white-blond hair and pleasant features said.

"I see," Dr. Curran said, a little surprised.

More hands and voices were raised, while a few holdouts remained quiet and pensive.

"I know you're afraid," Maria said, directing her eyes away from those who wouldn't look at her. "I know that everything we showed you is frightening, but this is our last chance. I am Inferi Boon Special Ops. I feel, think, and crave the freedom from the Scrags. When I enlisted in the Constabulary I knew that I may one day put my life on the line to protect this city. I never dreamed that I could continue to protect humanity beyond my death. I died over two weeks ago and yet I stand before you. I still care what happens to every citizen of this city...to you...to my family. I don't want any of us to face starvation and death. If you decide not to do this, so be it. I get it. I understand. My body feels foreign to me now. I don't feel alive. But I am still a soldier. And I will fight for my city." Her last words were raw with emotion as her air ran out and she had to force more air to her lungs so she could speak. Anger was pricking at her nerves and she suddenly couldn't see any damn reason why her fellow soldiers wouldn't do the right thing.

"Are you with me?"

Every soldier in the room stood up and let out a war cry.

* * *

Unexpectedly, Dr. Curran offered to escort Maria to her quarters. Maria was relieved when Dr. Petersen didn't follow. Chief Defender Omondi shook hands with her before she left the debriefing room. His wide smile said it all.

The two women walked in silence, their footfalls echoing through the long white corridor. Maria wanted nothing more than to lie down on her bed and wait for Dwayne's call. She wasn't tired physically, but emotionally she felt drained.

"I thought you were against the hard sell," Dr. Curran finally said.

Maria glanced toward her and grinned. "I was...I am."

"You basically called anyone not volunteering a coward and a traitor," Dr. Curran pointed out. "Not in so many words, of course, but the sentiment was there."

Lifting her shoulders, Maria slowed her pace.

Dr. Curran stopped and faced Maria. "Do you wish to tell me something?"

Maria set her feet apart and set her hands on her hips. "When I was in there, I think I finally believed we can have a successful mission. Looking at all of their faces and knowing what they're capable of, I felt this surge of hope fill me. Give us the right weapons and training and we can do this."

Dr. Curran laughed slightly as she rested her hand on Maria's shoulder. "I never doubted that for a second."

Once tucked away in her room, Maria showered and let her hair down. The alarm in her wristlet kept her alert as she settled onto her bed to study the file Dr. Curran had downloaded onto a pad for her. It contained maps of the valley and the pinpointed locations of importance, including the gate. The major obstacle to their mission was just the sheer number of Inferi Scourge filling the valley. They formed a massive wall of flesh that was going to be difficult to penetrate, or maneuver through.

After an hour of studying, her wristlet indicated that Dwayne was calling. She brought up the program and smiled as he came into view.

"Still at the office I see," she teased.

"I'm a workaholic. Besides, now I don't have you to rush home to," he answered, his eyes crinkling in the corners as he smiled. "How are you doing?"

"I'm doing fine. The other recruits are going to undergo the procedure soon. I get to guide them through their transition, then we start training for about two weeks."

"You sound excited." Dwayne's voice barely gave away his worry.

"I am. Today I think I finally believe that this is going to happen. We're really going to clear the valley. I think I believed it in theory, but now it feels real, tangible, possible."

Dwayne lowered his eyes as his smile grew bittersweet. "I hope you're right. I want nothing more than for you to return to me."

"And I will," Maria promised. "I love you."

"I love you. Until tomorrow night. I'll dream of you."

"I'll dream of you, too."

His face vanished and Maria felt a pang of loneliness cut through her. If she could cry, she would have for she realized that she had lied to Dwayne for the first time in their relationship.

She no longer dreamed.

Chapter 12

"So this is what it feels like to be dead," Chief Defender Obuya Omondi muttered.

Maria stood over him, her hand on his shoulder as Dr. Beverly Curran studied the various readouts pouring into her pad. "Kind of strange, huh?"

Omondi's brow slightly puckered as he lifted his head and studied himself. "I feel really odd."

The man's very dark skin and black eyes spoke of an African ancestry, but his voice was tinged with a rather posh accent. Most likely his family was from the British Isles. The refugees of the dead world tended to live together in enclaves reflective of their countries of origin. Not all the survivors of the great fall of humanity were interested in retaining the old world cultures, but enough did that languages were still being preserved despite English being the primary language of The Bastion.

"You get used to it eventually," Maria assured him.

"Feels a bit like I'm wrapped in a blanket," Omondi decided.

Dr. Curran looked more than pleased with the readouts. "Things are looking very good, Chief Defender. We're going to do a variety of tests just to make sure the transition was smooth," Dr. Curran said.

Maria's smile slightly faded at the doctor's words.

"How is the rest of the squad?" Omondi's brow was lightly furrowed with concern.

Maria was slightly jealous that the rest of the volunteers had been housed together while she was doing her duty as Dr. Curran's test subject. They had been able to bond as a unit while she had been isolated.

"Ready to follow in your footsteps," Beverly replied. She added with a slight smirk, "They're eager to join you."

A large smile spread across Omondi's lips. "I would expect nothing less. They truly are the best of the best." He flexed his large hands and wiggled his feet. His smile faded and he slowly exhaled. "This really does feel very peculiar. Do you really get used to it?"

Maria flexed her numb hand and drew a breath to speak. "Absolutely," she lied.

"How long before I will be ready to train?" Omondi asked. He forced himself to lie back, but Maria could see him flexing his muscles.

"Once all the tests are done. Thanks to Vanguard Martinez, your tests will go a lot faster and much more smoothly."

"I am grateful for that. I won't lie. I am very anxious to get out there and begin smashing Scrag heads." Omondi grinned at Maria.

"I feel exactly the same way," Maria responded.

Dr. Curran wore a look of amusement on her face as she stepped away from the table. "There will be time for that."

"I want to be there when my people wake up," Omondi informed the doctor.

"I'll see if I can arrange that," Dr. Curran answered.

Omondi's good-natured expression vanished as his eyes narrowed and his jaw tightened. "I was told I am in charge of this operation. It's my responsibility to make sure my people come through it safely. I will be at their awakenings. Is that clear?"

Dr. Curran's mouth dropped slightly in surprise, but then she regained her composure. "As I said, I will see what I can do. Come along, Vanguard Martinez."

Maria gave Omondi's shoulder a quick, reassuring squeeze then followed the doctor out of the room.

"There are too many heads to this beast," Beverly muttered angrily.

"Isn't the Chief Defender in charge of the operation?" Maria asked. "Isn't he the one calling the shots for our mission?"

"The line is blurred between where his mission begins and where mine ends," Dr. Curran confessed.

Sighing, she kept a brisk pace as they traveled the corridor toward the testing rooms. "Once this project was approved by the president it was no longer just an SWD project. I used to answer to my superiors. Now I answer to a committee consisting of every branch of the military and the government. Nothing is simple anymore on the bureaucratic end. Luckily for you, you don't have to deal with any of that. Your job is simple. Kill the Inferi Scourge and come home to your new life." Dr. Curran forced a smile onto her tightly-drawn face, as if to reassure Maria.

Though she didn't particularly like Dr. Curran, Maria could see that the woman genuinely cared about the success of the mission. It softened her anger against the scientist. She supposed that some sort of resentment was normal considering that Dr. Curran had *killed* her. "I can tell you that I may have transitioned a bit better if I had someone like Chief Defender Omondi there for me when I came to. I'm glad I was there for him today. I would like to be there for the next person who comes over as well."

Dr. Curran reluctantly nodded. "You have a point."

"I am not interested in the squabbles of the brass as long as the people volunteering for this mission are treated with the dignity they deserve."

"You're still angry at me, aren't you?"

"Do you blame me?" Maria raised an eyebrow.

"No, I don't." Dr. Curran took a hold of Maria's forearm and steered her into the scientist's private office. "Take a seat and I'll be right back."

With a sigh, Maria sat at the edge of a chair and listened to the door whoosh shut. The media feed was running on the screen over the doctor's immaculate desk. It was muted, but Maria read the feed at the bottom as the government propaganda filled the screen. So many promises were being made by the president that it created a sense of unease in Maria. Though hope had filled her the day before, now she felt a twinge of worry. If they weren't successful, the city would face a dreadful death.

Settling back in the chair, she waited for Dr. Curran.

* * *

Maria's return to cognizance was disorienting. Mr. Petersen was leaning over her, smiling his shark smile, his eyes gleaming in the light from the vid screen over the desk. Dr. Curran sat at her desk with her chin resting on her hand, staring at her with a tiredness that appeared to be bone deep.

"I...blacked out?" Maria glanced at her wristlet, confusion filling her.

"Well, we didn't need you up and about for a while, so we turned off the alarm to let you rest a bit." Mr. Petersen's smile widened.

His explanation was bullshit and they both knew it. The black outs didn't bring actual rest to her body. They had needed her out of the way for a while and had basically shut her off like a pad or computer. Her gaze flicked to the screen and she registered the time. She had been out for over six hours.

"While you were taking your catnap, we had a meeting, Dr. Curran and I, along with the oversight committee. It has been agreed that you and Chief Defender Omondi should be with the new Inferi Boon Special Ops as they awaken. It is believed that your presence will make the transition much easier." Mr. Petersen sat on the corner of Dr. Curran's desk, drawing a look of annoyance from her.

"You never thought you would get this far, did you? To actually creating Inferi Boon." Maria asked. "With this program. You're making it up as you go along, aren't you?"

Mr. Petersen's smile faded just a tad. "I wouldn't necessarily say that. But we are very pleased with you and Chief Defender Omondi. He has already passed his tests with flying colors. A very good start, don't you think?"

The disquiet she felt whenever in the presence of Mr. Petersen was beginning to grow into something akin to hate. She found it difficult not to despise him when he spoke to her as if she was a simpleton. He met her gaze comfortably, not at least intimidated by her pointed glare.

"I'm glad that he's doing well," she said at last.

"Aren't we all? Now, we—I mean, Dr. Curran— is about to perform the procedure on another of your comrades. We'd like it if you joined her once again."

Maria stood, giving him a curt nod. Dr. Curran stood, her shoulders slightly drooping.

Mr. Petersen hopped off the edge of the desk and slid his arm around Maria's waist, guiding her to the door. "We decided it's best if we don't make your comrades wait too long. We're bringing them all over in the next twelve hours. It will be a very long night."

"Why so soon?" Maria dared to ask.

"To hurry up your deployment, of course. There's a shining new world awaiting all of us once you accomplish your task," Mr. Petersen reminded her. "A brave new world."

"Did you ever read the book?" Maria asked, arching her brows.

"Of course," Mr. Petersen said in his disquieting voice. "And many others as well."

Dr. Curran gave Maria a warning look behind Mr. Petersen's back. Feeling like a co-conspirator, Maria fell into obedient silence. Mr. Petersen was baiting her in some manner and it was probably best to avoid any sort of confrontation with him. Again she wondered at his persistent white uniform with its lack of rank designation or even military affiliation. Maria seriously doubted he was the secretary to the admiral of the SWD. Who exactly he was and how much power he wielded over the entire project was a mystery. One that made her very uneasy.

* * *

After the third resurrection, Maria and Omondi were comfortable in the process. They worked well together, catching on to each other's cues and Dr. Curran's. After reach revival, the new Inferi Boon was transferred to the testing facility to ensure their transition was smooth.

The first three to be revived were veterans of the last push against the Scourge. All were Special Sergeants, the rank beneath Maria, and physically strong despite former wounds. Rom Mikado and Bob McKinney were both powerfully-built and took over ten minutes to return as an Inferi Boon. Leticia Cruz revived in five. She was the dark-skinned woman with the short-cropped hair that Maria had seen in the briefing room. Slightly shorter than Maria, she was lean and muscled. When she awakened so quickly, it startled all of them.

"Am I back?" she asked, her voice hoarse as she struggled to speak.

"Take a breath," Maria urged her. "It helps you talk."

"You've returned," Dr. Curran assured the woman.

"That was fast," Omondi noted, his dark brows furrowing over his eyes.

"The modified virus appears to affect humans in the same way the original virus did during the plague," Dr. Curran answered.

"Women and children changed quickly," Maria said, remembering her history.

"Or maybe I'm just more of a badass," Cruz suggested, getting the hang of taking a breath before speaking.

The next few soldiers were younger and more recently enlisted. Jameson was among the next group and revived in seven minutes.

"Can I kill zombies now?" he asked.

"Inferi Scourge," Dr. Curran corrected.

"Whatever," James said, struggling to speak above a whisper.

"You'll be killing them soon enough," Omondi promised.

It was disconcerting to see their fellow soldiers die and be resuscitated by the modified virus. Maria was glad that they didn't suffer through it alone as she had. All revived disoriented, but seemed relieved to have come back as Inferi Boon.

Dr. Curran appeared increasingly tired as the procedures wore on, her staff looking a bit haggard as well. Maria noticed a few taking stim-shots more than once. She didn't feel physically weary at all. Omondi didn't show any signs of waning energy either.

"I miss coffee," he whispered to her at one point, his dark keen eyes watching a few techs sipping some of the hot liquid.

"You're thirsty?"

"No, no. I was an addict. I always had to have coffee throughout the day. I think it's the habit I'm missing." He hovered over her shoulder, leaning over to whisper to her. Already there was camaraderie between them, a sense of *us* and *them* as they watched the doctor and her techs. "Do you crave food or drink at all?"

Maria shook her head. "No, no."

"Do you miss anything?"

She gave a short nod. "Dreaming."

"Dreaming?"

"Yeah. I miss sleep. Dreaming. Have you had the blackouts yet?"

"Three times."

"It's not like sleep at all, is it?"

Omondi frowned. "No, it's more like being dead."

"Exactly."

"But then again..." Omondi shrugged "...we are."

The procedures continued for hours. The only breaks were when the newly-transformed Inferi Boon were transferred to the testing rooms. Maria glanced at the clock on Dr. Curran's pad, discreetly noting the passage of time. When her designated time to speak with Dwayne passed, she sighed. She missed him so much.

Gideon Lanning entered the room in a white tech jumpsuit. Shoving his dark hair out of his face, he glanced around the room at his colleagues. If he was hoping for some reassurance, they gave him none. They treated him just as they had all the other volunteers. With a detached air about them, they strapped Gideon down as they had all the others. Because he was a lot smaller and leaner than the soldiers, the cuffs adjusted several times to capture his thin wrists.

"Gideon, you know what comes next," Dr. Curran said, leaning over him.

His eyes darted toward Maria, searching her face. She wasn't sure what he was looking for, but he seemed not to find any comfort. He closed his eyes and took several deep breaths.

"You volunteered, Gideon. You're not having second thoughts, are you?" Dr. Curran asked.

"No, no." Gideon shook his head. "It just feels different being on this end of the procedure."

Omondi laughed heartily. "It'll be okay, Gideon. Just a little prick and the world goes dark for just a little bit. You'll come back and feel like a new man."

The big man's laughter alleviated some of the tension that had been brewing in the room. Even Dr. Curran smiled one of her rare genuine smiles.

"Let's begin," Dr. Curran said.

Gideon opened his eyes, nodding.

Maria and Omondi retreated to a corner out of the way to watch. The techs finished preparing Gideon, then stepped back as Dr. Curran did a final check of his vitals. Looking up at the robotic arms retracted into the ceiling, Maria was glad that the transitions were now much more personal. With a nod of her head, Dr. Curran motioned to the lead tech who promptly administered the sedative.

Omondi bumped Maria's arm lightly with his elbow and indicated with his eyes Gideon's tightly clenched fists. Gradually, the fingers of the restrained tech unfurled and Dr. Curran did a read of his vitals.

Another injection resulted in all the monitors ceasing activity. As always, the moment of death made Maria uncomfortable. It was strange watching someone die willingly.

"Let's bring him over," Dr. Curran said.

The one thing Maria truly respected about Dr. Curran was that she didn't ask of her techs anything she was not willing to do herself. She had administered the last few injections of the Inferi Boon Virus, but this time deferred to the lead tech. Stepping forward, the man bent over Gideon and the hiss of the injector slithered through the quiet room.

"He's a little guy. He'll be back fast," Omondi whispered to Maria.

"How many do we have to go?" Maria wondered.

"About eight," Omondi answered. "Tired?"

With a smirk, Maria said, "No, you?"

"If not for this damn feeling of being wrapped in cotton I would say this is the best I've ever felt in my life."

"I know what you mean."

The ungodly howl of an Inferi Scourge ripped through the room. A tech dropped a pad and leaped from the table as Gideon thrashed upon it. More clamps erupted out of the table, locking over his limbs as the man fought against his restraints. Bloody foam flecked his lips as he gnashed his teeth, his eyes locked on Dr. Curran. She stood close to the table, her eyes wide, a stunned look upon her face. One of her techs pulled her a few feet away from the table as the large robotic arms unwound from the ceiling. They immediately began to take samples from the howling man.

"What the hell is going on?" Omondi demanded, stepping toward the chaos.

Dr. Curran regained her senses and began to quickly tap away on her pad.

Though the sight of the rabid Scourge that had once been Gideon terrified her on some primitive level, Maria advanced toward him. His gaze jumped from one tech to the next as tears rolled down his cheeks, his teeth snapping. Reaching Gideon, she laid her hand on his shoulder. Consumed with the need to spread the virus and kill, Gideon continued to fight his restraints. He ignored her touch and her presence completely.

"Gideon," she whispered. "Gideon, if you're in there..."

Foamy blood and saliva slid down his cheeks as he grunted, his body seizing. His eyes rolled up into his head. His body went limp, his clenched hands once more going still.

"I asked you a question, Dr. Curran. What is happening to him?" Omondi said, towering over the table.

Dr. Curran barely glanced at him. "Give me a moment."

"I want to know what is happening to my man now," Omondi persisted.

Whirling about, Dr. Curran glowered at him. "We're trying to assess the situation. I suggest you shut up."

Omondi fell silent, but his mouth was twisted into an angry grimace. He rested his hand on Gideon's arm, his stance protective.

Maria grabbed a sterile cloth from a nearby counter and wiped Gideon's mouth and face. No one stopped her. The techs and Dr. Curran attentions were intently directed at the monitors and their pads.

"We're not leaving you," Omondi whispered to Gideon, leaning over him. "We leave no one behind."

Resting her hand on Gideon's chest, Maria felt the stillness of his heart. "How did you knock him out? I didn't know we could do that to Scrags."

The robotic arms were busy depositing their samples into the machines set along one wall. Dr. Curran didn't look up as she answered. "We didn't knock him out. Like I said, we're trying to assess his condition."

"If you didn't knock him out, why—"

"I said, Vanguard Martinez, we're assessing his condition. Perhaps you had best leave the room while we work."

"We don't leave our people behind," Omondi said.

"You're not on the battlefield yet," Dr. Curran snapped back.

"Is it over?" Gideon's voice was a mere rasp.

Startled, Dr. Curran hurried back to his side. "Gideon?"

"Is it over? Am I turned yet?" Gideon stared at the doctor through cloudy eyes.

"Yes, it is. We had a slight...anomaly though. We're going to need to keep you here a little longer than we anticipated," Dr. Curran said swiftly.

"Anomaly?" Fear filled Gideon's eyes. "What happened?"

"You're going to be okay now, soldier," Omondi assured him.

Dr. Curran glared openly at Omondi. "We will have to do more tests. The rest of the procedures will have to be rescheduled."

"We need to move forward and soon," Omondi reminded her.

"I am aware of the situation, Chief Defender Omondi."

Silence seemed like the best option in Maria's opinion. She wasn't sure what she had just witnessed, but it had unnerved her. Omondi was a man of singular focus, as was Dr. Curran. They were already locked in a battle of wills. Maria kept her hand on Gideon's shoulder and his gaze slid toward her. Fear was in their depths, and she squeezed his shoulder, trying to reassure him.

The door to the room opened behind them. Maria was not surprised when she heard Mr. Petersen's voice.

"Chief Defender Omondi and Vanguard Martinez, could you please follow me?"

Reluctantly, Omondi stepped away from the table, giving Gideon a thumbs up. Maria smiled at the frightened man before following in Omondi's furious wake.

The door had barely slid shut when Omondi's proper tones, edged with anger, cut through the air. "You said the procedure was safe."

Mr. Petersen quirked a slight smile. "And it is. To most of you. We were aware there could be some..." he seemed to consider a possibility of words before opting to use Dr. Curran's. "Abnormalities may occur when dealing with experimental procedures. You must keep in mind that though Gideon is in good health, he is not a soldier. He does not have your strength and stamina. Apparently, this resulted in complications."

"Then give him the cure, Petersen."

It was clear Mr. Petersen didn't like the tone in Omondi's tone. Or perhaps he just didn't like taking orders. Maria wondered again who exactly the bland man in white truly was.

"We will assess his situation and give you a report later. But for now, why don't you return to your rooms. We will debrief you as soon as possible."

"If you suspected that one of us could have an adverse reaction to the procedure, I should have been told. I was given the impression that everyone selected for this mission wouldn't be in danger of complications." Omondi towered over Mr. Petersen, but it was obvious Mr. Petersen was not intimidated.

"Your presumption was erroneous. Now, follow me," Mr. Petersen said in a tone that made it clear he didn't expect them to argue further.

"What else aren't you telling us?" Maria said, not able to ignore her misgivings any further.

Mr. Petersen had started to turn away, but at her question, he swiveled back around on his heel. His cool gaze studied her for a moment, then he said, "The information imparted to you is all you need to do your mission. Is that clear?"

Maria and Omondi exchanged looks. She could see her superior officer's silent order to stand down in his body language and gaze. With a nod of her head, she fell silent and into step behind the man in the white suit.

She wouldn't be surprised if her and Omondi's wristlet alarms would be deactivated.

Chapter 13

Dwayne was reviewing weekly reports in his office late one night when Petra appeared in his doorway. She was already off duty, but was still in uniform. He lifted his eyes as she set a steaming cup of real coffee in front of him.

"Mind if I join you?" she asked.

"I'm busy right now," he said.

He tried to keep the irritation from his voice. There had been no word from Maria in two days and the silence was bothering him. Lindsey had promised to scrounge up what she could when he had contacted her a few hours before. To keep himself busy and distracted, he was trying to make a dent in the pile of reports he had to review before forwarding them to the commandant.

"Too busy to talk to me about a very interesting piece of information that fell into my lap by accident today?"

Dwayne set down his stylus and settled back in his chair. It creaked in protest and he made a mental note to oil its hinges later. "You're very good at getting my attention."

Her too-thin form folded onto a chair and she crossed her long legs. She always reminded him a bird: delicate in appearance, but acutely aware of her surrounds. Her thick hair was coiled into a tight braid down her back and not one curl dared to stray across her brow or neck. Commandant Pierce had once tried to snag Petra as her assistant, but Petra had somehow avoided the transfer. Dwayne appreciated her loyalty, but wondered sometimes what he had done to gain it.

"I assume that you have found other sources since you have not been asking me to gather information about the peculiar dealings in the SWD headquarters, or the constant chatter on the news vids about a top secret mission approved by the president." Petra's hawkish nose and keen eyes made her look distinctly like a predatory bird.

Dwayne slightly lifted his shoulders, his hands clasped at his waist.

A smile flitted across her lips. "I see. Well, I wonder if your other source of information knows that the SWD has initiated a full lockdown of their facility. Only the top brass is allowed to leave or enter the building. All other personnel have been detained inside."

Dwayne's stoic expression didn't change, but he felt his heartbeat speed up just a bit. "Has there been a contamination event inside the facility?"

Leaning forward, Petra rested her sharp elbow against his desktop and rested her chin on her hand. "This is the interesting part of the story. It's in response to several breaches. Apparently, the media used its sources to gain some important information about the top secret project the SWD is obviously implementing."

"I've seen nothing on the feeds. Commandant Pierce hasn't notified me of any additional security measures."

"That's because the journalists involved in the breaches were apprehended and are now incarcerated in the SWD facility. The official story to their news outlets and their families is that they're now imbedded with the SWD and will not be able to release their stories until the top secret operation is over."

Dwayne chuckled. "I just love how the top secret operation is all over the news and obviously occurring."

"It's marvelous, isn't it? Of course no one knows the true nature of whatever they're doing. There are rumors they have created a virus that will kill the Scrags, or a new weapon, or some sort of nanotechnology that will revert them to humans...in other words, everyone is guessing."

Dwayne exhaled slowly, adding this new information to what he already knew. Maria's silence could be a result of the lockdown and media blackout, but Lindsey had been certain her program could find its way through any security protocols. It was probably best that the SWD go on full lockdown during the mission. He hated to admit it, but he had been greatly unnerved at seeing Maria as an Inferi Boon. What had made it worse was seeing her smile on a dead face and her words tumbling from dead lips. It was difficult to reconcile that the woman he loved was now one of the creatures he had feared his entire life. In his nightmares, he saw her raging through the streets of the city infecting all who came into her path. And the dream always ended the same way. She would find him and tear into him, infecting him.

"A penny for your thoughts?" Petra narrowed her eyes.

"They want us to know that something is going on in the SWD," Dwayne said at last. "The government is doing nothing to hide the fact that something major is going on in there. The city is abuzz with excitement. They're building up the morale of the people and giving them hope. It's on purpose. A ploy. But why?"

Petra sat back in her chair abruptly, her eyes downcast as she visibly pondered the question. "To keep the population from seeing the truth."

Dwayne sighed, nodding.

"But what is the truth?"

He shrugged. "I can only speculate."

"The energy crisis maybe?"

"That's hard to ignore with the rolling blackouts."

Slightly biting her lip, Petra fell into deep thought. "I suppose," she said after a few long beats, "I could delve deeper."

"I would rather you just concentrated on the SWD. I need to know if you hear anything else come out of the SWD facility."

"Of course."

"Petra, I appreciate every little bit of information you have ever obtained for me. The commandant tends not to tell me everything I need to know to do my job effectively. You have always filled in the gaps. But these are very dangerous times. With the journalists being detained and the lockdown occurring, it's very clear that even you may end up disappearing behind SWD walls if you're not careful." Dwayne hated to frighten her, but he was concerned more than ever for everyone he cared about.

"I'll do my best." She deliberately looked at the clock. "I suppose I should get home to the kiddies and the partner."

Dwayne nodded. "It's late. Tell Robert hello for me."

"I will." She stood and he could see that she had fully regained her composure. "Don't forget the poker game on Saturday. Robert is planning on trouncing you."

Dwayne forced a grin. "I'm looking forward to it."

Petra disappeared through the doorway into the gloom of the hallway. He sighed as the office door slid shut.

It was stopped abruptly by a hand and he caught a glimpse of a familiar face. Since the building was not on lockdown, the door politely asked the person's name, but Dwayne knew she wouldn't want to be identified.

"Permission granted. Override protocols to identify," Dwayne ordered.

The door complied.

Lindsey shambled into the office and the door slid shut behind her. Leaning on her cane, she walked to his desk, a pad clutched in one hand. "I was waiting for her to leave," she said, scooting into a chair. Still in her uniform, she was as polished as Petra, but her injury was a sad reminder of all that was wrong with the city.

"What do you have for me?"

"Well, officially, I have a report on communication center equipment that you requested."

"I did?"

"You did. It's quite detailed and explained why you need to commission some new units," Lindsey said with a grin.

Dwayne smirked. "Do we have any in storage?"

"Warehouse Forty-Seven has six units that were misplaced a few years ago, but I found through a search of the updated inventory lists from this year."

"You're tenacious."

"I'm thorough." Lindsey grinned.

"But why are you really here?" Dwayne asked, his voice dropping as he took on a more somber tone. He knew Lindsey wouldn't have come if not for something very important.

Lindsey took a deep breath, then dropped a small drive on his desk. "Four communiques. Both from the SWD to Commandant Pierce. Both were top priority and maximum security. Both were scrubbed within seconds of transmission from both the sender and receiver."

"But you caught them," Dwayne said, impressed.

"I'm thorough," Lindsey reminded him.

"What are they about?"

"The SWD requested one medic, highly trained, doctor preferred in top physical condition that had to meet a certain biological profile. The commandant answered that she would dispatch one immediately to the SWD. And she asked why this request was not made when the other soldiers for the mission were selected." Lindsey's hands were visibly trembling.

"What was the answer?" Dwayne plucked the drive from the

desktop and stared at it thoughtfully.

"The answer was that the medic must fit the physical profile, or there could be the possibility of the Inferi Scourge Infection."

Dwayne looked at Lindsey quizzically.

"The fourth communique was not to the commandant, but from the SWD to the president. It was to inform him of the death of one of the soldiers in the Special Ops unit. Death by the Inferi Scourge Plague Virus."

Her words hit like a physical blow and Dwayne flinched. "Can you find out if it's Maria?"

"SWD implemented new security protocols today. The program I gave you can slice through it, but it's harder for me to transverse their system. *Of course*, I managed to get around their little roadblocks. It wasn't Maria. It was a SWD tech."

Dwayne felt guilty for feeling so relieved. "Any indication as to how he was infected?"

"An adverse response to the Inferi Boon Virus they're using. His body was destroyed and there is a cover story in place. There's a good chance Maria doesn't even know this guy died." Lindsey rubbed her nose and sighed. "This operation is really messy. It reeks of desperation."

"I have to agree." Dwayne lapsed into silence as he considered her news.

"Are you sure you don't want to go public with all of this?" The worry etched into Lindsey's brow matched his own.

Dwayne shook his head. "Maria believes in what she is doing. It gives me pause to usurp a mission that will free the city from the Scrags. But I am beginning to have grave reservations."

"So we won't do anything."

Dwayne nodded. "Not yet."

"I'll keep an eye out for more information."

"Thank you. You're a good soldier and a good friend, Lindsey."

She gave him a slight smile, then stood up. "I lost Ryan and a lot of other good people to the Scrags. I don't want to lose Maria. I have to believe she's okay...even if she's..."

"She'll come back to us," Dwayne said firmly. He had to believe it and he wouldn't stop believing it. He wanted Maria in his arms and far away from the dangers of the Inferi Scourge.

"I know you feel that what she's doing is the right thing, but does any of this make you nervous at all?"

Dwayne stared at the cooling mug of coffee sitting on this desk, then gave her a short nod. "Absolutely. But I believe in Maria and she is adamant that she is doing the right thing for all of us." His eyes strayed to the reports on the corner of his desk.

Standing, Lindsey leaned heavily on her cane as she turned to leave. Dwayne noticed her limp was always worse after a long day at work. He walked her to the door, hoping she didn't take it as an insult. With a grateful look, she clung to his arm until she found her balance again.

"I always used to believe that the more you know, the more peace of mind you will have. That is why I started hacking when I was a kid," Lindsey said, pausing in her steps so the door wouldn't open.

"Do you believe that now?"

"Fuck no. I think the more I know the more terrified I am," Lindsey admitted. "I'm still not thrilled about what the SWD has done to Maria, but I have to say I really hope they succeed."

Dwayne motioned to the door and it slid open. "Good night, Lindsey."

Once she was gone, Dwayne sank into his chair and held the small drive in his hand. Every day he felt like he had to fit the puzzle pieces together. The trouble was finding all of them. Like Lindsey he knew enough to frighten him, but ignorance was not bliss at times like these. His gut kept telling him something was wrong with everything happening around him. His only hope was that Maria would do her job and come home to him. In the end, he supposed that was all that truly mattered.

* * *

Again consciousness hit her like a fist. Her revived senses swiftly took in her surroundings. Her mind adapted to the new scenario, but not without anger building inside her.

Omondi sat across from her at a conference table. From the expression on his face, he had also just awakened. They had both retired to their rooms after the incident with Gideon. Obviously, their wristlets had not kept them stimulated and they had fallen into another black out.

Both of them checked their wristlets for the time and date. The function was disabled. Together, they glanced at the clock on the wall. It only told them the time, not the date.

"How long were we out?" Maria wondered aloud.

The doors on the far side of the room opened and Mr. Petersen, immaculate in his white uniform as always, and Dr. Curran, looking more haggard than before, filed into the room and were seated in the chairs at the end of the table.

"Good to see you again," Mr. Petersen said to the two soldiers.

Omondi's brow was heavily furrowed as he glowered at the man. "What's Gideon's condition?"

"I see we're straight to the point on that issue," Mr. Petersen said with a smile. "Would you like to tell them, please, Dr. Curran?"

Dr. Curran's blond hair obscured her face as she leaned over her pad. Maria had the impression she was trying to hide from the two soldiers glaring at her. Finally, she let out an exhausted sigh and sank back in her chair. "Gideon had an adverse reaction to the Inferi Boon Virus. We couldn't stabilize him. One moment he was lucid, the next he was mindless and tried to attack."

"And?" Mr. Petersen prompted her.

"We gave him the cure and revived him. He's in observation right now recovering. Understandably, he was shaken by the ordeal. He will be transferred to another facility to wait out the rest of the mission. He's earned his vacation," Dr. Curran said. She kept her eyes firmly directed at her pad, not looking up until she was done speaking.

"I would like to see him," Omondi said.

"That wouldn't be best at this time. Psychologically, he's a bit traumatized. We'll let his psychiatrist decide when it's best for him to interact with others," Dr. Curran answered.

"So another tech will be taking his place?" Maria asked.

"Actually, a medic from the Constabulary has transferred to the SWD and has already undergone the procedure. In fact, all of your people have successfully been revived."

"We were supposed to be there," Omondi said angrily. "This was agreed upon."

Mr. Petersen gave the big man a kind and understanding look that Maria didn't believe. "After the incident with Gideon, it was decided that having you in the room would be detrimental if something else occurred. You're not trained to deal with this sort of situation."

Omondi's huge hands flexed, then he sat back heavily in his chair, defeated. "When will we see our team and begin training?"

"Tomorrow," Mr. Petersen answered. "We just wanted to make sure you're both up to date on the latest situation now that we're moving forward. We thank you for your time," Mr. Petersen said.

The man in white and the scientist exited the room, leaving Maria and Omondi alone. Maria had no doubt that she'd be awakening in another room sometime tomorrow. She hated how they were using her blackouts to control her.

"It's bullshit," Omondi muttered.

"You don't think they cured him?" Maria asked, shocked.

"It's bullshit that we can't see him. I know you didn't have much interaction with him, but I did spend time with Gideon discussing his role in the mission. He's a good man and I do consider him a friend. That they won't allow me to see him is bullshit." Omondi's words were almost a growl.

"It's bullshit that they use the blackouts to shuffle us around." They were probably listening to her, but she didn't really give a damn at this point. Dwayne was probably worried sick about her.

"I am certainly not pleased about that either," Omondi agreed. "I realize this is not the Constabulary, but you would think the SWD would treat us with a bit more dignity."

Maria looked around the bland, white conference room, then back at Omondi. "Tomorrow will come a lot faster than you think, you know. We'll black out and tomorrow we'll wake up when we're supposed to head into training."

Omondi tersely nodded, then tapped his wristlet. "This better not act up when we're out there. I expect to have full control over our waking times. I understand that they feel we should regularly go into blackout to alleviate the emotional toll of our duty, but I want to control it. And I will make a fuss until I'm given it."

"Have you studied the new weapons?" Maria asked.

A large smile pushed away his glum expression. "Oh, yes. We shall have plenty of fun with those."

"Tomorrow," Maria said with a sigh.

"Which is just a blackout away."

"I wonder if we keep talking if it will prevent the black out from happening?"

"Want to talk all night like schoolgirls?" Omondi teased.

"And do each other's hair?"

Omondi swept his big hand over his nearly bald head. "Sounds like a fun time."

"Fuck it," Maria said, folding her arms on the table and cradling her head on them. "I'd rather get to tomorrow and start getting this fucking show on the goddamn road."

"That's how I like my soldiers thinking." Omondi teased. He folded his arms, too, and lowered his head. He gazed across the table at her. "Ready to save the world?"

"Ready and willing." Maria wanted desperately to talk to Dwayne. She couldn't reveal the program to Omondi, and there was no chance she would be revived in her room. With a sigh, she closed her eyes.

"See you tomorrow," Omondi's voice said.

"Tomorrow," Maria answered.

She never even noticed when she slid into torpor.

Chapter 14

Omondi chuckled as the squad of forty people practiced with their bolt weapons. Arms crossed over his chest, he stood next to Maria watching the squad dispatching targets erected across an indoor practice field. The Inferi Boon Special Ops were isolated from the rest of the SWD facility. They were never allowed outdoors and never left their dorms in the heavily-protected building they were assigned to.

Maria checked her pad, watching the stats scroll next to the names on her list. Each time a dummy was dispatched by a bolt weapon, it recorded every aspect of the attack.

"Jameson, you missed the brain stem!" Maria barked.

The young man gave the dummy an irritated kick and attacked the next one with gusto.

This time he registered a direct hit.

"We cannot leave any of the Scrags even remotely animated. The brain stem *must* be destroyed," Omondi reminded everyone in his booming voice. He glanced over at the readouts, surveying the stats.

"A few are hitting with one hundred percent accuracy," Maria assured him.

"We have a few below fifty percent," he noted.

"Newer recruits," Maria said. "Those from the SWD."

The Constabulary soldiers had undergone rigorous battle training, but SWD Security Officers had been taught to guard and detain people, not slay the Inferi Scourge.

"How's our medic?"

Maria pointed to the score next to the photograph of their newest member. His name was Michael Denman and he was one of their one hundred percent accuracy crew.

Omondi grinned. "I knew I liked him."

The Inferi Boon Special Ops were being deployed in three days and Maria was worried about a few of the squad members. Though there had not been any more adverse reactions like Gideon, a few were having trouble adapting. The lack of sensation and the inability to eat, sleep, or drink was a big adjustment for a few of the soldiers. A psychiatrist was meeting on a daily basis with the handful of people that were struggling. Maria envied them for the help they were receiving. She had been left to acclimate on her own and it hadn't been easy.

Thanks to Omondi's adamant appeal to the powers that be, all the soldiers now had the ability to control the timers on their wristlets. The SWD could still override the alarms if necessary, but Maria found it comforting to know that she could determine her wake cycles. Also, they were finally able to track time on their wristlets again. Dr. Curran had actually interceded on the matter. The faceless beings making decisions for the SWD had originally believed it was best if the Boon had no idea how much time they were losing. It was Dr. Curran's appeal that it was better for the psychological well-being of the Boon if they did know. Maria liked being able to track time. It was strange how knowing the time and date made her feel as though she was connected to the world and not apart from it.

Denman successfully maneuvered through his obstacle course,

scoring perfectly, before pulling out his own monitoring equipment and examining all the soldiers exiting with him. Though the soldiers were immune to the Inferi Scourge now, they could be injured in other ways. Denman would have to patch them up and keep them in top physical condition when out on the mission. Omondi and Maria had both sat in on his briefing when he was informed of his duties.

One aspect of the mission that Maria never considered was that one of the soldiers might experience what could be considered a life-threatening wound. Though it wouldn't kill the soldier while they were Inferi Boon, once they were restored to life any injury sustained during the mission would impact their health. It would be up to Denman to decide the course of action. Denman's credentials as a medical doctor was a comfort, but Maria wondered what would happen if someone needed emergency surgery.

"Those lower scorers need another round through the course. We can't afford any Scrags remaining alive out there," Omondi said in his proper tones. "Absolutely none."

"Good thing we don't get tired, huh?" Maria cracked a grin before returning her gaze to the action in front of her.

The soldiers wove through the crowded course filled with dummies. Each one carried a bolt weapon. It was a simple device with a long barrel and a trigger. The soldier just had to place the end of the weapon against the skull of the Scourge and fire. A bolt would slam out of the barrel, punching through the skull and obliterating the brain stem. The end of the bolt would expand, exposing sleek, razor sharp blades that whirled about like a fan before retracting, destroying as much of the brain as possible.

Since ammunition stores were running low, the weapon had been specially created for the operation. It was different from their rifles, so a few of the soldiers struggled with the mechanics of the device at first. The dummies also acted like the Scourge, moving side to side, whipping their heads about, not always staying stationary. It made hitting the target correctly a little more than difficult.

Omondi's dark eyes narrowed as Dr. Curran and Mr. Petersen appeared in the observation deck above the course. "I'll be glad when we're out there doing our job and not trapped in here being observed like lab rats."

"Agreed."

The last of the soldiers finished the course. Leticia Cruz was one of the last and was one of the higher scorers. Though smaller in frame than some of the others, she was heavily muscled and could easily hold her own. Her dark skin was slick with sweat and she playfully slugged Mikado as he tried to rub her head for luck. The taller Asian man with the devilish grin and high-cheekbones laughed. They were always teasing each other. It wasn't hard to see the attraction between them.

Most of the squad was bonding, but a few seemed to keep themselves apart. Jonathan Coleman only spoke when spoken to. He had already undergone two psych exams since being revived. He was one of the ones that Maria was worried about. Though he was scoring high, he avoided being too close to the others. He had been declared mentally competent for the job, but Maria wondered if he had found a way to fake his way through the tests.

McKinney, tall, blond, and powerfully built, was another one she was worried about. Not because he avoided the others, but because he was constantly trying to get affirmation from the others that everything was fine. Maria had caught him studying his cloudy dead eyes in a reflective surface one time and his expression had concerned her. But his jokes kept the mood light, so perhaps she was overthinking the situation.

Two soldiers she was not worried about were Ebba Holm and Jes Cormier. Both women were Constabulary veterans of the last push.

Cormier had been decorated for crashing her fuel-exhausted tiltrotor into the Scourge and buying time for another tiltrotor to airlift soldiers. Maria felt personally grateful for the woman, remembering the incident well. Cormier was of average height, with short black hair, green eyes, and a cocky grin. She always scored one hundred percent in her kills. Though she wasn't piloting a tiltrotor, she would be the driver of their personnel carrier.

Special Sergeant Ebba Holm had pale blue eyes and white-blond hair that were distinctly Nordic. She looked like a Valkyrie with her twin braids resting on her shoulders, and was six feet tall. She was an expert mechanic that had studied the schematics of the gate and was ready to do repairs. She was also a high-scorer and didn't seem the least bit phased by becoming Inferi Boon.

As for herself, Maria was ready to do the mission. She and Dwayne talked every night and despite what the SWD higher ups thought, having a connection to him gave her strength. Maybe that is why the other soldiers in the squad seemed a little desperate for affirmation from their superiors and comrades at times.

Omondi and Maria quickly reviewed all the stats, then ordered a few of the soldiers through the course again. There was no worry about physical exhaustion, just mental boredom.

"Think they'll be ready?" Omondi wondered aloud.

"Without a doubt," Maria assured him. "We can train them day and night if we have to."

"It's good to be dead," Omondi joked.

Maria smiled.

* * *

Dwayne maneuvered through the late night crowds on his way to his flat. It was Friday night and most of the citizens of The Bastion were out and about searching for something fun to do. Most of the bars were illegal, but the authorities looked in the other direction. He'd dropped by the pub for a sip of the latest moonshine, not really caring what was in it. He had a nice little buzz going and it was a relief after the long hours he'd worked. Exhaustion ate at him and he wanted to just lie down and sleep late.

Before Maria had left, he would have been looking forward to a long day with her, prowling through the markets looking for hidden treasures, or a day in bed reading and making love, or maybe a day sitting at the local pub watching the sports vids. It seemed like an eternity since she had left. He knew he was overworking himself in an attempt to mask her absence in his life. But when he was tired his loneliness was even more pronounced.

It was hard to love someone so deeply and yet watch them leave when duty called. It was the thing that had delivered a final death blow to his marriage to Barbara. She couldn't stand his long hours for years, but when he had been wounded in battle she had not been able to cope. Instead of drawing them closer together, his convalescence had been the end of his marriage. And the beginning of his new life with Maria.

The last details of the divorce had finally been settled upon and he would finally be free. The kids were doing a little better now. Hopefully, time would bring them healing so when he introduced them to Maria upon her return they would accept her.

Turning the corner onto his much quieter street, his apartment building came into view. It was just beyond an old subway station. The windows in the buildings lining the street were darkened in the late hour. Only a few were illuminated with the glow of a vid screen or lamp. It seemed unusually dark and it took him a second to realize all the street lamps were out. Stopping in mid-stride, he studied his surroundings. The stairways to the apartments were all drawn up and several SWD security cars were tucked into the shadows with their lights off.

"Excuse me, sir," a voice called out as two forms materialized out of the darkness. The facemasks of their helmets were an unyielding black. Most likely they were set to night vision or infrared vision. "Do you live in this area?"

"Yes, I do." He swept his wristlet over the identification unit one of the SWD officers was holding.

"Have you seen any unusual activity around the subway station today?" one of them asked.

"I was at work," Dwayne answered.

He was clad in civilian clothing and all the SWD security had checked was his address. SWD and Constabulary didn't always see eye to eye, so Dwayne shifted his weight, trying to look like a regular civilian. Maria joked that he always looked like he was at attention. "What's going on?"

"Just a minor problem with a criminal element," was the answer.

Behind him, Dwayne heard the whine of the gates set into the corner buildings being activated. On the far end of the block those gates were closing too. "This is looking a little serious."

"Just a report of a suspicious person hanging out around the subway exit. I'll escort you to your apartment building," the one doing all the talking said as he took hold of Dwayne's arm.

Relaxing his shoulders, Dwayne allowed himself to be herded toward his apartment building. Now that his eyes had adjusted to the darkness, he could see several SWD units sweeping around the buildings. Another group was checking the locks on the subway station's doors. Glancing up, he saw a woman staring down at him from behind a curtain as he was ushered to the retracted staircase of his apartment building. Dwayne swiped his wristlet over the sensor set into the wall and the staircase lowered.

"Stay off the street until further notice. This matter will be taken care of shortly," the SWD officer said.

Dwayne studied the dark visor covering the man's face, wondering if that was fear he heard in his voice. "I will. Thank you."

Minutes later, tucked into his apartment, he set a small camera in the window over his kitchen counter to record the activity below. It was old and didn't always get the clearest of images, but whatever it managed to capture he would send to Lindsey. His wristlet buzzed as a timer went off. It was time to call Maria. Hopefully, she would actually be able to answer tonight.

What remained of his earlier moonshine buzz was turning into a headache and he sat heavily at his small kitchen table. He quickly accessed the secret program and waited impatiently for Maria to answer. He hated when he wasn't able to contact her, but she had explained about the blackouts and the wristlet alarm. Supposedly she now had full control over the alarm in her wristlet, but they both knew the SWD could turn it—and her—off at will.

It took nearly a full minute for her to answer. It was an immense relief to see her face.

"Hey babe," he said, trying to keep the concern out of his voice.

"Dwayne," she breathed, relief filling her voice. "I miss you. I was afraid I'd miss your call again."

"They're keeping you busy, huh?"

"Extremely, but it's all good now that we're actually in training." She grinned in such a way he knew she was sincere.

"You look good," he said, and meant it. Her cloudy eyes bothered him, but her smile was genuine and gave life to her gray-tinged features.

"We're going in earlier than anticipated. I just got back from a briefing. Omondi and I are meeting in a few minutes to go over our plan one last time. This is such a huge relief. I'm so tired of training. I'm ready to be out there."

"That's my girl," Dwayne said, smiling at her affectionately. He had struggled with the idea of telling her about the death the SWD was covering up, but seeing her calm demeanor he knew it would be the wrong thing to do. Maria believed what she was doing was right. Until he was certain about what was really going on, he wasn't going to unnecessarily burden her. "Why did they move up the time frame?"

"I don't know. They just called us in fifteen minutes ago and told us to get ready. We haven't even notified the squad yet." Maria laughed with delight. "They're going to be thrilled."

Dwayne noticed that a strand of hair had worked its way loose from her bun. His fingers twitched at the thought of pushing it back behind her ear and kissing her. His whole body ached for her. "I can see you're thrilled."

"I am. You can't imagine." Her expression was rapturous.

"You be careful out there."

"I'm going to kick some Scrag ass!" A slight frown flitted across her expression. "Dammit. I gotta go. Omondi is pinging me."

"I'll talk to you tomorrow night. Love you."

"I love you, too." Maria blew him a kiss and was gone.

Rubbing his eyes, Dwayne tried not to think of his lover out among the Inferi Scourge. He knew she was immune, but it was difficult for his mind to accept it. He couldn't wait until this was all over.

Checking the scene out in the street below, Dwayne could barely detect the black-garbed SWD forces slipping through the night. They were definitely looking for someone or something. Maybe it was wrong for his mind to link the SWD security down below with the early deployment of the Inferi Boon Special Ops, but he had to wonder.

* * *

The room was filled with excitement as the squad gathered around the table where a holographic image of the valley hovered in full detail. There were no people in the room other than the Inferi Boon. The upper echelon had finally released their shackles on Omondi to take over full command. From this point on, he was calling the shots.

Most of the squad had been settled into their rooms watching vids or reading. A few had been in the rec room playing games. Jameson had managed to push his way through the cram of bodies to be at Maria's side. He kept grinning at her, excited.

"We're going to bust those fuckers up!" Jose Gutierrez, an SWD officer, declared from nearby.

"You know it!" Cruz high-fived him, quite a sight with her short stature and his height.

The high energy in the room was tangible. After two weeks of training and adjusting to their transformed bodies, the soldiers were desperate for some action. Everyone who enlisted always hoped to one day kill the Scourge, but they were part of a small force that was actually going to do it.

"Enough carousing, you bastards," Omondi growled, his voice laced with affection and his own vivacity. "Pay attention and listen up."

The din quieted as all eyes were drawn to the image before them.

Mary took a breath and started. "Every campaign against the Scrags failed because we have never had the resources required to eliminate them in such large numbers. When humanity arrived in the valley it was with what little we could salvage from a dying world. Food, medicine, farming and mining equipment and tech consumed a substantial amount of space in the storage facilities. Even before the great exodus here, humanity was dangerously low on ammunition and fuel. Our fathers and mothers salvaged what they could. Ironically, their faith in the gate and the valley was so strong, they didn't even believe they would need to stockpile weaponry."

"Stupid politicians," McKinney groused.

Chief Defender Omondi studied the faces of his people. "Now, we're nearly out of fuel and ammunition. This campaign will not fail because it is not dependent on resources, but on us. The Inferi Boon."

Maria nodded her head, continuing. "Fire-bombing is out of the question because of the mines. If we end up with a coal seam fire, we've just fucked our only chance at surviving in this valley. We will be burning the bodies of the Scrags, but there is no danger because we are above ground. We've been allotted enough fuel for our flame throwers to do controlled burns of the corpses. We've also been given fuel for the personnel carrier, but we estimate we have enough to last us the duration of our mission as long as we don't joyride all over the place."

"How many attempts have there been to eliminate the Scrags?" Denman asked.

Omondi looked very grim. "Too many to count. The position of the gate has always worked against the tiltrotors. They can't get close enough to set down without being swarmed. The one attempt to use some of the salvaged missiles that were stored in the city resulted in a dangerous cave-in of the subway tunnel near the hydroelectric station. We had a major breach in the subway system before it could be contained," Omondi answered. "That area is still considered the city's most vulnerable access point even though we did manage to seal the primary tunnel. There is a secondary one that did not retain damage. Luckily."

"Our primary objective is to close the damn gate. As long as it is open, the Scrags will keep coming. We still have large pockets arriving every few months. What draws them here, we don't know. They enter the valley and join the hordes already here." Maria slightly shrugged. "We just need to eliminate their only way into the valley. Then kill the ones trapped inside."

"The situation is as follows: the Scrags are up against the walls in every direction for nearly half a mile. They're an impenetrable wall of dead, stinking flesh."

"Kind of like Jameson," McKinney drawled, eliciting a few laughs.

Omondi's glare silenced the snickers.

"We can't deploy directly from The Bastion," Maria continued. "As you know, all the gates are sealed. As are all the service tunnels and the subway leading out to the various stations located all over the valley. The tiltrotors are our only option and they will draw in the Scrags immediately."

"What about the Maelstrom Platforms?" Denman asked from across the table. His thick brows were lowered over his keen eyes as he studied the holographic image.

Omondi and Maria exchanged glances, then the Chief Defender said, "We get one volley. A limited burst from the cannons along this side." He pointed to the hologram. "They will be targeting any of the Scrags breaking off from the crowd around the walls in pursuit of us."

"But if they see us as Scrags, why would they rush us?" Cruz asked.

"They'll rush the tiltrotor," Maria answered. "They always have. The good news is we'll be in a personnel carrier. We're hitting the ground running."

"We get to ride around in style," Jameson said with delight.

"Can't wait," Cormier said, grinning. "Gonna take us on a ride that none of you will ever forget."

"We just need a clear path to get the vehicle up to speed. We're heading to the gate first," Omondi continued, ignoring the interruption.

"Will they rush the personnel carrier?" Denman asked.

Omondi nodded. "We anticipate that they might pursue us. We could disembark and go on foot, but we decided against that. There are so many Scrags in the valley we would literally have to push our way through them. It will slow us down. The carrier will get us there faster. Our first objective is the gate. We get it closed, keep anymore Scrags from coming in, then we start to eliminate the Scrags in the valley."

The hologram revealed the plan in vivid detail. Maria watched with satisfaction as the armored personnel carrier sped past and through the Inferi Scourge horde. A grid descended over the map, overlaying the valley, sectioning it off.

"We will begin eliminating the Scrags closest to the gate and work our way toward the city. Each day, we will stack the Scrag bodies and burn them. We have been ordered to work sixteen hours a day. We then have four hours to ourselves. To read, talk, play games, to do as you please. We blackout for four hours." Omondi pulled the image around with his fingers and highlighted a few key points.

Watching the grayish faces of the squad, Maria could see that their joviality was giving way to rapt attention. It was fun to joke around to alleviate the stress, but in the end, they had a massive job to perform. As the briefing droned on, Maria marveled at the lack of tension in her body. There were no butterflies in her stomach, no tense muscles in her back, no headache or any other telltale sign of stress to deal with. It was actually really refreshing to not have to deal with any of the physical symptoms of anxiety. Though an occasional worrying thought would wind its way through her mind, she felt remarkably clear-headed.

"We will adapt our plan if needed once we're on the field, but I have confidence if we stick to our plan we will be done well before the six month end date," Omondi finished.

"Sounds good," McKinney decided.

"And to make things a little more interesting..." Omondi killed the map and chart took its place. "The SWD has approved a bonus system for most kills per day. The soldier with the most kills per day will be granted a gold star."

"Like in kindergarten?" Denman asked, looking amused.

"Exactly like kindergarten. These gold stars will be tallied at the end of our mission and based on how many you have acquired, you will be granted extra perks to your prefab house of your choice." Omondi grinned.

This elicited murmurs of excitement.

"Like extra wide vid screens?" Jameson asked.

"Oh, yes. Even extra rooms." Omondi winked at Maria.

She hadn't even known about this. It was a great way to keep everyone motivated during the long days of killing.

"Almost feels like an old-fashioned game show all of a sudden," Denman decided.

"A list of what you might be eligible for when this is all said and done has been downloaded to your wristlets," Omondi continued. "As for the rest of tonight, I would usually tell you to get some rest, but considering we're dead..."

Laughter filled the room.

"Isn't there a saying that you can rest when you're dead?" Gutierrez asked.

"And no rest for the wicked," Denman added.

"I guess it's flipped around now," Omondi said. "No rest for the dead cause we're taking down the wicked."

The briefing broke down as cheers filled the room and people excitedly chatted with one another. Maria overheard Jameson suggesting Cruz indulge him in a bit of necrophilia, which resulted in him being shoved off his feet. Laughter and high spirits would give way tomorrow to death and destruction. They all knew it, but there was a sense of invincibility now that they knew that the Scourge wouldn't identify them as victims.

It was Mikado who said it was like being a god.

Maria didn't remind him that sometimes even gods met terrible ends in old earth mythology.

Chapter 15

It felt like old times. Memories of the last time she traveled outside the walls of The Bastion assaulted her as she strapped herself into her seat in the personnel carrier. She almost expected to see Lindsey sitting across from her and Ryan grinning at her as he shamelessly flirted. Instead, Chief Defender Obuya Omondi was finishing securing the buckles of his harness.

The personnel carrier had been modified for their mission. An addition had been attached to the rear providing extra space for their equipment. The long, sleek armored vehicle wasn't the most comfortable to ride in, but it would provide a good base of operations.

Maria sat behind the driver and Omondi took up the space where the passenger seat in a regular vehicle would be. His monitors were up and running. Beside him was Michael Denman, their medic, and he was already checking on all the information being streamed from the armor and helmets of the soldiers crammed into the seats behind him.

"We're looking good. All units are transmitting," Denman informed Omondi.

The tiny sensors and cameras in their helmets would keep Denman and the SWD informed of their every movement.

Maria adjusted her bolt weapon beside her and glanced up the row of soldiers. The bravado was dissipating in the face of the actual deployment and she saw a few people whispering prayers. Crossing herself, she said her own silent prayer and closed her eyes.

A tremor ran through the personnel carrier as the tiltrotor latched onto the roof. The whine of the engines and the propellers beating the air was muffled by her helmet. Maria opened her eyes and glanced through the front window. As the tiltrotor lifted off, the world tilted to one side and the SWD facility came into view. Every window was filled with people watching the takeoff.

"Into the crucible," Omondi said hushed voice.

It was early morning on a Sunday. Not many people would be out in the streets of The Bastion. Their passage over the wall might not even be noted. Maria had seen the flight path and knew they were keeping it as low as possible to avoid too many sightings. Despite all the proclamations of the president, the mission was still top secret.

As the tiltrotor continued to angle away from the SWD headquarters, The Bastion came into view, gray in the gloom of the morning. The sun was barely beginning to peek over the summits of the mountains and darkness still filled the city streets. The lights in the government facility seemed to blaze in the darkened city. Maria knew that the president and his cabinet were probably watching the live feed transmitted from their helmets.

She felt eerily apart from the world, separated not only by the empty space below the tiltrotor and its heavy cargo, but by the grayish pallor of her skin, lack of breath, and quiet of her heart. Stillness filled her. Whereas before she would have been fighting her nerves, keeping her breathing regulated, and trying to calm a wildly beating heart, she was now in perfect quiet within her armor and helmet. The faces of her companions were contemplative behind the plastic of their visors. She wondered if they felt the same way, too. The SWD had made sure that the Boon were isolated from the rest of the facility. Even the pilots in the tiltrotor carrying them over the wall had no inkling of what they now were.

"We're Inferi Boon!" Maria said, her voice thick with passion.

Each soldier slammed one foot down and let out a war cry.

"Nothing can stop us!"

Another stomp and a cry.

"We *will* destroy the Scrags!"

Boom!

"We will free our people!"

Boom!

"We will not fail!"

Boom!

Cheers erupted and the silence fell away with its stifling deadness. Omondi grinned at Maria and gave her a thumbs up. Chatter started up among the soldiers, smack talk mostly, but it killed the quiet.

Denman glanced over his shoulder at her and nodded his head. She wasn't sure what he was approving of, so she gave him a quick nod back.

The tiltrotor banked again. Outside of the cockpit windows, the huge Maelstrom Platforms on the wall were an imposing sight. The tiltrotor sailed right between two of them and the world beyond The Bastion swung into view. The crowds of the Scourge were dark waves rippling across the valley.

"Damn," Cruz muttered. "That's a whole lot of Scrags to kill."

McKinney grunted. "I'll kill half on my own. I don't need you assholes."

"You better leave the other half for me!" Jameson's voice was a little high-pitched with excitement. "I'm getting myself a pool with my house!"

"I'm eyeballing a hot tub myself," Mikado chimed in. "Me and Cruz are going to sit back and soak in a hot tub of champagne when this is all over."

"Don't include me in your plans. I'm going to be too busy riding my electro-car around blasting my stereo," Cruz shot back.

The voices of the forty men and women anxiously waiting to set down filled her headset as they joked and ribbed each other. It was the best way to keep anxiety down before they landed. Soon they would be on the ground and speeding toward the gate.

The roar of the Maelstrom Platforms' opening fire drew everyone's attention forward. As the tiltrotor began to descend, the Scourge rushing toward the vehicle were destroyed by the barrage from the wall. Bodies dissolved as they were shredded by the Maelstrom Platform rounds. Blood clouds filled the air and the wipers on the cockpit windows of the personnel carrier cleared the red mist from the glass. Special Constable Jes Cormier, the driver, glanced over at Omondi.

"It's going to be messy down there," Cormier stated.

"We knew it would be," Omondi answered.

"Those guns are fucking awesome!" Jameson exclaimed as the Maelstrom Platforms continued to vaporize the Scourge rushing toward the tiltrotor and its cargo.

"Tiltrotors going silent in five seconds, Cormier. Get ready to roll," Omondi ordered.

Maria braced herself for the landing. The tiltrotor released the carrier and flew upward. A second later, the personnel carrier landed in the thick paste of the pulverized Scourge. The engine roared to life and Cormier slammed it into gear. The carrier treads sunk deep into the bloody mud before finding traction and surging forward. Maria quickly swiveled her chair around, summoning her console. It flipped out of the floor and over her lap. The radar and cameras on the outside of the carrier revealed a mass of Scourge heading toward them.

"How many more bursts do we get from the guns?" Maria asked.

Omondi was watching his readouts, too. "Status on the guns," he barked into his headset, speaking to the SWD directly. A growl emanated from his throat and he held up three fingers to Maria.

Frowning, Maria dragged her screen around looking for a viable path through the oncoming Scourge. "Punching in coordinates for where they should fire." She quickly transferred the information to Omondi's console, as well as Cormier's.

A quick nod from Omondi and the driver confirmed their course of action. Omondi transferred the coordinates to the SWD as Cormier swerved to avoid a mass of Scourge coming in from the opposite direction of the city.

"Maybe we should have walked," Maria muttered.

"Quicker to the gate this way," Omondi reminded her.

"Except that the Scrags think we're a meal on wheels," Maria answered.

"Platforms firing in three...two..." Omondi's voice vanished under the roar from the Maelstrom Platforms.

Looking up, Maria saw the Inferi Scourge just ahead of the personnel carrier dissolving into clouds of viscera. Cormier kept the carrier moving forward straight through the muck in the air and a few of the soldiers cheered as the windows were coated in blood.

"That's what I'm talking about," Jameson said, high-fiving Mikado.

The platforms continued to roar, punching a path through the crowd of Inferi Scourge. There was a hard jolt as the carrier found an old abandoned road. Cormier turned onto it and accelerated. A triangular-shaped plow extended out from under the nose of the carrier, the edges sharp and glinting in the growing light of the sunrise. The vehicle sluiced through the Scourge hurling themselves at the vehicle. Again the platforms sounded, shredding the Scourge before the vehicle.

"Exciting morning, isn't it, Vanguard?" Omondi said as he studied his console. "Bet you're glad you didn't sleep in."

"Wouldn't have missed it for the world." Maria's eyes never strayed from her readouts and screens. "Shit. We got a massive crowd coming up from the southwest. The guns won't be able to hit them at this range and we're not going to be able to push through."

"I see them," Omondi grunted. "Shit. Cormier, sending you a new course heading."

Cormier whipped the carrier about, the treads grinding a few Scourge into the pavement, then they were off the road again, bouncing across the wasteland.

The platforms roared one last time, creating a path through the ever-growing crowd of rampaging Scourge. Cormier continued to deftly wind her way through the massive throng, avoiding the worst clusters.

Glancing up briefly, Maria saw the faces of the creatures they had been sent to kill. As always, she was struck with how human they appeared. Their thrust out hands and screaming faces could easily be seen as a wounded person crying out for help. Instead, the Scourge were howling for the humans they believed were inside the vehicle.

Bending over her console, Maria continued to study the increasingly-complicated patterns of the Scourge as they flowed toward the carrier. The vehicle so far had been able to push its way through less-compacted areas of the crowd, but the Scourge were closing in on them far more swiftly than anticipated. They were terrifyingly fast and agile.

"Looks like you might get your walk," Omondi said, the images from his console reflecting on the visor of his helmet.

"It's getting tricky," Cormier declared. "See any paths for me?"

Maria slid her fingers over the screen scanning for any weak spots in the crowd. "Not yet. Looking."

"Vanguard, that situation from the southwest has become dire." Omondi's voice was clipped and hard, but the strain in his face said it all.

She could see the tidal wave of dead humans building and heading straight toward the carrier. The Scourge were clustering into one massive battering ram.

"Find a way past it, Vanguard!" Omondi ordered.

"Looking!" Maria's fingers swept back and forth over the map, her eyes skimming over the information swiftly. "No weak spots. They've closed in around us."

"Brace yourselves!" Omondi called out.

The wall of bodies struck the carrier, shoving it completely around. The soldiers inside braced themselves as the torrent of Inferi Scourge assaulted the carrier. The howling cries of the Scourge filled Maria with dread as they pounded against the sides.

Cormier quickly activated the protective shields that slid over the cockpit windows, blocking out the view of several Scourge trying to scramble over the plow, but only managing to cut themselves in half.

"Dead in the water," Cormier groused.

Silence filled the carrier as the soldiers awaited their next order. Denman's gaze was fastened on the readouts coming in from the soldiers. Maria didn't need to be told that the brain scans were all showing mass activity. Her head felt like it was about to explode. They had been positive they could make it to the gate without being overrun. They were only halfway there.

Omondi turned off his console and it folded back into the floor. Swiveling around in his chair, he looked into the faces of the forty men and women watching him.

"We walk," he said simply.

A few people exchanged nervous looks.

"We're Inferi Boon. We get out and they see that we're not...human and they will leave us alone. All they want to do is infect us. Make us what they're, but we are already the walking dead. There is nothing to fear." Omondi unbuckled himself and picked up his bolt weapon. "Let's get moving."

After deactivating her console, Maria slid out of her harness and joined the other soldiers as they prepared to disembark.

"We'll have to go out the top to avoid being crushed," Omondi said, motioning for Jameson to climb up and open the heavy hatch above them.

The young man quickly scaled the ladder to obey.

"Everyone keep together. Once the Scrags no longer identify us as potential victims, they will most likely remain where they're standing. We're going to have to push our way through." Omondi's eyes trailed over the soldiers crowded around him. "Nothing like an early morning walk, right, Vanguard?"

"Absolutely," Maria answered. She hung her bolt weapon over her shoulder and forced a wry smile. "I hear the view is pretty at this time of the day."

Omondi chuckled.

With a loud creak and a clang, the hatch folded open and the stench of the Inferi Scourge filled the enclosed space. The Inferi Boon Special Ops had a diminished sense of smell, but a few winced as the pungent scent of death washed over them. Maria was glad she didn't have to breathe. Since they didn't have to worry about breathing in any biological or chemical weapons, their armor was lighter due to the lack of air filters. Maria wished they had left them in.

"Let's go!"

Jameson's legs vanished through the hatchway as the soldiers fell into line. Maria took lead with Omondi right behind her. The bolt weapon on her back bounced against her hip as she moved and she adjusted the strap one last time before pulling herself onto the roof of the carrier. As she stood and surveyed the area, she was sure she was in hell.

The sunrise filled the sky with deep oranges, reds and pinks, making the clouds appear on fire. The twisted, snarling faces of the Scourge spread out as far as she could see. The sheer number was almost incomprehensible.

"We got a lot of heads to bash," Jameson said beside her, grinning.

"Yeah," she answered in an awed voice.

Making her way across the top of the vehicle, she pulled out her binoculars and pointed them in the direction of the gate. As expected, there were less Scourge up by the entrance to the valley, but the creatures from the southwest had compacted into a horde that was heading toward the carrier. Glancing at the display on her helmet visor, she saw it was empty of any new orders. They were truly on their own.

Omondi joined her, standing with his feet apart to keep steady on the rocking carrier. "Getting to the gate is going to take longer than we thought."

"Oh, yeah," Maria agreed.

"Why aren't they calming down?" Jameson asked. "They can see us, right?"

Twisting around, Maria saw that most of the soldiers were now on the roof, weapons ready, trying to stay balanced as the pitching of the carrier grew more violent.

Omondi glowered into the howling faces below him, then at Maria. His dark eyes held an unspoken question and doubt.

The crowd was even more raucous now that the soldiers were visible. The carrier was rocked hard to one side and a few people fell to their knees.

"Sir?" McKinney called out, his face strained behind his visor.

Coleman, at his side, leaned over to stare at the crazed creatures below. "Sir, they're not identifying us as Scrags, sir!"

Omondi moved so his back was to the soldiers and looked at Maria questioningly. She didn't know what to say. The Inferi Scourge were out of control below them and the carrier shuddered under their assault.

Again the carrier lurched to one side.

Maria heard a strangled cry.

"Coleman!" Cruz screamed.

"Coleman fell!" Mikado shouted.

There was a mad scramble to grab the fallen soldier. Maria reached the side, falling to her stomach, just in time to see Coleman dragged into the crowd. The outline of his comrades peering down at him was reflected in his visor just before he disappeared under the tumult of gnashing teeth and tearing hands.

"Our helmets! They can't see our faces!" Maria tore at her helmet clasps, trying to get it off.

Around her the Inferi Boon Special Ops hastily tore off their helmets. Maria leaped got to her feet and faced the crowd. The Scourge below her stared up at her, mouths agape, then started to fall silent.

"Spread out! Let them see you!" Omondi ordered.

Slowly, the Inferi Scourge howls faded as the crowd of undead saw their own kind standing above them. The need to bite and infect was what controlled their violence and as they identified the soldiers as Inferi Scourge, the need dissipated. Maria could literally see it in their faces as their jaws went slack and their gazes dropped. A low moan swept over the crowd.

"We need to get Coleman," Denman said from behind her. "Do you think it's safe?"

Together they moved to the spot where Coleman had fallen. Cruz was already there staring in silence at the Scourge clustered around the fallen soldier. Slowly, the Scourge that had attacked Coleman drew upright, falling into their torpor state.

"Mother of God!" Denman exclaimed. He scaled down the side of the carrier and into the crowd.

Maria followed, her hands shaking. She had caught a glimpse of what lay beneath the feet of the now quiet Scourge. Beside her Cruz and Omondi were also climbing to the ground. She dropped the last few feet, knocking aside the now still Scourge. Shoving a few more away, she knelt next to Denman. The gloom was thick near the ground in the shadow of the carrier and the undead. Denman had activated a light on his armor and was examining Coleman.

Examining the pieces of Coleman.

The armor was old and the many sharp fingernails and teeth had managed to rent tears along the seams of his arms and legs. One arm was completely torn from his body, another was a mangled mess. Numerous bites covered each.

Coleman's mouth was moving, but no words were coming out of his lips. There wasn't a throat to push air through, no larynx to speak. His neck had been torn open, bits of flesh strewn about his head. His spine was exposed and that was all that connected his body and head.

Omondi swore under his breath. Cruz gasped, but didn't say anything more. She knelt next to Coleman and rested her hand on his forehead through his shattered visor.

"I can't save him," Denman said in a stricken voice, looking at Maria. "Do you understand? He may be able to survive as a Boon, but we can't fix this. No medicine can put him back together. We can't resuscitate him like this."

"We'll med-pod him back," Omondi decided.

Denman rose to his feet and shoved a few Scourge out of his way to draw closer to Omondi. "I'm out here to fix wounds that may occur from physical rigors of the job or accidents. Nothing like this was supposed to happen. The SWD was clear on my directives. Any mortal wounds are to be considered fatal. I am supposed euthanize anyone with this sort of massive injury." He shook his head, agonized over the situation. "Dear God, he's already dead. If not for being Boon..."

"Is Coleman okay?" a voice called from above.

The soldiers were lined up along the edge of the vehicle attempting to watch. The forest of Scourge standing over Coleman blocked their view.

"No, he's not," Denman answered in a bleak voice.

Omondi glared at Denman, his jaw flexing as though he was chewing over the words he was going to speak. He briskly gestured for Cruz to stand back. Shoving Scourge away as she obeyed her commanding officer, Cruz stared at Coleman with sadness in her gaze.

Maria moved to stand at her side. It was a strange relief that she couldn't cry in this terrible moment. Coleman's eyes followed her and she averted her gaze.

"Chief Defender Omondi, I need to take care of this now. It's not right to leave him like this," Denman persisted.

Omondi's dark eyes glowered at Denman, then he gave a quick nod. "Do it."

Falling to his knees, Denman opened the medical kit that hung from his waist. He withdrew what looked like a smaller version of the bolt weapon.

"Coleman, I'm truly sorry," Denman said softly as the Scourge moaned and swayed around him. With more care than Maria expected, Denman turned Coleman's head, the last bits of muscle strung across his ruined neck tearing apart. Pressing the weapon against the base of Coleman's head, Denman hit the trigger. The bolt punched through the soldier's skull and whirred as the blades inside destroyed Coleman's brain.

Falling onto his backside, Denman covered his face with his gloved hand. "Oh, Jesus."

Maria glanced at her wristlet.

Thirty minutes into their mission they had already lost one of their own.

Chapter 16

Jameson drew his weapon, and with anger twisting his young features, slammed his bolt weapon against the skull of one the Scourge and fired. It grunted, its body thrashing, then fell to the ground.

"Sir?" Cruz asked, unsure if she should follow Jameson's bold action.

"Clear the area around the carrier," Omondi ordered, his voice gruff as he stared down at Coleman's broken body.

Weapons drawn, the Inferi Boon Special Ops butchered the creatures surrounding them. The metallic clang of the bolts punching through the Scourge skulls mingled with the moans of the swaying creatures. The Scourge didn't fight back or even seem aware of the danger around them. The creatures fell all around Maria. Their skulls were a ruined mess of broken bone and mangled brains. The sight was horrific, yet Maria felt emotionally removed from the slaughter. The memory of Ryan being torn away from her by the Scourge buffered her emotions.

The stench was still pungent despite her muted senses. Maria pulled a scarf from her pack and wrapped it around her head and over her nose. Using hooks from their packs, Maria and Mikado dragged the corpses away, heaping them into a pile. Arms and legs covered in decades of filth and dried gore wove together in a knot of death.

McKinney climbed into the carrier and tossed out a body bag. Anger strained his features as he knocked over a few Scourge blocking his way.

"He was fucking terrified to be out here," McKinney snarled. "I told him it was going to be okay."

"It's not your fault. It's no one's fault." Denman snatched up the body bag and carried it over to Coleman's body.

"We all knew the risks," Cruz said.

McKinney wagged his lowered head angrily. "Fucking Scrags."

"Calm it down, McKinney," Maria ordered.

Cormier patted the big guy on the back, then guided him away from Coleman.

It took all of Maria's willpower not to stare at the dead soldier's torn body.

"We fucked up," Mikado grumbled, hooking a dead child through the eye. With an angry tug, he hauled it onto the top of the stack. It flopped there like a doll, its dead face staring at the rising sun.

Maria snagged another one by the shoulder and dragged it over. Guilt tore at her and she wondered why they had never even considered the confusion their armor and helmets might cause. "No one ever really knew how Scrags could recognize their own from the living. Hell, some people thought they had a supernatural ability."

Mikado rolled his shoulders after dropping another Scourge on the growing pile of dead bodies. "Yeah, so now we know they visually ID us. What good does that do us now? Coleman is dead."

Glancing at the carrier and the discarded helmets, Maria sighed. "We won't make the same mistakes."

Mikado kicked at the stack of the dead. "Fuckin' Scrags. Coleman was a good guy."

Together they returned to the main killing area to gather more bodies. Mikado gruffly shoved over a few Scourge and dispatched them with his weapon.

"Just keep focused, Mikado," Maria said. She wished she felt something other than despair. Anger would serve her well right now, but the day had just begun and already things had gone awry.

Mikado hooked another corpse, this one a large man, and dragged it away.

Turning, Maria saw Omondi and Denman gently placing the pieces of Coleman's body in the body bag. Once the seal was activated, the body would keep until it was returned to the city. At least Coleman would get a decent burial, unlike the poor people turned Inferi Scourge.

Snagging another corpse with her hook, Maria towed it along behind her. It was heavier than it looked and its limbs caught on the ground a few times. Looking down, Maria saw it was a woman dressed in the tattered remains of a dress. Her shoes were long gone and her head was a mass of dirty red hair. It was terrifying how well-preserved the ISPV kept its victims. They looked fresh and newly-dead, yet Maria knew that this creature was older than she was.

"Check this out," Jameson called out. He was kneeling over one of the dead bodies. "It's wearing a diamond necklace. Can we, like, take it?"

"We don't rob the dead," Omondi answered in a grim voice. "Our orders are to salvage only what is useful."

With a slight shrug, Jameson hooked the creature and hauled it to another growing pile.

Omondi and Denman deposited the bag with Coleman's remains into one of the outer storage compartments of the vehicle. The sun was higher in the sky, hovering over the mountain range. It was growing warmer now, but sweat was a thing of the past. Maria felt like she always did since the procedure: cold and disconnected from the world around her. Glancing at the Scourge, Maria wondered if they felt that way, too.

"What do we do now?" Maria asked, observing the cleared area around the carrier.

"We move on to the gate," Omondi responded. "But first I need to report in. While I'm doing that, chart our way through this horde. It's going to be slow going if we have to kill everything in our path."

Maria saluted and slung herself up into the carrier. Cormier was already in the driver's seat running a diagnostic on the carrier. Activating her console, Maria quickly scanned the crowded valley. The Inferi Scourge that had been swarming the carrier no longer sensed prey and had slipped into torpor, but there were still Inferi Scourge traveling toward the carrier. Believing that the carrier held prey, the oncoming herd was marching through the Inferi Scourge that had entered torpor. It was likely that the new arrivals would attack the carrier.

Omondi leaned over her, staring at her readouts. "More are coming."

"The carrier is drawing them."

"The ones out there stopped when they saw our faces," Omondi pointed out.

"Yes, but the ones surrounding the vehicle identified us as the occupants of the carrier. The new ones will just see the carrier as the transport of potential prey. They'll surround us and attack," Maria answered. She watched the shifting mass approaching on her screen. "We can't use the carrier to go to the gate or we'll end up in the same position as before."

"We'll be constantly attacked by Scrags wherever we go. That will slow us down significantly," Omondi observed, his voice heavy with his frustration. "What do you advise?"

"Strip it down, activate its defense system, and leave it until we've cleared more of the valley." The dread that filled her was unexpected. Despite her transformation into an Inferi Boon, she was still unnerved by the massive horde. To not have shelter from them made her uneasy even though she had already walked among them without harm. Yet, it was hard to forget that some of them had torn apart Coleman.

"Agreed. Let's get what we need and move on. Cormier, shut it down and get ready to walk."

Cormier scowled at him, then shrugged. "Figures. I finally get a sweet ride to cruise around in and end up walking.

Omondi flashed the driver a sardonic smile. He climbed out of the carrier and soon his rich baritone was barking out orders.

Tracing over the screen with her fingertips, Maria marked a path through the Inferi Scourge in torpor. If the soldiers moved rapidly, they could avoid the larger horde about to descend on the carrier. There were snarls of Scourge all the way to the gate that would have to be destroyed. That would slow the squad, but then again part of their job was to destroy the Scourge.

Once she was done plotting their course, Maria transferred the information to a pad and secured her work station. Hopefully, the Scourge wouldn't tear the vehicle apart. Shoving the pad into a big pocket in her armor, she joined the others in collecting extra weapons and equipment.

Jameson snagged one of the toolkits for the gate and glanced toward Maria as she gathered up the backup bolts for the weapons. "It's not like I thought it would be," he said.

"What do you mean?" Maria attached the bag of bolts to the bottom of her backpack, snapping the clasps together.

"I thought it would be...different." Jameson shrugged slightly. "I thought they wouldn't look so..."

"Human," Cormier offered. "They look human under all the dirt and blood."

"That's why they fooled people in the beginning," Cruz reminded them. "They looked wounded and scared, not...what they are."

Scrunching up his face, Jameson shrugged his shoulders. "Up close it's just different."

"I can kill them," Holm said from nearby. "I don't care what they look like."

Jameson bristled. "I just meant it's not like in the vids, sir. It's different. They're different. I thought it would be more..."

"Fun," Denman finished. "You thought it would be like the action vids."

Holm chuckled, hoisting an extra gun over one broad shoulder. "At least they aren't howling for our flesh. I like them docile. It makes them easier to kill."

"Like shooting fish in a barrel," Jameson grunted.

"We have the upper hand. They always used to have it before, but now the rules have changed." Maria secured the lockers and motioned the rest of the soldiers out.

"I like these new rules," Mikado said, leaping from the carrier.

"So do I." Cruz followed.

Maria, too, felt uneasy with their circumstances, but they had to make the best of it. There were many unknown variables and no matter how meticulous they had been in their plans, something could always go awry. Coleman's death had certainly brought that reality home to all of them.

Once everyone had exited the vehicle, Cormier activated the defense system as she disembarked. It would sporadically unleash a high-voltage pulse that would fry any Scourge touching it. The driver sighed, heaved her pack onto her back, and sauntered after Maria.

"We need to hurry before that big group heading our way arrives. It'll be hell pushing through them," Maria called out as she joined the squad gathered around Omondi.

"How does it look?" Omondi asked.

Maria pulled out her pad and handed it over to her commanding officer. As he studied it, she swept her gaze over the Scourge encircling the squad. The howls of the approaching horde roused them from their torpor state. Their eyes were darting around, seeking out human prey.

"We need to move. They're getting stirred up," Maria said.

With a grim nod of his head, Omondi started off, gesturing for the squad to follow. Falling in behind him, Maria matched his stride. The Chief Defender deftly wove his way through the swaying forms. It was disconcerting how the Scourge's cloudy eyes shifted to watch him pass. Somewhere in the reanimated brains of the Scourge he registered as one of their own. Instead of attacking, they swayed and moaned.

Behind her Maria could hear the others shoving the Scourge out of their way. Agitated laughter and low conversation mingled with the growing howl of the approaching mob. The dead forest of flesh around her was constantly shifting, growing increasingly animated as the howling coaxed them out of their malaise.

A few bolt weapons sounded. Maria looked back to see a couple of the soldiers dispatching the undead. She understood their anger and the unease, but they needed to keep focused on their mission.

"Keep moving. We need to make it to the gate," she said in a firm voice.

A few of their faces registered annoyance, but the squad obeyed, trudging along behind her.

The steady stomping of feet over the well-worn terrain became a rhythm to her ears. There were small patches of grass and bushes along the path, but most of the valley had been worn away by the Scourge trampling across the ground.

Maria stepped over broken fences, barbed wire tangled around the rotting wood. The cattle and other farm animals had died of starvation after the gate had failed. The Scourge had no interest in animals, but there had been no way to rescue them. Their bones stuck out of the ground, the only markers of their passing. Maria was careful to step around the protruding ribs of one creature. It felt odd traveling across the remains of what had once been a prosperous cattle ranch. A human skull imbedded in the earth stared at them as they passed by a rusted vehicle. It was all a grim reminder of all that had gone so wrong with New Eden.

The howls of the Inferi Scourge rose steadily behind the squad. Maria cast worried looks at the carrier as it disappeared slowly from view, blocked by the growing crush of the Scourge. They were swarming the carrier.

The brisk pace picked up even more as the mass descended on their location. Maria kept an eye on her pad, calling out changes in their course as they marched. The Scourge heading toward the carrier were a wall of bodies moving rapidly toward the squad.

"Shit, look at them," McKinney muttered.

Maria paused in her steps to watch the horde sweep past their location. The sight of all the bodies pressed together in one big wave of death and destruction was almost too much to comprehend. The wails were so loud that Maria could barely hear the comments being made around her.

"Keep moving!" Omondi shouted over the din. "Keep moving!"

The Inferi Scourge were already riled up and the sound of a human voice caused a ripple of excitement to flow through the crowd. Torn, rabid faces turned in the direction of the soldiers and a large group of the Scourge switched course to pursue.

"Move!" Maria ordered.

She broke into a run, her pack and weapon beating against her back. Her heavy boots and armor weighed her down, but free of the physical constraints of a living body, she sprinted behind Omondi. The squad ran ahead of the pack of Scourge breaking off from the main herd. The howls of their pursuers grew louder and more desperate.

"They're coming!" someone shouted. "Run faster!"

Maria's heavy boots pounded over the ground as she ducked around the remains of a barn.

"Hurry!"

"They're closing in!"

The voices of the squad were edged with terror.

For a second, Maria lost sight of Omondi, then she burst into a clearing just beyond the barn and saw him leaping a low lying fence.

"Stop running!" Denman shouted. "Stop running!"

"No way! You saw what they did to Coleman!" Jameson yelled.

"Stop running! They're drawn to our movement!" Denman's voice was insistent.

Maria skidded to a stop. Whirling around, she saw Denman standing still, facing the sprinting creatures following him.

"Denman!" Maria cried out, fearing filling her. She was convinced he would suffer the same fate as Coleman before the Scourge realized his blood was dead, not living.

A howl erupted from Denman's lips as he flung out his arms. The Scourge slowed, their wild eyes studying the man before them. Howling again, Denman stood still.

"Obey him!" Maria ordered.

She raised her arms toward the Scourge and joined her voice with Denman's. Following their example, the squad's voices rose in an eerie imitation of the Scourge howl as they stopped running and stood together.

The Scourge stumbled to a stop, their wild eyes scanning the squad. Maria screamed at them, her voice a frightening sound even to her own ears. She clearly witnessed the moment the Scourge identified the squad as their kind. The desire to rend flesh and infect vanished from their faces and confusion replaced it. Sluggishly, the group of mangled creatures turned to follow the massive horde trudging toward the carrier.

Denman slowly rotated about and raised his finger to his lips. Nodding, Maria motioned for the squad to continue their trek.

No one dared to speak as the gate loomed in the distance.

Chapter 17

The sun had peaked in the sky and was starting its descent when the squad finally made it to the outskirts of the remains of the settlements surrounding the city. Time had eroded the structures, reducing them to mere heaps of ruined metal and plastic. The perimeter fences had long ago been knocked over and flattened into the ground.

"It's so freakin' huge," Jameson said in awe.

"Unlike someone we know..." Cruz joked.

Jameson threw her a nasty look before returning his gaze to the gate. "Seriously, that thing is massive."

Maria was just impressed as he was. The closer the squad moved toward the massive gate that cut off the only pass to the valley the more intimidating it became. It was a towering testament to the engineers who had constructed the last hope of humanity within the valley. The gate was set into a steel and cement wall that rose ten stories above the valley floor. The door itself was high and wide enough to allow the large trucks that brought in the building blocks used to construct the city.

"There is no way the Scrags pushed that door open," Cruz declared, anger tingeing her voice.

"How thick was it?" McKinney asked.

"Twelve feet," Maria answered.

"Wow," Jameson said. "No way in hell the Scrag assholes got in on their own."

"Which means someone had to have let them in," Denman pointed out.

"What kind of moron would do that?" Cormier asked.

"A moron with an agenda," Denman answered, then hurried to catch up to Maria. In a lower voice, he said, "What if we can't repair the gate?"

Maria gestured with her chin back toward Holm. "We have someone specially trained to deal with it, remember?"

Denman's face scrunched up, the freckles across his nose standing out against his grayish complexion. "I know I wasn't around for the training the month before transition, but we don't appear to have much margin for error."

Maria smiled ruefully. "No we don't. That is why we can't make any more mistakes. We can't fail."

Sighing, the medic shook his head. "We already lost one life and were almost attacked again. Being Boon isn't enough to survive out here, I fear."

"Then we stay sharp," Maria said briskly. "We didn't all give up our lives to be Boon just to come out here and fail."

"I didn't mean to-" Denman started.

"This is day one. We're adapting. We're learning. *We* can do that. *They* can't." Maria motioned toward the nearby Scourge staring blindly.

Falling back, Denman was swallowed into the ranks of the squad as Maria continued forward. Keeping her eyes on Omondi's back, she didn't look behind her. She knew what she would see: the anxious faces of her squad and the Scourge swarming the carrier in the distance.

And beyond that the city they were desperately trying to save.

* * *

The gate station came into view nearly an hour later. It felt as if they had been jogging toward it forever. The sun was even lower in the sky now. The whole day was slipping away as they pushed through the Scourge pockets and ran past the ruins of the old settler's homes and farms.

As they hit an old, cracked road, Omondi burst into a full sprint past the looser packs of Scourge. Maria stuck close to his heels, pumping her arms and racing against the gust of wind hissing through the open gate looming before them.

Beyond the gate were the high summits of the mountains.

It felt as though they were at the edge of the world.

Several crashed tiltrotors lay in wreckage near a turn in the road. The craggy outcropping hadn't allowed them to get very close to the station. The aircraft and its crew had obviously been overrun by the Scourge and crashed. Another testament to a failed attempt to close the gate. Since the gate failure, so much had gone wrong in the city.

The chain-link fence around the gate station was torn down, the rusted metal twisted into ragged teeth. Omondi leaped over a snarl of fence and pounded up the drive to the concrete and steel facility.

Maria couldn't take her eyes off the world beyond the gate. She could see an old road, gnarled with weeds, descending downward and out of sight. The mountains beyond the gate were topped in snow and thick clouds. She was mesmerized by the sight of the world beyond the valley. It was like a dream.

"Generator over there," Omondi called out, motioning.

"Got it!" Holm hoisted the heavy pack on her shoulder and kicked open the chain-link gate into an enclosure tucked into the side of the building.

The mummified remains of the guards who had worked at the gate were scattered across the walkway leading up to the guard station. Only bits of armor and mummified limbs tucked into thick leather gloves and boots remained of the men and women who had witnessed the failure of the gate.

"We'll need the codes to open the door," Maria called out to Omondi as he dashed up the stairs to the main entrance. She yanked out her pad to access the information.

"No, we don't," he answered in a grim tone.

Maria hesitated in her action. Omondi stood in the gaping doorway of the station. He stared inside with an expression that was difficult to decipher. Maria tucked away her pad as she climbed up the stairs and joined him.

The sunlight illuminated only part of the lobby, but it was evident there had been a battle. Bullet holes festooned the walls. Only armor suits revealed where the guards had fallen. But what Omondi was glowering at was a message left long ago scrawled across the wall in green paint.

"Gaia is free of the human scourge," Maria read aloud.

"What does it mean?" Cruz asked, joining them. She ran a gloved hand over her short hair, perplexed.

The rest of the squad gathered behind them.

"The Gaia Cult," Denman said with a sigh.

"What was that?" McKinney's confusion was matched by a few others.

"In the last days of human world, the Gaia Cult rose up to declare that Mother Earth, Gaia, was purging humanity. They said humans were a virus," Omondi explained. "They believed that once the last human had died, the Scrags would die, too. And then earth would be saved from us. They even claimed responsibility for the ISPV being released in Paris, London, and Moscow."

Maria had remembered the Gaia Cult being briefly touched on in world history, but now she knew they would have an even bigger entry. They had compromised the last settlement of the living. Stepping into the lobby, she activated the light on her wristlet and flashed it over the simple rectangular room. The plastic furniture was stained with time and blood.

"Holm, status on that generator," Omondi said into his wristlet.

The answer was the lights flickering on.

The room was rectangular and bland. The posters on the walls and style of the furniture indicated it had probably been some sort of recreational room for the guards. Omondi crossed the room to another doorway. It was also open. A desk had been wedged into the doorframe to keep it from closing. Sliding over the obstruction, Omondi disappeared into the next room.

Maria followed.

Monitors sprawled across one wall with a work station sprawled under the bank of screens. Sprayed over the monitors and the work station were the words "Gaia has reclaimed the world." Bodies were caught under the chairs and some of the monitors had bullet holes punched through their dark faces. Now that power had been restored, the flat screens revealed the view from beyond the valley. Cameras began to transmit images from the long road winding up the pass. Even the cameras at the base station at the bottom of the mountain range were operational.

"They would have seen the approach of the Scrag horde that attacked," Maria remarked.

"Whoever did this," Omondi pointed at the message, "must have killed the guards."

"The communication hub was completely destroyed. That's why there was no warning and the city never could regain remote access,"

Denman said, touching the wires spilling out of the destroyed workstation.

"But what brought the Scrags here?" Maria reached out to an operation console and began to quickly search through the recorded files. "This area is very remote."

Holm climbed over the desk in the doorway and joined them at the workstation. Her face was tense with concentration as she started her diagnostic on the gate.

A few of the squad members filed into the room behind them or lingered near the open door. Maria glanced at them, but said nothing. They were all in a state of shock. It had always been possible that sabotage had been behind the gate failure, but to see that it had been the Gaia Cult had stunned everyone.

"What did you find?" Omondi asked Maria, lingering over her shoulder as she searched.

"The cameras were recording until the generator failed. According to the timestamps, the generator went off just after the gate opened." Maria continued to scan the files, her fingers darting over the interface.

"That fits with what I found," Holm said. "The generator was sabotaged. The batteries were ripped out of it."

"Someone killed the guards, destroyed the communication and remote operations hub, and opened the gate," Omondi said in disbelief.

"Whoever it was didn't live very long after doing all that." Maria activated a screen showing a man and a woman yanking the batteries out of the generator and the screen going dark.

"Fuck," someone muttered behind her.

"They did this on purpose then died," Omondi said in a low, angry voice. "They butchered their own people and almost destroyed the last hope of humanity."

Maria pulled up more recordings. They told the atrocious tale of the ultimate betrayal. The base camp camera footage clearly revealed several trucks full of people luring a massive crowd of Scourge behind them. The people inside were yelling, but Maria didn't get the impression it was with fear, but with rapture. Each camera along the road recorded the same vehicles moving purposefully toward the gate just ahead of the horde of Inferi Scourge.

"They led them here." Holm shook her head, swinging her long blond braids.

There were even children in the trucks. Maria could see their frightened faces while the adults around them cheered with joy as the gate loomed before them. Sliding more camera views up onto the monitors, Maria watched the ascent of the Gaia Cultists and the Inferi Scourge. Now that the time frame was established for the arrival of the Scourge at the gate, she was able to swiftly find the recordings from the guard station.

Two men and a woman in the uniform of service workers parked outside the station and approached carrying what looked like a food delivery. When the woman fired the first shot into the face of a guard, the smile on her lips was eerie with delight. Systematically, the three people gunned down the guards as they advanced on the station. One of the male cultists was shot and killed on the steps, and the guard who shot him was moving to fire at the remaining two cultists when another guard killed him with a shot to the back of the head.

"Fuck me," Cruz's voice exclaimed. "One of the guards was a traitor!"

Maria glanced at Omondi. His jaw was set and his eyes were hard. Directing her attention back to the screen, Maria watched the two service workers and the guard kill everyone in the lobby. The door to the workstation was already propped open. Switching to the camera in the room, Maria slid back the timeframe.

They all watched as a guard at the console calmly turned and fired point blank into the faces of his two co-workers. He methodically destroyed the communication and remote access hub. Then he propped the door open and joined the Gaia Cultists in their killing spree.

"An inside job," Omondi whispered. He rubbed his chin with his fingers as he watched the monitors.

The room fell silent as the squad watched the traitorous guard and his cohorts enter the room they were now standing in and activate the gate. One of the men took out the green paint and gleefully left his claim to glory as the other two laughed and wept with joy. The vehicles entered the valley ahead of the Scourge and parked near the guard station. The occupants climbed out and rushed to form a circle. Holding hands, they turned their faces upward as the Scourge rushed toward them.

All the screens went black marking the moment when the generator had died.

Omondi leaned against the workstation, his eyes closed as he absorbed what he had seen. Finally, he opened his eyes and looked at Maria. "Transmit all the information back to the SWD."

Nodding, Maria started to compile the data for a full report.

"Holm, give me some good news," Omondi said, turning toward the tall blond woman.

"They didn't have time to sabotage the gate further. It's not even damaged. Just the remote access was disabled. I should be able to just close it and reactivate the locks," Holm answered. She had forgotten to take a breath before talking and her voice was ragged. Shaking her head, Holm returned her attention to the workstation. "We're lucky they only had enough time to make sure the city didn't know what was coming and disable the remote access. If they had done anything more to the gate..."

"Close it," Omondi ordered, his gaze on the live feed. There were only a few Inferi Scourge wandering on the road beyond the gate.

"Yes, sir," Holm answered, her fingers sliding over the controls.

Maria raised her eyes and watched as the massive gate trembled to life on the monitors. The room filled with a loud rumble as the floor vibrated beneath their feet. Behind her there was a scramble to get out of the room and witness the closing of the gate. Omondi leaned over the workstation with Holm and Maria at his side. The three watched the cameras outside record the second closing of the gate. It slid into place at an almost languid pace. A few Scourge were caught by the door and crushed. Maria felt the room shudder as the enormous door clanged shut and the locking mechanisms whirled.

"It's done," Holm said in an awed voice.

"Now we kill them all." Omondi lifted his bolt weapon and headed out of the room.

Maria finished with her download and followed with Holm on her heels.

* * *

Patience was a virtue that didn't come naturally to Dwayne. He had learned it over time, but it was still not an easy fit to his psyche. A long day at work had not distracted him sufficiently from worrying about Maria. She was beyond the wall now and far from him. He could no longer reach her, protect her, or hold her.

It was agonizing.

Flipping off the vid screen, he laid back on his bed. He had tried to watch an old film, but had been far too distracted. Lindsey had been unreachable all day, but that was not unusual for her. She would contact him when she was ready with information.

Checking his wristlet again, Dwayne fought the tug of sleep on his eyelids. He didn't want to sleep until he heard from Maria. Of course, she might not be able to find the time to contact him. That possibility was not something he wanted to consider. He longed to hear her voice.

Sleep had nearly won and he was gently dozing when his wristlet buzzed. Instantly awake, he rolled onto his side and activated the stealth program. The screen remained dark and he worried the call had been disconnected. Slowly, he realized he was viewing Maria in the darkness of the night.

"Dwayne, I can't talk long. Everyone is in torpor right now, but I need to be careful," she whispered.

He could barely discern the shape of her face and the glint of her eyes in the starlight. "Are you okay?" He knew her very well and there was tension in her tone that indicated she was upset.

"Things are worse out here than we thought they would be," she admitted. "There was an error in our planning and someone died. I doubt the same mistake will be made again, but..."

Dwayne squinted, desperately wanting to see her face. "I'm sorry, honey. You okay?"

"Yeah, I'm fine. It's just..." her voice faded, then he heard her take a breath. "What we discovered today was...someone opened the gate on purpose, Dwayne. The Gaia Cult tried to kill us all."

"Shit," he gasped.

There had always been theories of sabotage, but they were considered wild speculation. He felt as though he had been punched in the gut. It was unfathomable that someone had purposely tried to wipe out humanity.

"Somehow a group of survivors led the Scrags here and people inside the valley let them in. One of our own guards helped." Maria's voice was ragged. "I wish I could cry. Maybe it would make me feel better, but I'm just..."

"Maria, what you're saying is...unbelievable. It's so awful. I can't imagine how it felt to discover that."

"We're all in shock. We found the trucks of the people who led the Scrags to us. It had some of their literature recorded on pads. We'll bring those back to the city. I'm wondering if some of the city failures over the years have been the Gaia Cult. Maybe they're still active."

Dwayne again caught a glimmer of light in her eyes and again wished he could see her face. "All that information was sent to the SWD?"

"Yeah, but shouldn't they tell you? Aren't you in charge of protecting the city?"

"The commandant is very selective in the information she imparts to me. I can only hope that at some point she will draw me into this officially. I am trying to gather information using my own sources."

Maria sighed wearily.

"Maria, I'm so proud of what you're doing. You're amazing."

"I wish I felt amazing," Maria whispered. "I feel so lost out here. I didn't think it would be this overwhelming."

"It's your first night out there. You'll adapt. You can do this."

She was silent and he strained to see her face. Finally, she said, "You're right. I can do this. The gate is closed. This is the beginning."

"I love you, Maria."

"I love you, Dwayne," she answered. "I need to go."

The connection ended.

Slinging his legs over the side of the bed, Dwayne accessed the hidden menu again and sent a message to Lindsey. He would need her more than ever if there really was the possibility of a threat inside the city.

Chapter 18

"Today the killing starts and we don't stop until every Scrag in the valley is dead," Omondi said the next morning. "There is an estimated four million Scrags in the valley. I know that sounds like a lot when there are only forty of us, but let me show you something." Removing the bolt weapon from his back, Omondi pointed to Holm. "Set your wristlet timer for one minute. The rest of you count how many I kill. Holm, tell me when to start."

Holm fussed with her wristlet, then held up one hand. "Now!"

Omondi immediately started to dispatch the Inferi Scourge clustered around him.

"One...two...three..." the squad intoned together.

Maria watched, smirking slightly. Omondi was putting on quite a show as Scourge collapsed like fallen trees. It was quite impressive.

"...twelve...thirteen...fourteen..."

Omondi pivoted back and forth as his weapon slammed against the skulls of the creatures. His huge body was impressive among the mangled forms.

"...twenty...twenty-one...twenty-two...twenty-three..."

A few members of the squad began to laugh.

"...twenty-four...twenty-five..."

"Stop!" Holm cried out.

Omondi grinned, not winded, not tired, and lifted his bolt weapon over his head in triumph before sliding it back in its sheath. "How many was that?"

"Twenty-five," Jameson said, impressed.

"Each and every one of you can do that number or better. With the Inferi Scourge packed so tightly together, it makes killing them easier." Omondi rejoined the group. "There are forty of us. Multiply that twenty-five by forty."

"One thousand," Holm said, clearly startled.

"We can kill a thousand Scrags in one minute. One thousand. Let that sink into your minds. A thousand Scrags. In one minute. How many can we kill in one hour? In one day? In one month?" Omondi laughed heartily. "I've stunned you. Of course, not every situation around the valley will give us a prime killing ground such as this where they're packed so close together. Also, we have to salvage what we can from the bodies and burn them. So our numbers decrease significantly. But we can clear this valley in a matter of months."

The grins and nods of the squad coaxed a smile out of Maria. Omondi was quite good at stirring up good solid morale. The soldiers stood around him as he rolled a screen out on the ground and the holographic display of the valley appeared.

"We work each grid until they're cleared. We will start in this area since it's closest to the gate."

Maria listened as Omondi continued to lay out their mission. She knew it by heart, but she feigned attention. Soon the valley would be dotted with collapsible bins filled with anything of use they discovered on the bodies. They would be stacked neatly for later delivery to the city.

The dead moaned and swayed. In the distance the howling Scourge were still assaulting the personnel carrier. And beyond them, the city walls rose, impenetrable and imposing. There was no going home until the mission was done.

Her conversation with Dwayne the night before still haunted her. She was bothered by the constant breakdowns in the city in the years since the gate failed. Yes, the city was aging and so were the mechanisms that kept it running, but Maria wondered if people were still actively trying to find a way to exterminate humanity. She couldn't even begin to fathom why humans would actively seek to destroy other humans, yet she had witnessed that very act. Even more disturbing was the realization that after the last known pockets of humanity had been airlifted to The Bastion, other humans had remained alive outside. Was it possible that there were yet humans in the world beyond the valley struggling to survive against the Inferi Scourge?

Gripping her weapon, Maria refocused her attention on Omondi as he finished detailing the plans.

"We have a long day ahead of us. Let's get moving. Next break is in four hours," Omondi finished. He deactivated the holographic projection and folded up the screen. Tucking it into his jacket, he gave the squad a brief nod before walking over to Maria. He was taller and more powerfully-built than any of the other soldiers, yet there was an unexpected fragility in his gaze. Maria was learning to read his moods and this morning she suspected he was deeply troubled by their discovery of the gate's sabotage. She had transmitted the recordings to the SWD, but they had yet to respond. At least not so far as she knew. Omondi had not said anything to her if they had.

"Ready for the day, Vanguard Martinez?" Omondi asked.

"Absolutely, Chief Defender Omondi," she answered.

"Then let us begin." Omondi pulled his bolt weapon from its holster on his back.

"I'm right behind you." Maria echoed his actions and tailed him to a cluster of Scourge.

The first few kills were jarring. Maria hadn't expected to feel anything but relief at dispatching the creatures that had killed humanity. Instead, she almost felt as though she were betraying them. The creatures were docile when not riled to frenzy by the presence of humans. Their vacant eyes and soft moans gave them the appearance of bewilderment. Their eyes tended to roll about as the bolt weapons were fired, seeking the source of the sound. Maria wondered if they understood in any capacity that they were in danger. Though their eyes shifted in their sockets and a few Scourge looked around in confusion, none attacked.

Gradually, Maria was piecing together the truth about the Scourge. When in an overexcited state, any activity that could be associated with humans was enough to provoke them to attack. The squad had been speaking in very low voices to avoid activating the Scourge into hunting mode. The undead in torpor didn't even register the squad's presence.

Maria strongly suspected that those attacking the carrier wouldn't respond in the same manner. She was certain they would attack anything they suspected was human. Hearing a human voice would draw the attention of the rampaging creatures, but not those in torpor.

Her bolt weapon discharged and an old man crumpled to her feet. Stepping over him, Maria pressed the end of her weapon against the base of the skull of an adolescent boy and fired. The boy fell and she moved on to a middle-aged woman. All around her Scourge fell to the ground in final death. They didn't fight back. They didn't run. They just died. For so long the Scourge had been the monsters of her nightmares, but seeing them this close, she now also saw them as the sad victims of a devastating virus.

Yet, these were the same creatures that had killed Ryan and her father. Pity and hate struggled within her as she continued the gruesome task.

Eventually, the squad relaxed into their chore. Conversation started. It was stilted at first, but gave way to warm camaraderie. Maria found herself smiling despite their terrible task as the morning wore on. Jameson and McKinney were quite adept at a witty remark or two. Their chatter made the task easier whenever she had to stop and clean her weapon and wipe off her gloves. Holm and Mikado heaped the bodies into piles after doing a cursory search on each Scourge. It was surprising to see that there were actually items to salvage. Old communication devices, a few weapons, jewelry made of stainless steel, copper, silver and gold.

Maria began to note the little things about the Scourge: the diamond earrings in one's ears, the tie still clipped to one's shirt, the scissors still clutched in the hand of another.

"Got a nun over here," Jameson called out. "I'm not going to get in trouble with God if I kill her, right?"

"She's already dead. God won't get mad," McKinney answered.

"We'll have to bury her," Cruz said somberly. "Catholics don't believe in cremation."

"I'm sure God will overlook it in this case," McKinney said, his tone a bit dismissive.

"I don't believe in gods," Holm grunted, dispatching the nun in question. She hooked the dead woman and dragged her away.

"What if you're wrong?" Cruz called out after her. "What if God is out there?"

Holm hurled the nun onto the pile. "I'll be surprised and God can have a chortle over it."

Maria rolled her eyes, slightly shaking her head.

"I mock no one's gods." Omondi trudged past the squad lugging four bodies after him. "Just in case..."

"Sounds like a good policy," Cormier decided. "Playing it safe."

"Sometimes playing it safe gets you into the worst of trouble," Denman answered the young woman with a sardonic smile.

Maria glanced at him curiously. His words had held weight and underlying meaning to them.

"I'd rather play fast and loose and get in trouble that way. Fuck playing it safe." McKinney high-fived Holm as Cruz rolled her eyes.

The day wore on.

Though they had no need to eat or drink, the squad took a break after a few hours. Omondi walked away to report into the SWD, leaving the squad to their own devices. Most pulled out small pads to play games, watch vids, or read. They weren't able to communicate with friends or family, so most ignored their wristlets. Maria wished she could call Dwayne, but instead amused herself with a game on her pad. Holm decided to sunbathe and stripped off her heavy armor.

"Can we get tans?" Jameson wondered aloud, watching her disrobe.

Denman cast a look over his shoulder at the nearest Scourge. "I doubt it. They aren't even sunburned. The virus keeps them in stasis, exactly how they were when they died."

"I'm going to try," Holm said, closing her eyes under her sunglasses. She looked very pale against the dry-packed black earth of the valley.

"Shouldn't you keep your armor on?" Jameson asked.

"*You* should," Holm quipped.

Laughter rippled through the group and Jameson made a big show of stripping off his armor to lie next to the tall blond.

Maria watched over the top of her pad, amused, but not concerned. She was toying with the idea of taking off her armor, too. They were far from the Inferi Scourge that were frenzying near the carrier. She wondered if Omondi would make Holm and Jameson put their armor back on when he was done with his report. Returning her gaze to her game, she tried to keep her gnome that was riding a dinosaur alive as it traveled through a medieval setting.

Gutierrez put some music on and turned up the volume on his pad. It was very old rock music from a time when the Scourge didn't roam the earth. A game of poker started nearby with Cormier shuffling the cards while McKinney inflated a ball so he could play soccer with Mikado. Maria scrunched up her nose as her dinosaur died and left the gnome to fend off a pack of werewolves on its own. Her fingers danced over the screen as she maneuvered her little pink haired creature into an epic battle.

The sound of feet pounding on the hard-packed earth drew her attention from the game. For a moment she thought it was McKinney kicking the ball at Mikado, but a flash of movement drew her eyes toward the wall of Scourge standing a few hundred feet away. A figure exploded out of the densely packed crowd and raced toward them. As she scrambled to her feet, she took in the battered armor and desperate face of the running man. It took her another second to realize it was not one of her own people. He sprang toward Jameson and Holm lying on the ground.

"No!" Maria attempted to tackle the man, but only caught his feet, sending him sprawling.

Chaos enveloped the squad as they rushed in to help rescue Jameson and Holm. The snarls of the man and the screams from the soldiers filled her ears as she struggled to get a grip on the attacker. Holm shouted for help while Jameson cursed at the man clawing at them, attempting to fight him off. Holm managed to roll away, reaching for her weapon. Denman grabbed the man, trying to drag him off Jameson. The attacker kicked and twisted, smashing the bottom of his heavy boots into Maria's chest and stomach. She registered the impacts, but continued to grapple with the man. She managed to get her knees under her, heaving herself upward, getting a hold of the man's armor. Hooking both her hands into his collar, she tried to yank him away.

"Fucking shit!" Jameson screamed. "He bit me!"

Denman and Maria tried to heave him off the terrified young man. Spittle and blood flecked the man's face as he chewed the flesh he had ripped from Jameson's hand. He continued to fight, but he seemed more intent on devouring the bit of meat. Denman exchanged a startled look with Maria.

The squad tried to pin the attacker to the ground. He was abnormally strong and the bucking of his body knocked a few squad members away. Maria rested her full weight on his chest.

"Who is he?" Cormier screamed.

"*What* the fuck is he?" Maria gasped.

The attacker swallowed and grinned up at her. "Hungry," he hissed, and lunged toward her exposed neck.

Holm brought the bolt weapon down on the man's face. Blood burst from his ruined mouth and nose, spattering Maria and Denman, then Holm slammed the weapon down again, pulverizing his skull. The man finally stopped moving. Gasping, Maria fell back, her gloved hands wiping away the cold blood from her face. Denman sat back on his ankles as the rest of the squad let go of the corpse.

"He fucking bit me!" Jameson screamed. "He fucking tore a fucking chunk of fucking meat off my fucking hand!"

"Jameson, calm down," Omondi ordered jogging into view. "Denman, take care of him!"

Visibly collecting his wits, Denman got to his feet and hurried to Jameson's side, pulling his medical pack from his belt.

Maria stared at the ruined face of the man who had attacked them. He had looked alive, not like the Scourge. His eyes had not been milky, his skin had not been gray. And he had spoken. Yet, he had attacked as savagely as any Scourge. Rolling onto her knees, she leaned over the dead man.

Omondi knelt next to her and studied the man's armor. "Bastion Constabulary issue," he whispered.

"Yeah, I can see that. But no rank, no squad insignia." Maria searched the man's pockets.

"What happened?" Omondi asked.

Maria filled Omondi in as the squad gathered around Jameson and Denman.

"He didn't look like a Scrag," Maria finished in a low voice. "And....he spoke."

"What the hell? Are you sure?"

Maria replayed the scene in her head, then nodded. "Yes. I'm sure."

"What did he say?" Omondi asked, his brow scrunching above his dark eyes.

"One word: *hungry*," Maria answered.

A slight narrowing of his eyes gave Omondi a thoughtful, yet frightening look. Bowing toward her, he whispered, "Tell no one."

She acknowledged his order with the curt nod of her head.

"I'll report it to the SWD. Maybe they will be able to explain this."

"No I.D." Maria said with a sigh after looking for dog tags or other forms of I.D. "Nothing."

"Maybe he was from the last push."

"But why wouldn't he have I.D.?"

Omondi shrugged. "We'll figure it out. Now, we need to get back to work."

It felt as if the world no longer made any sense.

* * *

Physical exhaustion was a mere memory now and one that was quickly fading. Maria's memories whispered that her limbs should be tired, aching, and sore, yet they weren't. She felt strangely disconnected from the world, her own emotions, and her body. She ruthlessly killed the Scourge, dragged them to their funeral pyres, and watched them burn in the dying sunlight without feeling anything at all, physically or emotionally.

Her only real emotion throughout the day was worry when the first bonfire was lit. A whimper of fear slid through her as she wondered if the Scourge would be stirred into a rampage. Instead they scurried away from the burning pyre of their brethren. She supposed the fear of fire was innate in any creature. Watching the dead burn, she was glad that her senses were muted. Tucking her scarf up around her nose and mouth, she returned to killing.

The day felt particularly long. Their breaks were short and tense. The squad watched the Scourge with some trepidation. Fear that another anomaly might burst out of the horde and attack kept them all on alert. Speculation was high about what had spurred the Scourge to attack Jameson and Holm, but Omondi would silence anyone discussing the attack if he overheard.

"Keep focused. Keep alert," Omondi urged throughout the long, tedious hours.

It was nightfall when Maria's disassociation from the reality around her unleashed her from its numbing constraints and she felt the first sharp pang of remorse and fear slice into her mind. The world swam sharply into focus and she could no longer ignore the truth. Despite slaughtering the Scourge all day, the valley was still infested, and it would be months before she saw Dwayne again.

Turning away from the fires tossing sparks into the darkness, she was glad she could not cry. She felt the need billowing up from inside of her, constricting her throat, but her eyes would not give birth to tears. The heat from the fire washed over her back and she wished fervently that it could warm her cold flesh and give her life again. Squatting down, she crossed her arms over her chest and starred down at the hard-packed, black earth. He braid tickled her cheek and she flipped it back over her shoulder.

Closing her eyes, she tried not to see the faces of all the Scourge she had killed today. She tried not to smell their burning flesh. She tried not to wonder about the lives they lived before infection. And she tried not to think of all the Scourge still filling the valley and the world beyond.

"It feels like we've been out here an eternity already," Denman's voice said.

She opened her eyes and cast her gaze in his direction. He was kneeling next to her, fussing with his med-kit.

"We have a long way to go," she answered, jerking her chin toward the crowd of Scourge that started a few hundred yards away.

"Yes," Denman said, his voice painted with sorrow. "We do."

"Then we go home, get cured, and start a new life."

"A better life. My children will be thrilled to live outside the walls. I've asked for a farm near the gate actually."

"Already planning to get married and have kids?" Maria asked. She was glad he was speaking to her. It directed her thoughts away from the burning corpses.

"I *am* married and I *have* children," Denman replied.

"I thought all of us were unattached. I thought that was the recruiting requirement." Maria was surprised at his proclamation.

"Well, for my position they decided to make an exception."

"And you agreed to come out here away from your family?"

Denman nodded his head vigorously. "Absolutely. There are four of us living in a two room flat. The kids don't have a place to play." Denman sighed. "I just felt I didn't have a choice." Reaching out, he said, "Let me see your hands."

"Why?"

"Omondi is watching," Denman answered.

Yanking off her glove, Maria extended one hand. The atmosphere around them was suddenly conspiratorial.

Denman took her hand and studied it. "There is some concern that the virus will not keep the body in exactly the same condition it was in when we technically died. There is a possibility of skin breaks, blisters, and other concerns."

"Scrags don't get sick," Maria pointed out.

"They don't talk either," Denman replied. He took out some ointment and rubbed it on her knuckles.

"You heard it speak, didn't you?" Maria whispered.

A slight nod was followed by him gesturing for her other hand.

Maria complied quickly. "Why didn't you say anything?"

"What did the Chief Defender say?"

"He's not sure he believes me," she answered, shrugging.

Denman's brown eyes lifted to stare into hers. "I don't know anyone out here very well. I don't know you at all. But I watched you today. All of this bothers you more than it does the others. It bothers you like it bothers me. You and I heard that Scrag speak. He said he was hungry. He was wearing Constabulary armor."

"What do you think it means?"

"That the SWD is hiding something."

Maria tucked her treated hands back into her gloves and stood up. Denman followed suit, fastening his med-pack to his belt.

"They're not going to tell us. They want us to just do the job," Maria said at last. "So that's what we'll do."

Maria caught sight of Omondi studying their interaction and she flexed her hands, then gave him the thumbs up.

Recognizing they were under scrutiny, Denman said, "Good as new. Nothing major. If you notice any peeling around the knuckles, let me know." He sauntered off toward Mikado.

Maria smiled briefly at Omondi, then sat back down. Pulling out her pad, she couldn't wait to speak with Dwayne.

* * *

Dwayne stared at Maria's visage in disbelief. She had managed to slip away and turn on her pad to illuminate her face while they spoke. It was well past midnight and he was exhausted, but he didn't want to miss speaking with her. He could see the strain in her face and hear it in her voice.

"Are you sure it was constabulary armor?"

"Positive. Omondi and I wondered if he was from the last push, but neither of us recognized him. It's so odd. He didn't have any insignia or anything on his armor that would identify him."

"And he bit Jameson? That doesn't make sense."

"None of the other Scrags attacked us today. Even after the attack, they ignored us. After the last two days, I believe the Scrags respond to visual stimulus. If they perceive that a human victim is nearby it heightens their awareness. And once that happens, sound can draw them into attacking. The Scrags we were dealing with were docile today and then, this man, this...thing...just appeared and went after the two of us that were not in armor. He went for the vulnerable ones."

Dwayne sat at the edge of his bed, dumbfounded by what he was hearing. None of it made sense. "But why would it bite if you're obviously...a Scrag?"

Maria winced at his words and he instantly regretted what he had said. Shaking her head, she said, "He not only bit Jameson's hand, he ate what he tore off. Denman and I both saw him do it. And I'm not sure if Denman heard or not, but I know that the attacker said the word *hungry*."

"The Scrags don't eat their victims. They just infect," Dwayne said, mystified by what she was saying.

"I saw a Scrag bite and eat a piece of Stillson. I reported it, but no one believed me." Maria frowned. "Dwayne, I think the Scrag I saw bite Stillson was...I think it was in uniform."

Dwayne rubbed his chin with one hand while pondering her words. "None of this sounds right. At all. The Scrags don't eat us like those zombie monsters in the old vids. They bite to infect, not eat."

"Something is really wrong out here, Dwayne. Omondi got the squad to calm down and laugh it off after a while, but I could see in his eyes that he is just as concerned as I am. He wouldn't talk about it though."

"I'm going to look into it," Dwayne decided. "I'll find out what is going on."

"How?"

"My hidden sources," Dwayne answered with a wink. "I can see what I can uncover on this end, but you will need to be careful out there. It's obvious that there is a hell of a lot more going on than either one of us has been told."

Maria nodded. Her emotions played across her face, fluctuating from fearful to weary. At last she forced a small smile, "Never a dull moment, huh?"

"With us? Never."

"I still believe in what I'm doing," Maria said after a beat, her cloudy dark eyes staring into the camera. "We killed so many of them today. Men, women, young, old. Up close when they're in torpor they're such sad looking things, but then I remember what they did to the world, to my father, to Ryan, and it's so easy to kill them."

He listened because he knew she needed him to. There was really nothing for him to say. He couldn't imagine seeing the Inferi Scourge docile and up close like she was experiencing.

"It's so...intimate," Maria continued, pulling herself out of her thoughts. "I'm seeing who they were before they died, then setting them free."

Dwayne knew they were pushing it on the time limit, but he didn't want to let her go. He wanted to hear her voice and see her face. He needed to hear her speak and share her thoughts.

"Times up," Maria whispered sadly.

"I love you," Dwayne said.

"I love you," Maria answered, then was gone.

Sliding off his bed, Dwayne turned on his coffee maker and again sent a message to Lindsey. She still hadn't responded and he was becoming increasingly concerned. Sleep would be long in returning. He wasn't even sure he wanted to sleep after what Maria had told him. He was just pouring a hot cup of the freshly made coffee when his wristlet beeped that a message was incoming.

"Hello?" he said, answering in voice-only mode.

"I got your message," Lindsey said. Her voice didn't sound sleepy, but actually quite alert. "I'm working on what you asked for."

"There's more now."

"Shit. Really? How deep is this rabbit hole?"

Dwayne grinned despite the situation. "That's what I'm starting to wonder. The commandant was unavailable today. They're keeping me in the dark about the Gaia Cult situation."

"That's because they're preparing a huge media blitz on the subject. They realized that they can't keep the news of the gate closure away from the media much longer. The guards on the walls can see it's closed. Also, if they pull the guards on the wall, then the people in the city will notice."

"They should have thought of all that before," Dwayne said sourly.

Lindsey let out a sarcastic snort. "They did, but their initial plan was to eliminate the wall patrols. The president overrode that plan because he didn't want the population freaking out. He told them to make it work. Now they're in a quandary. They have to rework their story to the media."

"Interesting."

"Not all is well at the top."

"Which I know all too well," Dwayne admitted.

"So, what more do you have for me?"

Dwayne told her.

Lindsey drew in her breath and was silent.

"What is it?"

"Well," Lindsey hesitated. "Well, I'm not sure yet. But I did trace a few communiques from several years back that made it sound like maybe some of the Scrags were acting irregularly. Give me more time. I'll turn up something."

"Keep me in the loop and don't go quiet for so long."

"I have a life, you know. But I'll keep in touch."

The link went dead.

Taking a long sip of his cooling coffee, Dwayne knew for sure he wouldn't be sleeping anymore that night.

Chapter 19

The next morning, Dwayne was almost to the monorail station when his wristlet chimed. Activating it, he glanced down to see his eldest daughter's face. She was the spitting image of her mother when she was the same age and it always startled him. He loved Caitlyn with all his heart, but she also had her mother's temperament, which made her a bit difficult to deal with at times.

"Hey, honey, what's up?" he asked taking the metal stairs two at a time.

"Big news is about to break," Caitlyn said in a tone that was a little too brisk. It meant she was scared. "I thought I would warn you."

Dwayne hesitated as he reached the station. He stepped away from the other commuters. Caitlyn's job as an assistant to one of the vice president's secretaries was something she took very seriously. Regardless of him being the Castellan of the Constabulary, she never divulged any information to him. This was unusual for her. The tiny dot in the corner of the screen revealed this was a high security call.

"What is it?" Dwayne stared into his daughter's eyes. They were the only thing she had inherited from him. The same blue, the same intensity.

Sighing, she leaned forward. "The gate is closed. The official story comes out in an hour. The circumstances surrounding the gate closure are top secret." Caitlyn hesitated then said, "Daddy, I trust you not only as my father, but as the Castellan. I want you to know that. I don't know how much they will tell you, but..."

Dwayne felt his heart seize up. His little girl *was* afraid. He could see it.

"Don't let them keep you out of the loop," she said at last.

The call ended.

* * *

The face of an Inferi Scourge came into sharp focus as her vision was restored, and she thrust it away. She hated entering torpor so close to the hordes. Observing the rest of the squad, she saw that they were still in their blacked out state. Most laid on the ground to emulate sleep. It was a way to maintain a little distance between the squad and the undead around them.

Omondi was seated nearby. She was viewing him when his eyes suddenly focused. Startled, he studied the area, then cast a questioning look at Maria.

She shrugged.

They both checked their wristlets. They had been revived early. The sun was barely piercing the sky above The Bastion.

"What the hell?" Omondi muttered.

Their wristlets chimed. A quick message scrolled across the screens. The SWD would be contacting them within five minutes.

Pointing to an adjacent position, Omondi pulled out the screen from his backpack. In silence, they strode to where he had indicated. Though the squad wouldn't awaken until the SWD was done with their conference call, room was needed to unroll the screen. Omondi found an old dead tree trunk, and together they spread the screen and fastened it at the corners.

Unease had settled into Omondi's features, and Maria mirrored his feelings. The events of the last two days had been disquieting. The mission was supposed to be a simple endeavor, yet now appeared immensely complicated. It was difficult to put into words the myriad of thoughts that boiled within her mind. The silence between them was not reassuring.

Omondi linked his wristlet to the screen, and they waited.

Exactly five minutes later the screen activated. Mr. Petersen and Dr. Curran appeared, projected in all their holographic glory. Dr. Curran looked exhausted, but Mr. Petersen appeared calm as usual. Unexpectedly, Commandant Pierce of The Bastion Constabulary sat at the conference table as well. Her dark eyes and sharp cheekbones always made Maria think of a hawk. Her silvery-black afro was twisted into spirals that were wrapped into a bun at the nape of her elegant neck. She was beautiful, severe, and, according to Dwayne, borderline paranoid about everything.

"Congratulations on the closure of the gate," Commandant Pierce started.

"Thank you. It was a great success for us personally and for The Bastion," Omondi answered.

Commandant Pierce continued, "The death of Special Constable Coleman was an unexpected tragedy. We reviewed the report of his death. Though it was an unfortunate event, we learned new vital information about the Inferi Scourge. That we now know how they identify their prey is of great importance." She gave Dr. Curran a pointed look.

Dr. Curran didn't shrink under the piercing glare. "With the data we're now receiving from the field we do not anticipate any further setbacks of this kind. Now that we know specifically what stimuli compel the Inferi Scourge to attack, we can plan to avoid such situations again," Dr. Curran responded, her tone crisp and slightly defensive. "We will be updating the mission specifics accordingly."

Commandant Pierce's impassive appearance didn't alter when she spoke again. "I have been asked by the president to inform you that we're releasing the news of the gate closure to the public, and that a special ops team is destroying the Inferi Scourge. Initially we were going to wait to disclose this information, but the president feels it's in the best interest of the city if the population knows about the success we're incurring on the field. The fact that you're Inferi Boon will not be released to the media. Nor will your names. That aspect of the mission must remain secret. We will determine when to update the population on your progress as time goes on." The commandant paused, and instinctively, Maria knew what came next wouldn't be pleasant. "We're altering your work schedule to twenty hours a day."

"Understood," Omondi said with a brief nod of his head.

"We realize this may be emotionally taxing, but feel that the squad can handle the duress," Dr. Curran said with a short smile.

Maria didn't think the doctor believed her own words.

"Any questions?" Commandant Pierce asked.

"The Inferi Scourge from yesterday who spoke-" Omondi started to say.

"Vanguard Martinez heard a grunt and her mind interpreted it as a word," Mr. Petersen said swiftly over him. Mr. Petersen directed his gaze at Maria. "You're still adapting to your new environment. Your mind will play tricks on you. The Inferi Scourge do look remarkably alive at times, but they're not capable of speech."

Maria started to protest.

"We understand," Omondi answered, his dark eyes silencing Maria with just a look.

"Vanguard Martinez, your work has been impressive," the commandant said, directing her fierce gaze at Maria. "You will continue to compile the information you're gleaning from your observations and relay them through the Chief Defender. We would like you to work closely with Medic Denman on his reports as well. It's best if we keep communication between us to the minimum. The media will be watching closely, attempting to glean any information it can."

"Understood," Maria said.

Now that all the reports would be funneled through Omondi, that also meant any information coming from the SWD would be seen exclusively by the Chief Defender. Maria liked him well enough and trusted him to lead them, but she was bothered by the decision.

"We look forward to your progress reports, Chief Defender Omondi," the commandant said, then the screen went blank.

Just before the transmission had been cut, Maria had seen a worried look on Dr. Curran's face. Something was definitely amiss.

Omondi quickly folded up the screen. His jaw was set and tension edged his movements making them sharp.

"What do you think is really going on?" Maria finally dared to ask.

Omondi stared out over the valley, then toward the closed gate. It was obvious he was troubled, but at last he merely shrugged. "We have a job to do and we'll do it." He brushed past her and headed back to where the others remained in torpor.

Maria spiritlessly followed.

* * *

Commandant Pierce glanced up as Dwayne entered her office. He had been surprised by her late night summons. She was usually at home with her daughter by this hour of the night. The commandant's husband had died of a heart attack a few years after the birth of their only child. In spite of her often abrasive and dismissive manner, she was a devoted mother.

Seated behind her desk, she looked older than usual. Maybe it was the light from the lamp on her desk catching the silver in her tightly-woven hair, or how the shadows accentuated the lines around her face and eyes.

"Please take a seat," she said in an unusually tired voice. Her powerful demeanor and finely-toned physique never betrayed weakness. But tonight, everything about her appearance and conduct was weighed down with exhaustion.

Dwayne settled into the black leather chair. Her desk was pristine, the glass and chrome gleaming, but the clutter scattered across it was unusual. Many screens were opened on the desktop and pads and actual paper littered one corner. The photo of her deceased husband and their infant daughter was set at an angle so she could easily view them. Dwayne had never seen the photo before. It was odd to see such an object of sentimentality on the Commandant's desk.

Soft, short, pudgy with a receding hairline, blue eyes, and skin as white as snow: Leonard Pierce had been an opposite to his wife. The husband and wife had been a study in contrasts. Dwayne had met the man once or twice. He had been impressed with Leonard's humor and kindness.

His gaze drifted from the photo to Commandant Pierce.

"I loved him more than life itself. When he died, I thought I would never breathe again. I wanted to die with him, but I had Lucinda to think about. Sweet Lucy Lou, her father called her. She gave me a reason to continue living when all I wanted to do was die," the commandant said in a soft, weary voice.

Dwayne sat in silence, unsure of how to respond. He was mystified by her summons. It was best to allow her to reveal the reason for their late meeting on her own terms.

"She's everything to me, Castellan Reichardt. Lucy is my reason for life and breath. You're a father of three. I *know* you understand what I'm talking about."

"Yes, sir, I do."

Settling in her chair, the commandant raised her eyes toward the ceiling, but her gaze was unfocused. "Everything I do is for my daughter. Yes, I took a vow to the Constabulary and to the city, but at the very core of my being, every decision I make is to ensure the security of The Bastion so that my daughter can grow up to be the amazing woman I know she will be." Her right hand tightened into a fist.

"Does this concern the special ops clearing the valley?" Dwayne dared to ask.

With a sharp shake of her head, the commandant removed any hope Dwayne had that she would finally draw him into her confidence about the SWD secret mission. "No. I cannot speak of that mission. My involvement in the SWD mission to clear the valley is cursory at best." Her voice was bitter.

"I see." Dwayne understood perfectly. President Cabot had the commandant towing the line. The SWD was definitely firmly in charge of the mission Maria was on.

"I have called you in here because I was given recent orders that I have decided should be delegated to you. Because of the president's political maneuverings and grandstanding, the entire city knows that *something* is going on in the valley. Speculation is high as to how the valley is being cleared, but the specifics of the mission are not being divulged until after the mission is completed...if ever. The president needs for The Bastion citizens to be firmly focused on that mission. He wants them to have hope for a future without the Scrags." The commandant's voice was growing huskier with emotion. Sliding a report over to Dwayne, she said, "You must see this." She thumbed the corner of the clear sheet identifying herself as the reader. Instantly, the report appeared.

Dwayne read swiftly. His fingers began to tremble. "I thought they said that food production was up this year?"

"It is. But food production is only to supplement stores from before the fall of the gate. The Bastion has never been self-sufficient since the gate fell. We've been living off the stores for years now. Each year, despite the production of food, we're consuming vast amounts of stored food supplies. As the population grew, we consumed more. The government didn't halt the population growth because how else can humanity continue if it doesn't breed? The number of females still greatly exceeds the number of males. This whole situation has always been a conundrum. Everyone in the city knows that our situation is dire, but they don't know how truly bad it is." Commandant Pierce reached out and Dwayne handed her the report. Her face wore a neutral expression, but her eyes sparkled in the light from her lamp. "If something doesn't change, we will all starve to death within half a year's time."

"They're clearing the valley. Once the topsoil is removed and we begin farming again, the food crisis will be over," Dwayne said, his voice tight with emotion. The report had left him with a terrible empty feeling inside.

"If they fail, or take too long in securing the valley, food rationing will begin within the next two months. This is so we can stockpile what remains of our food resources in Section A."

"The fallback position." Dwayne knew all about Section A. It had been created specifically to sustain a small group of people for up to two years if the city was breached. It was heavily fortified with a water reclamation system and solar panels to provide energy. "Only four thousand people can survive in there."

Commandant Pierce tossed the report onto the stack of clear sheets resting on the side of her desk. "Though the president and the SWD are certain their *top secret* mission will be successful, the Constabulary has been ordered to prepare for the death of the city. In four months, if there is no successful push back of the Scrags in the valley, the healthiest of our population from ages eighteen to twenty-four will be moved to an area of the city that is being prepared now. The rations being set aside for them will keep them alive for possibly two years."

Dwayne's mouth and throat felt painfully dry. "I see."

"I've been trying to keep this from you, but I realize that eventually your sources will begin leaking this information. Most likely not only to you, but to the media. We could have a dire situation on our hands sooner than we think."

"Why are you telling me this?" Dwayne asked, his voice harsh with emotion.

"A small contingent of Constabulary soldiers and government officials will also be allowed into Section A. The list has already been made." Commandant Pierce drew in a deep breath, then slowly exhaled. "I often play the political game with aplomb, but sometimes that works against me. I offended someone in a high position. Though my name was originally on the list, my daughter's was not. She's only fourteen. I asked for her to be added. I was told that this was not possible. That it would mean removing a much healthier citizen with a better chance of survival, or robbing the survivors of experienced leadership." Her dark eyes met Dwayne's, her defiance clear in them. "All three of your children are on the list. And now you are, too."

"You removed yourself," Dwayne said in awe.

"I'd rather die with my daughter than survive without her. Once the evacuation begins to Section A, the city will spiral into chaos. There will be riots and bloodshed. I won't leave Lucy behind to endure that alone. I already informed the president of my decision. You're now officially in charge of preparing the evacuation to Section A and anticipating all security measures for the city."

"This may all be unnecessary if the valley is cleared," Dwayne reminded her. He was touched by her stance, shaken by her words, and afraid for the city, but he had faith in Maria. Even in the face of such calamitous news, he believed Maria and the men and women in her squad could save them.

Commandant Pierce's face regained its stone-like impassiveness. "These words stay between us. The mission has just begun and already there is reason for concern. I am beginning to wonder if the plan was viable to begin with."

Trying to maintain a professional demeanor, Dwayne shifted in his chair, trying not to ask her the many questions filling his mind. He already suspected why she was having misgivings, but maybe there were more happenings to which he was not privy.

"Of course, I cannot go into any detail other than to say that the task I have sanctioned you with is of the utmost priority. Though I hope the SWD will be successful in its endeavor to save us, my faith rests with the Constabulary and with you."

"If the SWD fails, Section A will only give us two more years of life."

"Two years where maybe you and the powers that be will be able to find a way to save the remainder of humanity." The commandant lifted her shoulders in a diffident shrug.

Dwayne recognized that she was trying to maintain her composure. He had known that there had to be a reason for the president being so forward about the mission to clear the valley, but he had never imagined it was to keep the focus away from the dwindling food supplies.

"I will do my very best," he said finally.

She pushed a pad across the desk toward him. "Your orders. The parameters of your assignment are clearly defined. You will report to me and I will report to the president and his council."

"Understood," Dwayne said, the heaviness in his chest worrisome and painful.

"As far as you need be concerned, the mission to clear the valley is not a salient component to your mission. In other words, prepare for the worst. Dismissed."

It took another two hours for him to read through all the details of his orders, and another thirty minutes to walk home in utter darkness. The curfew had passed and the city was dark. He was stopped by security patrols a few times, but a quick flash of his wristlet was all that was needed for him to continue on his journey.

When he finally secured the door to his flat behind him, he checked his wristlet. It was almost time for Maria to call. He couldn't wait to hear her voice, or see her face.

That night, Maria didn't call, nor respond when he called her.

And she wouldn't for the next two months.

Chapter 20

The world was full of death, fire, and endless days and nights of killing.

The day of the conference call, the SWD had reclaimed control of the wristlet alarms, locking out any chance of Maria reviving herself so she could speak with Dwayne. The loneliness that ached inside her only worsened every night before she fell into torpor. She missed him so much. She craved the ability to cry and to dream. Perhaps crying would have brought relief. Maybe her dreams would have been filled with Dwayne. Instead, she spent her days killing in the shadows of the high mountains and the city she had once called home.

The camaraderie of the early days had faded as the days droned on. The mixed group of SWD security and Constabulary often socialized apart. Sometimes there were tense moments, but overall the squad was working well together. Though Gutierrez was SWD security, he often hung out with Mikado and McKinney playing ball. Hopefully, the group would continue to integrate.

It was hard to find respite during the days of killing. Though there was still some joking and laughter during the breaks, it was easy to be foul-tempered when the small joys of life were missing. Even though they didn't need food and drink, they all missed sitting down to meals. Though they didn't need to sleep, being unable to find comfort in dreams was taxing.

As the first days faded into weeks and the weeks faded into a month, Denman lobbied Chief Defender Omondi for more down time for the sake of the squad's emotional well-being, but Omondi replied that the SWD had declined. They were on a tight schedule and the SWD was closely watching their progress.

It was hard to still feel human at the end of the first month. The squad could finally see their progress as they made their way through the valley. Each night the bonfires smoldered as they dragged the dead to the flames. As the bodies were cleared away, the ramshackle remains of the old settlements became visible. Old sealed subway stations were cleared of debris, listing fences were knocked down and used for kindling, pre-fab houses lay in broken ruins among the growing weeds. Little by little, the cleared areas began to sprout grass and weeds. Any bushes that had survived being trampled began to grow leaves. When the rain came, the ground was muddy and difficult to traverse, but the next day the valley was a little greener, a little more alive.

Some days were easier than others.

* * *

One day they had tallied up their kills and tried to figure out what nice additions they could add to their future home. There had been a lot of laughter and gentle ribbing as each person shared their dreams. Holm's desire for a cloned horse was met with some surprise, while Jameson's desire for a hot tub in bright red was to be expected.

"What about you, Vanguard Martinez?" Mikado asked.

Maria smiled at the thought of her and Dwayne sipping beers while staring out at the lake from their new home. "A nice porch that overlooks the lake. I'd like hanging plants, too. Maybe a nice barbecue pit to cook something other than soy protein."

"I cannot wait for them to start cloning livestock again!" McKinney said with a feral grin. "Damn, I want a steak so bad."

"You don't know what a steak tastes like," Cruz reminded him.

"It looks so good in all the vids. It has to taste good," McKinney responded.

"It'll be a few years before there will be enough livestock for actual meat on our tables," Cormier said in a sober tone. She blew her hair out of her face and sighed.

"I can wait," McKinney said. "It'll be worth it."

"What about you, Denman?" Cruz asked.

"A nice yard. For the kids to run amok," he answered simply.

"Kids, huh?" Cruz grinned. "I think I want one of those."

"Want to start practicing?" Jameson asked, leering playfully.

"With you? No. With him," she said pointing to Mikado, "maybe."

Mikado grinned at Cruz. Maria sensed the pulse of attraction between them and she missed Dwayne all the more. Jameson's face clouded with anger as he looked away from the exchange. Maria felt sorry for him, but the young man had been rather testy of late. He seemed more on edge than the others.

"Enough talking. Back to work," Omondi ordered.

There were groans all around as the squad broke up into teams. There were ten groups and Maria walked behind Denman, Jameson, and Cruz. The Inferi Scourge horde around the city had dissipated around the edges now that there was not a regular human presence on the wall. There were still thousands clamoring against the walls, but the din of their cries was muted now.

Maria slammed the end of her bolt weapon against the head of a Scourge and pulled the trigger. The bolt thrust out, whirled, then the Scourge fell. She barely glanced at its body before advancing on the next one. Denman worked beside her, efficient and silent. Ahead of them Jameson was giving Cruz a hard time. Though he was always joking, Maria sensed there was a bit of venom in his comments.

"This one has a better ass than you do," Jameson said, slapping the buttocks of a naked Scourge with long blond hair.

"It also has a bigger dick than you," Cruz grinned.

Maria smirked as Jameson yanked the Scourge around to realize it was a very young man. With a hard shove, Jameson knocked it over and dispatched it.

Cruz's laughter trailed on the wind.

There was a storm starting to move over the mountains and Maria dreaded working in the rain. If the downfall was significant, they might be able to take shelter in one of the decrepit houses nearby.

It would be Omondi's call and she doubted he would have any mercy on them. Since the conference call almost two months before, he was a somber, colder version of himself. Maria rarely saw him smile.

He looked like a man carrying a heavy burden.

Kicking the creatures over and killing them, Jameson was cutting a swath through the patch of Inferi Scourge they were destroying. He seemed in a particular fury today. Maria looked at him warily and noticed Denman watching him as well.

"Maybe you should calm it down just a bit, Jameson," Maria called out.

Jameson whirled around, his bolt weapon clenched in his hands. The grayish cast to his face seemed more pronounced in the shadow of the storm clouds sliding overhead. His mouth twisted into an ugly shape as he appeared to struggle with his emotions. He didn't answer. With a howl, he swung about and slammed his weapon downward. Instead of dispatching the bolt, he brought the weapon down again and again, smashing the Scourge's head into mush.

"Special Constable Jameson, calm yourself!" Maria shouted. She stormed over and gripped his shoulder, yanking him away from the Scourge.

Around them, the Scourge were stirring. Jameson's howl had broken their torpor.

"How can I be calm when there are so many?" Jameson shouted. "It never ends. There so goddamn many! Everywhere I look they're just standing there waiting to fucking die!"

Denman appeared at their side and rested his hand on Jameson's other shoulder. "Special Constable Jameson, I need you to sit down."

"They're all around us. It doesn't matter how many I kill, there are always more. All around me," Jameson gasped.

"Sit down," Denman said, his voice a soft order.

Collapsing to the ground, Jameson covered his face. His shoulders were shuddering, but no tears fell from his cloudy eyes.

Cruz crouched beside him, cradling her weapon in her arms. Her dark eyes were full of compassion as she whispered, "It's okay, Kurt. I'm here with you."

Pulling out his diagnostic equipment, Denman started to scan Jameson. Maria watched the Scourge around them slowly coming out of their torpor. Their dead eyes rolled about crazily in their sockets, seeking out human victims.

Maria squatted next to the others, her gaze scrutinizing their predicament. The Scourge were not riled sufficiently to respond to their voices, but she was unnerved by how quickly they had responded to Jameson's cry. It had sounded like a Scourge howl.

Overhead, thunder rolled.

Next to her, Denman studied the results of his scan, comparing them to a previous one. One of his tasks was to monitor their functions every day. The Inferi Boon Virus animated them, but it was unknown how the virus would affect them over time. Denman rubbed his chin thoughtfully.

Jameson's face was covered by his hands. Though his posture was that of a weeping person, Maria knew that tears were not falling. Cruz's hand rested on his arm as she whispered to him in a soothing voice.

"Is there an issue?" Maria asked.

"Emotional duress," Denman said quickly. "I told the Chief Defender that we're pushing too hard."

Eyes narrowing, Maria regarded Denman thoughtfully. He was lying and she knew it. Meeting her gaze, Denman didn't seem defiant, but afraid. They would have to find a way to speak in private.

A Scourge howl ripped through the air, instantly aggravating the Scourge around the soldiers. Their howls mingled with the original cry. A few Scourge lunged at each other, snapping their teeth in aggravation before realizing their prey was not before them. Maria motioned for her team to be silent as the Scourge surged around them, twisting around in circles, seeking out a human to bite and infect. Another howl pierced the growing din around them.

Maria shifted on her feet and cautiously stood, her bolt weapon clasped in her hands. The Scourge jostled her as they frantically thrust each other aside, seeking prey. Her wristlet vibrated. It was most likely the Chief Defender calling her, but she didn't dare speak aloud. She didn't want the Scourge mistaking her for prey and pouncing on her like they had Coleman.

Again a loud, terrifying howl rose above the Scourge cries. It was closer this time. Maria spun around on her heel, seeking out the source of the cry. She had a horrible inkling that they were being stalked. If there was another thinking Scourge out here—

Another knot of Scourge crashed into her, nearly knocking her over. She struggled to regain her balance under the onslaught. Widening her stance, she managed to stay on her feet as the stampede rushed past her.

"Hungry!" a voice snarled, then strong hands gripped her shoulders and yanked her backward.

"Fuck!"

Maria slammed her bolt weapon over her shoulder. It impacted with flesh and bone. Her feet slid out from under her and she fell out of the grasp of her assailant. Flipping onto her side when she hit the ground, she kicked out, striking the groin of the dark shape lunging at her. The impact was jarring, but she managed to drive the creature back a few feet.

Denman leaped over her and tackled the Scourge attacker to the ground. It writhed under Denman, clutching at his armor, its teeth gnashing. Cruz and Jameson flung themselves onto the creature and grappled with its flailing legs. Rolling onto her knees, Maria crawled rapidly to the struggle.

"I need a reading," Denman uttered through clenched teeth, trying not to draw the attention of the riled Scourge.

Maria nodded as she moved to help pin the attacker's upper body to the ground. Together, Denman and Maria pried the dirty, torn fingers from Denman's armor and pushed the attacker's arms downward. Denman rested his knees on one arm while Maria followed suit with the other. She pressed her hand against the creature's shoulder and leaned in, utilizing her weight to press the Scourge against the ground. The snarling face was covered in mud and deep wounds. It snapped its teeth at her, arching its neck, trying to bite her.

"Hungry!" he howled.

A sharp stab of terror flowed through her as Maria experienced a note of recognition at the sound of the voice. Peering into the ruined face, she saw brown eyes rimmed with golden lashes glaring up at her.

"Ryan?" she rasped.

"Hungry!" he screamed.

"Did he just talk?" Cruz whispered.

Denman shot her a dark look, shutting her up. He returned his gaze to his readouts.

"Ryan," Maria said softly, anguish filling her voice.

Maria was certain it was him. The stained and dirty hair had glints of gold in it and the brown eyes were rimmed with a slight border of green. His face was torn and ravaged by the bites of the Scourge. Sweeping her eyes over his torso, she saw that his armor was heavily damaged and his nameplate was gone. Risking the snapping teeth, she yanked on the armor fasteners and pried open the chest plate wide enough to slip her had inside. His skin was cold and clammy, but she found what she was looking for. She yanked the dog tags off his neck and pulled them out of his armor.

SPECIAL CONSTABLE RYAN SHERMAN the tags read.

Maria closed her eyes, overcome by grief and fear.

"Hungry!" Ryan shrieked, then his voice rose into an Scourge howl.

Opening her eyes, Maria stared at her old friend unable to fathom this living nightmare.

"Finished," Denman said, tucking his med-pad into his pack. He pulled out his weapon.

Maria's hand lashed out and gripped his wrist, stopping him. Denman stared at her curiously.

"He's my friend," she said in the softest of voices.

"Hungry!"

Denman hesitated as he studied her, then handed the weapon to her.

Maria clutched it in her hand and for a second considered throwing it away, but she couldn't bear to see what Ryan had become. He was howling in rage, his voice rising. He was like the other one. He wanted to bite, tear, and eat flesh. Ryan was no mere Scourge. He was something worse. Something terrifying.

Maria shoved the weapon against the side of his head, just behind his ear, and fired.

Chapter 21

Maria and Denman huddled together over Ryan's body as the swarm of Scourge streamed around them. Riled by Ryan's howls, the Scourge were on the hunt for human flesh. How long they would remain in an agitated state was uncertain. It was difficult not to make a sound as the Scourge trampled over Ryan's body. Each time a Scourge stared down at her, Maria returned their gaze. Her dead face and eyes were her best protection.

She slowly rose to her feet, Denman following her example. Cruz and Jameson also stood, the four of them standing shoulder-to-shoulder in a tight circle, facing outward. It appeared the Scourge in the distance were beginning to falter. With no potential victims in sight, the Scourge were gradually less agitated. The edges of the group fell into torpor and the crowd progressively calmed. It was a domino effect. The stillness rippled through the crowd, bringing the horde to a standstill. The howls faded into soft moans as the Scourge swayed in the strong winds of the coming storm.

Falling to his knees, Denman hastily unfastened Ryan's armor and tugged it open. Crouching, Maria stared in disbelief at the wounds. Ryan's chest and stomach were a ruin of flesh.

"What did this?" she whispered.

"Keep an eye out for the Chief Defender," Denman said in a quiet voice.

Jameson and Cruz hesitantly moved through the cluster of Scourge gathered around them. Methodically, they began to dispatch the creatures one by one, shaping a clear area around Maria and Denman.

Maria stood, her eyes scrutinizing the crowd, her weapon poised. Her wristlet buzzed again and she activated it.

"Status," Omondi's voice demanded.

"We were attacked by a Scrag," Maria answered truthfully. Omondi's face was dour and she could tell by the jostling of his wristlet camera that he was running. Most likely he was heading in their direction.

"Any injuries?" Omondi's dark eyes didn't betray a single emotion.

"No. We dispatched him. The rest of the Scrags are back in torpor."

"Excellent. We're on our way. I want to see the Scrag that attacked you," Omondi said, then cut the feed.

"Did you hear?" Maria asked Denman.

"Almost done," Denman responded. He was taking tissue samples while studying the grievous wounds.

"What the hell is going on?" Cruz asked, kicking an Inferi Scourge body out of her way and killing another. "I heard that fucker talk."

"Scrags don't speak," Denman answered in a neutral tone.

"Bullshit," Cruz snapped.

"I heard him. He said he was hungry," Jameson protested. "I heard him talk!"

"Me, too!" Cruz glowered at Denman and Maria, a look of betrayal on her face. "What the fuck aren't you telling us?"

"Drop it," Maria said in a firm tone.

"I heard it speak!" Cruz pointed at Ryan. "I heard it."

Maria winced, unable to think of Ryan as anything other than her friend. To have him considered any less was difficult for her to process. "I said to drop it."

"I'll talk to the Chief Defender about it then, Vanguard Martinez," Cruz said angrily.

"If you do, he'll disregard it." Denman yanked Ryan's armor closed and began fastening it back in place. "He has been ordered to disregard any anomalies out here."

"Why?" Cruz demanded.

"Because his job is to make sure we do ours. Efficiently, quickly, and without questions." Finishing his task, he stood up and quickly stowed away his med-kit.

Maria could tell that neither Jameson nor Cruz liked this answer even while seeing the truth of it. Both stared at the body at their feet.

"But if they can talk, or think..." Cruz trailed off.

"Like us," Jameson added, his eyes widening. "Shit!"

"It can't be. Ryan died in the last push against the Scrags," Maria said.

"You knew him?" Denman quirked an eyebrow at her.

"Yeah. He was one of my best friends. I saw him dragged down by a pack of Scrags. He's not like us." Maria shook her head. "I don't know what's going on, but we don't have all the answers."

Omondi and his group pushed through the wall of Inferi Scourge. The big man stopped at the body on the ground. "Constabulary," he breathed. Bending over, he searched for the dog tags.

Maria discreetly tucked them into her pack as she stepped away from the others. She didn't want to give Ryan's tags to Omondi. She could still remember her last moments with Ryan before he had been torn away. She had always mourned not being able to bury him, but now she could. The tags were sacred.

"So he just attacked you, randomly, for no reason?" Omondi asked, looking toward Maria.

"He was howling, stirring up the Scrags. He pulled them out of torpor. They all went crazy and then he attacked us while we were distracted." As the words left her mouth, she knew that Ryan had deliberately stirred up the Inferi Scourge. He had been hunting them.

"And then you killed it?" Omondi asked.

A brief silence stretched a little too long for Maria's comfort, but she wasn't sure how to answer. Would the others keep quiet?

"We held it down and I killed it," Denman said at last. "Then we remained silent and waited for the Scrags to re-enter their torpor."

Omondi straightened and studied their faces one by one. Behind him, Mikado, Holm, and Cormier stared at the body on the ground. Their faces were expressionless, but their eyes were full of questions.

"It said 'hungry,'" Cruz said in a timid voice, her eyes darting toward Maria. "We all heard it."

"You imagined it," Omondi said, dismissing her comment outright.

"No, it said 'hungry' and it was trying to bite Vanguard Martinez,"

Cruz insisted. "We all heard it."

"Scrags don't speak," Omondi said in a tone that made it clear the discussion was over. Swiveling about, he gazed down at Maria. "Don't you agree?"

"Scrags don't talk," Maria agreed. She could feel all eyes on her, but she kept her gaze locked with Omondi's.

"Burn the body. Keep moving. We have a long day ahead of us," Omondi ordered. He waded back into the throng of Inferi Scourge, his team shadowing him.

Grabbing Ryan under his arms, Denman pulled him toward a pile of Scourge.

With a growl of frustration, Cruz kicked a dead body. Jameson merely stared after Ryan, his hand tracing the bite on his hand.

Maria followed Denman.

It was difficult undressing Ryan for his funeral pyre. The wounds on his torso were terrible to behold. The armor wouldn't burn, so it would be stacked with other salvageable items. Denman helped Maria lift Ryan onto the top of the pile of bodies.

"I'm sorry about this, you know," he said at last.

"I saw them take him," Maria sorrowfully responded. "He sacrificed himself so I would survive."

Touching Ryan's torn cheek, Maria whispered a prayer in Spanish. Stepping back, she crossed herself. "None of this makes sense anymore," she said at last. Drawing the small, handheld flamethrower, she made sure it was loaded, then fired at the pile. A fire instantly roared to life. The flames spiraled above the pyre as thunder rolled and somewhere in the distance rain began to fall. The smell of burning flesh and ozone washed over her.

Timidly, Denman reached out and rested his hand on her back. Touched by his gesture, Maria gave him a sad smile. Deep sobs came from deep inside her and she wished she could cry. Though her eyes remained dry, her body shuddered with her despair.

* * *

"I have new orders," Omondi said hours later as the bonfires burned low and the squads sat in small huddled groups talking. He loomed over her, his face hidden by the darkness of the night.

Maria glanced up from the novel she was reading on her pad. "What are they?"

"We're dividing the squad. I have orders to take my half to the hydroelectric station."

Widening her eyes slightly, Maria set her pad aside. "I don't understand."

"It's not our place to understand orders," Omondi said in a tone that was both tired and rather cross. "We obey them."

The chastisement burned a little, but Maria refused to let it rile her.

Too much had happened during the day to let one more thing pile on top of her already overburdened mind. "I suppose they split the squad for us?"

Omondi handed over his pad and Maria scanned the list. It took only a few seconds for her to give Omondi a sharp look.

"Your squad is all SWD security."

"We're all Inferi Boon Special Ops," Omondi corrected her tersely. Yet there was something in his voice and posture that revealed his own misgivings on the situation.

"Of course." Studying the list, Maria began to realize that she truly didn't know the SWD security on the squad very well other than Gutierrez. They usually hung out in clusters on their own and though they did join in the joking, it was the Constabulary members of the squad that Maria interacted with on a more personal basis.

Peering over her shoulder, she recognized that even now, as the squad relaxed during their break, there was a visible break between the Constabulary and SWD soldiers. She returned the pad to Omondi and folded her arms over her chest.

"You will continue with our original plan and eventually meet up with my squad. We'll maintain regular contact and you'll need to send your reports to me."

"We only have one medic," Maria pointed out. Denman was staying behind. She was relieved that he wouldn't be departing, but she was also concerned about the health of the soldiers leaving with Omondi.

"We've been out here long enough to know what we need to watch out for," Omondi said dismissively. "We have our orders."

"And when do you leave?"

"Now," Omondi answered.

His expression was tense, his gaze fixed, and the lines between his eyes deep. Omondi was deeply upset about something and it was seeping out in his features despite his resolve.

"Tonight?" Maria arched an eyebrow.

"You'll be in charge of the wristlet timers for your squad now. The schedule will be transmitted to your pad. We'll have daily debriefs after our squad goes into blackout." Omondi's dark eyes peered into hers. "Though this is an unexpected alteration in our plans, remember: we're doing this for the citizens of The Bastion. We're soldiers in the soon-to-be-ended war for survival against the Scrags."

Maria nodded. "Yes, sir."

She followed in his wake as he made his way to the center of the soldiers enjoying their break. His formidable presence drew the attention of every man and woman. Maria could see trepidation fill the faces of a few while others merely looked curious. Omondi's booming voice filled the night air, drowning out the soft moans of the Inferi Scourge around the camp. He delivered the new orders in a strong, firm, commanding voice. Whereas Maria had sensed that he may have misgivings when he had spoken to her, there was no sign of those feelings when he addressed the squad. His strength, confidence, and charisma swept away the shock and dismay. By the end of his rousing speech, the split squad was cheering and ready for the next phase in their mission.

Within the half hour, Chief Defender Omondi and his newly formed squad marched into the darkness of the night, their forms slipping away into the moaning Scourge.

Maria wasn't surprised when Denman drew near.

"All SWD except for Omondi," Denman said in a discreet tone.

"I noticed."

"And right after the attack by the speaking Scrag."

"Yes."

Denman shifted on his feet and pretended to show her something on his med-pad. "In other words, they're keeping something from us."

Maria nodded silently.

Shoving the pad in his pack, Denman fully faced her, his eyes scanning her expression.

Finally, Maria said, "We do our job. We keep vigilant." In a much lower voice, she whispered, "And we try to figure out what the hell is going on."

* * *

Dwayne was fast asleep when his wristlet chimed. He instantly woke, his fingers instinctively sliding over the small interface. Heart pounding in his chest, he accessed the secret program. Relief filled him when he saw that the incoming call was from Maria.

Once her face filled the small screen, he found himself speechless. Even with her grayish pallor and murky eyes, she was beautiful. His body ached for her.

"Oh, God, Dwayne, I've missed you," she said, her voice rough with emotion.

"I've been going crazy hoping you were okay," Dwayne answered. "What happened?"

The face he loved so much became eerily still as Maria gathered her thoughts. "The Chief Defender had control of our wristlets and I couldn't override it."

"So how-"

"There have been some complications to the mission. The Chief Defender has departed with half the squad. I have control over my wristlet and those of my squad. Of course, the SWD could override it at any time, but at least I was able to contact you tonight."

Though the lines of her face tensed and Dwayne could tell she was overcome with emotion, no tears glimmered in her eyes. It was disconcerting.

"Maria, I'll always be here waiting to hear from you. I love you. I believe in you. I know you're doing a damn fine job out there."

"I saw Ryan," Maria said at last, startling Dwayne. "He attacked me. He wasn't like the other Scrags. He spoke like that other one."

"Another anomaly?"

Maria nodded. "It's damn apparent we're not being told everything. The virus must be mutating somehow. Thankfully, so far, there have been only two Inferi Anomalies. The rest behave like you expect Scrags to act, so we're safe in that regard. After Ryan attacked me today, Omondi split off with the SWD soldiers in the squad per the orders of the SWD."

"Suspicious." Rolling onto his side, Dwayne stared at the image of the woman he loved. He felt helpless. It ate at him that he couldn't rush out and protect Maria. Of course, he also knew she was fully capable of taking care of herself, but his natural inclination was to rescue her from a quagmire of hidden lies. "How are you handling all of it?"

"Doing what I learned from you. Keeping my squad focused on the endgame while keeping my eyes and ears open. Something is going on out here, Dwayne. Something is very, very wrong. I just wish they would tell us the truth."

"Maybe they told Omondi the truth and he's handling it," Dwayne suggested.

"Probably, but that doesn't help the rest of us. I can't help but feel we're in more danger than the SWD told us. I'd rather have the truth and deal with it."

"I'll see what I can do to help you with that," Dwayne promised.

"Ah, your mysterious connections, huh?" Maria lifted an eyebrow, slightly smiling.

"I have a way of finding out the truth," Dwayne said with a grin and a wink.

Her lips spreading into a wide smile, it was clear she knew what he was alluding to. They had spent hours upon hours together as they recovered from their injuries after the last push against the Inferi Scourge. They often worked side by side at physical rehabilitation and chatted often. He had known almost right away that he had deep feelings for her. After Barbara filed for divorce, he had decided to risk their age difference and find out if Maria felt the same way. The young soldier had been very good at keeping her feelings hidden, but he had sensed he was not alone in how he felt. It had taken him months before he had finally turned to her and said, "I'm going to kiss you now. Any objections?"

Maria had grabbed him and given him the most passionate kiss of his life.

"I still think that was entrapment," Maria said, laughing. "Find out what you can as long as you're not kissing anyone."

The sound of her laughter, though distorted slightly by the transmission, was a lovely sound. "I save all my kisses for you."

"You better." Her smile faded and she sighed. "I need to go."

"I love you, Maria."

"I'll try to keep in touch, Dwayne. And I love you."

The transmission ended.

With a weary sigh, Dwayne rolled out of bed and sent a message to Lindsey to meet him for lunch the next day.

Chapter 22

The kiosk was packed with people hurrying to grab lunch before returning to work. The smell of hot vegetable oil and the spices used to turn simple bland protein into a savory dish with vegetables and rice made Dwayne even hungrier. The tea simmering in his chipped cup smelled cinnamony and sweet. The kiosk was run by an older couple and was dependent on their personal rooftop garden. They weren't always open for business, but when they were, people rushed to drop off their daily protein ration so they could later enjoy it in a delicious dish. The proprietors soaked the protein in a delectable marinade that made the tasteless lumps into something divine.

Lindsey scooted onto the battered stool next to him, leaning her elbows on the wooden counter. The wood had probably once been a park bench. The grain had worn over time to a smooth polish. Everything in The Bastion was recycled. Lindsey was dressed casually and her blond hair was loose. It was her day off, but she had agreed to meet him.

"Name?" the cook, Sarah, asked Lindsey.

Lindsey answered and Sarah checked the list of people who had dropped off their protein ration earlier. "I'll get it on the fire."

"Thanks," Lindsey said, smiling, then swiveled toward Dwayne. "Enjoying the news?" She indicated the drone passing by showing the latest government-released vids of the closed gate."

"Exciting, isn't it?" Dwayne answered, sipping his tea.

"I heard they pulled all the wall guards last night. No more wall duty. Our special ops team out there is all we need. Speculation is that they have some sort of nifty new armor and weapons that the SWD developed just for the job."

"I heard that, too," Dwayne said, his tone casual. Sarah set a bowl before him, the rice steaming beneath green beans, bamboo sprouts, and snow peas. The protein was spicy and the steam made his stomach growl in anticipation. He tucked into his lunch, savoring each bite.

Leaning toward him, Lindsey said, "So, what's up?"

Dwayne handed her a small tablet. It was old and many of its features were broken or disabled. He had picked it up at a small street shop and entered some notes for Lindsey to study and investigate. It was a locked down device since it couldn't transmit. He didn't want any of his suspicions leaking out.

Lindsey thumbed it open, read a few lines and turned wide eyes in his direction.

He calmly sipped his tea and gave her the briefest of nods.

"Can I have mine to go?" she asked, pivoting around.

One of the two cooks looked up from the hot stove and nodded.

"Should I come by later?" Dwayne took a sip of his tea, his eyes following the drone.

"Not yet. When I have something solid, I'll let you know," Lindsey answered as her lunch was set down in front of her wrapped in paper. She snatched her meal and was gone.

He was just finishing his tea after swallowing the last bit of his meal when Dwayne saw a flash of navy out of the corner of his eye. Turning, he saw the shrewd black eyes of the commandant staring at him. Her ebony skin was slightly beaded with sweat. He glanced around for her usual entourage. There was none in sight. It appeared she had walked alone through the city, a surprising move on her part.

"I didn't know you came here for lunch," Dwayne said at last.

"You weren't in your office. Your assistant told me where you were," the commandant answered. She sat in the same stool Lindsey had perched on earlier and set her elbow on the counter. She stared at him openly and thoughtfully.

"I was hungry," Dwayne answered with a shrug.

"Can I have your name?" Sarah asked, her tired, wrinkled face neutral of any emotion, but her eyes slightly widened at the sight of the woman who was a regular on the news vids.

"I didn't leave off my ration," the commandant answered.

"I can only offer a vegetarian dish then," Sarah informed her. Sweat trailed down her face and she clutched her tongs in a shaking hand.

"That's fine. Make it extra spicy," the commandant replied, pushing a credit across the counter to Sarah. Without irony, she said to Dwayne, "A penny for your thoughts, Castellan Reichardt."

Dwayne shifted his weight on his creaky stool and regarded her thoughtfully. "On which matter?"

"The mission outside the walls," she answered.

"It's a massive success for the SWD," Dwayne said with the shrug of his shoulders. "If the news vids are to be believed."

"Exactly," the commandant said pointedly.

"How much do you know about their operation?"

She lifted one shoulder. "Enough."

"We transferred some of our best soldiers to the SWD a few months ago," Dwayne said, deciding to push a little.

The commandant arched her eyebrow.

"The special ops out there are our people, aren't they?"

There was the tiniest inclination of her chin.

"But SWD is getting all the credit."

Again, the barest of nods.

"And you don't like this."

"I play the game we all participate in." It was hard to hear her over the chatter of all the people around them and the sizzling of the oil in the big skillets on the stove.

"What do you want from me?"

In a voice that was barely audible, she said, "Your help."

Dwayne inclined his head toward her. He could see the anger, frustration, and fear in her eyes. "I'm doing as you ask. You've seen my reports."

"This is on another matter." Her eyes met his in an almost defiant way.

Dwayne sensed she was taking a risk just by broaching the unknown subject with him, even if her words were chosen in such a way that people outside their world wouldn't understand the true meaning.

"You have an uncanny knack of being one step ahead of me," she continued at a discreet volume. "In the past I have wondered how this happens, but my inquiries always came up short. Maybe you're a man of hidden talents, or hidden methods. Or maybe you're just that intuitive. Whatever the case, you always seem to know what you...shouldn't." She tilted her head slightly. "Continue this practice."

Dwayne sat back, folded his arms over his chest, and stared at her.

Commandant Pierce dismissed him with a look and turned her full attention to watching the cooks finish preparing her meal. He was clearly free to go. Dwayne gave her a slight nod that he knew she could see out of the corner of her eye, and slid off his stool.

He strode away into the crowd.

* * *

The carrier was not significantly damaged considering the amount of time it had been abandoned and left to the wrath of the Inferi Scourge. A few of the antennas were snapped off and a few of the outside compartments had been pried open, but otherwise the damage was minimal. Maria was impressed by the efficiency of the security system. Scourge bodies were piled up around the vehicle.

"Home sweet home," Denman joked as he walked alongside her.

"Doesn't look bad considering," Cormier said from behind them. She jogged ahead a few paces to get a closer view. The driver of the carrier flashed a grin their way. "This vehicle is so bad ass. I want to live in it when this is all done."

"We should go joy riding," Mikado suggested with a grin at Cruz.

Cruz returned the smile, lightly nudging him with her elbow.

"With the numbers down in this area, we could use the blades on the plow to kill the rest of the Scrags," McKinney suggested. His boyish grin was charming when it appeared on his face.

It had been nearly a week since the Chief Defender had departed. The first day or two had been quiet, but on the third day it was if the pall of grim anxiety had lifted. Without Omondi's dour presence and the reclusive SWD soldiers shadowing them, the Constabulary soldiers were in higher spirits than before. It was a relief to see them smiling and engaging in fun banter again.

Their duty was taxing on their minds, but every day the valley showed the results of their hard work. Maria had lost count of how many of the Scourge she had personally killed. The totals were transmitted from their weapons to the SWD and some of the soldiers kept a manual count. McKinney and Holm had tracked their every kill, but Maria really didn't want to know her number. She was tired of death.

"Clear the area around the carrier," Maria ordered.

Dragging the bodies away from the carrier was an easier task now that the area was cleared of most of the Scourge. Only a few straggler packs remained. By nightfall, they would be gone. Joining the rest of the squad, she helped gather the corpses into piles.

"Sir, I should get in there and make sure nothing is too fouled up," Cormier said. Her frame was virtually vibrating with the need to check out the vehicle.

"Give me a full systems report," Maria answered.

"Yes, sir!" Cormier grinned and darted away.

Holm and McKinney appeared to be in a competition as they dragged four Scourge each over to the burn piles. Amused, Maria smiled at their cajoling. Looking over her shoulder, she saw Cormier enter the vehicle.

"Let's take a break," Maria called out.

It was unscheduled, but she needed a moment. They were working harder than ever to destroy the Scourge. Even with half the squad gone, they were making enormous progress. Omondi was pleased with her nightly reports, but never relayed the actions of his own squad. The secrecy was beginning to annoy and frighten her.

The soldiers clustered together in small groups talking and relaxing. She noted Mikado and Cruz sitting aside from everyone else, discreetly holding hands. A few times they had sneaked off together, but they weren't the only ones. Since Omondi had departed, she had noticed a few clandestine hookups happening. A few jokes about necrophilia had been dropped in the early days, but now people craved to feel connected, to feel human. She didn't blame them. Her longing for Dwayne seemed to increase every day without him.

Mentally exhausted, Maria didn't feel like engaging in small talk. She strolled a short distance away, pulling her hair out of her braid and running her fingers through the silky waves. She was thankful for their recent dip in a pond. They discovered the Scourge avoided water and had been able to spend time washing up and relaxing instead of dragging the depths for the dead.

Squatting down, she ran her palm lightly over the soft grass and wildflowers that were growing now that the Scourge had been cleared. In the darkness of her days, the returning beauty of nature was a salve on her tortured thoughts. At times she felt like a ghost drifting through the valley. Separated from her family, friends and Dwayne, she was trapped in her own mind day in and out. Sometimes her mental fatigue was too much to endure. It was the small moments of respite that helped her survive emotionally through the long days.

A shadow fell over her and she looked up to see Denman smiling down at her. Crouching, he lightly touched the lavender petals of a wildflower. "Life is returning."

"It gives me hope," Maria admitted.

"Considering how much we're accomplishing out here, I would think you would feel very hopeful and excited." Denman cocked his head and stared at her thoughtfully. "More than three-quarters of the valley are cleared."

She directed her gaze at the fields of green spreading out behind them. "I'm tired of killing. None of this has felt right since the beginning. Omondi leaving after Ryan attacked has me on edge."

Denman nodded solemnly. "About that..."

"You're done with your analysis of your scans?"

Drawing in a breath so he could speak, Denman again nodded. "Ryan had been partially eaten. His ribs showed distinct bite marks. Human teeth. At first I thought that maybe when the Scourge tried to infect him they had mangled him, but I am pretty sure he was being consumed when he died."

"He said he was hungry. And I saw Vanguard Stillson have a piece of flesh torn off of him. I swear the Scrag was chewing it." Maria frowned, her fingers lightly brushing over the grass.

"He was even missing three ribs. They were broken and torn out of his body. The Scrags were never reported to consume their victims. I remember from history class that in the first days they were nicknamed zombies because they bit their victims and it was the bite that turned them. But they were never reported as consuming their victims. Never. Something out here has changed some of them."

"Maybe they're evolving into a more dangerous breed." Maria frowned. "Is that even possible?"

"Maybe. Maybe the virus mutated." Denman shrugged his shoulders. "Hard to say. It's not like we have proper equipment out here to make a proper analysis."

"True."

"Are you going to tell Omondi?"

Maria could feel Denman's worried gaze resting on her. "No," she said after a long pause. "No. I have a feeling he already knows anyway. I don't want him to know that you scanned the body."

"Agreed." Denman sighed. "These are bizarre times. But at least within a month or so, we get to go home. All of this will be behind us."

"I never thought we'd make it to this point," Maria confessed.

For weeks it had felt like the forest of Inferi Scourge was never-ending. The mass of ruined bodies had spread out in every direction, always in her vision, like ghosts haunting her. Then one day, she realized she could look to the south and see nothing but grassy fields and ruined structures. The trees and bushes were green and lush, and, to her surprise, she heard birds singing in the branches. Hope had filled her in that moment. She'd clung to that emotion even when she was in the killing fields.

"It's amazing, isn't it? Soon there will be houses out here with kids playing in the backyards."

"*Your* kids playing in *your* backyard," Maria pointed out with a smile. "Little Michael Junior and Felicity."

Denman's usually-sorrowful expression lightened significantly at the thought. "That would be heaven. Megan has an amazing green thumb. I can only imagine what she could do with a decent bit of land to cultivate." Whenever he spoke of his wife, Denman's face became absolutely handsome. The love he had for his family radiated out of him and made Maria happy and hopeful. Not only him, but her own future with Dwayne.

Bumping Denman's arm with her elbow, she said, "Maybe we can be neighbors. Have cookouts in my backyard."

They were fast friends now as well as sort-of co-conspirators in their pursuit of truth. It was Denman that kept her sane during the long days. They talked about their childhoods, their time in the service, Denman's family, and anything else they could think of. She wished she could share Dwayne with him, but she never felt comfortable with doing so. Though she could easily imagine Denman and Dwayne sharing a beer and getting along, she couldn't bring herself to talk about her love. The pain of their separation would become unbearable in that moment.

Denman became distracted. "I wonder what he's up to," he said, standing.

Maria turned her attention in the direction Denman was staring just in time to see Jameson slipping into the ruined remains of a pre-fab house. The squad was still gathered in the shadow of the carrier playing cards and chatting.

"I'll go check on him," Maria decided.

"He's been a moody son of a bitch lately." Denman stretched and fussed a little with his armor. After so many months, they were all tired of wearing it.

"I don't think all of this lived up to his very unrealistic action adventure dreams," Maria said with a light laugh.

"But he'll have great stories to tell once it's all over. He'll get plenty of women then," Denman joked.

Jameson was always trying to hook up with the women in the squad. He was always rebuffed. Holm called him a "deranged, horny little puppy." Now Jameson was called "Horn Pup" and he was not pleased with the nickname.

Maria walked briskly toward the house, stepping around the patches of weeds and flowers. She hated crushing the greenery under her heavy boots. The new life in the valley felt precious. A quick leap carried her over the ruins of the old fence and she landed in an overgrown yard. The building had collapsed at some point, leaving only one section still standing. Ducking, she crept inside.

Sunlight sliced through the broken roof illuminating the destroyed interior. The elements had taken their toll on the house and its furnishings. Wiring hung from exposed sockets and she stooped under broken pipes sticking out of the walls.

Maria opened her mouth to call out to Jameson when she heard a sound that she had not heard in months. It took several seconds for her mind to even process what she was hearing. Finally, it registered. It was the sound of someone eating. The slurping, wet sounds of biting and chewing were emanating from a nearby doorway. Slowly drawing her weapon, she crouched and edged forward. If another Inferi Anomaly was in the building, Jameson could be in serious trouble or worse. She knew they had cleared the building, but maybe the Inferi Anomalies were smart enough to evade them.

Sliding along a sloped wall, she held her weapon before her, ready to bludgeon anything that attacked her. Her feet were silent on the cold cement floor as she approached the sound. She was glad for her lack of breath and her body's inability to show the symptoms of stress. A sterile calmness filled her as she listened to the wet noises of someone gulping down food. Her thoughts flashed to what had happened to Ryan as she stepped through the doorway.

Instead of finding Jameson being consumed by an Inferi Anomaly, he was hunched over a kitchen counter shoving canned food into his mouth. Digging into the can in front of him, he pulled out a thick brown paste and thrust it into his mouth, eating ravenously.

"Jameson?" Maria lowered her weapon, confused by the sight. The Inferi Boon didn't eat, nor did they grow hungry.

Swiveling toward her, he kept chewing, his fingers dipping into another can. Dragging out green beans, he stared at her as he stuffed them past his stained lips.

"Jameson, what are you doing?" she asked in a soft voice.

"I'm so hungry," he gasped around the food he was eating. "I can't stand it anymore!" Turning his back on her, he grabbed another can from a cabinet and pried it open.

Maria quickly accessed her wristlet. "Denman, you need to get in here. Something is wrong with Jameson."

Pouring the contents of the can into his mouth, Jameson reached for yet more food. His body trembled as he fumbled with the cans.

"Kurt," Maria said in a gentle voice, using his first name. "Kurt, you can't be hungry. We don't need food."

"I *am* hungry!" he shouted. "I can't stand it anymore. Being so hungry all the time!" He swept the cans of food onto the floor and fell to his knees. With trembling fingers, he pried the cans open.

Maria could hear Denman's approach as he rushed through the ruined house. He burst into the kitchen and gasped.

"What the hell?"

Jameson didn't even acknowledge them as he continued to cram food into his mouth. He wasn't even fully chewing, just swallowing.

"He says he's hungry," Maria said, not able to comprehend what was going on before her.

"Hungry!" Jameson howled.

Maria and Denman froze, then both dropped into defensive stances. He sounded like Ryan and the first attacker.

"You can't be hungry. We don't need to eat because of the virus," Denman said in a very calm voice as he approached Jameson.

Covered in bits of food, gravy, and syrups, Jameson continued to eat with a ferocity that was disturbing. Squatting beside him, Denman pulled out his scanner and aimed it at the young soldier.

Belching, Jameson fell onto his side, gripping his stomach. "Hungry!" he howled again.

Maria pushed a table away and cleared the area around Jameson. Fear was slowly uncoiling within her and she could see Denman was unnerved as well. He was close enough to get a reading, yet at a safe distance.

With a blood-curdling cry, Jameson doubled over and violently vomited everything he had consumed. Great sobs of despair filled the room as Jameson fell onto his side again. His body seized with terrible tremors and he vomited again.

"What the hell is going—" Maria started to say but was cut off by Jameson's cry.

"Hungry!"

The soldier lunged at Denman, who scrambled out of his way. Jameson started to crawl after him but was seized by another spasm. Again he threw up. Instead of food, he vomited small pebbles and pieces of plants.

"Hungry!" Jameson cried again and hurled himself toward Maria.

Maria knocked him away with a powerful punch. Jameson fell into the kitchen counter and howled. Lurching forward, he screamed. Maria again hit him, knocking him to the floor. Denman grabbed one of Jameson's arms and twisted it up between the man's shoulder blades.

"I need restraints!"

Maria cautiously stepped forward as she activated her wristlet. "Cormier, bring me restraints immediately. I'm in the house."

"Yes, sir!"

Maria felt her disquiet growing. Maybe Jameson had just mentally snapped, but the distress in his voice as he howled was too similar to how Ryan and the other Anomaly had sounded.

By the time Cormier arrived with the restraints, Jameson was incoherent in his cries. Denman secured his arms, then hauled him to his feet.

Twisting around in Denman's grip, Jameson tried to bury his teeth in the man's neck. Luckily, Denman saw the movement in time and brought up his arm, deflecting the bite. Maria grabbed Jameson and flung him to the floor again.

"Hungry," Jameson howled.

"What the hell?" Cormier gasped, staring at Jameson in horror.

"What are we going to do with him?" Denman asked, stepping back from the raving soldier.

"Leave him here." Maria heard the coldness in her voice, but she saw no other choice. Jameson was incoherent and they couldn't drag him around with them. He had snapped, or worse.

"Leave him?" Cormier gasped. "What's wrong with him?"

"He's cracked," Denman responded in a tired voice. "He's mentally unhinged. There's no point taking him with us."

"We just can't leave him here," Cormier protested.

"Yes, we can," Maria said in a firm tone. "He doesn't need to eat or drink. He's fine here. I'll turn off his alarm and he'll go into torpor. He'll be safer here." Maria regarded the growling man at her feet. "We can't deal with what's wrong with him right now."

Writhing on the floor, Jameson's incomprehensible cries and howls tore at Maria's nerves. She knew she was right. There was nothing they could do for Jameson. They didn't even know what was wrong with him. Perhaps it was a psychotic break. They had all been under so much duress with little to no time for anything other than killing. But she feared it was something much worse.

"Did you scan him?" Maria asked Denman.

The medic was still staring at Jameson as he nodded.

"I want a full report as soon as possible." Maria turned to Cormier. "I want the carrier up and operational within the hour, and I want to run scans on the area."

Cormier saluted, stooped through the doorway and was gone.

Maria and Denman stood in silence over Jameson. Maria wondered how long it would take for torpor to come.

"The Anomaly bit him," Denman said after a minute or so.

Maria looked at him sharply. "What are you saying?"

"That out of all of us only the one bitten by an Anomaly is—"

The soldier at their feet screamed. "Hungry!"

Chapter 23

The door to the flat slid open and Lindsey stepped aside to let Dwayne in. Within an hour the city would be plunged into darkness as the mandatory nightly blackouts took effect. Only emergency services would retain power. That meant a curfew in all areas of the city. They didn't have much time to speak. Dwayne had come as soon as Lindsey had contacted him.

Dwayne was surprised to see another person in Lindsey's home. It was a lanky young man with wild dark hair falling over his brow. Slightly tilted eyes and strong cheekbones gave him a Slavic look. Dressed in jeans, a faded t-shirt, and flip-flops, the man regarded Dwayne with suspicion.

"Dwayne, this is my boyfriend, Vaja. Vaja, play nice." Lindsey slid into her chair and focused on her screens.

"I don't like you getting Linds involved with all this," Vaja said in a slightly accented voice. His pale blue eyes were accusatory. "It's not safe."

"I can't make Lindsey do anything she doesn't want to. At least not when we're off duty," Dwayne answered, flashing his more charming and disarming smile. He extended his hand to Vaja. "It's a pleasure to meet you."

Vaja reluctantly shook his hand and slumped against the ladder to Lindsey's elevated bed.

"Vaja is a very suspicious person. But helpful. He assisted with some of the inscription problems I was having. He has a brain like a computer."

"Which is why she likes me," Vaja said with a shrug.

"I don't have a lot of time before curfew." Dwayne rested his hand on the rail of Lindsey's bed and leaned over to peer at her screen.

"I love how no one is complaining about the mandatory blackout," Lindsey groused, her fingers flying over the screens.

"They're willing to sacrifice for the greater good now that they know the gate is closed and that they will soon be free of the Inferi Scourge," Vaja said sarcastically. "Exchanging liberties for security. Wasn't that what everyone did when the Inferi Scourge started to take over the world?"

"Didn't do us much good, did it?" Lindsey grumbled.

Dwayne frowned as he started to understand what Lindsey was loading onto her screens. "Security feed from the subway?"

"And sewers." Lindsey pointed at several vids as they played. "Remember that little incident you wanted me to look into?"

"When the SWD blocked off my neighborhood? Yeah, I remember."

"It just took me awhile to find these. They were deleted as soon as they were reviewed by the SWD."

"But nothing is really deleted if you know what you're doing," Vaja said with a grin.

"The night you saw that commotion outside the subway station in your neighborhood, there was a breach in the subway system. Not within the city, but outside."

The furrows in Dwayne's brow deepened. "Outside? The wall?"

"Yep. There was a breach in one of the old stations out in the valley.

The one next to the hydroelectric plant." Lindsey expanded one of the vid feeds. It revealed two shadowy figures huddled near the sealed door. It took Dwayne a second to realize they were trying to activate the panel and unlock the door.

"What's that they have between them?"

"Not sure yet, but whatever it was it had enough juice in it to activate the panel and watch..." Lindsey pointed to a section of the vid. On screen the door yawned open. Both figures slipped in before the security programs overrode the breach and shut the door.

"Who the hell are they? How were they outside the wall and not attacked by Scrags?" Dwayne couldn't believe what he was seeing.

"Just watch the vids. This is where it gets interesting," Vaja said, his smile cold and a little cruel.

Dwayne watched as the two figures rushed through the subway station, running to each locked exit, desperate to get out into the city. "Constabulary armor," Dwayne said, his fear growing.

"No insignias. No markings of any kind," Lindsey agreed.

Since the cameras were recording with night vision it was impossible to truly make out the faces of the two people running unheeded through the subway system. Reaching another exit, one started to try to open the door using a manual override.

"Which station is that?" Dwayne asked, though he already knew.

"The one in your neighborhood."

"They got that far into the city?" Dwayne checked the timestamp on all the vids. The two intruders were in the subway for close to two hours by the time they reached the station.

The figure on the screen worked feverishly on the manual override as the other person stalked back and forth. Their movements were somehow disconcerting, though Dwayne couldn't quite determine why.

"So at this point, the one trying to unlock the door manages to actually do it. But the door doesn't open. They've all been disabled so they don't open automatically when unlocked." Lindsey narrated as the rapidly-pacing one flung itself at the doors. Together, the intruders tried to pry it open. "They actually got the door to open six inches."

"And then..." Vaja pointed at the screen just as a search and destroy squad arrived. The screen was illuminated with gunfire, the flares blinding the cameras.

"Recovering the vids was the easiest part. Getting the SWD report on the incident was far more difficult, but I managed. Then it was encrypted. Which is when I asked Vaja to help." Lindsey pulled up the report.

Dwayne squinted as he read. "There are still words blacked out."

"That's how it was written. Those blank spots are deliberate. As if the person reading it would already know how to fill it in," Lindsey explained.

"So these unknowns that the SWD know about infiltrated the subway system and tried to break into the city," Vaja summarized.

175

"They killed the two in the station, but were afraid there would be more. So as they reviewed the security vids, they also dispatched a cleanup crew to make sure the neighborhood was secure."

Overwhelmed by the information, Dwayne shook his head in disbelief. "It can't be."

"That there are people outside the walls?" Vaja asked.

Lindsey was watching Dwayne thoughtfully. He suspected she had come to the same conclusion he had.

"No, that there are Scrags smart enough to infiltrate the city," Dwayne answered.

Incredulous, Vaja laughed. "C'mon. There has to be another answer. A human settlement has to be in the old facility. Maybe outcasts or criminals."

"If only it were that simple." Dwayne said nothing more, uncertain of how much Lindsey had divulged to her boyfriend. He hoped it wasn't much more than Vaja appeared to know. From the confused expression on the younger man's face it was clear he was having difficulty accepting what was obvious to Dwayne and Lindsey.

"How can Inferi Scourge be thinking?" Vaja asked at last. "All they want to do is infect. I don't get it."

Pressing her lips together, Lindsey began closing down the vids, saving all the information to a removable drive. She shot Dwayne a quick, furtive look. It was not difficult to ascertain she was beginning to worry about having drawn Vaja into the matter.

"Someone answer me," Vaja said sharply. "I helped you. I deserve to know."

"We don't know yet," Dwayne answered honestly.

Maria would have told him if any of her people had abandoned the mission. After her reports about the attacks by the speaking Inferi Scourge, it was clear to Dwayne that there was much more going on than the SWD had revealed to the public.

"Maybe they evolved," Lindsey said softly.

"The government, the SWD, whoever, knows that they're evolving then? Trying to get to us? Why haven't they said anything?" Vaja's voice was terse.

Dwayne remained silent, averting his gaze by staring at the tips of his boots. The young man was smart. Maybe too smart. Again, Dwayne wondered if it had been wise to involve Lindsey in this whole situation. It was becoming increasingly clear that the SWD and perhaps the governing powers of the city had gone to great lengths to suppress the information Lindsey had uncovered.

"Shit," Vaja exclaimed, throwing up his hands. "Shit! They made them, didn't they? The fuckin' SWD somehow made them and now they're trying to get into the city."

"We keep this quiet and among us," Dwayne said in an authoritative voice. "They're trying to suppress this information for a reason. They're going to great lengths to make sure that the general public and even the

Constabulary doesn't know about these...anomalies."

"Vaja will keep quiet. He's paranoid enough as it is." Lindsey's eyes said much more than her words. Dwayne knew they would need to talk when Vaja was not around.

"I don't want the fuckin' government coming down on me when we're this close to finally getting our home back. I want out of this godforsaken city. Do you think I'm going to ruin my chances of getting the fuck out of here?" Vaja growled. He paced back and forth, two sharp steps, then a quick turn, two sharp steps, then another turn. There wasn't much room in Lindsey's small flat.

Lindsey tossed the drive to Dwayne. He tucked it into his jacket and checked his wristlet. "I need to go. Keep this quiet. Lindsey, thanks for this, but you should probably stay out of the network."

"Agreed. This is getting really..." she shrugged, biting her bottom lip. "What could they do to us? If the SWD found out?"

Running his fingers lightly over the small drive, Dwayne stared at the young woman thoughtfully. "Honestly, I don't know. And I don't want to find out either."

Lindsey sighed, hugging herself.

"Good meeting you, Vaja. Thank you for your work," Dwayne said, extending his hand to the pacing young man.

Vaja snarled at him dismissively. "I don't think I like you. You may have gotten us killed."

"Vaja!"

"Lindsey, you need to stay out of this. We all do. We're so close to being free of this goddamn city."

"So sacrificing the truth for freedom is okay with you?" Lindsey asked pointedly.

Vaja stopped in mid-step. "No."

"That's all we're doing. Finding out the truth." Lindsey reached out and took her lover's hand.

"Why? What will you do with it?" Vaja rubbed her fingers, but stared at Dwayne.

"I'm not sure yet," Dwayne answered honestly. He had searched for the truth because of the woman he loved, but now it was much more than he had ever imagined. Lindsey had wanted to release the information to the news outlets when she had discovered the truth about Maria. He had stopped her. That had been the right choice. But now, Dwayne wasn't sure where the path of information they were uncovering would lead. There was enough trouble with the quickly-approaching food shortage and the possible evacuation to Section A.

"What do you mean you're not sure?" Vaja disdainfully regarded Dwayne, his lip slightly curled.

"We don't have the full story yet. We don't know exactly what the SWD has done. When we uncover the whole truth, we will decide what our next step will be." Dwayne would never risk Maria. The timing would have to be perfect if he were to use this information against the

SWD. Maybe this was what Commandant Pierce wanted him to do.

"Can we trust you?" Vaja asked, his eyes narrowed.

"You can," Lindsey assured him. Tears were brimming in her eyes. "He has more at stake than you realize."

"We'll talk soon," Dwayne said, then let himself out. The night was cool and he tugged his collar up around his ears as he walked. He had only a short amount of time before the city went dark.

He wished he could tell Maria what he knew.

She was in more danger than she realized.

Chapter 24

It was comforting to be seated in the carrier at her work console once more. Cormier was in torpor in the driver's seat and the rest of the squad was scattered around the interior of the carrier. Denman was slumped at his station. Maria toyed with the idea of waking him after she spoke with Dwayne. She wanted to discuss Jameson's condition in further detail, but their mission was so mentally taxing she felt too guilty to rob Denman of any of his downtime.

Her conversation with Chief Defender Omondi had been brief. He had appeared rushed and not interested in discussing Jameson's condition. Maria had spun the incident with Jameson as a mental breakdown. Omondi had readily accepted this explanation. She supposed Jameson's recent behavior had given credence to her story. She hated lying, but she was having grave misgivings about their situation. She mollified her guilty feelings over not fully reporting the details of the incident to Omondi because she was telling Dwayne, the Castellan of The Bastion.

Her wristlet chimed and she hastily answered. Dwayne's face appeared and she noted how much more silver was threaded into his hair. He had aged in the last few months. It was arrogant of her to think it was just because he was worried about her, but it made her feel loved nonetheless.

"Thank God," Dwayne said, obviously relieved. "Every night I fear you won't be able to pick up."

Maria slightly smiled at him. "If I can, I will. You know that."

"Remember those resources I said I was going to confer with over the recent events out there?"

Her smile faded. Dwayne's expression was quite grim. "What is it?"

"What we're calling the Inferi Anomalies are far more dangerous than you think. I have a feeling that Omondi and his squad are actively trying to track them down. You said they were headed to the hydroelectric station, right?"

"Yeah. But why is that significant?"

As Dwayne related the information he had acquired from Lindsey, Maria grew very still. Mind spinning, she swiftly pieced together the data he had uncovered with her own experiences on the field.

"Intelligent, speaking, cannibalistic Scrags..." Maria shook her head. "Unbelievable."

"It has to be what we're calling the Inferi Anomalies. A human couldn't survive out there all this time," Dwayne answered.

"I agree. There is no way a human could have survived out here. Impossible. It has to be the Anomalies, but the ones that attacked us didn't show any great intelligence. Cunning, yes. Ryan was obviously hunting us. But they only spoke one word."

"Hungry, huh?" Dwayne's frown deepened.

"Yes, and it gets worse." She told him about Jameson.

"The Anomaly bit him and only him?"

"Yes, and now he's suffering hunger pains."

"Maybe the altered virus from the Anomaly infected him? Can that happen?"

"Denman says it's possible. If we spoke to Dr. Curran, maybe she could determine if it is, but..." Maria sighed. "I don't trust her. I don't trust any of them."

"And you shouldn't," Dwayne said guiltily. "Not completely. There's something I haven't told you." In even tones, he told her about Gideon's death.

"They lied to me and Omondi! Why didn't you tell me?"

"To keep you focused on your mission. I knew you wanted to be on this mission. I felt that to tell you that the SWD was lying in some regards would affect you adversely."

"It would have," Maria admitted, but she was still annoyed. "I wish you would have told me last week."

"Would it have made a difference?"

Maria shook her head. "It really doesn't now either. I knew all along that something was wrong. I was lying to myself as much as they were. The question is does the SWD know what the Inferi Anomalies are?"

"Unknown. I assume Omondi hasn't kept you briefed on what he and his squad are doing?"

"Correct."

"I have my contacts searching for more information. As soon as I know something I will relay that information to you."

"Thanks, Dwayne. Knowing that you're working on my behalf makes this...bearable." She could see the concern in his keen blue eyes and knew that he could see the emotional devastation in her own.

"I love you," he said.

"I love you."

He was gone.

Closing her eyes, her thoughts rested on him. He was tenacious and he was a man of his word. He would do everything he could to keep her informed even though her superiors saw fit to keep her and the others in the dark. Her anger against the SWD and Omondi was growing. Jameson's condition was a sign that not all was well and that they were all in danger.

But if Dwayne was searching for answers, she knew he would find them.

Words from a previous conversation slithered through her mind. He had teased her about how he always found out the truth. The allusion to their beginnings had made her smile. It had taken her a very short time to fall madly in love with him, but she had been keenly aware of the ring on his finger. She had avoided revealing her feelings at all costs even though she saw him every day during physical therapy. They often chatted on their return walk to their rooms. Even though she had been resolute about not emotionally investing her heart in him, she had cherished those long slow walks. One day she had noticed the ring was gone. She had wondered if he had merely forgotten to wear it.

"I'm going to kiss you now. Any objections?" he had said.

There was no hesitation as she had pressed her lips to his and let him claim her heart. That kiss had been like no other she had ever shared with anyone. In his arms, she had felt so safe, so loved, and so cherished. The passion between them had been overpowering.

Her eyes still closed, she touched her lips...remembering.

Intertwined, they hid in the shadows of the building, sheltered by a giant oak tree. The scent of his freshly washed hair mingled with the flowery fragrance of her own shampoo. His body was hard and strong as it pressed against her. His lips were both loving and demanding as they kissed. She'd never wanted the kiss to end even when her breath was gone and her knees shook. Her fingers dared to slide under his shirt as he buried his hands in her hair.

"We should go somewhere...private and talk," he finally whispered against her lips.

They had managed to make it to her room, but the talking hadn't come until much later...

* * *

"Dwayne," she whispered, waking.

Sitting bolt upright in her chair, Maria stared at the console in shock. Checking her wristlet, she saw that it had not buzzed her into consciousness. She had not been in torpor.

She had been asleep.

Confused and reeling, she swung out of her chair and stumbled to the open doorway of the carrier, sidestepping the bodies of her squad frozen in the torpor. Leaping to the ground, she stared up at the starry sky above. Her body felt oddly alive as she processed what had just happened. A nervous giggle flitted from her lips as she felt the pleasant sting of arousal burning between her thighs.

She felt alive.

Pressing her hands to her neck, she felt no pulse. She ceased to breathe, and felt no need for air.

But she felt...aroused. She had fallen asleep.

What did it mean?

Then she heard a scream emanating from the collapsed building nearby. Anguished cries were caught by the wind and swept away, diminishing their sound, but she knew what it was.

It was Jameson crying out in hunger and pain.

He had not fallen into torpor.

* * *

The screams emanating from the collapsed house were full of desperation. Denman and Maria hesitated in the darkened doorway.

"And his wristlet alarm is off for sure?" Denman asked again.

Maria felt agitated by his question. She gave him a curt nod of her head.

They had left the squad behind in torpor. It was best not to rouse them until they had a handle on the situation. Before they had left the carrier, Maria had performed a quick scan of the area. So far, Jameson's screams had not stirred the Inferi Scourge that were within a two mile radius.

Slipping into the house, Maria heard Denman follow.

They found Jameson where they had left him. He had managed to sit up and was tucked into a corner of the dining area off the kitchen. Reclining against the wall, he was crying out as his body seized. Flashing a light toward him, Maria was shocked to see tears streaming down his face.

"Denman!"

"I see it!" The medic scrambled over the remains of the dining room table and chairs and squatted next to Jameson.

Spit flecked his lips as Jameson wept. His red and swollen eyes stared at Denman in fear.

"Jameson, I need you to remain calm, okay? I need to take some scans and a few samples of your tissue so we can figure out what is happening to you," Denman said in a soothing tone. "I need you to not try to bite me. Do you understand me?"

Jameson nodded, but seemed unable to actually answer.

"Do not try to attack me, or I will leave you here."

"Hungry!" Jameson sobbed. "Hungry!"

"I know. Just let me do my job, okay? We'll figure out what is going on."

Jameson curled in on himself, trembling violently, his lips pressed tightly together.

Denman glanced at Maria. She gave him a swift nod. If Jameson attacked, she would move in.

Maria stood nearby watching as Denman cautiously performed a variety of tests on the sobbing young man. It was obvious that Jameson was in terrible pain. He was trembling violently and his teeth were chattering.

After twenty-five minutes, Denman finally finished his tests. "Kurt, I appreciate your cooperation. I'm going to transmit these results to the SWD and we're going to get you help. Do you understand?"

"Hungry!"

"We're going to get you help." Denman tucked away his med-pad and calmly joined Maria across the room. A slight jerk of his head directed her outside.

Stepping out into the cool night air, Maria felt relieved to be away from the sobbing man. Jameson was an idiot at times, but no one deserved to be in such agony. She couldn't imagine why the torpor hadn't come.

"I need to send this information to the SWD immediately. Omondi is in torpor. You're going to have to do it directly," Denman said in an urgent tone.

"What's going on?"

"His...vitals are wrong."

"Vitals?"

"He has a pulse, Vanguard Martinez. A faint pulse, but it's there. You saw him weeping. We can't produce tears. He can. Honestly, right now he's half alive and half dead. Some of his biological systems are working again, while others are not. I think the best way I could describe what he is experiencing is...he is in death throes."

"Are you fucking kidding me?" Maria gawked at Denman in disbelief. "How can this be?"

"I don't know! It's not like the Inferi Anomaly scans I took. This is different." Tugging his med-pad out, he tapped a few commands into it then handed it to Maria. "On the left side are our readings. On the right, Jameson. In the middle, the Anomalies."

It didn't take a medical degree to see the vast differences. "What could have caused this?"

"I don't know. As far as I know none of the other Boon are suffering any of these symptoms. We have to get this information to Dr. Curran. I don't think Jameson will re-enter torpor. We leave him here and he's going to starve to death."

With a sigh, Maria nodded her head. Uplinking the med-pad to her wristlet, she made the call to the SWD.

Within the hour a med-pod was lowered from a tiltrotor. Maria and Denman had already removed Jameson from the house. He lay on the ground whimpering and trembling. They had to move fast before the Inferi Scourge were completely drawn out of their torpor. They were two miles away, but they could move fast when hunting.

Maria pulled open the med-pod as Denman lifted the restrained man in his arms. Jameson howled, but didn't struggle. Together, they pushed him inside and worked to secure the harnesses around his quivering limbs.

"Special Constable Jameson, you're going to be okay, do you hear me?" Denman shouted at the man over the roar of the tiltrotor hovering overhead.

Jameson gave a slight nod as he stared at them with wide eyes.

Maria wondered if Denman's words were the truth, but she reached in and gave Jameson's shoulder a reassuring squeeze. "You performed admirably. Good job, soldier." The fact that he was no longer trying to bite them gave her hope that he would be okay.

Stepping back, she watched Denman press a med-tag to the young man's sweaty flesh just above his collar and activate it. The medics onboard would be able to monitor Jameson remotely until he was back in the city. Sealing the med-pod, Denman backed away.

"He's secure," Maria said into her wristlet.

"Aye, sir," the pilot's voice answered.

The med-pod lifted off the ground and slid upward until it

disappeared into the underbelly of the tiltrotor. The craft swung around in a wide arc and headed back to the city. As the roar of its rotor's faded away, Maria could hear the howls of the Scourge.

"They're coming," Denman said in a weary voice.

"Time to wake the others," Maria said.

Together, they sprinted to the carrier.

Chapter 25

The carrier careened into the Scourge stampeding toward it just as the sun broke over the horizon. The razor-sharp plow sliced through the bodies like a heated knife through butter. Special Constable Jes Cormier expertly swung the vehicle around, making another pass through the rabid creatures.

Jostled about by the sharp turn, Maria glanced up briefly to view the carnage through the splattered windshield before returning her gaze to her screens. "Maintain your heading until you're clear of the crowd, then take another pass."

Behind her she could hear the excited whoops and chatter of her squad. Maria had awakened the soldiers and quickly outlined their plan of action. She was done fighting the Scourge by hand. With so much of the valley cleared in their area, she was ready to use the carrier as a weapon.

"Brace yourselves!" Cormier called out just before the carrier slashed through the Scourge mass.

Scans of the valley revealed how much they had cleared in the last few months. The main clusters were around the city walls and near the hydroelectric facilities. That there were vast areas of open space was breathtaking to behold.

The carrier cleared the raging Scourge herd and swung around for another pass.

"You almost have this herd wiped out," Maria said to Cormier.

"I like this way of dealing with them much more," Cormier answered as the carrier accelerated forward.

Grinning, Maria answered, "So do I."

The carrier left a large swath of blood, gore and body parts in its wake.

* * *

The bonfire burned brilliantly against the backdrop of the blue mountains rising above the valley. They had utilized the carrier's plow to build an enormous bonfire. The Scourge bodies smoldered and the stench of their cooking flesh made Maria's eyes water.

Shocked, she lifted one hand to her eyes.

"Denman," she gasped.

Turning, he gazed at her curiously. She pointed to her eyes. Denman gaped at the tears trailing down her cheeks. He reached out and swabbed the corner of her eye with the tip of a finger.

Looking around at the remaining squad members, Maria saw they were unaffected by the fire. Denman rubbed the tear between his gloved fingers, then drew out his med-pad. In silence, he scanned her as she waited impatiently.

"What's happening to me?" Maria asked finally.

Denman shook his head. "I don't know. I'm reading miniscule changes but nothing like what Jameson was going through. Should I report this?"

Maria pondered his question and abided her instincts. "Not yet." They were probably a few weeks away from clearing the valley if they could maintain their pace. "Just keep me informed."

* * *

Maria relished the feeling of being at a work station doing something other than destroying the Scourge. Maria and the Chief Defender were plotting out the final push against the Scourge.

They had numbers from the SWD on how many Scourge the squad was clearing on a daily basis on average and how many remained; therefore, they could estimate how much longer it would take to wipe out the rest of the hordes.

Omondi's image was located in a corner of her work station screen. "It appears we're looking at two more weeks until completion of the mission."

"The number changed slightly with Jameson out of the picture. He was our most efficient killer."

"We'll make up for his absence with taking only one hour of torpor a day."

"The last psych exam Denman gave us says we're all on the verge of mental exhaustion. Can we risk pushing ourselves even harder?" Maria tilted her head so she could see Omondi's face. It was emotionless as usual. She rarely saw the man smile.

"SWD is adamant that we continue around the clock." Omondi rubbed his chin. "I just don't know how we can reach their projected end date otherwise. They're unyielding that we meet that date."

Maria studied the various bits of information displayed on her screen. "Are they certain about the Maelstrom Platforms?"

"Yes, they're going to destroy all the Scrags around the wall once we clear out everything else."

"They want a big final bang, don't they?" Maria smirked.

She could imagine the news vids now. The platform guns destroying the last of the Scourge gathered around the wall. Of course, there would be no vids of the long endless days they had spent destroying the Scourge.

"We have our orders." Omondi studied the numbers on his pad. She could see the weariness around his eyes. "We will soon be done with all of this and it will be just a nightmare to be forgotten."

It was the most human thing he had said in a very long time and Maria was glad to hear it. It was a strange solace that he too was affected by the endless killing.

"How are you progressing toward the hydroelectric plant?"

"Steadily making progress. I estimate we'll make it there in the next three days. We had to clear out a massive gathering of Scourge near one of the old subway stations."

"I just don't understand why we have left the hydroelectric plant until last," Maria said, tapping her finger lightly on the screen. "With the energy shortages I would expect it to be one of the first places we would clear."

"We started near the gate because that was where our first objective was located," Omondi answered, lifting his shoulders dismissively.

"Any word on Jameson?" She had been putting off asking the question, trying to avoid any topic that might annoy her commanding officer. He was very good at avoiding giving her direct answers.

"Psychotic break. His mind had difficulty believing he no longer had to eat. He became obsessed and..." Omondi mimed breaking something in half. "Dr. Curran will be sending Denman some guidelines to help identify any warning signs in the rest of the squad."

The bold-faced lie left Maria stunned, but she managed to maintain a neutral expression. The SWD was either lying to Omondi, or had told him to lie about Jameson's condition. Certainly the SWD knew that Denman and Maria were intelligent enough to discern that the readings they had taken of Jameson were not the norm.

Maria decided to push just a little and see how deep the lies were. "Do they have any theories as to why that one Scrag tried to eat Jameson?"

It was if an invisible blast door slammed down between them. Omondi was suddenly an ebony statue staring at her in cold silence. She was very glad he was far away and only an image on her screen.

"The Scrags are rabid undead monsters. We cannot assume to know everything about them considering how long we've been trapped in the city. Keep that in mind, Vanguard Martinez."

"Yes, sir," Maria said softly.

Denman was watching her from his console. The rest of the squad was in torpor, but she had kept Denman awake. They had both been hoping for answers to Jameson's condition.

There was terse silence for a few more minutes as Omondi transmitted new orders to her console and Maria reviewed them.

"We can continue utilizing the carrier for at least a day," Maria decided. "Once we hit this area there will be too many Scrags to risk it."

"Agreed," Omondi answered. "We'll speak again tomorrow night. Dismissed."

The feed was cut off abruptly.

Maria sighed wearily.

"Do you think he's lying for them? Or are they lying to him?" Denman asked.

Shrugging, Maria settled back in her chair. "I'm not sure about any of this anymore."

Denman rubbed the top of his head, mussing his short brown hair. "We're doing the right thing clearing the valley."

"I agree."

"But I strongly suspect the SWD didn't fully understand the modified virus they gave us. We're their grand experiment."

"Their greatest success so far," Maria said.

"I am concerned about what happened to Jameson and your tears."

"I'm not hungry."

"Not yet. So far all the tests have shown is that the virus is now allowing your body to produce tears and saliva. Nothing else has changed."

"It's nice not having a dry mouth," Maria observed, smiling slightly.

"But why this change? Why now?" Denman clutched his fist, pressing it to his lips. "This isn't making sense."

"I'm dreaming."

"What?"

"I've been dreaming for a week."

He stared at her incredulously. "Are you sure?"

"Maybe." She shrugged. "I feel different when I revive. More alive."

"I should set up a scan for when you enter torpor."

They both started when Maria's console beeped that there was an incoming message. She answered immediately and was surprised when Dr. Curran's face filled the screen and not Chief Defender Omondi's.

"Dr. Curran, this is unexpected."

"Vanguard Martinez, I'm glad I caught you before you entered torpor."

Like Dwayne, the doctor appeared to have aged in the last few months. Dark circles shadowed her eyes and the lines around her lips had deepened.

"How can I be of service, Dr. Curran?" Maria tried to keep her voice neutral, but a hint of her hostile feelings toward the doctor crept into her words.

Dr. Curran gave her a weary, yet sardonic smile. "I am contacting you for a variety of reasons. I should let you know now that we are on an encrypted channel and no one knows I have contacted you directly."

Maria lifted her eyebrows. Questions flitted across her mind, but she opted not to speak, and just listen. It was best to be silent and allow Dr. Curran to say her piece. Maria was far too on edge to be truly civilized.

Dr. Curran waited for Maria to speak, but when she didn't, she plunged ahead. "I am still examining Special Constable Jameson and have fully reviewed the scans and reports you sent me. This was the first I was informed of Special Constable Jameson being attacked and bitten by one of the Scrags."

"I sent a detailed report to the SWD when it occurred," Maria protested.

"As I said," Dr. Curran said rather crossly, "this is the first I have heard of the attack on Jameson."

"Did you hear about the attack on me?"

"Were you bitten?"

"No, but the Inferi Anomaly who attacked me tried to bite me. He also spoke. Just like the one who bit Jameson."

"Inferi Anomaly?" Dr. Curran arched an eyebrow.

"It's what I've been calling the two Scrags that attacked us. Both appeared to be trying to bite and devour flesh. And they both spoke. They're not like the other Scrags. I'm fairly sure the second one was actively hunting us." Maria quickly detailed both attacks in her own words. Denman slipped out of his chair and stood on the other side of her console, out of sight of Dr. Curran, listening intently.

"You're certain they spoke? Both of them?" Dr. Curran was scribbling notes on her pad.

"We reported this previously," Maria said, exasperated.

"I remember that Mr. Petersen told you that you were imagining things, but I didn't..." Dr. Curran's voice faded away as she quickly wrote, her stylus flashing in the lamplight in her office. "And Jameson is the only one that has been suffering the reported symptoms, correct?"

"Yes, that's correct. None of the rest of the Boon on my squad is suffering hunger pains or has scans similar to the ones that Medical Specialist Denman took of Jameson." Maria watched the blond woman rapidly writing and dared to look toward Denman. He pointed to his eyes and then to Maria.

"What is going on with Jameson, Dr. Curran?" Maria asked.

Dr. Curran returned her gaze to her vid screen and regarded Maria thoughtfully. "A mutation of the ISPV."

"And this wasn't expected, I take it?"

"No, it was not," Dr. Curran admitted. "The Inferi Anomalies and Jameson have hunger and limited language skills in common. Is there anything else you noted?"

Hesitating for a moment, Maria ignored Denman as he mimed at her. "Jameson appeared more...human than the Anomalies. Alive. He was weeping and his face was flushed."

"An astute observation." Dr. Curran sighed and made more notes.

Maria had the strong desire to reach through the transmission and rip the pad out of her hands.

"And no one else is experiencing any changes at all?"

Denman continued to point at his eyes.

"I dream now."

Dr. Curran set the pad down and gaped at her. "What?"

"I dream during torpor." Maria stared at the woman steadily. "What's happening to us?"

"I...don't know," Dr. Curran said, confusion filling her eyes.

"Jameson didn't go back into torpor after his eating frenzy. We left him alone for hours. His wristlet alarm was disabled. I did it personally. But he never slipped into the blackout. I want to know why."

"Is anyone else experiencing this?"

"No. At least not yet."

"Have you said anything to Chief Defender Omondi?"

"No, I have not."

"Don't. I want you to report only to me in regards to any changes your squad is experiencing physiologically." Dr. Curran's voice was clipped and fierce.

"He is my commanding officer, Doctor."

The doctor slammed her hand down on her desk. "Vanguard Martinez, do you really believe that if I trusted Chief Defender Omondi I would be talking to you? He's the puppet of Mr. Petersen and the Black Ops of the SWD. Even though I was appointed by the President of The Bastion to supervise this mission, vital information has been withheld from me at every turn. I am trying to help you and your squad survive out there. Mr. Petersen is more interested in covering up the SWD's mistakes."

"Excuse me?"

"Do you really believe this is the first time we tried this? Do you?" Dr. Curran shook her head in disbelief. "There are four failed missions that haunt the SWD past. This is the closest we've come to success. All other missions failed."

It all began to click in Maria's mind. "The Anomalies are the soldiers from the failed missions."

"Yes, they are. And they've been trying to get back into the city for years. The modified virus they were given mutated. They began to crave...flesh. Human flesh. The SWD cut them off and left them to rot outside the city. But they didn't die. And like Jameson, they never went into torpor. Your squad is the SWD's first success with a modified ISPV. You're *my* success. It wasn't until I inherited the project that the SWD had any success in modifying the virus sufficiently to create you and your squad."

"Omondi is tracking down the Anomalies, isn't he?"

Dr. Curran nodded briskly. "The Anomalies, as you call them, have been located around the hydroelectric station for years. The service tunnels and subways have long been sealed off, but they have concentrated their efforts to getting into the city in that area."

"And they succeeded," Maria whispered. She thought of her father dying under the city as he fought the Inferi Scourge that had mysteriously invaded the sewers.

"A few times." Dr. Curran drew in a deep breath and exhaled, obviously trying to calm herself. "Listen to me, Maria. I'm trying to help you. I want you to succeed in your mission. You'll send daily reports to me that will have thorough scans of every squad member. You will send the information via this encrypted channel. Record the data I am sending you now. It's a back door into our system."

"If we're becoming Anomalies, you can stop it, can't you?" Maria asked in a rough voice. Her brain was buzzing with all the information she was processing.

"I believe I can help you as long as you send the data."

"Jameson is still alive, isn't he?" Maria asked abruptly.

Dr. Curran's eyes narrowed slightly, then she gave Maria a curt nod.

"Of course."

"Why should I trust you?"

"Because you have no choice and you know it."

Maria let out on explosive breath. "Very well."

"Keep this between us. There is more at risk here than just your career, you know."

"I understand."

Dr. Curran folded her hands together and leaned toward the vid screen. "I am trying to help you. Whether you believe that or not, it's the truth. Now, keep me informed of any changes in any of your squad members."

"Very well."

"I'll be in touch."

The screen flashed then her image was gone.

Maria raised her eyes to meet Denman's intense stare.

"Holy Christ," Denman finally said.

"Fuck them all," Maria grunted.

"Why didn't they tell us about the Anomalies?" Denman exclaimed.

"Because they fear we'll end up just like them," Maria snapped. "Isn't that obvious? That's probably the reason they have accelerated our schedule. They want us to finish before we become Anomalies!"

"Shit!"

"Wait!" Maria frowned. "Ryan died in the final push. He couldn't have been in a mission."

"When the Anomalies bit him, they transferred the modified virus to him."

"Which made him one of them."

Denman's eyes widened slowly. "Oh, fuck. That means if the Anomalies bit the soldiers who fell in the last big push against the Scrags..."

"Then there are a lot more of them than the SWD realizes."

Chapter 26

Sometimes the truth brought no comfort. Dwayne stared out the window of his office at The Bastion and wondered if the future was as bleak as it appeared. The plans for the evacuation to Section A were finalized and preparation was underway. Each of the Constabulary mini-stations scattered across the city were fully stocked with electro-shock rifles, riot gear, and tear gas. Patrols had been steadily, but discreetly increased. Even the notices that would be sent to the select few chosen to survive in the dying city were prepared for delivery at a moment's notice. His thoughts lingered on his children for a second before focusing on the great wall in the distance.

Somewhere beyond that wall was the only woman he had truly ever loved, and he was powerless to help her.

Maria's news about the previous attempts at creating Boon soldiers had been disconcerting enough without the additional information about the Inferi Anomalies. He could tell by her expression she had been keeping more from him. Something about the tilt of her head and the way her eyes shifted when he asked her how she was doing had revealed more than she intended.

Something was horribly wrong.

His chest ached with the thought of her far beyond the wall and untouchable. The longing he felt for her was so intense it hurt.

Maybe this was what the commandant had wanted him to uncover. The truth about the Inferi Boon and their mission. She had hinted none too subtly that there was a good probability that the mission could fail and that the Section A fallback plan would be implemented. Perhaps she knew about the failed missions and suspected that this one would also fail. Maria was concerned with the acceleration of the plans to clear the valley. He had not told her about the food shortage or Section A.

With a sigh, he realized they were both starting to keep secrets from each other.

It was plausible that the hastening of the mission was due to the food shortage and the anticipation of implementing the Section A fallback plan. But in light of the new information about the Anomalies, Dwayne feared it was because the SWD believed that the Boon would devolve into Anomalies as well.

He wished he had asked Maria more questions.

Behind him his door sounded. He knew it was Petra arriving for their daily meeting. She was unhappy with him. Though she hadn't said anything outright, it was clear from her manner that she knew he was not being completely forthcoming. It was difficult to see her struggling with the planning of Section A. None of her family was on the evacuation list.

"Come in," Dwayne called out.

The door opened and he pivoted about to greet Petra.

Instead, Commandant Pierce stood in the doorway.

"Sir?"

"I need you to accompany me to the SWD headquarters," she said, her beautiful face impassive. "There's been an incident."

* * *

Maria scanned their location in the valley again and was satisfied to see that there was no significant migration of the remaining Inferi Scourge hordes. Being able to utilize the carrier's equipment was a godsend in these circumstances. Every night Omondi was demanding higher and higher kill numbers. Maybe it was just her imagination, but she was beginning to feel tired.

Of course, over the last few days she had started to feel a lot of things that had been absent since the SWD had made her Boon. Denman was scanning everyone on a daily basis. So far Maria was the only one that was dreaming and showing any noticeable differences. Perhaps it was her imagination, but the strange numbness that had encompassed her since her transformation felt like it was fading.

Dr. Curran was not very obliging with any hypothesis she had as to what was occurring. Denman cursed his basic field kit and wished he could be assisting her. Maria just wanted to know what was happening. Would they end up Anomalies, or worse? And was there a cure?

"Cormier, it looks like we have a clear path for five miles. Once we hit the five mile marker, come to a stop. We'll have to deal with that cluster on foot," Maria said.

"Yes, sir," Cormier answered and swung the carrier onto the cleared road.

The chatter behind her was muted. They had already been working for most of the day. They were all mentally and emotionally exhausted. With so much of the valley clear, they just wanted to finish their mission and go home. With the end so tangible, so close, it made the days seem longer. They had already been working for ten hours, but had another twelve hours before they faded from the world.

Maria wondered if she would dream again.

Her wristlet chimed. It was a call from Chief Defender Omondi. It requested a secure connection. Maria tugged her helmet out from beneath her console and slipped it on. She quickly patched the call through to her helmet's feed. Omondi's face appeared on her visor, battered, torn, and flecked with blood.

"Vanguard Martinez, I need you to immediately re-route your squad toward the hydroelectric station. We're presently pinned down and need backup immediately."

Her fingers dashed across the screen on her console, quickly scanning for a clear path to the hydroelectric station. Omondi's squad had done a good job clearing the way. Only a few patches remained, but they wouldn't be able to drive all the way to the station without risk of being overrun. There was still a large horde to contend with that was located near Omondi's location. The carrier would definitely rouse them. She quickly did the calculations on how long it would take to reach the station.

The scan of the hydroelectric station didn't reveal a concentration of Scourge as she feared. "Sir, where are you?"

"We're trapped. We're under siege by some..." Omondi frowned deeply.

"Sir?"

"Those talking Scrags..." he said with some reluctance. "Like the ones that attacked Jameson and you."

"Anomalies," Maria breathed.

"Is that what you're calling them?" Omondi sighed wearily, rubbing his brow. "There were a lot more than we anticipated. They're also armed. Projectile weapons. Handmade. Our bolt weapons are useless against them unless you bludgeon them." He laughed bitterly.

"You went there looking for them?"

"I'm not supposed to be telling you any of this, Martinez. In fact, I was told to stay put until I hear back from the SWD, but we're not going to make it if they break through the doors. They're deranged. Insane. They don't just bite to infect, they fucking eat you." Omondi shook his head in disbelief. "I'm down to five squad members, including myself. I've been ordered to stay put. By the time they decide how to rescue us, it may be too late. Come get us."

"Understood, sir."

Omondi rubbed his face, smearing the blood across his features. "Vanguard...tell your squad what is going on. Don't let them come in here blind. And arm them."

"I could put in a request for weaponry from The Bastion," Maria ventured. "Surely they won't be opposed to us rescuing you."

"Vanguard, they're saving all the remaining ammunition for their big finish. They're not going to waste it on us." Omondi's dark eyes flashed with barely-contained anger.

Maria peered past the image of Omondi projected on her helmet visor to her console. She knew he was right. Ammunition was a scarce resource. Though Omondi wasn't saying it directly, she understood precisely what he was saying.

They were expendable.

"We're on our way," Maria said at last.

Omondi nodded his head and cut the transmission.

Tugging off her helmet, Maria spun her chair around to face the squad. As she suspected, their attention was already focused on her. Cruz looked especially worried, her hands clutching her bolt weapon tightly. It saddened Maria to realize that at this point the squad expected the worst after what had happened to Jameson.

"We're heading in to rescue the Chief Defender and the other squad. They're pinned down in the hydroelectric station. We need to get there quickly, but unfortunately I don't believe we can take the carrier all the way there."

"I don't understand," McKinney said, confusion on his face. "Who has them pinned down?"

Out of the corner of her eye, Maria caught Denman's sharp look in her direction. Words caught on her tongue briefly as she considered the potential fallout of what she was about to do, yet what did it matter anymore. The SWD had betrayed them all by not disclosing vital information. They were all at risk as long as the modified ISPV was in their system. She was a soldier of the Constabulary and sworn to protect The Bastion at all costs. The Anomalies were a danger to The Bastion. They had to be stopped. Waiting around for the SWD to get their heads out of their asses was going to get the rest of the squad killed.

Stepping forward, she crossed her arms over her chest, took a deep breath, and told her squad the truth.

* * *

The area surrounding the carrier was a mess. Items retrieved from the Inferi Scourge dead lay scattered in heaps. After burning the bodies, the squad had left the containers filled with the salvaged goods stacked in heaps to be recovered at a later time. Maria had Cormier drive to each pile along their route to the hydroelectric station so the squad could rifle through them for any potential weapons.

"More knives," McKinney said with a sour look, handing them to Maria.

The containers were the ones filled in the first days of the valley clearing. Maria didn't recall there being anything more exciting than a few hunting knives. There was an old gun with no bullets on one body, but that was all.

"What did you expect?" Holm rolled her eyes and kept digging.

"We're wasting time," Denman decided as he kicked over a container.

Maria shaded her eyes as she looked toward The Bastion and the heavy crowd of Scourge gathered at the base of its walls. The last estimate of Scourge destroyed since they entered the valley had been over three million. Now they were down to hundreds of thousands gathered around the city perimeter. The end was near, but not close enough.

"We're up against projectile weapons. We can't wear our helmets until we're past the Scrags, so we're vulnerable any way you look at it." Maria handed Denman a dagger and slid the other one into a sheath on her arm. It had a rusty blade, but she didn't care. It might help at some point.

Cormier jumped out of the carrier and ran over to them. "I think I figured out how to get to the station without going on foot and wasting time."

"Let's hear it." Maria followed Cormier back to the vehicle as the squad finished up rummaging through the containers.

"We'll have to make a first pass by the hydroelectric station by skirting around the horde that is located just before it. We need to pull them behind us. They'll definitely pursue us." Cormier leaped into the carrier and led Maria over to the navigational computer tucked in beside the driver's seat. "Once they're following us, we'll head over here at full speed." She pointed to an outcropping of rocks that bordered the foothills.

"You're thinking about looping around that formation and heading back, aren't you?"

"Absolutely. That passage used to be part of a major supply line that encircled the valley. If the scans are correct, the road isn't that bad off. We can pull them into the area between those rocks and the base of the mountain, then kick up some speed and head around the formation, doubling back. If we have enough speed on us, they're not going to see where we went. The road splits off in three directions from that point. Back to the hydroelectric station, another to The Bastion, and a third to the far side of the valley."

"I like it," Maria said, nodding.

"The trick is not getting hemmed in."

"I think we might have a solution," McKinney said from behind them.

Holm held up the compact flamethrower they used to incinerate the bodies. "I say we burn them alive."

"She's kind of a genius," McKinney said with a grin.

"If I was a genius, I would have thought of this before." Holm set the flamethrower down on the floor, kneeling beside it. "We have twenty of these and the fuel for them is stored in this vehicle, right?"

"You're thinking of creating bombs?" Maria arched her eyebrows.

"No, sir. Actually one big flamethrower." Holm motioned to McKinney, who handed over his flamethrower. She set them side by side. "Like most Bastion weaponry, these are pieces of shit, old as hell and equally clunky. But they were created to store easily and save space." Holm hooked the flamethrowers together using the clasps that were used to secure them in storage units. "I say we string these babies together, bind them to the top of the carrier and use them to burn anything trying to follow us. That'll slow them down for sure."

Maria grinned slowly. "Cormier can you outrun and outmaneuver a mass of burning Scrags?"

Cormier smirked. "Hell yeah. I've been studying the scans for hours. I know exactly where I need to go. We will not have a repeat of that first day."

"Then let's make this happen!" Maria ordered.

"Yes, sir!" Holm, McKinney, and Cormier all answered.

Maria's work station paged her just in that moment. Leaning over, she opened the feed. To her surprise, Dwayne's face filled the screen.

"Vanguard Martinez, we've noted that you are en route to the hydroelectric station," he said crisply.

"Yes, sir," Maria answered in a cautious voice.

Near her, her three squad members looked pensive.

Dwayne's expression was pure business and she felt slightly intimidated. It had been a long time since she had interacted with him as her superior officer.

"And why is that?"

"Chief Defender Omondi and his squad are pinned down. We're on our way to rescue them," Maria answered, sliding into her chair. She wasn't sure if a reprimand was on the way, but she was ready to kill the feed and disobey him. She would rescue the others.

"Very good. I've been asked to coordinate the rescue effort with you," Dwayne said, a slight hint of warmth entering his gaze.

"That's the best news I've heard all day," Maria said with relief.

"Let's discuss logistics and exactly what will be required for this rescue," Dwayne continued.

"What's required is weapons," Maria said. Sliding the dagger out of her armor, she held it up. "This is not going to hack it against creatures armed with projectile weapons."

Lifting his eyebrows, Dwayne inclined his head in agreement. "I'll see what I can do."

Chapter 27

"The situation is grave," Dr. Curran said. "Chief Defender Omondi has lost most of his squad and the Anomalies have him trapped. They've retreated to the basement shelter, but are now pinned down."

The men and women seated around the table, all members of the government, upper echelon of the SWD, and the president's council, shifted uncomfortably at her words. Dwayne's own daughter, Caitlyn, was seated behind the Vice President. She was studiously taking down notes and ignoring her father. Dwayne respected his daughter's professionalism and directed his attention to the doctor seated across the conference table. A holographic image of the hydroelectric station slightly obscured his view, but he didn't need to see Dr. Curran to know she was afraid. It was in her voice.

"Is that what we're calling them now? Anomalies?" Mr. Petersen scoffed.

"Would you prefer we call them your previous failures?" Dr. Curran answered briskly.

Mr. Petersen started to retort, but the president said, "Enough squabbling. Keep to the facts at hand, Dr. Curran." President Cabot's voice was as stiff as his manner. He was angry, his usually-amicable public face set into a stern expression.

Mr. Petersen sat back in his chair, but said nothing.

"Chief Defender Omondi and his squad were our best chance to wipe them out. The Anomalies are a growing danger to this city. The recent breach into the subway tunnels proves this," Dr. Curran continued. "A breach, I would like to point out, that I was not aware of until today."

"You're told what you need to know," Mr. Petersen said with a reptilian smile.

Dwayne had met the man only a few times previously and didn't care for his manner. Though Mr. Petersen was at the heart of the SWD mission, Lindsey's deep forays into the SWD system had not revealed one shred of information on Mr. Petersen. That was the perfect reason to fear him. He was most definitely SWD Black Ops.

"The Inferi Anomalies, as you call them," the president said, motioning to the hologram, "are only at the hydroelectric plant?"

"That is uncertain," Mr. Petersen admitted.

"They're congregating there because it's the most vulnerable access point into the city and they know it," Dr. Curran said crossly.

"Why didn't we clear that area first?" President Cabot glowered at the silent people at the table.

Again the men and women who held the greatest power in The Bastion averted their eyes and shifted about in their chairs. They were obviously ill at ease with the discussion. There was a desperate aura about them. Perhaps they, too, were terrified of the days to come if the Inferi Boon failed.

"We didn't know the Anomalies still existed," Mr. Petersen said after an uncomfortable pause. "After their last push into the sewers, we killed most of them. We did an inventory of the dog tags collected and all but five were accounted for."

"May I point out that this information was kept from me and I am hearing it for the first time now," Dr. Curran said, her steely gaze fastened on Mr. Petersen.

"This mission was doomed from the start." Commandant Pierce's tone was icy and her dark eyes were cold as she regarded Mr. Petersen. "You kept me and the Castellan out of the planning stages of this mission. We're only here because you need our help to salvage what is left of your plans."

"The SWD's primary mission is to destroy the Inferi Scourge. Your mission is to protect the city," Mr. Petersen said in a voice that was slightly on edge. "There was no need to include you in our mission."

"Yet you conscripted the best of our people to do the actual dirty work," Dwayne pointed out.

"SWD security is also part of the mission. In fact, Chief Defender Omondi's squad that was nearly destroyed today are all SWD personnel." Mr. Petersen looked equal parts smug and contrite.

President Cabot pointed a finger at Mr. Petersen. "I was told that you would have the valley ready for the big final push within the week."

"Mr. President, there have been—," Mr. Petersen started to answer.

"What is the Constabulary doing to resolve this issue, Castellan?" the president asked, directing his focus to Dwayne. "I understand you were brought in once we lost contact with Chief Defender Omondi."

"Vanguard Martinez and her squad, consisting of Constabulary soldiers, are on their way to the hydroelectric station to rescue the Chief Defender and his team," Dwayne explained. He had spent most of his morning receiving intel from the satellite feeds and observing Maria's trek across the cleared valley toward the last infested area.

"Any ideas as to why we lost contact with Chief Defender Omondi?" the president asked.

"We lost contact with the chief defender's squad soon after he reported that the Inferi Anomalies had ambushed him and his people at the hydroelectric station. We believe he fell back to the basement shelter after communication became an impossibility."

"But we are in communication with Vanguard Martinez?" the president asked.

"We are." Dwayne could see that the president was pleased to have direct answers. It was clear that the power struggle between Dr. Curran and Mr. Petersen was annoying the president.

"Will we have a quick resolution to this issue?"

Dwayne caught the president's slight shift in his weight toward him and the commandant. He was starting to freeze out the SWD, which was exactly what Dwayne and Commandant Pierce wanted. "By the time we spoke with Vanguard Martinez, she and her squad were already on their way and had a solid rescue plan."

"Vanguard Martinez has requested that we airdrop weapons for them to use against the Inferi Anomalies," Commandant Pierce added.

"I would advise against that," Mr. Petersen interrupted. "We have the Inferi Scourge exactly where we want them for our big...finale. If we send out aircraft now, we could pull the Inferi Scourge out of the range of the Maelstrom Platforms. That would mean we would have to have the Inferi Boon kill off any of the stragglers and—"

"This would add time to the mission projected end date," Dr. Curran added with a sigh. "But it would be worth it to make sure the squads survive and kill the Anomalies."

"Show me the position of the Inferi Scourge right now," the president motioned to the hologram.

Mr. Petersen changed it to show a scan of the valley. The Inferi Scourge glowed red against the brilliant blue hues of the projected valley, mountains and city.

"Can we handle them with the platforms?" President Cabot again looked to the Constabulary officers.

Dwayne kept his face neutral. He didn't like where this line of thinking was going. "Based on our previous experience battling the Inferi Scourge with the Maelstrom Platforms, I would say yes."

"Only the ones around the city. Those clusters east of the city are out of range," Mr. Petersen hurriedly added.

"Do we have the firepower and fuel to eliminate what's left of the Inferi Scourge with the tiltrotors?" the president asked.

Dwayne's spine stiffened. Next to him Commandant Pierce's eyes narrowed.

"That is a question for the SWD. They conscripted the Maelstrom Platforms and the remaining ammunition per your order," Commandant Pierce said in a terse tone.

"Other than the ammunition on reserve for the Section A evac, we don't control the ammunition stores. The SWD does," Dwayne added grimly.

President Cabot directed his stern gaze at Mr. Petersen. "Well?"

"We have sufficient ammunition to clear out those pockets," Mr. Petersen admitted. "But it will be a significant drain on our resources. That weaponry was set aside for the final elimination of the Inferi Scourge around the wall."

"We need the Inferi Boon to finish their mission," Dr. Curran said firmly. "Destroying the Anomalies must be a top priority."

"But we might risk extending the mission when we're on the verge of a severe food crisis," the president said in a cold tone. "We can't afford to have riots in the streets. If we are forced to begin restrictions, the city will lose faith in us and we will have a mess on our hands. I was promised that this time there wouldn't be a failure with the Inferi Boon."

"There won't be," Dr. Curran said quickly.

"Let us drop weapons to our people." Commandant Pierce leaned toward President Cabot. "Let us do our job efficiently and with proper weaponry."

"We can't risk drawing the Inferi Scourge away from the wall." Mr. Petersen gave Dr. Curran a withering look. "Don't you agree?"

"The Anomalies need to be our concern," Dr. Curran argued. "They have already breached the subway and sewer systems. They're a real threat to this city's security. Arm the Inferi Boon and let them deal with the situation. If the aircraft does draw Inferi Scourge away from the wall, let the Inferi Boon deal with them."

"If we end up extending the mission, the food crisis will not be avoided," Vice President April Sims said, daring to finally speak up. "We're already gambling with the belief that we can start producing crops as soon as the valley is cleared and safe."

President Cabot gave her a withering look.

Dwayne couldn't keep his silence on the matter anymore. "Instead of preparing for Section A and potential food riots, we should have warned the citizens long before now. If there is a delay in this mission, there will be serious ramifications because this administration has not been forthcoming with the populace."

"I will remember your words," the president said crossly.

Caitlyn shot a worried look at her father and he winked at her reassuringly. Caitlyn had yet to understand how truly messy things could be at the upper levels of government, but she was certainly learning swiftly.

"He's right," Commandant Peirce spoke up. "We're teetering on the edge of extinction, our only hope resting on the people we killed and made into Inferi Boon to do our bidding and we won't even arm them against the Anomalies?"

"We already had to deal with one delay by pulling Special Constable Jameson out of the field. That tiltrotor pulled an estimated twenty thousand Inferi Scourge away from the city walls. We can't afford to do that again." Mr. Petersen's bland face was becoming eerily calm.

"At the rate the Inferi Boon have been killing, that is not even a half day delay. At one point the squads were killing eight hundred Inferi Scourge a minute." Dwayne was well-acquainted with all the numbers since the commandant had insisted on his inclusion at the meeting.

"That was when the Inferi Scourge were packed so tightly together that our people had to hardly move to be within killing reach of the next one. Now they're more scattered and it takes much longer. The kill counts have decreased. Especially since they lost Jameson. He was a blood-thirsty one." Mr. Petersen's voice was calm and accommodating, but his smile was shark-like.

"He *was* a blood thirsty one?" Commandant Pierce's voice was like knives, sharp and cruel.

"He died unexpectedly yesterday," Dr. Curran said, averting her eyes.

"A sad loss. A true hero," the President said. His words sounded well-rehearsed and empty.

"The point is that we cannot *afford* delays. Our fuel, food, and ammunition stores are nearly depleted. If we do not clear the valley within the next week, we will have to implement Section A," Mr.

Petersen said. "And that is not acceptable."

"And you're not on the evacuation list, are you?" Dwayne gave the man a mirthless smile.

Mr. Petersen rewarded him with a bland look and a slight shrug. "I have the city's interests at heart."

"If the Inferi Boon don't have sufficient weaponry to fight off the Anomalies, this conversation will be moot. They will fail. We will fail and the Section A evacuation will commence," Commandant Pierce said. The sharp beauty of her face only added to the power of her words. "If the Inferi Boon are our only hope, then give them the damn weapons."

"If there is a delay-" Mr. Petersen started.

"Give them the weapons," the president said. His glum face was turned toward the hologram of the valley. "One aircraft. Air drop the weapons. But after the Inferi Boon destroy the Anomalies, we will launch our final assault on the Inferi Scourge."

"The pockets of Inferi Scourge along the eastern edge of the valley-"

"Mr. Petersen, you said that we had the weaponry for one final assault, so plan to eliminate those pockets of Inferi Scourge as well. I do not want any more delays. I'm done with this Inferi Boon, Inferi Anomaly, Inferi-fucking-Scourge business! Clean it up! Give the city a gawddamn show and keep us from starving to death. You said you could do it. Then fucking do it." The president glowered at the silent people gathered around the table then turned his scorching gaze to Mr. Petersen. "Am I clear?"

"Absolutely," Mr. Petersen answered.

Dwayne noticed he wasn't the only one suppressing a smile.

"Then we're done here," the president said, rising to his feet.

Dwayne and the commandant swiftly moved to intercept the departing leader as he entered the corridor. His staff looked nervous and sufficiently cowed by the president's outburst. He was well-known for his temper away from the news cameras and his face was flushed, the veins in his neck standing out sharply.

"President Cabot, a word please," Commandant Pierce called out, trying to edge around a security officer.

The handsome man with the killer looks and wide grin that was so pleasing to the public fastened a glower upon the commandant that was far removed from his public face. "The meeting is over, Commandant Pierce."

"Yet the Constabulary continues to play a secondary role in this infamous finale the SWD has planned. I have towed the line and done as you wished for months now, but I know if I had been included in this mission from its inception we would be much closer to success instead of a potential disaster." Commandant Pierce met the president's stare without fear and with a touch of defiance.

"The Constabulary was responsible for one of the worst losses of life and resources The Bastion has endured since the gate failed. Your final push was a disaster."

"Yes, and my predecessor resigned in the aftermath. I am not Commandant Young."

The president chuckled. "You'll have to do better than that."

"I'm sworn to protect this city," Dwayne said. "That's the role I play. I should have been included in the planning of this mission and its implementation. The SWD has security officers, not trained military men and women. There is a huge difference in their training. Why else would have the SWD asked for the best of the Constabulary soldiers?"

The president motioned his security aside as the vice president lingered just behind him. A small smile on her lips revealed clearly how much she enjoyed seeing the president put on the spot. Caitlyn stood just behind her, watching with keen interest.

"You do have a point there. And I do commend you for the performance of your soldiers out in the field. It's obvious from the number of Inferi Scourge that they have killed in the last few months that they're strong and capable men and women. Whereas the SWD security forces suffered a painful loss today, your people are still in play. So well done. But that doesn't take away the fact that both of you have been a part of the dismal failures of the Constabulary in the past and the SWD has implemented a successful plan of action. Let me repeat that in case both of you hard heads didn't catch that. The Constabulary failed in its plan for a final push. *Failed*. Yes, you were both lower-ranking officers at that time, but you had a part in the planning of that mission. I don't trust failures." The president was smiling, but his tone was lethal. "That is why you weren't given a seat on the planning council and the SWD has taken point on this mission."

"This mission is on the verge of failure because we were not included," Commandant Pierce protested. "The SWD has made grandiose plans to eradicate the Inferi Scourge in one big show for the city to relish, but we have not been consulted. In fact, we just received the bare details of the planned action today."

"We're still reviewing the plans the SWD has proposed to determine if they will be effective," Dwayne added.

The president folded his arms and smirked slightly. "You're involved in this operation at this point only because Commandant Pierce and Dr. Curran pushed for it. I don't like including people who have a personal stake in an operation."

"Excuse me, but we all have a personal stake in this mission," Commandant Pierce protested. "If it fails, we all die."

Dwayne knew what was coming before the president directed his gaze toward him.

"But you're not fucking Vanguard Martinez."

Caitlyn's eyes widened, but Dwayne couldn't worry about his daughter at this moment. It was a cheap shot by the president to knock him off his game, and he was not about to relent. Millions of lives were on the line.

Commandant Pierce barely acknowledged the comment. Her eyes briefly shifted toward Dwayne, then she riveted her gaze directly on the president. "We've been studying the SWD plans for the elimination of the Inferi Scourge around the walls. The Maelstrom Platforms will not kill all the Inferi Scourge. Some will be missed. They might scatter. The Inferi Boon will have to track them down and eradicate them. The trained soldiers of the Constabulary can assist them in clearing the valley now that the number of Inferi Scourge are significantly reduced. If you allow us to plan the mission, we can assure that there will not be an evacuation to Section A."

"The SWD is in charge. It's staying that way. You two should be more concerned about the potential of initiating Section A and preparing for possible riots if food production over the next few months does not reach expected levels. This isn't over yet. We're just trying to make sure we all have a chance at surviving. You have your orders."

"You can't keep playing the SWD and Constabulary against each other," Commandant Pierce protested.

"Why not? It's keeping you both on your toes and finally getting results," President Cabot answered before pivoting away and striding up the corridor.

Dwayne watched as the vice president, his daughter, and the entourage of council members and security hurried after the president. Caitlyn glanced over her shoulder one last time, anger and pride mixed in her eyes. Dwayne had a feeling he'd be getting an irate call from her later. In some ways she was very much her mother's daughter.

Commandant Pierce waited until they turned a corner before swinging around toward Dwayne. Her dark eyes were livid.

"That could have gone better," Dwayne dared to say.

"Vanguard Martinez, huh?" The lightness of her tone in contrast to the angry set of her jaw and tense body surprised him.

"We were trying to be discreet."

A slight smile crept onto her full, dark lips as she nodded. "Good for you."

"I keep my personal life out of my work," Dwayne said in a hushed tone.

"Of course, you do. That is why I have always trusted you to do what is right." Standing with her hands behind her back, she sighed. "I should have spoken up long before this point."

"President Cabot does hold grudges, doesn't he?"

"He's nefarious about it." Commandant Pierce shook her head. "This is ridiculous. We shouldn't be squabbling. We should be united in this effort."

"My thoughts exactly," Mr. Petersen said, stepping around her and flashing his pearly white teeth. "Certainly you must understand the need for there to be a chain of command? The SWD is firmly in control of the situation despite the changes that have been...requested in today's meetings. I understand that you may feel the Constabulary will not receive the proper amount of credit once we have destroyed the Inferi Scourge, and you're most likely correct. But at least we can all take heart that you will handle the possible upcoming food shortages with a deft hand."

"You're an insidious little shit," Commandant Pierce said in a low voice. "And my question is are you the man at the top or are you sucking someone's dick to remain their lap dog?"

Mr. Petersen simply smiled.

"SWD Black Ops may try to keep a low profile behind the ruse of Admiral Kirkpatrick and you as his adjutant, but if you blow this mission, I'm sure the president would be more than happy to drag you all out into the light and expose you for your failures."

"Strange how the political maneuvering has become more cumbersome the closer we come to success," Mr. Petersen said in a light voice. "And how clumsily it's handled by some while others manage to get everything they desire."

"We teeter at the edge of extinction and all the SWD is concerned about is usurping the Constabulary and moving into a position of power."

Dwayne stood next to his commanding officer feeling more proud of her than he ever had before. She was pure steel.

"Ah, you're mistaken," Mr. Petersen said with his fake little smile. "Commandant Pierce, we *are* in power."

With that chilling comment, Mr. Petersen strode away.

"Who is he really?" Dwayne wondered under his breath.

Commandant Pierce shook her head with irritation. "He's a loathsome creature."

"I better get back to the SWD Command Center and oversee the rescue mission."

"Keep me abreast of the situation. I'll join you shortly. I'll show that little runt how clumsy I am at political maneuvering. I still have a few trump cards."

"Yes, sir." Dwayne turned to depart and saw Dr. Curran staring at him from down the corridor. Realizing he had spotted her, she looked away, busily scribbling on her pad.

Disconcerted, he departed.

Chapter 28

Tucked behind her work console as the carrier sped across the valley, Maria tracked the progress of the carrier while conversing with Dwayne. After months of monotonous killing, the squad was galvanized to be facing an enemy that had the capacity to respond with intelligent action. Their fear and excitement were tangible as they spoke in hushed voices. Tucked on top of the carrier, Holm and McKinney were manning the rigged flamethrowers.

It was difficult for Maria to contain her composure every time she spoke to Dwayne. His low, soothing voice was a balm to her exhausted mind. The warmth in his blue eyes stirred within her the desire to slip into his arms, press her face to his neck, relish his warmth, delight at the touch of his hands on her skin, and feel his heart beating against hers.

Outwardly, she managed to maintain her professional demeanor.

"We're keeping away from the remaining Scrag herds. A few are following, but shouldn't be an issue," Maria informed Dwayne.

"There doesn't seem to be any major shifts in the remaining herds," Dwayne agreed.

"We should be at the rendezvous point in fifteen minutes."

"I wish we didn't have to do the drop so close to the hydroelectric station," Dwayne said with a dour look on his face.

"Time is of the essence." Maria's gaze darted to the front of the carrier, where Cormier deftly drove the large vehicle. Through the window she could see the distant shape of the station next to a large lake. Tall pine trees dotted the foothills beyond the glimmering dark waves. It was the exact location she dreamed of having a home with Dwayne. The thought warmed her.

"Has there been any communication with Chief Defender Omondi?"

"Nothing. We can't reach him since he took shelter in the basement," Dwayne answered.

Maria briefly touched his image on her console. Despite the weariness about his eyes, his calm strength emanated outward, soothing her fears. She had been surprised when he had personally logged on to coordinate with her, but the sight of Commandant Pierce and Mr. Petersen lingering in the background had spoken volumes. The operation must be considered a high priority to have the Constabulary and SWD upper echelon working together.

The jostling of the carrier drew Maria's attention to the front window. She could see several thick masses of Inferi Scourge slowly rousing as they approached. Cormier was fast to redirect the carrier path so they wouldn't be cut off by the creatures.

"It's getting tricky out here, Castellan." Maria did another scan of their position. Several of the stagnant Inferi Scourge masses were beginning to move in their direction.

"The tiltrotor is en route. You're right on schedule," Dwayne assured her.

"Any chance of air support?" Maria lifted an eyebrow at him.

"I'll see what I can do."

His feed cut off and Maria grumbled under her breath in Spanish. She hated it when politics became entangled in the matters of the

Constabulary. It was worse now that they were in the field and desperately needed some assistance. They were so close to finally being done with this mission, but it was becoming even more harrowing the closer they got to completion.

"We got some Scrags in pursuit. May I fry them, sir?" Holms voice asked in Maria's ear bud.

"Transmit what you got. Let me look," Maria answered.

Immediately the feed from Holm's helmet began to play on her screen. The ravaged faces of the Inferi Scourge gave her chills. Their wide, distended mouths and crazed milky eyes would forever haunt her nightmares. Even over the gentle roar of the carrier's engines and the chatter behind her, she could hear their howls.

"Fry 'em," Maria answered.

Immediately the feed was filled with white hot flames. With satisfaction, Maria watched the creatures enveloped in the inferno dropping away, setting others in their horde on fire. The thrashing fiery bodies fell behind.

"That was beast," Mikado said from behind her.

Maria grinned and kept an eye on the screen. The carrier was barreling toward the rendezvous point and sweeping past stirring masses of Scourge. She felt a trickle of sweat slide down her brow and she wiped it away with annoyance. A second later, her eyes widened as she looked down at her gloved hand.

"Denman," she whispered urgently.

He glanced over at her and she pointed to the beads of sweat on her brow. With a gasp, he grabbed his med-pad and rushed to her side. Maria forced herself to focus on the mission at hand and not the steady, slow thumps within her chest. When they had started, she wasn't sure, but she could feel her heart sluggishly pumping in her chest.

Dwayne's feed came back to life. "We can give you limited air support and it looks like you're going to need it. You burned out the ones that were in pursuit, but there is a mass of several thousand heading to cut you off. I'm redirecting you toward a new rendezvous spot."

"Yes, sir," Maria said and shared the information with Cormier.

"It's getting crazy ahead," Cormier called out.

"Just follow the route the Castellan sent us," Maria answered. Out of the corner of her eye, Denman looked stoic, but she could see that his hand was trembling. She pressed a palm to her neck and felt moist flesh and a slow, steady throb of a pulse. On impulse, she positioned her own feed on her screen and studied her face. Her eyes were vivid and dark again. The murkiness was gone.

"This is incredible," Denman whispered as he finished his scan and studied the readings.

"I don't have time for this right now," Maria said in hushed tones.

Denman leaned toward her, his exhaled breath tickling her ear.

"You're alive, Vanguard."

Fear pierced her freshly-beating heart. If she was alive again, then that meant she was probably in more danger than anyone else on the squad. She swallowed hard and stared into Denman's eyes.

"Is there a problem?" Dwayne's voice asked.

Maria returned her attention to the screen before her. The commandant was hovering over Dwayne's shoulder. "A minor problem that has been resolved, sir." She gestured to Denman to return to his work station.

Reluctantly, the medic did as he was ordered.

There was no time to contemplate what was happening within the cells of her body. She was on a mission to save Chief Omondi and his squad and that had to be her priority. Lowering her hand out of view of the camera, she flipped on her armor's cooling system. She was relieved when it activated. The Boon armor was not standard issue. They had been stripped of some of the systems unnecessary to the Boon.

"That Scrag horde is moving in fast, sir," Cormier said worriedly.

"I'm watching them. Maintain top speed and we should bypass them."

"Aircraft is almost to the rendezvous spot," Dwayne said in the corner of her screen. "It has pulled off a good chunk of Scrags from the wall."

Maria watched the fresh information fill her screen and then swore. "It's going to make our loop around difficult with them coming in from that angle."

"The tiltrotor will fire at the horde coming from the wall. You just concentrate on evading the one coming from behind."

She could see the concern in his eyes and the tightening around his mouth. He was apprehensive and so was she.

The images on her screen were growing more and more worrisome as the surge of Scourge continued toward the carrier. Omondi and his people had cleared a lot of the area, but they had been concentrating on clearing a way to the hydroelectric station, not eliminating all the pockets of the Scourge. They had left quite a few clusters with high numbers for Maria's squad to deal with.

"I'm going to have to slow down slightly," Cormier called out. "I have debris in the road and we don't need to pop a tread."

"Keep an eye on that horde," Maria ordered. "We'll have to risk our treads if we're going to outrun them."

"This parade is getting bigger," Holm's voice said. "We're picking up a lot more now. Should I blast them?"

Dwayne and the commandant were deep in a muted conversation. Maria frowned then sighed. "Do it. Contained bursts. We want to get some distance on them, not set the whole area on fire."

The footage from Holm's helmet was perturbing. The carrier didn't exceed fifty-five kilometers per hour. The Scourge were terrifyingly-quick on their feet. A human being could in theory run nearly as fast as the carrier, but would never be able to sustain the pace or the speed. The ISPV eliminated the physical barriers. The Scourge were closing in as Cormier slowed the carrier.

"Cormier, I need you to accelerate or we're going to have a serious problem on our hands in just a few minutes," Maria barked.

The squad had fallen silent as the tension began to rise. A few were craning their heads to peer out the windshield or view Maria's screens. The Scourge rushing in from the east was a growing tidal wave of dead flesh that was about to crash onto the path before them.

"I have a barbecue back here, but they just keep coming," Holm's voice said in Maria's ear.

"Continue with short bursts. Keep them off of us."

The Scourge set aflame were quickly consumed and fell away, but they were being just as swiftly replaced with fresh bodies.

"You're going to cut this really close, Vanguard," Dwayne's voice said as he came back online.

"We had some debris in our path." Maria ran another scan of the road, then keyed in a new path to Cormier. "We're going to have to off-road it to reach the drop zone." She deliberately ignored the pack of Scourge that had followed the aircraft toward the rendezvous site.

The carrier bounced off the road and barreled through a gnarled field. It slowed fractionally, allowing a few Scourge close enough to touch the carrier. Maria hit her feed to Holm seconds before Holm opened fire with the flamethrower.

"Holm, hold your fire!" Maria shouted.

The weedy field sprang to life, flames sweeping outward from the carrier, setting the world ablaze.

"Fuck!"

"Report in, Vanguard!" Dwayne's voice was pure steel.

"We have a situation on our hands. We have a brushfire."

Maria watched in horror as the flames spread through the cleared field, burning high and bright. In her ear bud she could hear Holm and McKinney screaming. The flames licked across the surface of the carrier as a claxon rang out. There was a mad scramble behind her as Holm and McKinney dropped through the hatch, their hair on fire. Denman doused them with a fire extinguisher as Cormier activated the carrier fire controls.

"Did you disengage the flamethrowers?" Maria shouted the two scorched soldiers lying on the floor.

A massive explosion rocked the carrier. The safety straps pressed hard into her armor, making Maria gasp, and the carrier shimmied. Cormier's inventive swearing filled the carrier as she fought for control of the vehicle.

"That was behind the carrier," Cormier shouted. "It wasn't us!"

Swiveling her chair about, Maria saw Holm holding up her thumb. Unable to talk through her burned lips, the soldier tried to smile.

"Good job, Holm." Maria gave the woman a quick salute.

Crouching over the wounded, Denman was already spreading salve on their blistered faces and heads as the other squad members helped them out of their burning armor. The stink of scorched flesh was nauseating.

"The fire is diverting that horde," Dwayne said in a calmer voice.

"I have two soldiers with grievous wounds." Maria could now see the tiltrotor hovering above the road.

"I can keep going," McKinney choked out. "It doesn't hurt...much. Not being able to feel much is really nice right now."

"Requesting a med-pod for both of them," Maria continued.

She almost swore when Dwayne's feed was muted and she could see Mr. Petersen and Commandant Pierce arguing furiously behind him.

"I'll be fine," McKinney protested. "Ebba just can't talk. No big loss there."

Holm hit him in the stomach with her fist as Denman continued to treat her badly burned face.

"Mikado, Cruz, get ready," Maria ordered.

"Yes, sir," they chorused.

"We're almost there," Cormier said excitedly. "And we've got a minute or two before the Scrags reach us."

The carrier bounced up over the incline then was on the worn road again. The treads slid slightly, then caught the asphalt, the carrier fishtailing slightly. The tiltrotor was a welcome sight. Already the crew on board was lowering the desperately needed weapons.

"Negative on those med-pods," Mr. Petersen's voice said in her ear.

Maria had been watching the onslaught of the Inferi Scourge and her eyes flicked toward the spot where Dwayne's precious face had been. Instead the completely bland, yet disturbing face of the SWD mystery man was on the feed.

"I have two badly wounded soldiers, Mr. Petersen."

"Are they able to fight?"

"Yes," McKinney said from behind her.

She assumed the thumbs up was Holm agreeing.

"Medic?" Maria glanced at Denman.

Denman helped strap Holm and McKinney into some backup armor. "They're Boon. They can keep going," Denman said reluctantly.

Despite her composure, Maria wanted to reach through the feed and strangle Mr. Petersen. His snake-like smug smile was infuriating.

"Keep to the plan, Vanguard," Mr. Petersen ordered.

"Arrival in thirty seconds," Cormier called out.

Directing her attention to Mikado and Cruz, she saw they were crouched next to the door waiting.

Cormier slammed on the brakes, pitching everyone forward. "We're here!"

"Go!" Maria ordered.

Mikado slid the door open and vanished. Cruz followed. Their helmet cameras sent a feed to Maria's screen. As they ran toward the squat black box on the road, she felt her heart speeding up. Twisting away from the console camera, she tried to discreetly wipe the sweat off her brow and upper lip.

Outside the carrier, Mikado and Cruz reached the box. They activated it and squat wheels pushed out of the bottom of it. Gripping handles that unfurled from the box, Mikado and Cruz ran it toward the carrier as the tiltrotor began to fire at the wave of Inferi Scourge approaching from the city.

The wildfire in the field beside the road was burning itself out and the Scourge that had been pursuing closed in once more.

Mikado and Cruz reached the carrier and slid the box right up to the doorway. They activated the loading mechanism and claws extended from the carrier, gripped the box, then slid it up on a track into the carrier. The two soldiers scrambled in after it. Maria breathed a sigh of relief as Mikado slammed the door shut.

"Go, Cormier!"

"Yes, sir!"

Cormier shoved down on the accelerator and the carrier lurched forward. Excited words were exchanged as Mikado and Cruz opened the box and handed out actual rifles.

"Oh, sweet, baby. How I missed you so," McKinney said and kissing sounds followed.

Cruz handed one to Maria along with several clips. "Vanguard, it's good to have actual weapons."

"That it is," Maria agreed. "Give me one for Omondi. Some of you double up on weapons for the survivors."

The carrier accelerated on its course that would loop around the rock formation between the foothills and the city. All they had to do now was lose the horde of Scourge following them, make their way back to the hydroelectric station, and save the day.

Chapter 29

The acrimony in the command center was a distraction Dwayne didn't need. It was insulting to have Mr. Petersen looming over the shoulders of the Constabulary officers. Dwayne literally felt Commandant Pierce's fury burning every time Mr. Petersen insinuated himself into command decisions.

The command center at the heart of the SWD facility was crackling with excitement. The usual boring day-to-day tasks were set aside as the men and women specifically selected to oversee the rescue of the stranded squad directed their attention and expertise to the task at hand. They were a combination of SWD and Constabulary personnel. The commandant had not put up much of a fight once she was able to pull in her own people and place Dwayne at the head of the operation.

Leaning over a communication console, Lindsey was consumed with finding a way to reach Chief Defender Omondi. She was busy adjusting the communication dishes set around the valley in an attempt to locate his feed. If anyone could find a way to contact Omondi, that person was Lindsey.

Meanwhile, Dwayne communicated directly with Maria. To see her in danger was difficult, yet he had to put aside his personal feelings and concentrate on the mission. Like any man, he wanted to protect the woman he loved, but he also felt a surge of pride at her strength and ability to lead her squad.

Watching the feed from the tiltrotor, Dwayne felt his anxiety swell as a massive wave of Inferi Scourge rushed toward Maria's position. The aircraft shredded the creatures moving on an intercept course with the carrier. The heavy guns pulverized the running corpses, creating a clear path for the carrier. The vehicle slid through the bloody remains of the Scourge and barreled down the abandoned road.

"How many in that swarm behind them?" Dwayne asked the soldier at the console beside him.

The young man promptly ran a program to calculate the number. "Close to ten thousand."

Commandant Pierce leaned over his shoulder and peered down at the many screens before Dwayne's post. All the information being gathered by their staff was relayed to his station. "It appears that their plan might work if they can get some distance on that horde."

"Agreed, but they lost valuable ground securing the drop."

"How are we doing on ammunition on that tiltrotor?"

Dwayne tapped on the screens and a window popped up revealing the exact number. "The guns are down to half."

Commandant Pierce pointed to the primary screen that revealed the carrier as it sped alongside the rock formation. The remaining Scourge from the group that had broken off from the crowd around the city fell behind the carrier, joining the larger horde. "Once they double-back, they should have a clear shot back to the hydroelectric station," Commandant Pierce noted. "Have the tiltrotor fire at the leading edge of that horde. I want them to exhaust their weapons on the front of that crowd. It will give the carrier more distance, but also provide obstacles for the Scrags following behind."

"Agreed," Dwayne answered, then immediately transmitted the

order to the tiltrotor pilots and gunners.

"They're performing well, aren't they?" Mr. Petersen said, joining them. "I can't help but admire Vanguard Martinez. She really is the exemplary soldier you said she was, Commandant Pierce. You were wise to recommend her to be the first of our Boon."

Dwayne ignored the man. It was obvious that Mr. Petersen had heard the president's accusation. And there was no reason to believe that Commandant Pierce would volunteer Maria as some sort of slight against Dwayne. He was sure she had been genuinely surprised to find out about his relationship.

"Yes, I was." Commandant Pierce fastened her stony gaze on Mr. Petersen.

With a slight smirk, the man walked on to check in with the SWD personnel at their stations.

"We're putting more ground between us and the Scrags," Maria's voice said. On one corner of his screen he could see her dark eyes glancing toward the camera. He loved how they glimmered like obsidian. He had missed that when-

Dwayne sat up straight and stared intently at Maria's eyes. Commandant Pierce was talking briskly to Lindsey. He stole a quick look in Dr. Curran's direction, then returned his gaze to Maria. Maybe no one else noticed in the heat of the moment, but he knew Maria's face intimately. Her eyes were as dark and clear as they had been when she had been alive.

"Castellan Reichardt," Commandant Pierce's voice said, cutting through his flurry of thoughts. "We were able to get through briefly to Chief Defender Omondi. It's confirmed he is still holed up in the basement of the facility."

"Relaying that information to Vanguard Martinez. Do we have the schematic of the hydroelectric station yet?"

One of the SWD officers said, "Yes, sir. Transferring to you and Vanguard Martinez now."

The commandant squeezed his shoulder as she leaned over him again. "Keep focused," she whispered.

He gave her a short nod. She probably thought he was ruffled by Maria's presence on the mission, but it was her clear dark eyes that had him unsettled. As soon as he was able, he was going to have a word or two with Dr. Curran.

On the screens around the command center, the carrier sped along its path toward the point where it would reverse course. Hopefully, the maneuver would be performed out of the sight of the pursuing Scourge.

"Is our little surprise ready?" Commandant Pierce asked.

Dwayne gave her a brisk nod.

"Good," she gave Mr. Petersen's back a fierce look. "He'll have a fit. I'm going to enjoy this."

The cameras on the tiltrotor continued to transmit the aerial view of the carrier on its fast-paced journey toward the end of the rock wall.

The old underpass appeared to be in good condition. Dwayne hoped the carrier would be able to maneuver swiftly around the curving road.

Keeping one eye on Maria as she toiled at her console inside the carrier, he observed all facets of the unfolding events. Lindsey cursed under her breath at her work station, attempting to contact Chief Defender Omondi again.

On screen the carrier started to reduce speed as it exited onto a curving off ramp that ducked under the road before emerging on the other side to end at a three-way intersection. Commandant Pierce folded her arms over her breasts as she stared at the primary screen. The sheer force of her will that the carrier succeed was a palatable energy. Dwayne silently prayed as he prepared to signal the tiltrotor.

For a few seconds the carrier vanished from the screens as it journeyed through the underpass. When it emerged unscathed and turned onto the road that would carry it to its destination, Dwayne exhaled and transmitted a signal to the tiltrotor.

The screens flashed as the aircraft fired two missiles into the side of the stone formation. Massive explosions blinded the cameras, filling the screens with white light.

"What the hell was that?" Mr. Petersen twisted about in his chair, glaring at Dwayne and the commandant.

"Missiles," the commandant answered with a wry smile. "You have heard of those?"

As the images on the screens returned to normal, the passage the carrier had taken was blocked by a massive landslide. Part of the Scourge horde was buried under the dirt and boulders. The rest of the horde scrambled around the edges of the destruction, their path redirected away from the escaping carrier.

"I didn't sign any clearance for you to use missiles! Those were in reserve for the final attack!" Mr. Petersen snapped.

"Well, at least now the mission is back on track," Commandant Pierce said with an even bigger smile.

"I didn't approve of the use of those missiles! All the remaining stock was to be used in the—"

"They got the job done. Let it go," Dr. Curran spoke up from across the room.

Mr. Petersen glared at her, but fell silent. With one last thoughtful look at the commandant and Dwayne, he swiveled about to peer at his console.

Lindsey gave Dwayne a wide grin before returning to her task.

"Now let's hope they find our people and get them out of there safely," Commandant Pierce said.

Nodding, Dwayne tried to sweep away his worrisome thoughts to concentrate on the next dangerous step of the mission.

* * *

The carrier roared down the road, the Scourge horde that had been following it stuck behind the barricade created by the tiltrotor. As the aircraft returned to the city, Maria focused her attention on mapping out the rescue mission using the schematic of the hydroelectric station. There was no power in the building, so they would have to wear their helmets and rely on night vision.

Leaning over her, Denman muted her feed. "I transmitted your readings to Dr. Curran."

She threw him a dark look, her brow furrowing. "Why?"

"Because she might be able to figure out what is happening and how much danger you may possibly be in."

"I'll be okay. I have armor," Maria said in a low, tight voice.

"I'm not talking about just the Scrags attacking you, but...the Anomaly situation. What if you're becoming one of them?"

Her frown deepened, but Maria understood his concern. She shared his fear. "Fine, but you should have told me first."

"The standing order is to send her all our readings. This does concern us all. You were the first of us. Whatever is happening to you most likely will happen to us. Maybe Jameson's transformation was accelerated by the bite."

Denman had a point. She had been transformed into Inferi Boon weeks before anyone else. So far she was the only one other than Jameson who was showing signs of the virus mutating in her system. It had to be the virus that was restoring her to life.

She gave him a curt nod, dismissing him. Opening up her feed, she said, "Unless there is significant damage to the interior of the facility, I have our projected path to Chief Defender Omondi mapped out." Maria watched the screen as Dwayne reviewed her plans. Her heart was beating regularly now, slower than it should be, but at a steady pace. She felt flush with life and it was a terrifying sensation.

"The road is clear and we should be at the hydroelectric station within ten minutes," Cormier said crisply. The driver had been performing admirably all day and Maria had already noted this in her log.

Directing her attention forward, Maria gazed at the massive white granite dam that bisected the lake that was fed from an underground river. The station was tucked on the shoreline. It not only housed the massive generators, but had also been a recreational facility for the people living in the valley. Maria had seen vids of the old playgrounds and picnic areas where people had relaxed during bright sunny days. There was a museum, educational facilities, recreational hall, and small restaurant all tucked into the building. Now the long squat building with its broken windows looked like a prison.

"It's almost pretty," Denman said as he returned to his station.

The medic had applied fresh ointment and bandaging to Holm's face. She still couldn't speak, but the virus was doing its job preserving her. It upset Maria that they weren't going to airlift her wounded people, but there was not much she could do other than file an angry complaint later.

Checking her screens, she was relieved to see no Inferi Scourge movement toward their location. The carrier had pulled the horde away from the station just as they had planned.

"Vanguard Martinez, your retrieval strategy appears solid," Mr. Petersen's voice said in her ear. "But perhaps you should clear the station before retrieving Chief Defender Omondi and his people from the basement. We need to make sure all the Anomalies are destroyed."

"The last report from the Chief Defender was that they were in a dire situation," Maria pointed out curtly.

"Rescue the Chief Defender, Vanguard Martinez. Our people's retrieval is your top priority," Commandant Pierce said briskly. "We will deal with the Anomalies afterward."

"Very well," Mr. Petersen said, his voice cold.

The carrier reduced speed as it neared the drive that led to the building. Inspecting her weapon one more time, Maria ignored the bland little face on her screen.

"You must retrieve all the dog tags," Mr. Petersen continued. "We must make sure all the Anomalies are destroyed."

"How do you know how many there are?" Maria asked.

Mr. Petersen closed his mouth and stared into the camera for a long moment. "We don't."

"Vanguard Martinez, we have the utmost confidence that you will do an excellent job," Commandant Pierce's voice cut in.

"Thank you, sir," Maria answered, and donned her helmet. She redirected all the information she needed to the visor before abandoning her console. Dwayne's feed was framed in a small square on the left hand side of her visor. It was a comforting sight.

"Helmets on, weapons at the ready," Maria ordered.

The squad shoved their helmets onto their heads, securing the clasps and activating their displays and cameras. The bolt weapons and rifles hung from their shoulders, extra ammunition tucked into their belts.

"We keep to the path I've laid out. We kill any Scrags and Anomalies we come across. Remember, short bursts. Conserve your ammunition. Aim for their heads. Retrieve any dog tags you find on the bodies. Mark the location of the corpses on the schematic I have sent to your helm-units. This is different from fighting the Scrags. Anomalies can think and function at a much higher level. According to Chief Defender Omondi they have created projectile weapons. Our armor is older issue, so we're vulnerable. Don't play the hero. Take cover if you need to. We go in, we rescue the squad, we clear the building. Understood?"

The "yes, sirs" echoed within her helmet.

"Cormier, bring us to a full stop at the front entrance."

"Yes, sir. Almost there."

The carrier shuddered as Cormier applied the brakes. The vehicle decelerated near the front of the building. The once-white granite walls of the facility were stained dark from the passage of time and the elements. There was no sign of movement outside or inside the building.

Maria studied the faces of her squad behind their visors. The men and women returned her steady gaze, resolute and ready to do their job. The bandages covering most of Holm's face didn't hide her determined stare.

With a sharp little jerk, the carrier came to a stop. Maria stared out the front window at the silent building. Dark clouds were sliding over the mountaintops, casting dark shadows over the lake. The last thing they needed was rain.

"Mikado, open up this tin can," Maria said.

"Yes, sir!"

Mikado sprang forward to obey, Cruz right on his heels. Together they jumped out and covered the rest of the squad as they disembarked.

"Cormier, secure the carrier on your way out." Maria leaped to the ground and nodded with approval at the squad's quick deployment and efficient securing of the area. They were not just killing machines sent to exterminate the mindless Inferi Scourge anymore. They were soldiers again.

Following in her shadow, Denman motioned toward the approaching storm. "Not good. Visibility will already be an issue inside."

"That's what night vision is for," Maria responded.

The defense system buzzed as it came online when Cormier slid the door shut. The battered vehicle had seen better days, but it had held up admirably. Cormier joined the squad, her weapon at the ready.

"Let's do this," Maria said in a fierce voice and headed toward the building.

Chapter 30

The glass crunched under her boot heels as Maria approached the empty floor-length windows that had been destroyed long ago when the gate had failed and the Inferi Scourge had rampaged through the valley. The white stone around the empty windows was discolored. Furniture and heavy objects that had once been stacked against the glass lay in rotting piles just inside the building. The menacing gloom within the massive lobby made Maria's sluggish heart beat faster.

Mikado and Cruz led the squad, quiet and graceful as they scanned for any sign of the enemy. They were the first to peer into the abandoned building before slipping over the windowsill and being absorbed into the darkness. The small lamps on their helmets switched on, beams of light streaking across the sad remains of a vanquished world.

"Keep alert," Maria said, trailing McKinney and Holm into the building. Denman was right behind her.

There were signs of battle all around her. Bullet holes were punched deep into the interior walls. The once-white walls were moldy and streaked with dark blots. It didn't take much of an imagination to know the stains were the markers where blood spilled long ago. The smashed remains of the lobby chairs and tables littered the floor. Bits of broken bones and a few shattered skulls were strewn about.

"Must have fought like hell," Cruz said in a soft, almost reverent voice.

Cut off from the city, whoever had taken shelter within the building had been doomed. Maria wondered how long the windows had held before surrendering to the onslaught to the Scourge. The lights from the helmets cast shadows across the walls, mimicking wraiths.

The squad spread out across the lobby. Every possible hiding spot was checked.

One by one, seventeen different voices said, "Clear."

The schematic on Maria's visor altered to show the lobby free of the Anomalies. Next they would enter a corridor that opened to the offices of the administration of the facility. At the far end would be the stairwell that would lead down to the basement. The doors opening to the corridor were straight ahead. One was slightly ajar, the thin line of the blackness that dwelt beyond the doors an ominous sight.

Maria signaled for Mikado and Cruz to advance. The rest of the squad fell back from the doors, staying out of the range of any possible fire.

"Switching to night vision, "Mikado said, then took up his position next to the door. He silently counted down on his fingers with Cruz, then they shoved the doors open. Keeping in cover, they both peered into the darkness, their helmets illuminated in a ghostly glow.

"We've got bodies," Cruz said, her voice slightly wavering.

"Gutierrez." Mikado's voice as grim. "What's left of him."

"Advance with caution," Maria directed.

The small schematic on her screen altered to pinpoint the position of Gutierrez's body. Flipping on her night vision, she watched the world fade to shades of blue and gray.

With practiced perfection, the squad moved into the wide corridor.

Closed doors lined either side. Breaking into smaller groups, the squad began to open each door. Every time a door yawned open and the darkness beyond faded to washes of blue to reveal its secrets, Maria felt her heart thud a little harder. The offices were trashed, the desks tossed against the walls, chairs shattered into pieces of plastic and metal. Computer terminals were ruined monuments of another time. Personal photos in broken frames were faded, moldering mementos of lost lives.

One by one, the rooms were checked and secured. Meter by meter, they crept toward the door that would open to the stairwell. Gutierrez's body lay at the far end, his face turned toward them on a shattered neck. Maria tried not to see the ravaged body, stripped of muscle and skin. As he neared the corpse, Denman cautiously crouched next to the dead soldier.

"Entry wound is above his left eye. Exit wound is..." Denman's face was an eerie mix of various shades of blue and gray as he looked up at Maria. Gently he turned Gutierrez's head so Maria could see the thin metal pipe sticking out of the back.

"Projectile weapons, Omondi said," Maria remarked, keeping her voice as calm as possible. "Do you see this, Castellan?"

"We see it. Proceed with extreme caution."

Maria could hear the slight fear in his voice and her eyes flicked toward his small image.

Denman stepped back into formation and the group pressed forward. Again, Mikado and Cruz were first through the new set of doors. One of the doors hit the wall with a harsh sound and an echo followed.

They were at the top of the stairwell.

The squad filed onto the landing. Maria stepped up to the rail and peered cautiously into the blackness below. The night vision displayed the long spiral of stairs and a blank square of concrete floor at the base. She was straightening when she saw something flash through her line of vision followed by a metallic clank. The sound of receding footfalls ricocheted up the stairwell.

Immediately, she stepped back and thumbed off the safety on her rifle. "Watch yourselves. There are some below."

Holm plucked a thin piece of pipe that had landed near Maria's location.

"Definitely armed," McKinney said sourly.

Mikado and Cruz stepped onto the stairs, keeping away from the railing, carefully heading downward. Their footfalls rang through the blue-washed darkness. The descent into the basement was terrifying. At least in the valley they could see the Scourge coming toward them and have some sort of idea of where an attack may originate.

Scuffling noises from below brought the soldiers to a stop. Mikado quickly peeked over the rail. He barely dodged an object that shot up from below. Cruz sent a short barrage of gunfire into the darkness beneath the stairs before the attacker darted out of range.

Holm reached down and picked up a long thin pipe. Though she couldn't speak, her eyes said it all. The Anomalies were definitely armed.

Continuing downward, they hugged the walls, trying to stay out of range of fire. Maria's gaze stole upward when her hearing picked up a different sound. A shadow was leaning over the rail peering down at them.

"They're above us!" she called out.

The sound of the Anomalies' weapons discharging sent the squad into defensive positions. The pipe projectiles clanged against the wall and stairwells, missing their targets. Maria could see the thin objects hurtling at her from above and below. She dodged and ducked, trying to avoid them. The gunfire bursts from the Inferi Boon were deafening.

The cold Anomaly bodies were registering as ghostly wisps on the night vision. Cursing, Maria darted around Mikado and fired down the final length of stairs. She could see the Anomalies at the bottom darting back and forth out of cover.

"Move down!" she ordered.

Maria fired at a shape ascending the stairwell and heard it scream.

Advancing into the basement, she continued to pull the trigger of her weapon, scattering the Anomalies on the basement floor. Mikado and Cruz were right behind her, helping her pin down the Anomalies. Their opponents continued to attack, but the inaccuracy of the makeshift weapons gave the squad the advantage. Maria registered that a few of her people were hit on her helmet readout, but none were down.

"Fuck! They hit my helmet! I'm blind!" Cormier screamed.

"Get Cormier!" Maria ordered, ducking around a corner and firing point blank into the body of a man standing there. He staggered back as the bullets punched through him.

"Hungry!" he screamed, then lunged at her.

A bullet to the head stopped him cold and he fell to her feet.

"Fuck! Fuck!" Cormier's voice rang out. "Get them off me!"

The cries from above became desperate. McKinney's shouts of anger and the staccato of gunfire deafened Maria. Her helmet started to register squad losses.

Screams and shouts filled the cramped space as Maria, Mikado, Cruz, Denman and Holm managed to find refuge behind a reserve generator. Maria could now see the Anomalies scurrying from cover to cover in the long corridor that led to the shelter that the Chief Defender and his squad were bunkered down in. The ambush was carefully thought out and the enemy had prepared. The only reason Maria and the others had found any protection was because the Anomaly she had killed had been overwhelmed with hunger and abandoned his position.

"Vanguard Martinez, we have five people immobilized up there," Denman whispered urgently.

"I can see my readout," Maria retorted.

The gunfire from above was steady and purposeful.

"Let them do their job, you do yours," Maria added, firing again. "McKinney, report in."

"Got rushed! Have some wounded. Cormier...I think they took her...Got two above me still firing. We're moving down."

"Cormier, report," Maria said. "Cormier."

There was no answer.

"Fuck," Cruz whispered.

Studying her schematic, Maria knew they were trapped. They couldn't move in any direction without being gunned down. The flashes in the darkness from the corridor were blinding as a fresh barrage of pipes, nails, and other sharp metal scraps were fired at high velocity at them. The metal objects sang against the generator as they impacted.

"We're almost to the bottom," McKinney's voice said.

"Hold your position," Maria said.

There was a lull in the attack from the Anomalies.

"Castellan, I need an analysis fast. How much time do we have between their barrages?" Maria asked. Her eyes flicked to Dwayne's image. She could see others gathered around him. At her request there was a flurry of movement. The feed was starting to cut out and soon she knew she would lose communication as she zeroed in on the Chief Defender's location.

"Twenty seconds," Dwayne's voice answered.

An explosion of sound and a hail of metal fragments exploded against the generator.

"They have to reload whatever they're firing," Maria said softly to her people. "The second the lull hits, rush them. It's our only chance."

"Understood," was the answer from McKinney.

"Watch who you're firing at. We're coming in from the dead-end on the right. Move when I say."

She waited through two more lulls and attacks before uttering the words she dreaded.

"Go!"

Skidding around the generator, she charged forward. The shapes of her squad rushing in from the staircase were a blur in her periphery. Mikado and Cruz were just ahead of her. McKinney leaped over a barricade, firing as he landed amidst the Anomalies on the other side. Maria and Denman hit another barricade, toppling the stacked machinery over on top of the howling creatures on the other side. Gunfire and the strange staccato sound of the Anomaly weapons filled the corridor. Darting around a barrier, Maria fired into the face of an Anomaly. Mikado was just ahead of her, heading toward the huge weapon the Anomalies had been firing at them. A counter sprung up on her visor screen, warning her that the weapon was nearly reloaded.

"Mikado!" she shouted, falling back behind one of the barricades, taking cover.

The barrage erupted again. Cruz and Mikado screamed at the same time.

Mikado's armor reported his death, his status flashing red on her screen.

"Denman," Maria gasped.

She could see him analyzing all the data pouring onto his med-screen in his helmet. He shook his head.

"Eviscerated," Denman said.

Cruz continued to scream, her gun firing. Maria had no idea where the soldier was located, but the squad was now up against the first set of barricades. She had caught a glimpse of the massive gun and the Anomalies clustered behind it before she'd been forced to seek cover.

The flying pieces of metal skidded across the concrete floors and punctured the walls and ceiling. Then the gun fell silent.

This time the Anomalies were waiting for the Boon. Their projectile weapons fired as the squad rushed them. Maria barely caught a glimpse of Mikado's torn body before she was in the thick of things. She felt a hard punch to her chest, but her armor resisted. The pipe projectile clattered to the floor, but her body hurt like hell. She fired at the Anomalies trying to cut her off as McKinney tossed one over his shoulder, heading for the gun. The countdown on her helmet was moving swiftly to zero and she could see the ghostly form of the gunner feverishly reloading.

"McKinney, toss me!" Cruz shouted. She lay on the floor, wounded, clutching her weapon to her chest.

Maria barely had time to register what the two soldiers were doing before an Anomaly attacked her. It was a woman, her murky eyes terrifying in the night vision blues. The female Anomaly tried to fire her weapon directly at Maria's helmeted head, but Maria knocked it aside and sent a blast of bullets through her enemy's torso. The woman staggered a few feet, drawing a razor sharp piece of metal from a sheath. Maria fired into the Anomaly's face just as the countdown hit zero.

Dropping to the floor, Maria saw McKinney hook his hands under Cruz's armpits, hoist her off the floor and hurl her small body over the massive gun. Cruz fired as she fell, targeting for the gunner. Her aim went wild, but Cruz fell into him, sending both sprawling.

The squad scrambled forward as the Anomalies set upon Cruz. Their grunts and cries and Cruz's screams mingled with the blasts from her weapon. McKinney shoved the massive barrage gun over onto its side and scrambled over it toward the Anomalies attacking Cruz.

"Watch your fire!" Maria's voice rang out as she followed in McKinney's wake.

The Anomalies were trying to stab through Cruz's armor and shatter her helmet, their metal weapons glinting in the flash of gunfire. Mayhem descended in the narrow space. It was difficult to even get close with Cruz's weapon discharging.

"Cruz, hold your fire!" Maria's voice was harsh against the din.

Though there were only five Anomalies still on their feet, the narrow space between the barricades they had erected in the corridor gave them the advantage. Maria stumbled as she crawled over the debris the creatures had packed into the narrow space as cover. Cruz's cries rang in her ears. McKinney's huge form loomed ahead as he shoved the Anomalies off of Cruz and fired at them.

Maria kicked over the body of an Anomaly tucked behind some old terminals. Its wild eyes glared as it gnashed its bloody, broken teeth. She swore she heard it utter "hungry" just before she killed it.

The gunfire ceased at last.

The blood and viscera were black in the night vision. Her helmet was reading multiple causalities, but she was waiting for Denman to update the stats. The Boon could take some serious wounds and remain on their feet. Denman moved swiftly through the carnage, scanning the Boon as McKinney dragged the bodies of the Anomalies to one side, stacking them.

"Are you getting the dog tags?" Maria asked.

"Yes, sir," McKinney answered, dangling them from one hand.

"Holm, watch our rear," Maria said.

The mute soldier nodded her head, taking up position.

Cormier's stats read as KIA on her screen. Maria doubted that stat would change. There were Anomalies still in the building above, that much was certain. Some of the KIA's began to change to WIA/BR and she sighed with relief.

Cruz staggered out of the gloom to her side. The smaller soldier's helmet was dented on one side and her armor had some tears. Black blood ran down over the plates in the gray/blue murk of the night vision.

"Wounded in action and battle ready, huh, Cruz?" Maria said, slightly smiling.

"Those bastards suck," Cruz grumbled.

"I don't remember being trained in the fine art of being pitched like a football," Maria said wryly.

"It seemed like a good idea at the time," Cruz whispered, her dark eyes settling on the broken body of Mikado. Several of the other squad members had pulled his pieces to one side.

Maria laid her hand on Cruz's shoulder gently for a second, then moved forward to where McKinney stood ready to advance.

"Straight shot to where they're holed up," McKinney said in a somber voice.

"We go slow," Maria said. "We need to be cautious. They've been here a lot longer than we have."

More of the KIA's altered to WIA/BR. Maria glanced back toward Denman as he continued his scans and sealed wounds. Holm and several other soldiers lingered near the first barricade, watching the stairs. Maria didn't like being in this area. It was a killing zone.

Her screen flashed as Denman finished his task. Three KIA's remained: Cormier, Mikado, and a big burly soldier named Klosk. She sighed, composing herself.

"What's the delay?" Mr. Petersen's voice said, interrupting her moment of silence. His voice sounded distant, the connection wobbly and fading.

"Securing the area before advancing," Maria said briskly.

"We need you to-"

Maria cut off the feed. Dwayne would have to calm down Petersen. She didn't have time to deal with him. Besides, she was about to lose all communication as they moved down the corridor.

"McKinney, lead the way."

Chapter 31

"Back off and let them do their job," Dwayne uttered.

"She cut my feed!" Mr. Petersen said, his usually placid expression flushed with anger.

"They're trying to survive right now. They're in the middle of a battle. They don't need you interfering with what they're doing," Commandant Pierce added.

Dwayne stood with his feet apart, arms folded, glaring at the smaller man. "We lost three people in that action. We don't need to lose any more. There are obviously more Anomalies than you projected, aren't there?"

Mr. Petersen's gaze darted toward Dr. Curran. She was standing nearby clutching her pad against her chest. It was difficult to read her expression, but Dwayne suspected she was just as surprised by the numbers of Anomalies the Boon were encountering.

"What haven't you told us?" Commandant Pierce demanded. "What are you keeping from us?"

"This was unexpected," Mr. Petersen said, his usual blandness ruffled. "We were not expecting this many. We thought that maybe there were half a dozen at the most."

"They're not equipped to deal with the resistance they're encountering. If you had even the slightest idea-"

"Commandant, I believe they're some of the soldiers from the last push." Dr. Curran cleared her throat before speaking again. "The Inferi Anomalies infected them."

"So how many are there?" Commandant Pierce's dark eyes were hard as stone.

"I don't know. I couldn't even begin to speculate." Dr. Curran lowered her eyes, her uneasiness clear.

"I need to speak to the president." Mr. Petersen glowered at Dr. Curran, then spun about on his heel. He motioned to two dark garbed SWD security officers to follow and walked briskly from the command center.

"He will not keep the Constabulary out of this! Castellan, you're in charge!" Commandant Pierce strode out after Mr. Petersen.

Dwayne caught Lindsey's eyes for just a second, then he returned to his work station. Dr. Curran drew closer, lingering just over his right shoulder.

"What else do you know that you're not telling me?" Dwayne asked the scientist.

Dr. Curran remained silent for so long, he looked up at her questioningly. There was definitely an internal struggle behind the woman's eyes. "Nothing that will affect the mission."

"Are you certain? Because if—"

"Yes, I'm certain," Dr. Curran answered.

Dwayne returned his gaze to the vid screens and the many fuzzy images filtering in from the basement of the hydroelectric station. He didn't trust anyone anymore but himself, Lindsey and Maria. The city was increasingly a dark and dangerous place.

* * *

When the dented metal door swung open, Chief Defender Omondi's face was the first thing Maria saw as he peered out at her.

"Vanguard, you're a sight for sore eyes," he said. The bluish light from his helmet gave him a spectral appearance, but his smile was genuine. Stepping into the narrow corridor, he appraised the soldiers clustered into the narrow hallway. The remainder of his squad hovered just behind him, waiting.

"We were hit pretty hard. We lost three." Maria handed over the extra weapon she had been carrying for him, then some ammo.

"There are a lot more of those bastards than we were told," Omondi agreed.

"We killed eleven on the way down." McKinney dangled the dog tags from one hand.

Omondi took them somberly. "There are a lot more than that."

"We know." Maria sighed. "And we're basically in the perfect place for an ambush."

"They'll be waiting for us upstairs." Omondi brushed past Maria, moving down the long corridor. "I never should have obeyed the order to enter the basement."

"Who told you to come down here?" Maria asked, anger edging her words. She followed in his wake, weapon at the ready.

"Mr. Petersen," Omondi answered.

Maria didn't respond. The feed to The Bastion was coming back online as they drew closer to the stairwell.

When they reached the heavily barricaded area, Omondi squatted next to the bodies of the Anomalies. He flipped on his helmet's light. He pulled their eyelids back, exposing their filmy eyes.

"These aren't the ones." Omondi killed the light, stood, and peered up the hallway.

"What do you mean?" Maria asked, dread filling her.

"The ones with the red eyes are the truly dangerous ones. I would call the ones down here drones. They're hungry bastards and fodder for their leaders. The ones with the red eyes are truly sentient in every way. But I didn't see too many of them. Maybe three."

As they continued to the stairwell, Omondi took control of the squad as his helmet finally picked up the feed from the command center. Maria was surprised when Omondi allowed her to keep the feed active in her helmet. She was glad he finally seemed willing to include her again in command decisions.

Arriving at the base of the stairs, they cautiously moved onto the steps. Weapons pointed upward, the squad hugged the far wall as they climbed. Maria felt her pulse accelerating again, a disconcerting feeling after it being absent so long. Her breath sounded abnormally loud and labored in her ears. She wondered if everyone else could hear it through her feed.

The squad reached the top of the stairs without incident. Omondi and Maria exchanged worried looks. The doors that opened to the stairwell were slightly ajar. The hallway beyond it would be perfect for an ambush. The tension between her shoulder blades was increasingly painful and she wished her armor wasn't so old. She was used to armor that responded to physical ailments with injections of painkillers or relaxants. Rolling her shoulders, she watched as McKinney and Holm proceeded ahead to open the doors. Scrutinizing the squad, she saw Cruz with her head tilted down, staring into the darkness below. It was no secret that Mikado and Cruz had been involved. Maria felt for Cruz, but there was no time to mourn right now. Denman saw Maria's scrutiny and tapped Cruz's shoulder, then gestured to pay attention. Cruz obeyed.

Maria directed her gaze to beyond the doorway.

The hall was also empty. Gutierrez's body was gone.

Reenacting the same procedure they had followed when entering the building, the squad crept ever so slowly toward the lobby at the far end. Door by door, room by room, they advanced cautiously. Each step was measured, each action stealthy. No one spoke, obeying Omondi's silent hand signals.

Maria was painfully aware of her beating heart and heavy breath. She muted her feed as a precaution. The rifle in her hand felt heavy and cumbersome. The building was oppressive in its darkness and stillness. The claustrophobic atmosphere weighed on her as they slipped into the main entrance area. The squad would have to curve around the lobby to reach the stairwells that led to the higher floors. It was the only way up since the elevators were dead.

Outside the empty windows a soft rain pattered against the broken asphalt. She flicked her night vision off and the world returned to the normal hues of an overcast day.

"Come out!" a male voice echoed through the lobby.

Omondi signaled to stop.

A figure shifted into view just beyond one of the windows. Even though the mysterious stranger was in silhouette it was clear that he was in armor and held a weapon. The squad immediately took cover. Maria slid down the wall behind an overturned table, Denman crouching adjacent to her.

"We realize we were...hasty in our attack on you earlier. We're not so...hungry now. We can think clearer now that we've fed." The man's voice was strangely familiar. It had a rich baritone to it and the hint of an accent.

Maria felt her heart speed up.

"Please, come out. We're all soldiers of the Constabulary of The Bastion. We're all Boon. We're brothers and sisters." The voice was calm, collected, and sounded reasonable.

It gave Maria the shivers.

Omondi was speaking in his helmet, but his feed was isolated from the squad as he contacted the command center.

"Please, come out. We won't attack. You have far superior weapons and can easily destroy us. We're in the open. Exposed. We wish only to talk. To discuss our situation. You may not realize it yet, but you're in just as dire a situation as we are."

A touch on Maria's arm drew her attention to Denman. From the concerned look his face, she discerned he had come to the same conclusion that she had. This was one of the original Inferi Boon.

"How do we know you won't attack?" Chief Defender Omondi called out.

"We have more in common than you realize. We're your future. What you will become. Do you think you will be allowed back into the city? We weren't. Do you think if there was a cure for us, they wouldn't have administered it? Instead, they cowered behind their wall hoping we wouldn't find a way back in. They betrayed us and they will betray you."

The restless shuffling of feet and shifting of bodies indicated that the squad found the stranger's words just as disconcerting as Maria did.

"Come out. Speak to us. See your future. We have to work together to get into the city and force them to cure us," the voice continued. "Come out and see what you'll become."

Omondi crawled over to Maria. "Keep the squad back and ready to respond if they attack."

"Are you sure you want to do this?"

Rubbing his lips together, Omondi nodded. "I cut the feed with command. I want to know what the fuck is going on out here."

Maria bobbed her head in agreement. "Understood, sir."

Omondi stood and cautiously approached the window. Maria and the others shadowed him, careful to keep under cover. The Chief Defender's imposing form neared the window and he peered out at the stranger standing in the rain.

"Come out, brother," the man said.

The Chief Defender obeyed.

* * *

Watching the vids, Dwayne slowly rubbed his chin, concentrating on the feed from Maria's helmet. She had muted her feed, and Omondi's had gone dark unexpectedly. Something was going on and he didn't like it.

"Vanguard Martinez, what is the status of the Chief Defender? I have lost his feed," Dwayne said curtly.

Her feed reopened, and she answered, "He has advanced in front of the squad. There appears to be an Anomaly outside the main entrance."

She wasn't answering his question directly.

"He cut it off on his end," Lindsey said, answering his earlier question.

Dr. Curran drew closer to Dwayne's station again. Concern and fear played over her features, deepening the furrow between her eyebrows and the lines around her mouth.

"Vanguard Martinez, I need for you to advance so I can see the Chief Defender," Dwayne instructed.

"Yes, sir," came the answer.

The camera on Maria's helmet continued to transmit a clear signal as she appeared to crawl toward an open window. He could hear her breathing and he shifted uncomfortably in his chair. The virus was definitely altering her, and he wondered what secrets the SWD was keeping about the virus from the Constabulary.

Gradually, the image of Chief Defender Omondi came into view. He stood just outside of one of the broken windows. Standing before him was a soldier in Constabulary armor that was dripping with blood and rain. The man's close-cropped wiry, curly hair glistened with droplets of water as the sun crept out from behind the dissipating storm clouds.

"Find out who that is," Dwayne ordered and the young man at the work station nearby immediately began scanning the databases.

"I know who it is," Maria's trembling voice said. "It's my father."

Her feed went dark.

* * *

Maria could barely believe what her eyes were telling her, but she knew the face of her father too well to deny the truth. Vanguard Mariano Martinez stood face to face with Chief Defender Omondi. He looked exactly how she remembered him. Dark curly hair, wide shoulders, tall frame, and skin a shade or two darker than her own. But his dark eyes were gone. In their place were gleaming red eyes and the warmth of his smile was replaced with cold cruelty.

"Who are you?" the Chief Defender asked.

"Vanguard Mariano Martinez of the Constabulary," he answered.

Out of the gray, misty rain appeared more figures. Two more people in Constabulary uniforms stepped into view. They, too, had the disturbing red eyes. One was a woman, the other a man. Both were smeared in blood. What was keenly unsettling about them was that, unlike the Inferi Scourge and the Anomalies, their faces were not vacant of thought. Their disturbing red eyes were obviously appraising Omondi.

"Special Sergeant Amber Alkan, Special Constable Gareth Reese and I are the only survivors of the fourth Inferi Boon mission," Mariano said.

"What happened to the first three missions?" Omondi asked, his demeanor calm, but his voice demanding.

Mariano smirked and glanced at his two companions. "Should I tell him?"

"He's on his way to joining us," the woman responded.

Her pale skin looked ghastly beneath the layer of blood and bits of flesh that was bit by bit sluicing away with the rain. Her brown hair was tucked away from her blood-smeared face. She wore a beret with a Constabulary emblem on it. The man standing behind her was as dark as night, tall, and leanly built.

"The first mission was a failure. The Inferi Boon turned Scourge within forty-eight hours. The SWD barely contained them from starting a new outbreak. The second mission was more successful. The squad went through training and were sent into the sewers to clear out some of the Scrags that had found their way into the system through a faulty hatch. They never returned. They turned into Scourge and were destroyed later by the third mission. They cleared out the sewers and exited through the hydroelectric plant. That mission cleared out a good portion of this area before turning Scourge. The fourth mission—us— we were the most successful. We never turned Scourge. But we became something much more dangerous."

"You're Anomalies. Cannibals. Feeding off of the dead and living." Omondi's words were tight and hard.

"Anomalies?" Mariano laughed. "I like that. We call the ones we turned Aberrations."

As Maria watched, more mutated Scourge crept out from hiding places. These Aberrations, as her father called them, also wore Constabulary uniforms, and Maria recognized a few among them, including her former commanding officer, Ren Stillson. They looked closer to the Scourge with their murky eyes and swift, jerky motions, but there was something intelligent and desperate in their gaze. There were over fifty of them.

"You created these others?" Omondi scrutinized the bloodied creatures standing at a distance. Though the Aberrations didn't make any hostile movements, Maria was unnerved by their presence. They were obviously of the same ilk as the mutated Scourge they had fought in the basement.

"We hunger. The hunger is madness. It drives us. At first we tried to assuage it with the food we salvaged from the farms, but it was never enough. Then we..." Mariano faltered, a spark of his humanity showing for a moment. It made Maria's heart ache for him. "One of us went mad and bit one of the Scrags. The flesh...it...helped with the pain of the hunger. For a while. When the Constabulary tried to expand the perimeter, a few of us were close enough to attack, bite, and feed. Our victims rose as Aberrations. They are simple-minded creatures, but they do as we tell them. They know if they help us, we can get back into the city and feed."

"We will not help you," Omondi said in a dangerous voice. "We came out here to save the city, not destroy it."

"You're going to be what we are! Soon the hunger will be so great, the pain of it so overwhelming, you will do anything to placate it!"

The madness in his eyes and voice were terrifying. Mariano wouldn't be reasoned with. That was painfully obvious. The loving father she once adored was gone. He had been replaced with a cold, calculating creature.

Maria shifted her weight, moving into a better position to fire if required. Against Omondi's orders, she signaled the squad to move into an offensive position.

"So you're going to invade the city you swore to protect and kill its people?" Omondi asked incredulously.

"We will make the SWD cure us! We will kill until they realize that to survive they *must* cure us!" Mariano shouted. "We gave our lives to save the city and it abandoned us!"

"We're soldiers of the Constabulary. It's our honor to give our lives in service to protect the last of humanity. It's a sacred duty," Omondi growled out.

"We're your future! We're what you will become! Soon you'll be tearing into flesh just to slake the pain in your gut and the madness in your mind!" Mariano took a dangerous step toward Omondi, his body coiled as if to strike. Pointing an accusing finger at the Chief Defender, Mariano said, "Do not act the innocent! You came looking for us! You knew we were here all along! Did you tell your people? Did you warn them of what they'll become?"

Out of the corner of her eye, Maria could see the uneasy movements of the squad. Holm turned her head to look at Denman, then at Maria, her eyes questioning.

"There's no happy ending for us! There is no cure for the Inferi Boon Virus. Or the Inferi Scourge Virus. They lied to all of us! We came out here to fight their war and we killed for them until the hunger was shredding us. We were going mad with the agony." Mariano pointed at himself. "I listened to my commanding officer beg the SWD for med-pods. He begged them to come get us. We were in unbearable agony, immobilized, desperate. They refused us. Our Med-Specialist reported our condition faithfully to the SWD, recommending immediate evacuation before we worsened. They refused. And when they realized we had become what they fear most, they stopped answering us. They sent a virus to our wristlets, deactivating them. They thought we would black out and cease to be their concern. But we didn't. We stayed awake, hungry, and mad."

"So you're the reason why they finally shut down the subways." Omondi slightly moved his weight to one side, a casual move, but one that placed his hand closer to his weapon.

"When there were more of us, we were able to breach the system a few times. Our last incursion was a few months ago. We had collected the weapons left behind when the mission to expand the perimeter failed. We salvaged what we could from the armor and equipment left behind. We failed and lost many of our...Anomalies. It's difficult to..."

Mariano wavered on his feet slightly. "It's difficult to think when the hunger is so intense. Only living flesh makes it go away entirely. The flesh of the Scourge only takes the edge off of it. "

"You killed Inferi Boon!" Omondi's voice was a sharp bark of anger.

"We *hunger*!" Mariano bared his teeth.

Maria felt tears in her eyes. This was the man who had meant so much to her, altered, changed, and monstrous.

"Did you eat each other? Did you attack each other?"

There were uneasy looks among the three.

"Did you?" Omondi persisted.

"The hunger creates insanity. There were incidents in the beginning, but we banded together to try to fight the hunger." Alkan's voice was cold, devoid of emotion.

"But you hunted us like animals and killed us. Ate us!" Omondi seemed even bigger and more imposing.

Mariano took several sharp steps toward him and screamed, "We were hungry! We were irrational and...and..."

"You're irrational now!" Omondi lashed out and gripped the man by one of the straps on his armor. Shaking him, Omondi shouted, "We're Constabulary! We protect the city! We protect each other!"

"I want to go home! I want to see my family! I want to not be a monster!" Mariano bellowed in Omondi's face, his red eyes wide and frantic.

Alkan and Reese began to walk swiftly toward the two grappling men. The Aberrations tracked behind them.

Maria cursed as she lifted her weapon, aiming at Alkan. "Holm, take out Martinez if you have to."

The other woman nodded.

In the time since her father's death, Maria had longed to see him one last time. To hold him in her arms and tell him how much she loved him. It was cruel irony that she was able to see him one last time just to watch him die. Maria activated the exterior speaker on her helmet.

Mariano and Omondi continued to shout at each other, each struggling to wrestle the other man to the ground.

"Release him, Vanguard Martinez!" Maria shouted, her voice strong.

Mariano froze, his gaze searching along the blank face of the building.

"Step away from the Chief Defender now!" Maria ordered.

"Maria?" Mariano questioned. He pulled away from Omondi, his red eyes sweeping back and forth over the empty windows.

Taking a deep breath, Maria steadied her nerves. "*Si, papa.*"

"*Mi hija, ¿dónde estás?*"

Maria tentatively stepped into view, her gun swinging toward her father in a slow arc. His red eyes fixed on her and she feared he would attack. She was not a Scourge, Boon, Anomaly, or Aberration. As the seconds ticked away, she realized she and the others were something very different. Dr. Curran had created a new creature altogether.

"Speak to me as an officer," Maria said in a tense voice.

"You're here. One of us," her father said. He was utterly shocked by her appearance and he released Omondi.

She nodded.

Omondi drew his weapon. "Tell your people to fall back, Mr. Martinez."

Mariano hesitated, then waved his hand. The Anomalies and Aberrations ceased stalking toward the building, but their stances were that of predators, waiting and watching.

Mariano studied his daughter's face. "Maria, do you know how Inferi Scourge identify each other?" Mariano's red eyes shifted to gaze into her eyes.

The other creatures were staring at her as well.

"Sight," Maria said at last.

"No. The virus within our blood tells us who is one of us and who is not. Maybe it's the virus whispering in our cells like a communal brain, or maybe it's somehow hidden in your scent. I look at you and I *know* you're Inferi Boon. Everything inside of me says you're one of us. Yet, you look human."

Maria shifted her weight slightly. "What's your point?"

"Inferi Scourge cannot think for themselves. They're creatures of instinct. If the virus inside of them says you're one of them, then they will not attack. Right?"

Maria shrugged. "They can be dangerous when stimulated by the possibility of prey."

"Sure. But when you're standing face to face with one, far away from the...humans, they know you're one of them. They're not going to wake up and attack you."

Narrowing her eyes, Maria wondered what he was driving at.

"*Mi hija,* I'm not Inferi Scourge. I can *think*! I can *see*! I can choose my actions. Right?" Mariano grinned at her, his red eyes disturbing with their brightness.

"What is your damn point?" Omondi demanded.

"My point is that I can choose to go against the virus. I can decide for myself what I will and will not do. If I wanted to, I could attack you, kill you, devour you because I can *think and override* my instinct that says you're Inferi Scourge!" Mariano noted her discomfort at his words. "Of course, I would never do that to my own daughter. But I have to ask, *mija*...what are you?"

Omondi's gaze shifted toward Maria. "Vanguard?"

"I'm Inferi Boon," Maria finally answered. "Just like you. Just like the people you murdered and ate!"

Mariano's mad eyes were fever bright. "Then what you are...it's in us. If it's in your people, then it's now in us." He grinned with delight, turning toward his two companions. "It's in us! We'll be what she is!

The humans will not realize what we are until it's too late!"

The echo of the short bark of the rifle rang out around her. Mariano slumped to the pavement. Within a second, both sides opened fire. The projectile weapons of the Anomalies and Aberrations propelled shrapnel through the air. Maria fell to the ground to avoid the onslaught. She could see her father's slack face in a pool of blood. She felt both relieved and sorrowful at the sight.

Omondi snagged her arm as he barreled past her, dragging her behind him. Hurtling her through the window, he followed. They both crawled into cover.

"I'm activating my feed and reporting in," Omondi said, his eyes fastened to her face. She could see the disbelief in his expression. He could now see what her dead father had witnessed. Maria was no longer a dead thing. She was alive.

Sliding onto her knees, she caught an Aberration in her crosshairs and fired.

Chapter 32

When the doors to the command center opened and Mr. Petersen entered, followed by the president and his council, Dwayne knew that what was about to happen wouldn't be to his liking. Commandant Pierce stepped into the room after the primary entourage and sought out his gaze immediately. Dwayne rose to attention.

"Castellan Reichardt, you and your people are dismissed," President Cabot said. His demeanor and voice were devoid of his earlier briskness. If anything, he sounded slightly afraid.

"Mr. President," Dwayne started, but saw the commandant shaking her head. Instead of voicing his protest, Dwayne saluted and slipped past the gloating Mr. Petersen. Lindsey and the other soldiers of the Constabulary slid to their feet and followed him.

"Dr. Curran, thank you for your dedication to this mission, but we're no longer in need of your services," the president said as he turned to face the beleaguered scientist.

"I am still collecting data from the field," Dr. Curran started to protest.

Mr. Petersen gently took her by the arm and escorted her across the command center. She walked with him, confused and alarmed. "You've done a splendid job, Beverly, but your services are no longer needed in this matter."

More SWD personnel filed into the room, pressing past the exiting Constabulary people. Dwayne was nearly to the doorway when Admiral Kirkpatrick stepped through. Wearing his white uniform, many medals, and silvery hair and beard with pride, the leader of the SWD gave him a bright, triumphant smile. The man was legendary at seventy-five years of age. He had won battles against the Inferi Scourge before the final fall of humanity. He alone retained his rank from the armies before The Bastion Constabulary was created. Rarely seen in public since he had assumed command of the SWD, he was a mysterious figure that drew much speculation from the media. He only appeared at the most prestigious events. Dwayne was startled when the admiral gripped his hand, shook it, smiled, then walked on. A bit dazed, Dwayne stared after him in surprise. With Mr. Petersen at the forefront of the Inferi Boon project, he had speculated that perhaps the admiral was ill. This appeared not to be the case.

Commandant Pierce motioned for Dwayne to hurry and he crossed through the threshold into the corridor. The Constabulary soldiers stood waiting along with Caitlyn. Dr. Curran was virtually shoved into the hallway by Mr. Petersen.

"Your contributions to our impending victory are appreciated. I shall make a notation of each and every one of your excellent execution of your duties." Mr. Petersen smiled one last time and the door shut.

Dwayne gaze flicked upwards to watch the panel above the door. It turned red. They were locked out.

"What are we going to do?" Lindsey asked.

Commandant Pierce lifted her finger to her lips, then gestured for them to follow her. Dr. Curran stared at the locked door in confusion and Dwayne lightly touched her shoulder.

"Why don't you come with us?"

Dr. Curran nodded and fell into step with him.

Caitlyn was leaning against the wall giving her father her notorious dagger eyes. She shoved off with one elbow and strode alongside him.

"Don't you have work to do?"

"I've been dismissed for the day," Caitlyn answered. "I think I'll tag along with my dear *old* dad, if you don't mind."

Dwayne slightly smiled as he wrapped his arm around her shoulders. "Your dear *old* dad is glad you're coming along."

"Not when you hear what I have to say," Caitlyn warned him.

Sighing, Dwayne suspected he was going to get an earful about Maria. Fear and desperation tore at him as he thought of Maria facing down the creatures he had briefly glimpsed on the monitors. He had faith in her abilities and those of the other soldiers, but he worried about Maria's safety.

The sooner they were back at the Constabulary, the quicker they could find out what exactly was going on.

* * *

The Aberration fell to its knees, blood exploding out of its torn throat. Maria's next shot sheared off its head.

There were at least fifty yards between the attacking Aberrations and remaining Anomalies and the building. And they were advancing quickly.

Maria ejected the cartridge from her gun and reached for another one. She was shocked to find only one left. "I'm running low on ammo," she called out.

"We all are," Denman grunted, firing at her side.

Maria slammed the cartridge home and aimed at another Aberration. Stillson was as fast in his new incarnation as he had been in life. He moved swiftly from cover to cover, darting between the stone benches and massive empty cement planters where lush decorative foliage had once bloomed. Maria kept trying to get a bead on him, but he seemed to know she was tracking him and kept dodging out of view.

The Anomalies called out to the Aberrations, ordering them to move in. Maria had lost track of the Anomalies once her father had been killed. She still didn't know who had fired the shot, but she suspected it was Omondi. As the gunfire echoed around her, she tried not to think of her father's broken body on the ground. Her squad depended on her.

"That fucker is fast," Denman grunted, trying to pin down Stillson.

Maria was about to answer when Aberrations attacked from a flanking position. They had swung around to pin the Boon into the building. Maria redirected her aim, Denman following her example. They opened fire, their guns unloading their precious ammunition.

Her helmet screen was full of information. Omondi's voice echoed in her head. His orders were precise and wise. The squad was barely keeping the Aberrations at bay.

"The gunfire is going to draw the Scrags," Maria said, carefully aiming at the charging Aberrations.

There were more than they had realized. Many more. She tried not to fire randomly, but to make every shot count. Yet, the Aberrations were closing in as the Anomalies continued to shout out orders. As the Aberrations' weapons clicked empty, they discarded them and charged the Boon, wicked blades in their hands.

Several Aberrations reached a window on the far side and leaped through the ruined facade. Holm cut them down as McKinney continued to cover her. Another breach further up the line had the Boon pinned down

Maria saw her ammo counter was going to reach zero soon, and she felt her heart accelerating. "Almost out."

"So am I," Denman said grimly.

"Fuck." Maria fired her last shot and swung her rifle around onto her back. She was reaching for her bolt weapon when Stillson darted out from his nearby position, charging her. He, too, was out of ammunition, and tossed his makeshift weapon as he ran. Even without the projectile weapon, he was incredibly dangerous.

"Hungry!" he roared.

Snagging the dagger she had tucked into her armor, she took a deep breath and leaped out of the window. She met Stillson head on. Ducking under his first blow, she swiped her dagger at his hamstring. The rusted blade slipped across the hard casing of his armor. Allowing momentum to carry her, she rolled past him, tumbling onto her hip before pushing up with her hands. He twisted around and swung his huge fist down at her helmeted head. The power of the blow sent her reeling, falling onto her hands and knees. Another blow to the back of the helmet jarred it loose as the feed and readouts went dead. Maria kicked out, slamming her boot into his kneecap, knocking him off balance. As he fell, she whipped the broken helmet off her head and got to her feet.

The chatter of weapons dissipated. Now the Boon and Anomalies fought hand-to-hand, blades flashing, bolt weapons wielded like clubs, and curses and howls filled the air.

Before Stillson could get to his feet, Maria battered his head with her helmet. Blood splattered her as she brought the helmet down repeatedly. Stillson growled an ungodly noise and snagged her arm as it descended toward him again. Yanking her off her feet, he tossed her to the ground. As she tumbled, Maria lost the helmet, but managed to hold onto the dagger. She rolled to her feet.

Flipping her braid back over her shoulder, Maria crouched on the ground. Near her, Stillson's dropped blade glinted in the fading sunlight. Keeping watch on Stillson as he wiped the blood from his eyes and clambered to his feet, Maria reached out and snagged the blade.

"Hungry!" Stillson howled, then charged.

Heart thundering, Maria sprang into action, avoiding his desperate, angry blows. She was faster than he was and used it to her advantage. His ruined face bayed in anger as he thrashed about, trying to snag her as she darted around him. There was no way she could cut through his armor. His exposed head was her only hope.

Another Aberration clutched Maria's arm as she attempted to slip past Stillson to attack from behind. Punching the female Aberration in the face, Maria knocked her back. Another swift kick to the chest sent the female Aberration sprawling. Maria barely twisted out of the way of Stillson's mighty fist and fell beside the stunned Aberration. Shrugging off the bolt weapon and rifle harnesses, she spun onto her knees. Stillson kicked her in the chest, toppling her to the ground. He dove forward, trying to pin her, and she skirted away just before he impacted with the earth. The blades still clutched in her hands, she scrambled onto Stillson. The huge Aberration started to push upward as the female scrabbled at Maria, trying to grip her.

Digging her knees into Stillson's sides, Maria rammed the dagger in her left hand into the woman's neck. She ripped the blade out through the flesh, tearing out the Aberration's throat. With her other hand, she thrust the knife into Stillson's meaty neck. The female Aberration attacked again. Maria slammed the dagger down into her skull. The creature fell as Stillson rose fully to his feet, Maria riding his back.

She clutched the empty rifle harness attached to his chest armor and wrapped her legs around his waist to secure herself. Yanking the knife out of his neck, she hacked at it as he twisted around, yowling in rage. Concentrating on killing him, Maria couldn't allow herself to think of the man he used to be.

Denman tackled both of them to the ground. Stillson landed on his side, pinning Maria partially under him. His huge hand closed on Denman's throat as the med-specialist rammed his small bolt gun into the side of Stillson's throat. Bucking wildly, Stillson dislodged Denman. Maria yanked the knife out of Stillson's flesh and pounded it into his skull over and over again. She didn't even note when he stopped moving.

"He's dead," Denman gasped, pushing the heavy man off Maria. He gripped her blood-slicked hand and dragged her to her feet.

Breathing heavily, but not feeling truly winded, Maria's eyes scrutinized the battle scene around them. Most of the Aberrations were dead. Only a few remained fighting. Some of the Boon were also dead. A few Aberrations were crouched over one fallen Boon, tearing at his face. Omondi dispatched them with mighty blows from his bolt weapon.

Maria could hear the swelling cries of the Scourge as they rushed toward the station. Gripping Denman's hand, she gazed at him with frightened eyes.

"You're not human," Denman said with certainty.

The last of the Aberrations finally fell and the remainder of the squad stood in the blood drenched entrance of the building. Holm was badly wounded and leaned against McKinney. Cruz was barely standing. Omondi stood covered in blood and gore, a somber expression upon his face.

The howls of the Scourge grew louder.

"We should get in the carrier and get out of here," Maria finally said.

"No need." Omondi pointed toward The Bastion.

Maria turned to see tiltrotors rising above the city walls.

"They're coming to get us," Omondi said, relief in his voice. "This is nearly over."

* * *

As soon as Commandant Pierce and her entourage arrived at the Constabulary, she dispatched most of the staff to the Constabulary Command Center.

"We need Special Sergeant Rooney," Dwayne said, motioning for Lindsey to stay. He knew Lindsey would be able to find out the status of the Inferi Boon soldiers. He kept assuring himself that Maria could handle herself out on the field and that she was fine. But he wanted confirmation.

"Very well," the commandant answered, then directed her focus to Dr. Curran. "You and I need to speak."

Dr. Curran's mouth twisted into a sour shape, her eyes staring at her pad intently.

"Dr. Curran, are you listening to me?"

"Yes, I am, Commandant Pierce. But I don't know how I can help you. I am SWD." She added as an afterthought, "At least I think I still am."

"Don't be so sure," the commandant said.

Turning, she briskly led Dwayne, Caitlyn, Lindsey and Dr. Curran into the heart of the Constabulary. Dwayne was surprised when they arrived at his office. Petra looked up from her desk as they passed and he motioned for her to follow. She quickly fell into step. Once inside the room, Commandant Pierce motioned for him to lock it.

"Room lockdown. No transmissions in or out until I specify," she said.

Dwayne lifted his eyebrows at the commandant.

"My office is bugged," she answered with a shrug.

Lindsey put a finger to her lips, tugged out a pad that appeared to have been modified, and swept the room. Petra watched Lindsey thoughtfully while Caitlyn nervously took her father's hand. Dr. Curran merely sighed and sat down heavily in a chair.

Commandant Pierce looked at Dwayne curiously, then slowly grinned as she fit the pieces together. "You're one step ahead source, huh?" She pointed to Lindsey.

Dwayne shrugged.

Petra arched an eyebrow, looking slightly insulted.

"I am a man of many resources," Dwayne admitted.

That mollified Petra and amused the commandant.

Lindsey climbed onto a chair and laid her pad against the wall. She swiftly tapped away on it before jumping back down.

"We're clear now."

"We need to find out what is going on out there," Dwayne started.

"It can wait. We have other matters to deal with," Commandant Pierce said, holding up a hand. "Have faith that our people can defend themselves."

Dwayne started to protest, when Dr. Curran started to get to her feet.

"I don't know why I'm here," Dr. Curran said.

Commandant Pierce shoved the doctor into the chair. "Stay right here, Dr. Curran. Trust me. Be glad we made it back to the Constabulary."

"What are you talking about?" Dwayne asked.

"We're in the middle of a coup d'état," Commandant Pierce answered simply.

"What?" Dwayne felt the blood rushing out of his head and he felt a little faint for a second.

"She's not lying, Dad. I was there," Caitlyn said somberly.

"Admiral Kirkpatrick is about to seize control of the entire city. The president was informed today that he should be prepared to resign for the greater good of the people. Admiral Kirkpatrick made it very clear to the president and the council that the SWD is not to be reckoned with. They're going to clear the valley with what remains of our armament, then take full credit. Therefore, in a few weeks, when President Cabot announces that despite the victory over the Inferi Scourge there is still a dire food shortage and that he is declaring martial law until the crises is over, he is going to take the brunt of the blame. He will later resign and Admiral Kirkpatrick will officially take over."

"What the hell?" Dwayne stared at the commandant incredulously.

"I was informed by Admiral Kirkpatrick that he expects my full cooperation and that of the Constabulary. I told him he has it. Of course, I was lying." Commandant Pierce folded her arms over her breasts. "I was a fool. I should have realized what was happening. They weren't preparing for a Section A evacuation. You have provided them with the solution to the food riots. Strip away the evacuation and what do you have left?"

Dwayne felt a cold chill whisper down his spine. "Specific plans on how to control the population, where to assign the armed forces..."

"Exactly." Commandant Pierce shook her head in disbelief. "How could I have not seen it? All the food supplies have been compiled in one secure location that the SWD now controls. They control the food. They control the armaments of the city. They control the president.

They control everything. And we were all blind fools."

"Is this why they sent only one squad out to kill millions of Scrags? To give them time to maneuver? To build public support?" Dwayne leaned back against his desk, his jaw dropping in amazement. "Dammit, it's so perfect!"

"What's happening?" Petra asked softly. "I don't understand."

Lindsey handed Petra her pad. "Read this. It's my summary of what has been going on outside the wall. I've been preparing it just in case I have to leak it to the press."

Commandant Pierce started in surprise, then laughed. "I was about to say we're fucked since we have no proof of what has been going on. I see I was wrong."

"Oh, if you need proof, I have it," Lindsey assured her.

"And I have the backups." Dwayne grinned at Lindsey despite the sick feeling in his gut.

Caitlyn joined Petra in reviewing all that Lindsey had compiled.

"We've all been so expertly played. Even today. All that fuss about the Inferi Boon and the weapons. It pushed the president to order the clearing of the valley. Which is what they wanted. He played into Mr. Petersen's hands, giving the official order that seals his doom." Commandant Pierce hung her head. "We were fools."

"Once the president signed off on the attack, that gave the SWD everything they needed. They can now move forward legally...until they force the President's hand." Dwayne rubbed his face. "He gave them the city."

"It's rather amazing. I should have never let them keep me out of such vital planning and kept you, Castellan, in the dark of what I knew." Commandant Pierce paced back and forth before Dwayne's desk. She would give her head a shake every few seconds, the look of disbelief not leaving her features.

Dr. Curran stared down at her pad, her silence disconcerting.

Dwayne lightly touched her shoulder, pulling her attention to him. "There has to be a way to sort this out, right?"

"It doesn't matter, Castellan Reichardt. We were all pawns and it's too late now." She looked years older now. It was evident she had not realized the full extent of the conspiracy within the SWD, if at all.

"We can release the information Lindsey compiled," Dwayne suggested.

"If we leak the information about how the SWD cleared the valley, the citizens of The Bastion won't care. They'll be thankful to the SWD for freeing them from the Inferi Scourge." Dr. Curran slumped in her chair. "They've won. They have control."

"We'll just have Maria tell them that they—that *you* lied to her!" Lindsey leaned heavily on her cane, glaring at the doctor. "You totally fucked her up and didn't even tell her what you were doing."

"I did what I believed was right," Dr. Curran said defensively, then deflated again. "It doesn't matter anyway. Maria won't be able to tell the media what happened out there."

"If the SWD confines the veterans of the mission, won't that be suspicious?" Petra asked.

"I have important information about that," Caitlyn said softly. Her vivid blue eyes gazed at Dwayne sadly as she reached out and took his hand in hers. Dwayne could feel his daughter's fingers trembling and he wanted to pull her into his arms and comfort her like he had when she was a little girl. "Sometimes Secretary Mayburn forgets I'm still in the office, or maybe he just doesn't care about security clearance. He sometimes speaks openly about confidential matters. I've just ignored it until today. I overhead something that really bothered me."

Leaning toward her, Dwayne tried to give her a reassuring look. "What is it, Caitlyn?"

With a sigh, she tucked her blond hair back from her face, her wristlet catching the lamp light, flashing brightly for a moment. Obviously struggling with words, or maybe having second thoughts about confiding in the people in the office, his daughter took a moment before responding. At last she said, "The soldiers clearing the Inferi Scourge from the valley...they're not coming back."

Dwayne stared at her, mouth agape, trying to process her words. "What?"

Commandant Pierce lowered her eyes as Lindsey swore impressively. Petra sat down heavily in a chair, clutching Lindsey's pad. Dr. Curran sighed sorrowfully.

"They're not letting them back into the city, Dad. I know they're Constabulary soldiers. They're your people. I was afraid that you were part of that decision until I heard all of this. But I should have known better."

"Shit," Dwayne exhaled. "Shit."

"It makes sense in a terrible way," Commandant Pierce said angrily. "The SWD created its own thinking Inferi Scourge, used them to clear the valley, and will dispose of them to ensure there's no risk of further infection. There was never any cure for Maria and the others. It's all been a lie, hasn't it, Dr. Curran?"

Dr. Curran shifted around in her chair so she could glare at the commandant. "I've been working on a cure since I successfully made Vanguard Martinez into the first viable thinking Inferi Scourge. All other scientists before me had failed, but she was perfection. I did lie to her and the others. I knew that there was a possibility that they would be destroyed, but I didn't think it would really happen. Mr. Petersen swore that he would give me the time to develop a cure. I modified the virus. I was convinced I could discover a way to turn it off."

"And did you?" Lindsey spat out. "Did you find your fucking cure?"

Dr. Curran began to laugh, hysteria edging the sound. "I never had to find a cure!"

Dwayne gripped the armrests, leaning down to gaze into her face, his anger barely held in check. "You're allowing them to die!"

"That's not what I mean!" Dr. Curran waved her pad at them. "I received some very important intel today that no one but I has seen. The SWD doesn't possess this information, not that it would change anything."

"What are you talking about, you stupid bitch?" Lindsey shouted.

"Stand down, Rooney," Commandant Pierce ordered, her expression curious.

Dwayne glared at the scientist. "Make yourself clear. Now."

"The modified virus I gave the Inferi Boon was the closest we had to the original virus."

"Original virus?" Commandant Pierce arched her eyebrows. "The Inferi Scourge Plague Virus?"

"No, no." Dr. Curran poked Dwayne in the chest. "Get out of my face and I'll tell you."

Dwayne complied. It was probably the best idea because he was close to losing his temper. He tried to estimate how much time he might possibly have to start a public groundswell to bring the Inferi Boon back into the city. It would probably take them another few days to completely clear the valley after they killed the Anomalies.

"The original virus was a gift. We, humanity, didn't realize it at the time. A gift that landed in the ocean and every nation on earth raced to discover what had fallen from the heavens and still remained visible on satellite and radar."

"You're talking about extraterrestrial?" Lindsey said in a dubious tone.

Dr. Curran nodded. "Oh, yes. It was. What was discovered in international waters was a capsule that contained several strange containers. One had the most beautiful fabric ever seen by human eyes. The others contained mineral specimens. And one contained vials of the virus." Dr. Curran sighed. "The *original* virus."

"I don't remember any of this from history," Petra said in a cross tone. "I don't believe it."

"Well, for once the nations of the earth cooperated in keeping humanity in the dark about what had been discovered. The Unified Nations of Earth Council determined that since there was no message within the capsule, we had to regard it as a possible weapon. The virus and other objects were secured at the Unified Nations of Earth Disease Control Laboratory. It wasn't until nearly a decade later that it was discovered that the virus samples had been stolen one by one over the years. The Inferi Scourge Plague Virus appeared soon after. The virus I used to create the Inferi Boon was recovered from the laboratory of the United Eastern Seaboard States of America. According to the data recovered alongside the virus, it had only been modified slightly."

"What is your point?" Lindsey shouted at her.

"My point, little girl, is that we were idiots!" Dr. Curran stood up and held out her pad. "We were fools! We began altering and experimenting with the virus before we even knew what it was meant to do!"

"There wasn't a message. You said so!" Lindsey's face flushed red beneath her blond hair.

"There was a message, wasn't there?" Commandant Pierce said in a soft, dangerous voice.

"The fabric...scientists didn't realize until much later, when it was far too late, that it was the fabric that held the message. The actual weave itself was a language. The virus was a gift. Immortality, perfect health. The minerals, building blocks for utopia. Somewhere, out there, we have benefactors." Dr. Curran sighed wistfully. "Though if they have been watching for the last one hundred years, I'm sure they regret their gift. By the time we understood what the virus was for it was too late. No pure sample of the virus remained, and the Inferi Scourge were nearly done finishing us off."

"The virus you gave the Inferi Boon was not altered as much, so what does that mean?" Caitlyn asked.

"It means that the virus is doing what it was originally intended to do. It's restoring the Inferi Boon slowly back to life. I've been keeping close tabs on Maria Martinez without the SWD's knowledge. No, I didn't trust them either. The virus is restoring her, healing her. Already I have seen some dramatic changes in her scans that she may not even be aware of yet."

"What does that mean for the rest of us?" Petra asked, her hand pressed to her breast. "We're going to be immortal?"

"The last of the virus is in the Inferi Boon. Out there." Dr. Curran waved her hand. "Everything was destroyed once they were dispatched. All samples of the virus were eliminated. Gone. This was our last ditch effort in every way. If the Inferi Boon failed, we'd all die anyway."

"Immortality is in Maria's veins and the SWD don't even know it," Lindsey said in awe.

"No. They don't. I didn't even realize it until today. And now it's too late," Dr. Curran said with a heavy sigh.

"We must have a few days until they clear the valley. If we compile all the information we have and release it to the news media, we can undermine the SWD," Dwayne said. The passion in his voice revealed that his control had slipped and he struggled to regain it.

"Maybe," Dr. Curran said thoughtfully.

"I'll start right away." Lindsey snatched her pad back from the still stunned Petra.

"It's already too late," Caitlyn said softly. "They're going to wipe out the Inferi Boon today. That was what I was going to tell you. They may already be dead."

"That's why they sent us out of the command center!" Commandant Pierce's fury was tangible. "Of course!"

Dwayne felt his anger fade away into an almost paralyzing numbness. All hope of saving Maria was fading fast.

"Her wristlet!" Lindsey shouted at Dwayne! "Call her!"

With trembling fingers, he activated the secret program, praying that he wasn't too late.

Chapter 33

Maria cleaned the dagger on her armor, her eyes on the approaching tiltrotor. Shoving the blade into the sheath on her armor, she stood with her feet apart to steady herself. She felt slightly lightheaded from the blows Stillson had administered, but the pain he had inflicted was quickly receding.

Denman stood beside her, his hand on her shoulder. "We're almost out of here."

Tears pricked at her eyes. Thoughts of Dwayne filled her mind and she longed to feel his arms around her. She wondered how long it would take for the Boon to be returned to life.

"I have to admit," Omondi said in a raspy voice, "that I felt they had abandoned us. But when you came to rescue us with the SWD's blessing, I knew I was wrong."

The Boon drew together, some limping, others being carried. Out of the forty that had started together, Maria was horrified to see only ten remained.

McKinney held up both Holm and Cruz, his big boyish face in a grin. "I'm going to get shitfaced the second I'm alive," he decided.

Cruz's tiny frame sank to the ground. Sobs without tears rocked her as she clutched her hands prayerfully before her. "We can't even bury our dead."

Maria knew she was speaking of Mikado and she reached out to touch the smaller woman's head gently.

Cruz gazed up at Maria and whispered, "But it was worth it, right?"

"Yeah," Maria assured her. "It was worth it. We saved humanity."

"We're heroes," McKinney declared, relishing the word. "We're fucking heroes. I want a statue. A big one."

Omondi laughed despite everything. "Well, you deserve it. We all do. Especially our fallen."

Holm tried to speak, but what emerged from her mouth were barely words or sounds. But Maria could make out the gist of it. She had said Cormier's name.

"Gather around," Omondi ordered, digging into his pack. He withdrew small flares and struck them against the ground. They lit up as he formed a circle around the remaining survivors of the Inferi Boon Special Ops.

Maria's wristlet buzzed against her skin. It wasn't the jolt sent to activate her nervous system, but the buzz to indicate Dwayne's call was coming in. Startled, she gazed at the wristlet in confusion. It buzzed again, an urgent sensation against her battered flesh.

No one around her seemed to notice. They were all staring intently at the fleet of tiltrotors whirling over the approaching Inferi Scourge. There was a flash from the lead aircraft and then the earth below it was on fire, the Scourge caught in an inferno. The Boon cheered. More flashes from the other tiltrotors were followed by a conflagration on the ground.

Maria's wristlet kept buzzing. Unsure of what to do, she glanced over her shoulder. The carrier loomed nearby. She hesitated, but a quick look at the squad told her they were too busy watching the beautiful sight of the tiltrotors destroying the mob of Scourge heading their way.

As quietly as possible and trying not to draw attention, Maria hurried toward the carrier. She heard footfalls and cast a quick look over her shoulder to see Denman tailing her with curiosity in his eyes. Ducking around the carrier, she activated the secret program.

"Honey, I'm coming home. Can this wait?" she said with a grin.

"Maria, run! Hide! The SWD issued a kill order for the Inferi Boon!"

She only had a second to register Dwayne's terrified expression before she heard another volley of missiles hitting the ground. Denman stood near her, staring at her wristlet in confusion.

"What do you mean?" Maria finally asked.

"Run! They're going to kill all of you! Hide!"

"We need to warn the others!" Maria gasped. She grabbed Denman's arm, yanking him after her.

As she was about to clear the side of the carrier, she saw the last of the Inferi Boon Special Ops waving frantically at the approaching fleet of tiltrotors. They were cheering and leaping, overjoyed at the sight of the lead tiltrotor moving steadily toward them.

Denman yanked her backward.

"Omondi!" Maria screamed.

The big, beautiful black man with the wonderful smile threw out his arms to welcome the tiltrotor crew. It was the last she ever saw of him as the crew on the aircraft unleashed their arsenal and the Boon was engulfed in a firestorm. The tiny form of Cruz disappeared in a wash of fire. McKinney and Holm staggered briefly out of the blaze before being engulfed again.

Denman dragged Maria around and pulled her after him. She instinctively ran with him in the shadow of the carrier, then bolted around a low wall that encircled the station. Hunched over, they scurried along the wall, waiting for the blast of fire that would engulf them. The tiltrotors continued to hover as they fired at the carrier and the building. Flaming debris filled the scorching hot air and Maria choked as they fled. Reaching the side of the building, they broke into full sprints now that they were out view of the tiltrotors.

"Keep running!" Denman shouted. "Aim for the lake!"

The massive building next to them shuddered as eruptions within the concrete walls resounded through the dying day. In the distance, the Maelstrom Platforms roared to life. This was it. The final push. The day the Inferi Scourge would be completely wiped from the valley.

As they arrived at the rear of the building, Maria saw that the ground sloped straight into the dark waters of the lake. More explosions rent the air, hot wind and ash swirling around her. Denman ran straight into the waves lapping up on shore.

Casting a hasty look over her shoulder, Maria saw that some of the tiltrotors were moving on to attack other locations, but the ones remaining to destroy the station were drifting their way. She wasn't sure they had been seen.

Wading into the water, she felt her armor pulling her down. Gasping, she pressed on into the shadow of the dam. Denman vanished beneath the waves, then reappeared further away. He didn't have to breathe anymore, but her lungs were functional again.

She dove under and tried to swim through the murky water, fish and underwater plants flowing around her. The armor kept dragging her into the deeper depths of the blue lake. Kicking furiously, she held her breath. Finally, afraid at how deep she was sinking, she swam toward the surface. It took many hard, fast kicks to get her even near the top. Denman emerged from the murk, gripped her under the arms and helped her swim upward.

They crested the waves halfway along the dam. Maria's lungs ached, but she was surprised at how far she had managed to swim. Denman's hands tugged at her armor, unclasping it. In the shadow of the dam, they bobbed on the choppy waves as more fireballs erupted out of the station.

The Maelstrom Platforms growled to life again in the distance and the world was full of smoke.

They managed to disconnect the top of Maria's armor from the bottom half and let it sink away.

"Better?" Denman asked.

She nodded, feeling more buoyant. Her undershirt stuck to her skin, but the water felt wonderful.

"Okay, we keep along the dam until we can get to those trees over there." He pointed to a thin line of pines growing up against a steep incline. "We need to get into the foothills."

"Do you think they know we're alive?" Maria asked.

Denman lifted his wrist out of the water and stared at his wristlet. Maria followed suit. They were water resistant devices and the shiny surfaces reflected their frightened faces.

"I saw you talking to someone. Can they help us?"

Maria hesitated, then nodded. Sliding her finger over the surface, the screen activated. She quickly accessed the hidden program.

"Maria, it's Linds. I have your feed redirected to me now, not Dwayne." Lindsey appeared to be at a workstation in the Constabulary. "I am jamming the feed from all the Inferi Boon wristlets right now. How many of you are alive?"

"Me and Denman. That's it."

Denman sank into the water so just his eyes were visible above the waves. He was watching the tiltrotors moving over the station. So far, they had not been spotted.

Lindsey's shocked expression transformed swiftly into one that was all business. "Okay. That'll make it easier. They're attempting to confirm that all of you are dead using the wristlets. I'm trying to come up with a false transmission that will make them think you were inside the building. Meanwhile, you two have got to get away from that area. It's fuckin' ground zero."

The Maelstrom Platforms continued to roar. Somewhere in the distance, more explosions filled the air with fire.

"Is Dwayne there?" Maria asked.

"I'm here," her lover's voice said from off camera.

"I love you," she sobbed.

"Keep going, Maria. You can do this. You and Denman need to find a safe place to hide. We're going to get you out of this." Dwayne's voice was calming. He bent over Lindsey's shoulder to peer into the camera. "I love you. Keep going. This isn't over."

Maria nodded.

"I'm killing this connection. We'll be in contact," Lindsey said, then vanished.

The screen dissolved into the shiny silver of her wristlet.

Denman kicked so that his mouth was out of the water so he could speak. "We need to move. One of them is starting to search the shoreline. Deep breath, hold it as long as you can."

Maria nodded, then dove.

* * *

Caitlyn's big blue eyes stared at the vid screen as the SWD transmitted live coverage of the destruction of the remaining Inferi Scourge. Dwayne gently rested his arm over her shoulders to comfort her.

Beyond the walls of the Constabulary facility, people were filling the streets to watch the coverage on the drones rolling along the streets. Cheers filled the night. The sound of the Maelstrom Platforms firing on the walls echoed throughout the vast expanse of the city.

The Constabulary Command Center was eerily silent. The SWD had replaced them as the protectors of the city and the officers watched the battle on the vid screens. Commandant Pierce sat in her command chair watching with a grim expression on her face. Lindsey and a few other communication officers worked vigilantly on the far side of the room.

Dr. Curran sat at a station watching the magnificent show on the screens. "Every last bit of ammunition, every last bit of fuel, every last bit of weaponry is putting on the biggest fireworks show in history."

"They knew what they were doing," Dwayne said, barely contained anger in his voice.

"They will worship the SWD as their salvation. We'll just be their foot soldiers when the food riots begin." Commandant Pierce sighed.

"Dad?" Caitlyn whispered, her hand resting on his.

"Yeah?" She looked younger than her age. He could almost see the child in the young woman. "What is it?"

"The woman who is out there. The vanguard?"

Dwayne nodded, not sure if he liked where she was going with her line of questioning.

"Do you love her?"

There was no other way to answer. "Yes. I do."

Caitlyn smiled ruefully. "You're going to save her, aren't you?"

"She saved me once. I owe her," Dwayne said with a shrug. "Plus, I'm not sure how to live without her."

The doors to the command center slid open and Petra hurried in. Her usually impeccable persona seemed ruffled in light of all she had learned. She strode to Dwayne's side and gave Caitlyn a slight smile.

"What is it?" Dwayne asked his harried assistant.

"My media sources informed me that the President is set to go on the air within the next hour to announce the destruction of the Inferi Scourge. He also will reveal the details of the sad death of the Special Ops who died tonight during the assault on the hydroelectric plant. The official story is that their tiltrotor crashed, killing all on board."

"Then when we reveal the truth of the matter, what do you think the reaction will be?" Dwayne asked.

"They won't care," Dr. Curran said tiredly. "The people won't care because it means all the Inferi Scourge in the valley are dead. All of them. Even the Inferi Boon."

Petra pursed her thin lips together, then nodded. "I agree."

"So how do we usurp the SWD?" Caitlyn asked.

Dwayne glanced toward Lindsey and her minions working away. "We hope that our little hacker over there can piece together what the SWD did in an attempt to take over the government illegally. And we save the President from being removed from office."

"He's a prick," Caitlyn said, disapproval in her voice.

"Yes, but it's better to have an official elected by the people, than a dictatorship," Commandant Pierce reminded her.

"So no one is going to care about Vanguard Martinez and her people? That they were slaughtered trying to save us?" Caitlyn shook her head. "I don't believe it."

"They won't care right now," Petra corrected her. "They will once they realize how the SWD manipulated the situation. Plus, Dr. Curran is going to lie and tell everyone there was a cure, right, Dr. Curran?"

Dr. Beverly Curran, brilliant scientist and former member of the SWD, looked up at them with weary eyes and said, "Anything to fuck over Petersen." And grinned.

* * *

The hard bark of the trees, the scratching branches and nettles, and razor sharp rock wall had Maria's exposed arms and neck covered with cuts and welts. Her boots and the lower half of her armor were weighted down with lake water that sloshed as she climbed through the foliage lining the lake.

In spite of the hindrance, they were still moving faster than she expected. Part climbing, part hiking, the trek was tedious and dangerous, but she still didn't feel tired from all the exertion. There were odd internal twinges that were a little alarming though. A few had been sharp pains that had made her gasp for breath, but nothing that incapacitated her. Denman didn't dare stop to scan her, so she kept her mouth silent whenever a wave of pain rippled through her.

The hydroelectric station was now far behind them. The sun had set on a fiery valley filled with death and destruction. The wind carried the sound of the Inferi Scourge howls, the tiltrotors firing, and the Maelstrom Platforms. Maybe it was her imagination, but she thought she heard a great crowd crying out in triumph. The Inferi Boon had reduced the numbers of the undead masses so significantly, the battle was extremely short-lived. Now the valley was filled with smoke from the smoldering fires. It was providing greatly-needed cover to her and Denman.

The sparse tree line they were moving along ended abruptly just ahead. They would have to sprint across open ground toward the foothills. The formations were steep, but Denman was hoping the higher they climbed the more hiding places they might find.

"What about the last two Anomalies?" Maria wondered aloud. "Did you see what happened to them?"

Denman shook his head. "No, no. Though, I somewhat suspect they may have ducked into the carrier. At least, let's hope so."

With a sigh, Maria scrambled over some roots jutting out of the rock, tilting her head to gaze up along the steep incline that seemed to rise up to the very top of the mountain itself. She wasn't too sure how well she would be able to climb. The pains in her body were worsening.

"Okay, we need to run until we reach that patch of pines over there, then start climbing. There are plenty of boulders and spots to hide up there." Denman pointed to their destination as she stepped closer to him.

"Okay. I'm ready."

"You sure?" Denman touched her sweating face lightly with one hand. His hand was icy against her skin.

"Yeah, I'm sure." Maria gave him a slight smile. "I'm a total bad ass."

"So I noticed." Denman said, returning the smile.

"I'm glad you're with me," Maria said, tears suddenly in her eyes. In her mind, she saw Omondi and the others engulfed in flame.

"I'm glad I'm here." Denman enfolded her in his arms and rested his chin on her shoulder.

Clinging to him, Maria felt hot tears sliding over her flushed cheeks. "If we make it we have to have that barbecue by the lake. Just your family and mine."

"I'd love that," Denman answered. He pressed a kiss to her forehead. "You and Megan will be best friends. I know it."

"You and Dwayne will get along really well."

"You'll have to tell me more about him when we're somewhere safe."

Maria peered into the darkness as Denman stepped away. A handful of tiltrotors were skimming low over the ground. The rest of the fleet had returned to the city. There would most likely be patrols and cleanup crews out in the valley for weeks before declaring it officially cleared. Denman and Maria hopefully wouldn't be trapped out here that long. Evading the patrols for so long would be difficult, if not impossible.

Denman extended his hand toward her. She took it.

Together they ran across the wide expanse of empty land through trails of smoke drifting on the wind. The city loomed to their left, alive with lights. Behind them were the smoldering remains of the hydroelectric station. Their heavy boots pounded against the dark earth and patches of new grass. The foothills loomed beyond a thin smattering of pine trees that were black in the pale light emanating from the city and moon.

Plunging into the deep gloom of the trees, they were among the Scourge before they realized it. A cluster of thirty or so stood in the pines staring silently toward the rock face of the mountain.

Maria gasped, her heart beating violently in her chest. She tugged at Denman's hand, trying to escape his hold and the Scourge surrounding her.

Instead of letting her go, Denman pulled her into his arms. Cradling her against him, her back to his chest, he slowly scooted them past the swaying forms. Maria clutched his forearms with her fingers, her eyes wide with fright.

She was alive again. Would they sense her?

The Scourge remained silent as they passed. None even acknowledged their presence.

"Your father said that it's the virus inside that tells the Inferi Scourge which are their own," Denman whispered.

Maria kept herself pressed against the hard surface of Denman's armor. They moved carefully in sync past the swaying Scourge, the pine needles and dry twigs crackling under their feet. The milky eyes and vacant faces didn't alter in the wake of their passing. At the edge of the trees, Denman let Maria slip from his arms and took her hand.

Studying the path they had just taken, Maria noted that not one Scourge had awakened from its torpor. For a second she considered going back and hitting one of them to see if it responded.

Instead, she followed Denman over the rugged ground.

Chapter 34

"Dad, this is so beast!"

Dwayne couldn't help but grin at his son's exuberance. Studying his child, he could see his genetics stamped on his features. This was true immortality. Not a virus. One generation carrying forward the genes of the former. "Hunter, is Allison with you?"

"Yeah! We're out near the capital with our friends. You should be here. It's wild!" Hunter's face kept blurring across the screen as he was jostled about by the crowd.

Allison's cute face peeked at her father. It was off-center on the screen, but he could see her bright blue eyes gazing at him happily. "Dad, this is so freakin' cool! The Maelstroms sounded like thunder! This party is so wild. I wish you were here with us! We keep trying to reach Caitlyn, but I guess she's working."

Caitlyn shook her head, keeping out of frame. Like her mother, she wore her emotions too clearly on her face. It was best if her younger siblings didn't see her, or they would know something was amiss.

The twins scrunched their faces together so they could both gaze into the camera and smile at their dad. Dwayne felt his heart stutter and the overwhelming love he had for his kids stole his voice for a few seconds. The twins chattered on about all they were seeing, gleefully carried along by the crowd converging on the capital building.

"No more Inferi Scourge," the crowd was chanting.

"Dad, come see us soon, okay? We totally need to celebrate as a family," Hunter said excitedly. "Maybe you and mom won't even fight."

Dwayne chuckled. "Maybe. I love you both. You know that, right?"

"We love you, Daddy!" Allison shouted as the chanting of the crowd drowned out all other sound.

"You're beast, Dad!" Hunter yelled, then cut the feed.

"Beast?" Dwayne looked at Caitlyn curiously.

"Old slang that is making a comeback. I'm pretty sure it's a compliment." She hesitated. "You're not going to tell them."

Dwayne shook his head sorrowfully. "Can you tell them goodbye for me?"

The sheen of tears made her eyes sparkle as she nodded. "Yeah."

Commandant Pierce was overseeing crowd control per President Cabot's request. Constabulary patrols were in the streets trying to maintain order. The command center was once again a hub of activity. Dwayne and the others had relocated to another room off the main center. Vaja had joined Lindsey and wore a special badge on his worn and patched black sweater. Dr. Curran had finally shaken off her malaise. She was on a secure workstation diligently putting together a report that would be leaked to the media.

Petra slid in through a door, struggling to heave the heavy bags she was carrying into the room. They had SWD emblems on them. Dwayne rushed over to alleviate the burden. The heavy black bags contained everything he would need.

"You're the best, Petra," he said with a grin.

"I just hope you don't get yourself killed," she said with a sigh.

"I'll get Maria and Denman back in here safe and sound," Dwayne promised.

Petra stared at him for a long moment, then said, "Chances are you won't. But if anyone can pull this off, you can."

"Thanks for the vote of confidence." Dwayne dragged the bags to one side of the room and opened them to examine their contents.

"Dad, I just got a call. I have to go. They expect me down at the capital." Caitlyn drew near, running her hands over her blond hair to smooth it.

Standing, Dwayne gave his daughter a firm hug. "Take care."

"Don't die, Dad," Caitlyn whispered into his shoulder.

"I won't give your mother that satisfaction," Dwayne said with a wink.

Caitlyn laughed. "You're the best, Dad. I know I don't tell you enough. But you are."

Touched, Dwayne squeezed her shoulder. "I love you, Caitlyn. And you've been a pain in my ass more times than I can count, but I couldn't be prouder of the woman you've become."

"Thanks, Dad." She pressed a kiss to his cheek then hurried out of the room.

Dwayne scanned the small room with its banks of work stations. All the vid screens save the ones Petra, Dr. Curran, and Lindsey and Vaja were working on showed the massive crowds descending on the capital. Most of the Constabulary and a big chunk of the SWD security would be occupied taking care of the crowds. He had to move fast to have any chance of saving Maria and Denman.

Rifling through the bags, he began to organize his armor, weapons, and supplies. He was busy checking the systems on the armor when Dr. Curran's high heels appeared in his vision. Looking up, he saw her pinched face staring down at him.

"Can we speak?"

"Certainly."

Rising, he stared at her curiously before leading her into the commandant's ready room. Fresh coffee was bubbling in a pot and heated containers of food waited for the commandant and her staff whenever they were able to get a break. As the door shut behind them, Dwayne and Dr. Curran sat at the small conference table in one corner of the room.

"I lied to you," Dr. Curran said in her point-blank way of speaking.

Dwayne squinted at her, confused. "What do you mean?"

"In the SWD it's very competitive among the scientists. Everyone has been trying to find a cure to the Inferi Scourge Plague. Ever since this city was created, the SWD has tried to find a way out of this horrific mess we've made for ourselves. My whole life I dreamed of finding that solution. I never modified the virus I told you I used. It was a small sample, lost in the massive cold storage vaults. That is the one I used on Maria Martinez. The virus administered to the other members of the squad was modified from the one used in the failed attempts."

254

"What are you saying?"

"Denman can't come back into the city. He will turn into an Anomaly. And Maria can't return because she has immortality in her veins." Dr. Curran sighed, rubbing her eyes. "You can't go out there, risk your life, and bring them back. They both need to die out there. I suppose, ironically, the SWD is right."

"If Maria is the solution to mortality, she should come back into the city!" Dwayne protested.

"Why? So another SWD scientist can figure out how she returned to life? I've been reviewing my data. I can fool some people with it, but it won't take long for someone in the SWD to realize that something is amiss. And once they see Maria on the news vids, *alive*, what do you think will happen?" Dr. Curran stared at him pointedly.

"They'll isolate her. Test her. Maybe if we discover a way to mass infect—"

"I am *assuming* that she is immortal. I don't know for certain. My data is preliminary. She is back to life, but for how long?" Dr. Curran tapped her pad thoughtfully. Her eyes grew distant as she pondered the situation. "I may be jumping to conclusions, or hoping in vain. Something wonderful is happening to her, but I'm not truly certain of the end results. Maybe after you kill her you can bring me a sample of her tissue and blood."

Regarding the scientist with cold anger, Dwayne didn't speak. Dr. Curran was already scribbling away on her pad. Dwayne thought of all the lies that had been told from the very beginning. He was also haunted by Gideon, the man who had immediately turned into an Anomaly when given a modified version of the virus. Dr. Curran said the virus given to Maria was without modifications, but what did that mean? For Maria? For the city? Or maybe it was all a lie. Maybe Curran just wanted her handiwork dead and a new sample to work on.

Dwayne closed his eyes, pressing his knuckles against his lids. "You said you modified it. You can create a cure."

"I modified a virus that was already doomed to fail. I gave Maria the virus from the vault on a reckless whim." Dr. Curran snorted. "Call it scientific curiosity or just plain stupidity. Neither can be brought into the city. They're both unsafe."

Opening his eyes, Dwayne fastened his fierce gaze on the woman. "You doomed them all."

"I wanted to save them!" Dr. Curran insisted.

"You lied and doomed them. Denman has to die because you lied! Maria can't come home because she'll end up in the bowels of the SWD as an experiment because you're not sure what she has truly become! You fucking lied, Dr. Curran, and people have lost their lives."

"I thought there was hope when Jameson was infected with two different viruses, but he ended up going feral just like the others! I thought there was a chance that I would solve the Inferi Scourge problem and I had to take the risk!"

Dwayne slammed his fist down on the table, making her jump.

"If you go out there, you must kill them both," Dr. Curran insisted. "I don't want this, but it's the truth. I don't have enough data and if you bring Maria back..."

"Maybe you just don't want someone stealing your specimen!"

"Do you really believe the SWD will just roll over and die once the truth is revealed? Mr. Petersen is Black Ops. He planned all of this. Can't you see that? Hell, Admiral Kirkpatrick is probably just his pawn. He probably has a way to escape prosecution just in case something does go wrong. He's not going to let go of an asset like Maria once he ascertains what she is. You can't trust him!"

"I can't trust you!" Dwayne said in a voice close to a growl.

"I was wrong, but for all the right reasons. Mr. Petersen and even the president will use Maria for their own means. And if I'm wrong about her virus, then what?"

Dwayne stared at her, resisting the urge to strike her. "I'm going out there."

"You can't bring them back! You can't bring her back. You have to kill both of them."

Shaking his head, Dwayne stared at the woman incredulously. "You really don't feel remorse for what you've done, do you?"

"She's contagious."

"With immortality. Or so you suspect."

"She's contagious, Castellan. Hell, if she kissed you, you would be infected!"

He stared at her.

"You and I both know that even if I'm right in my suspicion about her virus, it will only serve the people in power, not the city."

Dwayne leaned toward the doctor. "Tell me something, Doctor. If this virus gives you immortality, why did you kill her before administering it?"

"To see if it would bring her back...and it did." Dr. Curran covered her face with her hand. "Ironically, I probably didn't even have to kill her. I could have given her the virus and it still would have altered her. Probably faster."

"Would she still have been able to walk among the Inferi Scourge?" Dwayne was weighing all she was telling him carefully.

The doctor shrugged. "Maybe. Possibly. Probably. Who knows?"

Rubbing his face, Dwayne tried to calm his chaotic thoughts. "So what you're telling me is that you're not sure that Maria coming into the city is even safe. Not just because you might be wrong, but because you might be right."

Dr. Curran pressed her thin lips together, then slightly nodded. "You have to kill them both. Bring me back a sample. Maybe...her legacy can be fulfilled after extensive testing. Maybe after the city has settled down and the coup is behind us, maybe then we would be able to explore the possibility of a virus that grants immortality when minds are rational and not rash."

Dwayne looked at her sharply. He suspected the scientist was insane, or worse. Conniving enough to hide the truth to forward her own secret agenda. But what was the truth? He was beginning to suspect that the immortality virus was a lie, too. Maybe Maria wasn't as special as the doctor claimed. Maybe the doctor just wanted a sample of the Inferi Boon virus since all the others had been destroyed. So many maybes...so little truths.

"Keep this between us until I tell you otherwise."

"You have to kill them both!"

Standing, Dwayne ignored her pleas, his mind already sorting through all his options. By the time he left, he knew what he had to do. He was the Castellan of the city and he would fulfill his duty.

* * *

Denman found the cave shortly after midnight. It was high up on the mountain and for several terrifying minutes they had scaled the rock face in plain view of the valley below. Thankfully, none of the tiltrotors were patrolling in the area. When they reached an outcropping, Denman hoisted himself up into a narrow opening before stretching his hand out to Maria. Gripping his wrist, she used the treads of her boots to give her leverage against the rock.

Scooting back, Denman hauled her through the gap. Maria gasped in the cold air and tasted dust and mold. It took several minutes for her eyes to adjust to the darkness, but little by little the details of the space they were squeezed into began to emerge.

The ceiling was very low. There was no way they could stand and they could barely sit with their backs straight. There were large boulders pressed around the entry. At some point the opening had been larger, but a rockslide had nearly plugged up the entrance. Denman activated his med-pad and used the light from its interface to crawl deeper into the cave. Maria followed, the rocks biting into her hands and dirt dusting her face and skin. They squeezed through a very-pinched curve in the tunnel to emerge into a much larger space.

The dim light from the med-pad illuminated the roughly-hewn walls and jutting rocks. Maria crawled onward cautiously. Denman slid into a crouch and slowly rotated, the brightness of the pad pushing back the shadows.

"Maria," Denman whispered. "Don't move."

Startled, Maria froze in place. Following Denman's frightened gaze, she saw that she was next to a pinned Inferi Scourge. His coveralls were mere scraps, but he appeared to be a workman. He lay silently, his eyes staring directly at Maria. His hand rested on the ground near her arm.

With very precise movements, Maria rolled onto her side and pressed against the rocks. Using her feet, she scooted herself past the creature.

Denman crawled over to the Scourge and studied it up close while Maria cleared the creature and hurried to a safe distance.

"Looks like he may have tried to hide up here when the gate failed and ended up in a landslide."

Shivering, Maria rubbed her arms as she watched Denman.

"Maria, remember what your father said. I don't think he was full of shit." Denman scowled slightly. "I really never talked to you about this, but one of the things that always bothered me when I was out among the Scrags was that I felt...them."

"What do you mean?"

"I felt connected to them. I know I'm not the only one. When I spoke one on one with squad, they said the same thing. We were more a part of the Scrags than we were a part of the humans in the city. It was the most frightening part of becoming what we are." Denman rubbed his upper lip thoughtfully as he sat back on his ankles. "Do you know what I mean?"

Maria shrugged. "Maybe. I don't know. Kind of. I never thought about it in any great detail."

"You're stronger than the rest of us," Denman conceded.

Maria laughed, shaking her head. "No. I'm not. I'm scared out of my fucking mind." Another rolling pain slid through her body and she flinched.

"Another one?"

"Yeah. Worse this time." Maria clutched her stomach as another spasm ripped at her insides. "Fuck."

Denman scooted over to her, scanning her.

Sweat slid over her cheeks to her chin as yet another twist of her guts sent her over onto her side.

"It's getting worse, Denman," she grunted. It was if waves of dreadful agony were washing over her. Until now she had been able to ignore the occasional twinge and jab, but now it was nearly unbearable. "Fuck!"

Denman gently rolled her onto her back and pressed his very cold hand to her forehead. "You have a fever."

"You're freezing cold," Maria retorted.

Chuckling, Denman nodded. "Yeah. Comes with being dead." He slanted over her and stared into her eyes as he used the pad to shine light in her eyes.

Maria gasped.

"What is it?" Denman asked worriedly.

Rings of bright red rimmed the irises of Denman's brown eyes. Fear gripped her as she gazed at her friend.

"Maria?"

Touching his cold cheek, she stroked his flesh, realizing that something was terribly wrong with both of them. Her body was seized in another swell of anguish.

"Denman," Maria whispered, thinking of his wife and kids waiting for him at home. She thought of him sitting by the lake with Dwayne sharing a beer. Memories of his friendship and devotion throughout their ordeal brought tears to her eyes.

"Maria, you're scaring me," he said in a tender voice. His hand gently pulled her hand from his face and he held it to his still chest.

"You've been a good friend," she said at last.

"And so have you. Soon, we'll be home with our families and this will all be a nightmare. I promise." He kissed her hand and laid it on her chest.

Maria doubled over as another wave hit her. Shivering, she was relieved they had found shelter before she had been crippled by the terrifying spasms.

"Maria," Denman whispered, peering down at her with his red-ringed eyes. "How long ago did you start to feel hungry?"

"I'm not," Maria answered, her teeth chattering.

"Strange," Denman said, shrugging. "I am."

The tidal wave of pain hit her and shoved her consciousness down into a place of darkness tinged with red. Struggling to remain awake, she gripped his arm. But the red waters of agony swallowed her whole and she faded from the world.

* * *

"You'll exit here and head directly to this area. That subway exit is very close to where Maria's wristlet is reporting they're holed up," Lindsey said, pointing to the holographic image projected above the table.

In his armor, Dwayne felt more like a soldier than he had in a long time. His backpack was packed with everything he needed to get to Maria. Petra had even provided weaponry for both of them with silencers.

The holographic image was reflected in the dark eyes of Commandant Pierce as she studied the route Dwayne was taking out of the city. They were the only three in the small room off of the command center. Petra and Vaja had retired to the ready room to eat and rest upon Commandant Pierce's not-so-subtle hint. Dr. Curran had been assigned quarters inside of the Constabulary and was under guard. Dwayne had not told anyone about their discussion.

"Where does he exit the city?" Commandant Pierce asked.

Lindsey pointed at the subway entrance that was sealed at the bottom of the Constabulary. "I can make sure they don't detect it opening. Any of the others will take more time."

"Then I'm willing to risk it." Commandant Pierce decided. "Once we get Denman and Martinez back inside the city, we'll be able to secure them inside of the Constabulary for their own protection."

Lindsey nodded in agreement. "Vaja and I almost have the worm ready that will deliver all the nice goodies about the SWD to every wristlet in the city. I can also, technically, take over the newsfeed."

Commandant Pierce laughed. "Where did you find her?"

"Lindsey? Her dad and I were friends," Dwayne answered.

Lindsey glowed under the praise. She was crippled physically, but her mind was her true weapon.

"I think she's due for a promotion," Commandant Pierce decided.

"Aw, shucks, ma'am, I mean, sir." Lindsey blushed.

"So at oh eight hundred hours you can make sure every single person in the city will have all the information?" Dwayne asked.

"Absolutely. Vaja even uncovered the little stash of deleted communiques from Admiral Kirkpatrick to Mr. Petersen where they laid out the entire plan for the coup against the government." Lindsey's grin widened. "Add in the Inferi Boon, the manipulation of the food resources, the crippling of the Constabulary-"

"And you have all the steps of a coup d'état." Commandant Pierce rolled her shoulders and set her hands on her hips. "We have them. Despite their maneuverings, the Constabulary outnumbers them."

"If we can successfully pull this off, we will have stopped a hostile takeover of the city. The Constabulary will never be under the heel of the SWD again," Dwayne said confidently.

"So are you ready?" Lindsey asked.

Dwayne snagged the holographic image and dragged it to his wristlet. It loaded onto the device and vanished from the table. "I'm ready."

"Okay, just one more thing." Lindsey handed him a small drive. "This will update the program installed on Maria's and your wristlets. It will also install the new program on Denman's wristlet. It completely blocks out the signal to the city, but gives you the ability to contact me and each other. If you get stuck out there, just stay low until the dust settles."

"I'll send someone out to get you," Commandant Pierce promised.

Dwayne slightly smiled. "This moment reminds me of why I am proud of be part of the Constabulary." He saluted the commandant.

Her lips parted in surprise, then returned it. "I always believed in you."

"Thank you. That means a lot to me. Thank you for allowing me to do this."

"No one else has as much as you on the line. I know you will do your best to save her," the commandant answered, and a flicker of sadness betrayed her. She was thinking of her husband. Unlike Dwayne, she couldn't save the one she loved.

Dwayne glanced over at Lindsey. She was studying him with an intense gaze. He felt as if she was hacking into his brain the same way she hacked into computers. With a hitch in her step, she slid into his arms and hugged him tightly. Startled, Dwayne gently embraced her.

The surprise on the commandant's face was comical, but she

shrugged it away.

Pushing Lindsey gently out of his arms, Dwayne said, "Thank you for everything."

Lips pressed tightly together, Lindsey nodded.

Picking up his helmet, Dwayne headed toward the door. "Petra hates goodbyes. Let her know I left, okay?"

Lindsey nodded again.

"We'll see you soon," Commandant Pierce called after him.

Dwayne nodded and ducked out the door into the narrow corridor that would take him to the lift that would deliver him to the lower levels of the Constabulary and the city.

Chapter 35

The old subway tunnel was as black as the darkest depths of the ocean. If not for his helmet's night vision, Dwayne never would have managed to take one step. There were no external lights of any kind and the darkness was absolute. Lindsey had done exactly as she had promised and unlocked all the blast doors. Now he rode along the old track on a maintenance cart as fast as he dared. The old contraption shook as it rumbled over the ground. The length of time it would take him to pass under the wall and reach the foothills was of some concern. He needed to beat the sunrise.

His wristlet buzzed and he answered, the feed immediately transferring to his helmet. Denman's face flickered into view. Dwayne was immediately alarmed by the man's bizarre eyes.

"Castellan Reichardt, I have a bit of a predicament. Vanguard Martinez has collapsed."

"What do you mean?" Dwayne demanded.

"I don't think it's actually a bad thing. My scans are confusing me. I can't seem to think straight. I suppose it's the stress of the day. But...I think her body is repairing itself. All the damage inflicted on it over the years. If I were to hazard a guess, I would say that she's in a healing coma."

The knot between Dwayne's shoulders lessened slightly. "How are you doing, Denman?"

Denman smiled slightly. "I think I'm about to follow in her footsteps. The virus appears to be altering me, too. I'm feeling a bit...tired. And hungry."

"I'm on my way to you now."

"Good to hear, sir."

Shifting Maria's arm, Denman disappeared from view for a moment. Dwayne caught a brief glimpse of Maria's serenely-sleeping face. He would do anything for her.

Denman's uncanny red-ringed eyes came back into view. They were eerie and disturbing. Perhaps Denman was on the verge of becoming an Inferi Anomaly. If so, Maria was in danger.

"Denman, why don't you meet me at the subway exit? I'll send the coordinates to Maria's wristlet now."

"Don't you need me to help carry her?" Denman asked, worried.

"No, I brought some equipment with me. I'd like to get you back into the Constabulary as soon as possible as a precautionary measure. There's no use you both being stuck outside the wall."

"I understand." Denman nodded briskly. "When should I leave?"

"Now. I'll be there within the hour, but it may take you some time to arrive at the rendezvous."

"Agreed. I'll see you soon, Castellan."

The feed went dead.

Dwayne accelerated.

* * *

"Maria," Denman's voice whispered through her dreams of pain and darkness. Shadowy figures lurked in the recesses of her mind, calling out to her. Denman's voice was one of them.

"Maria, can you hear me?"

She wanted to answer, but her lips wouldn't form words. Deep inside of her a spider was weaving her back together again. It hurt like hell.

"Maria, I have to go. But it's going to be okay. For both of us."

Screams died in her throat and echoed in her mind instead. She had seen his eyes and knew he wouldn't be all right. He was going to become the very thing he had tried to destroy.

"Goodbye," Denman's voice said.

Maria struggled to escape the weaver in her body, stitching her pieces back together again.

* * *

"Lindsey, I've reached the subway door," Dwayne said into his wristlet. Standing at the top of the steps of the defunct subway station, he felt as though he were standing in another time. The station was nearly perfectly preserved except for the thick layer of dust and the spider webs draped in the corners. Old vid screens waited to come to life again, running general announcements and advertisements. It was a world he would never see.

There was silence, then her voice said, "Deactivating the locks now."

Dwayne watched as the blast doors retreated into the walls and the heavy locks twirled to life. Sluggishly, the doors to the valley crept open. The weapon in his hand felt deadly as he cautiously inched up the dirt encrusted steps toward the world above. Thick clods of dirt crumpled under his boots as he hesitated on the stairs. He could hear the tiltrotors in the far distance still making sweeps over the valley. The Maelstrom Platforms were silent. He had seen the footage on the vid screen. A thick, gory paste was all that was left of the hundreds of thousands of Inferi Scourge that had surrounded the city.

A figure darted out of the darkness. Raising his weapon, Dwayne waited in silence. The bluish haze of the night vision washed over Denman as he leaped over the bent rail at the top of the stairs and landed near Dwayne.

"Good to see you, sir," Denman said with a wide grin and a salute.

Dwayne returned the salute and patted Denman on the shoulder. "How's Maria?"

"Unconscious still, but her readings were better. The virus is amazing. Whatever Dr. Curran did to our batch is just stellar. I'm feeling the changes myself. Honestly, I'm so damn hungry right now I can't wait to have a decent meal. Maria isn't having hunger pains, but I know that biochemistry may have an effect on which symptoms emerge first." Denman's eyes shifted constantly. Dwayne was rather glad he couldn't see the red ring edging his brown eyes.

"Where is she exactly?" Dwayne asked, revealing the holographic image he had downloaded to his wristlet.

"Right here," Denman said, drawing on the image, revealing a path to a cave high on the rock face.

"Excellent." Dwayne saved the information and it fed into his helmet.

"Are you sure you can bring her down alone?" Denman asked apprehensively.

"I'm sure. I got the equipment I need." Dwayne hesitated, feeling uneasy about the task at hand. "You did a good job. Your family will have a good life out here." Dwayne thought of his own kids being able to finally step outside the high walls and felt a lump in his throat.

"I think of my kids running around in a big yard and my wife being able to have a real garden and I *know* it was worth it." Denman sat on the steps, his body slightly shivering. He kept rubbing his hands together in an anxious manner. "How's the Constabulary going to explain our return?"

"Commandant Pierce has a plan to reveal everything the SWD did to seize control of the city, including what was done to the Inferi Boon." Dwayne kept an eye on Denman and the top of the stairs. They were crouched in the darkness, not visible to the tiltrotors circling the city.

"So our story will be told. People will know what happened to all of us." Denman nodded, looking satisfied.

"Yes," Dwayne promised him. "People will know what happened to all of you."

Denman stared longingly at the doorway to the subway. "Sir, I hate to rush you, but I'm starving and I'd love to contact my family tonight."

"Of course," Dwayne said and extended his hand to Denman. "Thank you for taking care of Maria."

"She's a dear friend. We all must have a drink together one day." Denman shook his hand before rushing down the last few steps to the doors.

Dwayne activated his wristlet. "Lindsey, open the door to the subway."

She didn't answer this time, but the locks to the door audibly clicked. Denman gave Dwayne a quick salute, then stepped through the doorway.

Dwayne shot him twice in the head. The silencer rendered the shots completely inaudible. With a sigh, Dwayne trudged down the stairs and pushed Denman's legs through the doorway.

"Lindsey," he said into his wristlet as the door swung shut, obscuring Denman's body.

There was a long pause, then she said, "Yes?"

"Denman was an Anomaly. Dr. Curran must tell Commandant Pierce what she told me about the virus she gave everyone, but Maria. His body *must* be destroyed immediately."

Another pause. "Understood." A longer pause. "You're not coming back are you?"

"No, I'm not."

264

"What are you going to do?"

Dwayne stared down at the weapon in his hand. "What I have to do."

He cut the feed.

* * *

Former Castellan Dwayne Reichardt's trek across the valley was not without its share of danger. A few times he had to lie among the Inferi Scourge that were burned to a crisp to avoid detection by the circling tiltrotors. Petra had managed to secure one of the most recent upgraded versions of the SWD armor through unknown means. Its mean black countenance was sleek and beautiful, but its internal workings were near magic. They could hide him from scanners and allowed him to blend almost seamlessly into his surroundings.

A daily runner, it was easy for him to maintain a swift pace as he headed toward the area that Denman had pinpointed as Maria's hiding place. He reached the base of the outcropping and began to scan the face for a path upward. Movement registered on his helmet and he whipped around.

A thin pine copse was a few feet away and the wind rustled the branches. Feeling on edge, he checked his map.

Again, movement drew his attention.

Shapes within the trees were beginning to move. Dwayne raised his weapon and aimed for the nearest form. As it stepped into the clearing, the twisted face of an Inferi Scourge snarled. Dwayne shot it, the head snapping back as it tumbled to the ground.

Within a second's time, Scourge were pouring out of the trees, racing toward him, howling. Though his heart was racing, he kept calm as he aimed precisely at each creature, firing off a single shot. Their heads exploded, their bodies crashing into the ground around him. Stepping carefully backward, he tried to maintain a safe distance from the creatures dashing out of the shelter of the pine trees.

The ammo counter hit zero. With his left hand, he calmly drew his other weapon and fired. Not as accurate as he was with his right, the bullets hit the Scourge below their screaming faces. He adjusted and managed to kill the last three just as they reached him. The last Scourge fell into his arms and he shoved it off, blood and brains pouring out of its head.

Dwayne reloaded both weapons and took several deep breaths to still his thundering heart. He had to holster the firearms to climb, but he comforted himself with the idea of being able to see the Scourge from a high distance before they could reach him. From his bag, he drew out the special climbing gear Petra had secured for him and attached the grips to his gloves and boots.

Soon he was moving swiftly over the massive boulders and heading toward the rock face that would lead him to Maria. His heart heavy inside of him, he resolutely climbed higher.

* * *

Darkness greeted her when she finally awoke. Pushing herself up on one elbow, Maria activated her wristlet. The glow from the screen filled the cave around her. She considered trying to contact Dwayne, but was afraid to do any more than pull up the blank starter screen.

Shoving her braid over her shoulder, she scooted over to the wall. "Denman?"

A strange dream flitted through her memory.

He had left her, hadn't he?

A cramp made her shudder. It wasn't the same as before. It was different, yet familiar.

The heavy armor was still damp inside and uncomfortable. Unlatching it from her body, she slid out of it and rubbed her hands down over her still damp leggings. Another cramp made her flinch. Something moist and warm trickled against her thigh. Mystified, Maria touched the dampness, the light from the wristlet revealing the dark red of blood.

"What the hell?" Pressing her hand to her abdomen, she pressed inward where her uterus used to be. She was rewarded with another cramp. Tears filled her eyes as she yanked up her undershirt and stared at her stomach and chest.

All her scars were gone.

Running the light from her wristlet over her arms, she saw smooth, tan skin with no keloids.

"Oh, God!" she gasped. "Oh, God!"

"Maria?" Dwayne's voice called out.

"Dwayne?" Maria wiped the blood off her fingers onto her leggings and crawled forward.

A light crept out of the long, low tunnel and illuminated her. She could see a figure in black SWD armor and a sleek helmet heading toward her.

A low growl made her skin crawl.

"Dwayne, there's a Scrag! It's pinned near the entrance to this area. Be careful."

The Inferi Scourge let out a low howl, its eyes going wide as it strained its hand toward Dwayne's dark shape as he drew closer.

"I see it," Dwayne answered, pressing his body against the far end of the tunnel. He scooted around the Scourge and crawled toward her.

She waited until he was close, then Maria flung herself into his arms. They clung to each other for several wonderful moments. Her love for him rendered her speechless as she savored the feel of him against her, even if he was clad in armor.

"I'm here," Dwayne finally said, his voice rough with emotion.

Together they unlatched the helmet from his armor and set it down beside them. The external lights from it illuminated the familiar lines of his face and his intense blue eyes. Maria's hands flew to his cheeks and she stared at him with tears in her eyes.

"You came for me," she whispered.

"I love you," Dwayne answered. "How could I not?"

Wrapping her arms around his neck, she rested her forehead against his cheek. His scent filled her with joy and made her body sing with need. Locking his arms around her, he clung to her, his face buried in her hair. She was glad she had taken a dip in the lake. At least she didn't smell like death now.

"I missed you so much, Dwayne."

"I missed you, too." Dwayne pressed a kiss to her cheek. His gloved hands smoothed her hair as he stared into her face. "God, you're beautiful."

Behind him the Inferi Scourge hissed and howled as it twisted beneath the boulders that had crushed its lower body.

"You're a little grayer," she teased him, touching the hair at his temple. Tears trailed down her cheeks.

"I aged a million years waiting for you," he murmured, kissing her neck.

Rubbing her hands over his hair, she leaned her head on his shoulder. "I never want to be apart again."

"I couldn't agree more. Never again will I let you out of my sight for more than a few minutes."

Pulling back, Maria gazed into the face she loved so much. "Are you here to take me home?"

Dwayne tenderly worked her braid apart and ran his hand through her hair languidly. The silky strands of her hair slid over the black glove like dark waters. He shook his head.

"I can't take you home," he said at last.

Maria frowned at his words. "What do you mean?"

"The Scrag didn't rouse until I came, did it?"

Maria stared at the creature that was trying to rip itself in half to reach Dwayne. Returning her gaze to Dwayne, she wondered what he was trying to say. "No, it was quiet until you came."

Dwayne cupped her face gently and stared down into her eyes. A smile was pulling up on the corners of his mouth. The joy of their reunion was clear in his eyes, yet Maria was disquieted.

"Dwayne? What is it?"

"You're not Inferi Boon or a Scourge. Not an Anomaly. But you *are* some kind of Inferi. Dr. Curran told me a long and twisted story. I don't think I fully believed her until this moment. Frankly, I think she's fucking insane." Dwayne kissed the tip of her nose and nuzzled her cheek. "But I can feel your heart beating and see your beautiful dark eyes are clear."

"Where's Denman?" Maria asked, suddenly beginning to understand.

Dwayne sighed sadly. "I killed him. I had to. He *was* an Anomaly. You're not."

Maria gasped, her thoughts spinning. "Why not? We were all given the same..." Maria bit her lip, shaking her head. "We weren't given the same virus, were we?"

As she listened to Dwayne explain all that had occurred, Maria stared at him in stupefied silence.

"Denman's eyes were changing. He was hungry." Maria sat back on her heels, sorrow filling her.

"The entire squad would have become Anomalies, except for you," Dwayne took her hands and kissed them. "You're the gift literally sent from the heavens."

The Scourge continued to thrash, its eyes fixated on Dwayne.

"All of this because they thought it was a weapon and it was...immortality? Perfect health?"

Dwayne nodded.

"I'm going to live forever?" Maria couldn't even comprehend the notion completely. "Have perfect health?"

"And be able to walk among the Scrags."

Eyes widening, Maria touched her stomach in awe. "Dwayne, I think my uterus and ovaries grew back!"

He chuckled. "Isn't that a good thing?"

She grimaced. "I have my period."

"It always appears at the worst time," Dwayne joked.

Maria playfully glowered at him, then her hand returned to her belly. The full impact of what the return of her reproductive system meant struck her like a thunderbolt.

Dwayne could see it in her eyes and lovingly traced his fingers over her cheek. "Your scars are gone. All of them. And you can be a mother, if you choose to be."

Maria struggled to grasp it all. "I can't go back because of what I am..."

He nodded.

Maria all of a sudden understood why he had come so far for her. Out of fear that she was an Anomaly, he had come to set her free. Instead, he had found that the mad ramblings of Dr. Curran were true.

"You came to kill me."

Dwayne sighed softly.

Maria licked her lips and drew his hand against her cheek. "And you weren't planning to go back."

"There is no life for me without you. I realized that tonight. My kids are grown and happy. I've done my best for them. My life is entangled with yours and if tonight I had to..."

She had never seen him cry in all their time together, but a tear slipped down his rugged cheek. Brushing it away, she kissed the wet trail on his skin.

"But just in case," he said with a soft chuckle, "I had Petra secure everything we would need to escape the valley together."

"I can walk among the Scrags...out in the world," she said in awe. "Go anywhere..."

"Yes, you can."

Maria stared into his eyes, understanding. "What about you?"

"Kiss me and I can join you," Dwayne whispered, touching her lips with his gloved fingers.

"Do you want that? Eternity?" Maria asked, her emotions making her voice soft.

Dwayne didn't hesitate. He leaned down and pressed his mouth to hers. She clung to him as they kissed. Her lips parted his and she licked the tip of his tongue.

"Stay with me forever," Maria whispered against his mouth.

Drawing away long enough to gaze into her face, Dwayne answered, "I want nothing more."

The Inferi Scourge at their feet was silent. As they had slept, it had returned to torpor. Maria bent and touched its head. It didn't stir. Dwayne squatted next to her and laid his hand over hers. The Scourge was silent, its eyes staring blindly.

Dressed in the sleek black SWD armor Dwayne had brought her, Maria ruffled the Scourge's hair lightly.

"Goodbye," she said, then killed it with a sharp blow to the head with the butt of her gun.

Dwayne stood and in the light from his armor she could see that the gray was nearly gone from his hair. His scars were now a memory and the lines in his face were diminishing. After sleeping for nearly twenty-four hours, he looked younger and stronger than ever. Maria's transformation had been slowed by her being killed before the virus was administered. Dwayne's had been smooth and easy due to being alive.

Stepping close to him, she rested her hand on his chest and he smiled at her warmly.

"Where will we go? she asked.

"Anywhere we want, I suppose," he answered. "The whole world is ours now."

Their helmets tucked into their packs, their wristlets updated and secure, Dwayne and Maria crawled through the tunnel. Stealthily, they scaled the rock face, moving higher and higher. The grips on their gloves and boots allowed them to climb easily and quickly. Strong winds buffeted them as they ascended the mountain, the air growing thinner, but their lungs easily adapted.

A few times they stole looks at the city far below them. In the moonlight, it was dark and dreary. The valley around it spread out like a vast canvas waiting to be painted with the colors of rebirth.

"Think they'll make it?" Maria asked.

"With Commandant Pierce busting heads, without a doubt," Dwayne assured her.

When they reached the snowline, they crunched over the icy drifts. Sometimes they found pathways, other times they balanced on narrow ledges. At last, they were high enough that the valley and the city were far below, hidden beneath soft clouds.

Not even breathless or tired, they stood together, arms about each other's waist staring down at the world they had emerged from. The cold wind flecked with ice pellets and snow nudged at their faces.

Together, they turned and gazed outward at the world yet to be discovered. It spread out before them, white and serene under a vast sea of stars.

"Ready?" Dwayne asked.

A kiss was his answer.

Together, hand in hand, they trekked into the unknown world.

Author's Final Note
(Please don't read until you finish reading the book)

I absolutely love THE LAST BASTION OF THE LIVING. I hope you did, too. I love the power of Maria and Dwayne's love, their individual strength, their ability to stand on their own, and yet come together as a powerful team. When I wrote the last line, I wept. I was so happy to have finally completed their story.

It's been a wonderful experience to write a novel that has a complete story contained within its pages. Dwayne and Maria find their peace at the end of the tale and wander off into an unknown world. What comes next? Who knows? I think that is what I love best about the end of the novel: it allows the reader to imagine all sorts of wonderful adventures for the two.

I hope you enjoyed it as much as I.

Rhiannon Frater
May 7, 2012

About the Author

Rhiannon Frater is the award-winning author of the As the World Dies trilogy (The First Days, Fighting to Survive, Siege,) and the author of three other books: the vampire novels Pretty When She Dies and The Tale of the Vampire Bride and the young-adult zombie novel The Living Dead Boy and the Zombie Hunters. Inspired to independently produce her work from the urging of her fans, she published The First Days in late 2008 and quickly gathered a cult following. She won the Dead Letter Award back-to-back for both The First Days and Fighting to Survive, the former of which the Harrisburg Book Examiner called 'one of the best zombie books of the decade.' Tor is reissuing all three As the World Dies novels. You may contact her by sending an email to rhiannonfrater@gmail.com or visit her online at rhiannonfrater.com. You can find out more about the As the World Dies trilogy and world by visiting astheworlddies.com.

—Author photo courtesy of
Mary Milton

30278136R00160

Made in the USA
Lexington, KY
25 February 2014